Born in 1802, the son of a high officer in Napoleon's army, Victor Hugo spent his childhood against a background of military life in Elba, Corsica, Naples, and Madrid. After the Napoleonic defeat, the Hugo family settled in straitened circumstances in Paris, where, at the age of fifteen, Victor Hugo commenced his literary career with a poem submitted to a contest sponsored by the Académie Française. Twenty-four years later, Hugo was elected to the Académie, having helped revolutionize French literature with his poems, plays, and novels. Entering politics, he won a seat in the National Assembly in 1848; but in 1851, he was forced to flee the country because of his opposition to Louis Napoleon. In exile on the Isle of Guernsey, he became a symbol of French resistance to tyranny; upon his return to Paris after the Revolution of 1870, he was greeted as a national hero. He continued to serve in public life and to write with unabated vigor until his death in 1885. He was buried in the Panthéon with every honor the French nation could bestow.

THE TOILERS OF THE SEA

BY VICTOR HUGO

IN THE TRANSLATION BY
ISABEL F. HAPGOOD

A SIGNET CLASSIC

SIGNET CLASSIC
Published by New American Library, a division of
Penguin Putnam Inc., 375 Hudson Street,
New York, New York 10014, U.S.A.
Penguin Books Ltd, 27 Wrights Lane,
London W8 5TZ, England
Penguin Books Australia Ltd, Ringwood,
Victoria, Australia
Penguin Books Canada Ltd, 10 Alcorn Avenue,
Toronto, Ontario, Canada M4V 3B2
Penguin Books (N.Z.) Ltd, 182–190 Wairau Road,
Auckland 10, New Zealand

Penguin Books Ltd, Registered Offices:
Harmondsworth, Middlesex, England

Published by Signet Classic, an imprint of New American Library,
a division of Penguin Putnam Inc.

First Signet Classic Printing, November 2000
10 9 8 7 6 5 4 3 2 1

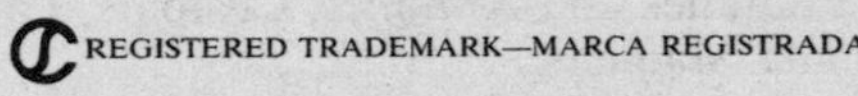

Printed in the United States of America

TABLE OF CONTENTS

PART ONE • SIEUR CLUBIN

BOOK FIRST • WHAT A BAD REPUTATION IS COMPOSED OF

BOOK SECOND • MESS LETHIERRY

BOOK THIRD • DURANDE AND DÉRUCHETTE

BOOK FOURTH • THE BAGPIPE

BOOK FIFTH • THE REVOLVER

BOOK SIXTH • THE DRUNKEN HELMSMAN AND THE SOBER CAPTAIN

BOOK SEVENTH • THE IMPRUDENCE OF ASKING QUESTIONS OF A BOOK

PART TWO • GILLIATT THE CUNNING

BOOK FIRST • THE REEF

BOOK SECOND • LABOR

BOOK SECOND • GRATITUDE PLAYS THE DESPOT

BOOK THIRD • DEPARTURE OF THE "CASHMERE"

I DEDICATE THIS BOOK

TO

THE ROCK OF HOSPITALITY AND LIBERTY

TO THAT NOOK OF ANCIENT NORMAN SOIL

WHERE DWELLS

THE NOBLE LITTLE RACE OF THE SEA

TO THE ISLE OF GUERNSEY

SEVERE YET GENTLE • MY PRESENT ASYLUM

PROBABLY MY TOMB

V. H.

PREFACE

Religion, society, nature; these are the three struggles of man. These three conflicts are, at the same time, his three needs: it is necessary for him to believe, hence the temple; it is necessary for him to create, hence the city; it is necessary for him to live, hence the plow and the ship. But these three solutions contain three conflicts. The mysterious difficulty of life springs from all three. Man has to deal with obstacles under the form of superstition, under the form of prejudice, and under the form of the elements. A triple *ananke* [necessity] weighs upon us: the *ananke* of dogmas, the *ananke* of laws, the *ananke* of things. In *Notre-Dame de Paris* the author has denounced the first; in *Les Misérables* he has pointed out the second; in this book he indicates the third.

With these three fatalities which envelop man is mingled the interior fatality, that supreme *ananke,* the human heart.

VICTOR HUGO

HAUTEVILLE HOUSE, March, 1866.

THE CHANNEL ISLANDS

I

THE OLD CATACLYSMS

THE ATLANTIC wears away our coasts. The pressure of the Arctic current deforms our western cliffs. The wall which runs parallel to the coast is undermined from Saint-Valéry-sur-Somme to Ingouville; large blocks of stone crumble, the water rolls clouds of pebbles, our ports are filled with sand or stones, and the mouths of our rivers are barred. Every day a portion of Norman earth is detached and disappears under the waves. This prodigious work, now abated, has been terrible. The immense buttress of Finistère was a necessity to keep the sea back. One may judge of the strength of the flow of the Arctic current, and of the violence of its effects, by the hollow which it has made between Cherbourg and Brest.

This formation of the Gulf of La Manche, at the expense of French soil, took place in pre-historic times. The last decisive raid of the ocean on our coast, however, has a fixed date. In 709, sixty years before the advent of Charlemagne, the action of the sea separated Jersey from France. Other points of land formerly submerged are, like Jersey, visible. These points, which jut out of the water, are islands, and are known by the name of Norman Archipelago.

A swarm of laborious humanity dwells there.

To the industry of the sea, which made a desert, has succeeded the industry of man, which made a people.

II
GUERNSEY

GRANITE in the southern part, sand in the northern part; here steep slopes, there the downs; an inclined plane of meadows with rolling hills, relieved by rocks; for a fringe to this carpet of green wrinkled in folds, the foam of the ocean; the whole length of the coast flanked batteries, fortified towers; from place to place, all along the low beach, a massive breastwork, intersected by battlements and stairways, invaded by the sand and attacked by the waves, the only besiegers to be feared. The mills dismantled by the storm—some in Valle, others in Ville-au-Roi, in Saint-Pierre-Port, in Torteval—are turning yet. On the steep shore are places to anchor; on the downs the flocks; the shepherd's dog and the drover's dog meet there and work; the little carts of the city merchants gallop in the hollow roads; often black houses, tarred at the west on account of the rains; cocks, fowls, dungheaps; everywhere Cyclopean walls. Those of the old port, unfortunately destroyed, were very much to be admired, with their formless blocks, their powerful stakes and heavy chains; farms surrounded by forests; fields walled to the height of support by projecting lines of dry stone, drawing on the plains an odd chess-board. Here and there a rampart around a thistle, thatched cottages built of granite, huts with vaults, cabins built to resist a bullet; sometimes in the wildest place a small new building, surmounted by a belfry; this is a school; two or three streams in the bottom of the meadows; elms and oaks; an especial kind of lily, found only there—the Guernsey lily. In the busy season, the ploughs drawn by eight horses; in front of the houses large haystacks placed in a circle surrounded by stones; heaps of prickly furze; occasionally gardens in the old French style, with trimmed yew trees; boxwood precisely cut; vases of shells or pebbles, mingled with orchards and kitchen gardens; amateur flowers in the gardens of the peasants; the mountain laurels among the potatoes; everywhere on the grass rows of seaweed of primrose color. There are no crosses in the graveyard; instead, slabs of stones, looking in the moonlight like standing white ghosts; six Gothic steeples on the horizon; old churches, new dogmas; the Protestant rites lodged in Catholic architecture. In the sands and on the capes, the sombre Celtic enigma dispersed under its different forms, large cut stones, long stones, fairy stones, rocking stones, sounding stones, galleries, cromlechs, dolmens, pouquelaies, all kinds of antiquities; after the Druids, the priests, the pastors; the remembrance of the fall from heaven; on one point, Lucifer in the castle of the Archangel Michael; on the other point, Icarus on Cape Dicart; almost as many flowers in summer as in winter. This is Guernsey.

III

GUERNSEY

(Continued)

THE land fertile, rich, strong. No better pasturage. The cheese is celebrated, the cows are noted. The heifers of the pastures of Saint-Pierre-du-Bois equal the laureate sheep of the plain of Confolens. The agricultural committees of France and England award honor to the *chefs-d'œuvre* produced by the furrows and meadows of Guernsey. Agriculture is furthered by a very extensive inspection, and an excellent network of communication gives life to the entire island. The roads are very good. Where two roads branch off, a flat stone with a cross on it is placed on the ground. The oldest bailiff of Guernsey, the one who held office in 1280, the first on the list, Gaultier de la Salte, was hanged for judiciary injustice. This cross, called the bailiff cross, marks the place where he knelt for the last time and where he offered his last prayer.

The water of the little gulfs and bays is enlivened by the *corps morts* (objects firmly fixed on the shore or on the bottom of a roadstead for the mooring of vessels); large towboats decorated with sugar-loaf patterns in squares of red and white, equal parts of black and yellow, dyed with green, blue and orange, lozenged, veined, marbled, float with wind and tide. In some places can be heard the monotonous song of the workmen towing a vessel and drawing the tow-rope.

The laborers have a no less contented appearance than the fish dealers and the gardeners. The soil, permeated with powdered rock, is rich; the manure, which is composed of the river sediment and seaweed, adds salt to the granite, whence an extraordinary fertility; vegetation thrives wonderfully; magnolias, myrtles, daphnes, rose-laurels, blue hortensia, fuchsias, abound. There are arcades of three-leaved verbenas, also walls of geraniums; oranges and lemons ripen in the open air, but grapes ripen only in hot-houses; there they flourish. The camelias are trees; in the garden the flowers of the aloe trees are seen growing higher than a house. Nothing could be more rich and prodigal than the vegetation concealing and ornamenting the coquettish fronts of the villas and cottages.

Guernsey, attractive on one side, is terrible on the other. The west is laid waste, being exposed to the blasts from the open sea. There, the breakers, squalls, creeks where vessels are stranded, repaired boats, heath, waste lands, hovels, sometimes a low and tottering hamlet, lea flocks, the grass short and salt, and the general appearance of extreme poverty.

Lihou is a small barren island quite near, and accessible at low tide. It is full of brushwood and burrows. The rabbits of Lihou are familiar with tides. They leave their holes only at high tide. They set man at defiance. Their friend, the ocean, isolates them. These numerous animals are in their wild state.

By digging in the clay of Vason Bay trees are found. A forest is discovered there under a mysterious covering of sand.

The vigorous fishermen of this wind-beaten west make skilful pilots. The sea is peculiar in the Channel archipelago. The bay of Cancale, which is quite near, is the place where the tides rise higher than anywhere else in the world.

IV

The Grass

THE grass at Guernsey is the ordinary grass; however, a little richer. A meadow in Guernsey is almost like the lawn of Cluges or of Géménos. You find there *fétuques* (a kind of grain), grass suited for grazing, as well as ordinary grass, besides the soft brome-grass, with the grain growing on the top of the stalks; then the canary grass; the agrostis (red top), which produces a green dye; the darnel rye-grass; the millet, which has a woolly stem; the fragrant vernal grass, the sensitive plant, the weeping marigold, the timothy grass, the foxtail, whose grain looks like a little club; the feather-grass, used for making baskets; the lyme grass, used for steadying shifting sands. Is that all? No; there is also the cock's-foot grass, whose flowers grow in clusters; the guinea grass, and even, according to some native agriculturists, the lemon grass;

also the bastard hawkweed, with leaves like the dandelion, which marks the hour; and the sow-thistle of Siberia, which foretells the weather. All that is grass; but no one cares for this grass; it is the grass indigenous to the archipelago; it needs the granite for sub-soil and the ocean to water it.

Now, imagine a thousand insects running through and flying above this, some disgusting, others charming. Under the grass the longicornes (insects with long antennæ), longinases (insects with long proboscises), weevils, ants occupied milking the grubs, their cows; the driveling grasshopper, the small beetle, ladybugs, *bête du bon Dieu*, moles, *bête du diable*; on the grass, in the air, the dragon-fly, the wasp, the golden rose-beetle, the bumble-bee, the lace-winged fly, ruby-tailed flies, the noisy volucellæ, and you will have some idea of this sight filled with material for thought, which is offered at noon of a June day on the ridge of Jerbourg or Fermian Bay to a dreamy entomologist and to a poet who is also something of a naturalist.

Suddenly you perceive a little square green slab of stone under this sweet green grass, on which are engraved these two letters, "W.D.," which mean War Department. That is right. Civilization must be apparent. Without that the place would be wild. Go on the banks of the Rhine; search the least-known nooks of this scenery; in certain respects the landscape is so majestic that it seems pontifical; it seems as though God is nearer there than elsewhere. Plunge yourself into the solitary fastness of the mountains and into the silent places of the forests; choose, for instance, Andernach and its surroundings. Pay a visit to that obscure and impassable lake of Laach, mysterious in its wildness; no place more August. Universal life is there in all its religious serenity; no trouble; everywhere profound order in the midst of apparent natural disorder. Walk with a softened heart in the wilderness; it is delightful as the spring and melancholy as the autumn; wander at random; leave behind you the ruined abbey; lose yourself amidst the sweet peace of those ravines, amidst the song of birds and the rustle of leaves; drink, from the hollow of your hand, the water from the springs; walk, meditate, forget. A roof is seen; it marks the angle of a hamlet buried under the trees; it is green, fragrant, charming, covered with ivy and flowers, filled with children and laughter; you approach, and at the corner of the cabin, covered by a brilliant rift of shadow and sunlight, on an old stone of this old wall, under the name of the hamlet, *Liederbreizig*, you read: *22d. Landw. battalion, 2d Comp.* You thought yourself in a village; you are in a regiment. Such is man.

V

The Perils of the Sea

THE "overfall"—read *break-neck*—stretches along the entire western coast of Guernsey. The waves have torn it up skillfully. At night, on the edges of dangerous rocks, strange lights are seen to warn or to deceive, so it is said. These are believed in by the sea rovers. These same rovers, bold and credulous, distinguish under the water the legendary holothuria. This infernal marine nettle cannot be touched without setting one's hand on fire. Such a local appellation as Tinttajeu, for example (from the Welsh, *Tin-Tagel*), indicates the presence of the devil. Eustace, who is Wace, says in his old verse:

When the sea begins to toss,
And the waves to trouble cross,
Black the sky, the cloud is dark;
Danger near! Look to thy barque!

This Channel is as unsubdued to-day as in the times of Tewdrig, of Umbrafel, of Hamondhû the black, and of Knight Emyr Lhydau, who took shelter on the Isle of Groix, near Quimperlé. In these parts of the ocean there are dramatic effects which must be distrusted. This, for example, is one of the most frequent caprices of the ship's compass in the Channel Islands: a storm blows to the eastward; it becomes calm, a complete calm; you breathe; that calm lasts sometimes an hour. Suddenly the storm, which has disappeared in the southeast, reappears at the north; it took you before in the rear; it faces you now; it is the storm turned round. If you are not an experienced pilot, accustomed to the place; if you have not profited by the calm and taken the precaution of tacking the ship while the wind was turning, all is over; the vessel goes to pieces and founders.

Ribeyrolles, who died in Brazil, wrote from time to time, during his stay in Guernsey, a personal memorandum of daily facts, a leaf of which lies before us:

> "*1st. of January*. New Year's Gifts. A storm. A ship coming from Portrieux was lost yesterday on the Esplanade.
> *2d.* Three-masted vessel lost at La Rocquaine. It came from America. Seven men lost; twenty-one saved.
> *3d.* The packet boat has not arrived.
> *4th.* The storm continues. . . .
> *14th.* Rain. Landslide, which killed one man.
> *15th.* Stormy weather. The *Fawn* could not sail.
> *22d.* Unexpected sudden storm. Five disasters on the western coast.
> *24th.* The storm continues. Shipwrecks on every side."

There is scarcely ever any repose in this corner of the ocean. From this place the cries of the gull echo for ages in this endless squall the verses of the restless poet of ancient days, Lhyouar'hhenn, that Jeremiah of the sea.

But the bad weather is not the greatest danger of the archipelago; the squall is violent, and its violence is a warning. You return to port, or you close-reef the sails, taking care to give the lowest part the greatest emphasis. If the wind blows strong, you brail up everything, and you can come through all right. The great dangers of these latitudes are the invisible dangers always present, and the finer the weather the more they are to be dreaded.

In these emergencies especial care is necessary. The sailors of the western part of Guernsey are very skillful in managing a ship in a way which might be called preventive. No one has studied so thoroughly as they the three dangers of a quiet sea, *le singe, l'anuble*, and *le derruble*. *Le singe* (swinge) is the current; *l'anuble* (dark place), the shallow water; *le derruble* (which they pronounce *terrible*) is the whirlpool, the navel, the funnel of underlying rocks, the well beneath the sea.

VI
The Rocks

THROUGHOUT the Archipelago the coast is almost uncultivated. These islands have charming interiors, with a stern and uninviting approach. The English Channel, being almost a kind of Mediterranean, the sea is short and choppy, the billows are resounding, which produces a strange hammering of the cliffs and the heavy crushing of the coast.

Whoever follows this coast passes through a series of mirages. At every turn the rock tries to deceive you. Where do these illusions originate? In the granite. Nothing stranger. Enormous stone toads dwell there, come out of the water, no doubt, to breathe; giant nuns hurry to and fro, leaning over the horizon; the petrified folds of their veils have the form of the waving wind; kings with Plutonic crowns meditate on large thrones, which have not been spared by the breakers; some creatures buried in the rocks extend their arms aloft, the fingers of the open hands visible. All this is the shapeless shore. Approach. There is nothing more. The stone is worn away. Here is a fortress, a defaced temple, a chaos of ruins and demolished walls, all the ruins of a deserted city. Neither city, nor temple, nor fortress exists; it is only the sea-cliff. In proportion as one advances or retreats, clears the shore or turns about, the bank varies; no kaleidoscope changes more quickly; the views alter to form again; the perspective is deceptive. This block appears like a tripod, then it looks like a lion, then like an angel opening its wings, then like a seated figure reading a book. Nothing is more changeable than the clouds, unless it may be the rocks.

These forms appear grand, not beautiful. Far from that; they are sometimes revolting and hideous. The rock has wens, cysts, blotches, knobs and warts. Mountains are the protuberances of the earth. Madame de Staël, hearing Monsieur de Chateaubriand, who had rather high shoulders, speak slightingly of the Alps, said: "Jealousy of the hunch-back." The great outlines and the great sublimity of nature, the cradle of the ocean, the profile of the mountains, the shade of the forests, and the blue of the heavens, are composed of elements of intense discord mingled harmoniously together. Beauty has its lines, deformity also has its own. There is the smile and also the grin. Disintegration has the same effect upon the rock as upon the cloud. The one floats and decomposes, the other is stationary and disintegrates. A remnant of the agony of chaos remains in creation. Brilliant things have their scars. An ugliness, sometimes dazzling, is mingled with things most magnificent, and seems to protest against order. There is a grimace in the cloud. There is a heavenly grotesqueness. Each line is broken in the water, in the foliage, on the rock; and it is impossible to tell what parodies may be seen there. Irregularity reigns. Not an outline is correct. Large? Yes. Pure? No. Examine the clouds; all kind of faces are drawn there; all kinds of resemblances are seen there; all kinds of figures are sketched there. Look there for a Greek profile! You will find Caliban, not Venus. You will never see the Parthenon there, but sometimes, at nightfall, a grand table of shadow, resting on two door-posts of cloud and surrounded by blocks of sea-fog will roughly sketch, here in the fading twilight, an immense and prodigious cromlech.

VII
Country and Ocean

AT Guernsey the manors are monumental. Some of them have, along the road, a frontage of wall set like an ornament and pierced with a carriage gate and a pedestrian gate, side by side. In the jambs and arches, time has hollowed out deep crevices in which the tortula moss shelters its germinating spores, and where it is not unusual to find bats sleeping. The hamlets under the trees are decrepit and old. The cottages have the aged quality of cathedrals. A stone cabin on the road from les Hubies has a niche in its wall containing the stump of a small column and this date, "1405." Another on the side of Balmoral displays on its front, like the country houses of Hernani and Astigarraga, a sculptured coat-of-arms cut right in the stone. At every step the farm-houses show their windows with lozenged panes, their stair towers, and their Renaissance archivolts. Not a door that has not its horse-block of granite.

Other huts have formerly been boats; the hull of a boat, turned over and supported on stakes and cross-beams, forms a roof. A vessel with its keel uppermost is a church; with the arch downward, it is a ship; the recipient of prayer, reversed, subdues the sea.

In the arid parishes of the western part, the common well with its little dome of white stonework, in the midst of the untilled lands, looks like a marabout from Arabia.

A perforated beam, with a stone for a pivot, closes the hedges of a field; one can recognize by certain marks the sticks which the hobgoblins and witches ride astride at night.

Pell-mell on the slopes of the ravines are displayed the fern, the bindweed, the wolf-rose, the holly with its crimson berries, the white thorn, the rose-thorn, the Scotch dane-wort, the privet, and the long, pleated thongs called "collarettes of Henry IV." Amidst all this grass there multiplies and prospers an epilobe with a husk very much liked for food by the asses, and which the botanist with elegance and modesty calls by the name of Onagracea. Everywhere thickets, hedges of yoke-elm trees, "all kinds of tares," green copses, in which warbles a winged world, laid in wait for by a creeping world; blackbirds, linnets, redbreasts, jays; the goldfinch of the Ardennes rushes with its jerky motion; flights of starlings manœuvre in spirals; elsewhere the greenfinch, the goldfinch, the Picardy jackdaw, the red-footed crow. Here and there a snake.

Little waterfalls, brought through troughs of worm-eaten wood from which the water escapes in drops, turn the mills, the nose of which is heard under the boughs. In the yards of some of the farms may still be seen the cider press and the old circle of hollow stone in which the wheel turned as it crushed the apples. The cattle drink in troughs like sarcophagi. A Celtic king has perhaps rotted in this granite case from which the cow, with Juno eyes, is peacefully drinking. The woodpeckers and the wagtails come in a friendly way to steal the grain from the fowls.

At the shore everything is tawny. The wind blows away the grass burned by the sun. Some churches are covered with ivy which reaches as high as the belfry. In places in the wild heather a rocky excrescence is turned into a thatched cottage. Boats stranded on the beach, for want of a harbor, are supported on large stones. sails of vessels seen on the horizon are rather the color of ochre or salmon yellow than white. On the side facing the rain and the north wind the trees are covered with a fur of lichens; the stones themselves seem to take precautions and possess a covering of moss, well grown and thick. There are heard murmurs, whisperings, the cracking of branches, sudden flights of sea-birds, some with a silver fish in their beaks; an abundance of butterflies, varying in color according to the seasons, and all kinds of hollow sounds in the sonorous rock. Grazing horses gallop across the heath. They roll, bound, stop short, allow their manes to be tossed in the breeze and look before them on the waste of waters which roll on indefinitely. In May the old rural and marine buildings are covered by stock gilly-flowers; in June by wall lilacs.

In the dunes the batteries crumble. Disuse of the cannons is profitable to the countrymen; the nets of the fishermen dry on the port-holes. Between the four walls of the ruined Block-house, a wandering ass, or goat fastened to a stake, browses on the thrift grass and the blue thistle. Half-clad children make merry there. In the paths can be seen the hop-scotch games they trace there.

In the evening the setting sun, radiantly horizontal, slants in the hollow roads, lighting the slow return of the heifers as they linger to taste the hedges on the right and left, making the dog bark. The barren capes of the western shore plunge down in a waving line behind the sea; a few rare tamarinds shiver there. At twilight the Cyclopean walls permit the daylight to shine aslant their stones, making long crests of black lacework on the top of the hills. The sound of the winds heard in these solitudes gives one the sensation of extreme distance.

VIII
Saint-Pierre-Port

ST. PETER PORT, or Saint-Pierre-Port, capital of Guernsey, was formerly built of carved wooden houses brought from Saint-Malo. A beautiful stone house of the sixteenth century still stands in the Grand' Rue.

Saint-Pierre-Port is a free port. The city is situated in a chaos of valleys and hills clustered around the Old Port as if they had been held in the grasp of a giant. The ravines make the streets, stairs shorten the turns. Excellent Anglo-Norman teams gallop up and down the extremely steep streets.

In the large square, the market-women seated on the pavement in the open air are wet by the winter showers; but a few steps away is the statue of a prince. A foot of rain falls in a year at Jersey and ten and a half inches at Guernsey. The fish dealers fare better than the vegetable gardeners. The fish market, a large covered hall, is furnished with marble tables, on which are handsomely displayed the hauls of fish, which are often wonderful in Guernsey.

There is no public library. There is a mechanical and literary society, also a college. As many churches are possible are built. When they are finished they are approved by "the Lords of the Council." It is not unusual to see wagons passing through the street carrying wooden ogive windows, presented by such a carpenter to such a church.

There is a court-house. The judges, dressed in purple robes, give their judgment in a loud voice. During the last century butchers could not sell a pound of beef or mutton before the magistrates had chosen theirs.

Many private "chapels" protested against the official churches. Enter one of these chapels and you will hear a countryman explaining to the others Nestrorianism—that is to say, the difference between the Mother of Christ and the Mother of God, or teaching how the Father is power, while the Son is only a limited power, which very much resembles the heresy of Abelard. Many restless Irish Catholics attend these meetings, so that the theological discussions are sometimes punctuated by orthodox fisticuffs.

Sunday stagnation is the rule. Everything is permitted on Sunday except drinking a glass of beer. If you were thirsty on "the holy Sabbath day" you would scandalize the worthy Amos Chick, who is licensed to sell ale and cider on High Street. Sunday law—sing without drinking. Except in prayer, they do not say, "My God," but instead, "My good." The word good replaces the word God. A young assistant French teacher in a boarding-school, having picked up her scissors, exclaiming, *"Ah, mon Dieu!"* was dismissed for having sworn. These people are more biblical than evangelical.

They have a theatre. A private door opening on a corridor in a deserted street. The interior resembles the architecture adopted for hay-lofts. Satan is not surrounded by luxuries, and is badly housed. Opposite the theatre is the prison, another dwelling of the same individual.

On the north hill, at Castle Carey (solecism, we should say, Carey Castle), there is a precious collection of pictures, most of them Spanish; were it open to the public, it would be called a museum. In certain aristocratic houses there are curious specimens of Dutch painted tiles, with which the chimney-piece of the Czar Peter at Saardam is adorned, and of those magnificent faïence coverings, called in Portugal *azulejos*, products of a great art, the ancient manufacture of fine earthenware, revived to-day more beautiful than ever, thanks to men like Dr. Lasalle, of manufacturers like Premières, and to pottery painters like Deck and Devers.

The causeway from Antin to Jersey is called Rouge-Bouillon; the faubourg Saint-Germain of Guernsey goes by the name of les Rohais; beautiful streets abound, well laid out and intersected by gardens. In Saint-Pierre-Port there are as many trees as roofs, more nests than houses, more sounds of birds than of carriages. Les Rohais has the grand aristocratic air of the fashionable parts of London, and is white and clean.

Cross a ravine, pass over Mill Street, enter a sort of niche between two high houses, ascend a narrow and interminable winding staircase with unsteady flagging, and you are in a Bedouin city—houses, foundries, narrow lanes with broken pavements, burned gable ends, dwelling-houses going to ruin, deserted rooms without doors or windows, where the grass grows; beams crossing the street, ruins barring the passage, here and there a shed inhabited by little naked boys and pale women; one would mistake it for Zaatcha.

At Saint-Pierre-Port, a watchmaker is called a *montrier*; an appraiser, an *encanteur*; a whitewasher, a *picturier*; a mason, a *plâtreur*; a foot-doctor, a *chiropodiste*; a cook, a *couque*; one does not knock at the door, but *tape à l'hû*. Madam Pescott is "custom-house agent and ship-furnisher." A barber announced in his shop the death of Wellington in these terms: "The commander of the old guard is dead."

Women go from door to door reselling, in small quantities, things bought at the bazaars or markets. This industry is called *chiner*. The *chineuses*, very poor, gain a few farthings with great difficulty. Here is a quotation from a *chineuse*: "You know, it's very nice; I've laid aside seven sous this week." One day a friend of ours passing by gave five francs to one of them; she said: "'Thank you very much, sir; this will enable me to buy at wholesale."

In the month of May yachts begin to arrive; the bay is filled with pleasure boats, most of them rigged as schooners, some as steam yachts. Such a yacht costs its owner one hundred thousand francs a month.

Cricket prospers, boxing declines. The temperance societies reign; very useful, let us acknowledge. They have their processions and their banners, and make an almost Masonic display which softens the hearts even of the tavern-keepers. The wife of the tavern-keeper may be heard saying in the *patois* to the drunkards, while serving them: "Drink a glassful, not a bottle."

The population is healthy, beautiful, and good. The prison of the city is very often empty. When the jailer has prisoners at Christmas, he gives them a little family banquet.

The local architecture has its peculiarities, of which it is tenacious. The city of Saint-Pierre-Port is faithful to the queen, to the Bible, and to sash-windows. In summer the men bathe nude; a pair of drawers is immodest; it attracts attention.

Here mothers excel in dressing their children; nothing is prettier than the variety of little toilettes coquettishly designed. Children go about alone in the streets—touching and sweet evidence of confidence. The little ones take the babies.

As to the fashions, Guernsey copies Paris. Not always; sometimes the brilliant reds or crude blues show the English alliance. However, we have heard a local milliner, advising an elegant native, protesting against indigo and scarlet, and adding this delicate observation: "I find that a color which is ladylike and genteel is a happy inspiration."

The maritime carpentry of Guernsey is renowned; the wharf is crowded with repair shops. Boats are drawn up on the beach by the sound of the flute. "The flutist," says the master carpenter, "works harder than the workman."

Saint-Pierre-Port has a Pollet like Dieppe and a Strand like London. A man of the world will not be seen on the street with an album or a portfolio under his arm, but he will go to the market on Saturday carrying a basket. The passage of a royal personage has been made a pretext for a monument. The dead are buried within the city. The college street closely skirts two cemeteries on its right and left. A tomb of February, 1610, is part of a wall.

L'Hyvreuse is a square of grass and trees, which can be compared to the most beautiful squares of the Champs-Elysées of Paris, with a view of the sea in addition. In the glass cases of the elegant bazaars one can see announcements such as this: "Here is sold the perfume recommended by the Sixth Regiment of Artillery."

The city is traversed in every direction by drays loaded with barrels of beer or with sacks of pit-coal. The pedestrian can still read other announcements here and there: *"Here a fine bull is lent as heretofore."* Again: *"The highest price is given for marbles, lead, glass, and bones." "For sale—New kidney potatoes of the best quality." "For sale—Stakes for peas; some tons of oats for chaff; a complete set of English doors for a parlor, as also a fat hog. Mon-Plaisir Farm, Saint Jacques." "For sale—Yellow carrots by the hundred, and a good French syringe. Apply at the Moulin de l'échelle Saint André." "It is forbiden to dress fish and to throw out the refuse." "For sale—An ass giving milk,"* etc., etc.

IX
JERSEY, ALDERNEY, SARK

THE Channel Islands are portions of France which have fallen into the sea and been picked up by England. Hence a complex nationality. The Jerseymen and the Guernsians are certainly not involuntarily English, but they are French without knowing it. If they know it, they make a point of forgetting it. One can tell that, somewhat, by the French they speak.

The archipelago consists of four islands—two large ones, Jersey and Guernsey, and two small ones, Alderney and Sark—without counting the islets: Ortach, the Casquets, Herm, Jethou, etc. The islets and reefs in this old Gaul are usually called "Hou." Alderney has Burhou; Sark has Bréchou; Guernsey, Lihou and Jethou; Jersey, les Ecréhou; Granville, Pirhou. There are also

Capes Hougue, la Hougue Bie, Hougue-des-Pommiers, Houmets, etc. There are the Isles of Chausey, the rock Chouas, etc. This remarkable root of the primitive language, *hou*, is found everywhere—in *houle* (the swell of the sea); *huée* (hooting); *hure* (boar's head); *hourque* (a hulk); *houre* (an old word for scaffold); *houx* (holly); *houperon* (shark); *hurlement* (roaring); *hulotte* (brown owl); *chouette* (screech owl), from whence is derived *chouan*, etc. It is perceived in the two words which express the indefinite *unda* (a wave) and *unde* (whence). It is also found in the two words which express doubt, *ou* (or) and *où* (where).

Sark is half the size of Alderney, Alderney is quarter the size of Guernsey, Guernsey is two-thirds the size of Jersey. The entire island of Jersey is exactly the size of the city of London. It would require two thousand and seven hundred Jerseys to equal France. According to the calculations of Charassin, an excellent agronomist, France, if it were as carefully cultivated as Jersey, could sustain two hundred and seventy millions of men—all Europe. Of the four islands, Sark is the smallest, and is also the most beautiful. Jersey is the largest and the prettiest. Guernsey, wild and gay, partakes of the charms of both. At Sark there is a silver mine, unworked because of the smallness of its yield. Jersey contains fifty-six thousand inhabitants; Guernsey thirty thousand; Alderney, four thousand five hundred; Sark, six hundred; Lihou, one only. The distance from one of these islands to the other, from Alderney to Guernsey and from Guernsey to Jersey, is the stride of a seven-leagued boot. The arm of the sea between Guernsey and Herm is called the Little Russel, and between Herm and Sark the Great Russel. The nearest point of France is Cape Flamanville. At Guernsey the cannon of Cherbourg can be heard and at Cherbuorg the thunder of Guernsey.

The storms in the Channel archipelago, as we have said, are terrible. Archipelagoes are the abodes of the winds. Between each island there is a corridor which causes a draft—a law bad for the sea and good for the land. The wind blows away malaria and brings shipwrecks. This is a law of the Channel Islands, as well as of other archipelagoes. Cholera has passed over Jersey and Guernsey. In the Middle Ages, however, there was such a furious epidemic in Guernsey that the bailiff burned the archives to destroy the plague.

In France these islands are usually called *English islands* and in England *Norman islands*. The Channel Islands coin money; copper only. A Roman road, which can yet be seen, led from Coutances to Jersey.

It was in 709, as we have said, that the ocean snatched Jersey from France. Twelve parishes were engulfed. Families now living in Normandy possess the lordships of these parishes; their divine right lies under the water; that is the fate of divine rights.

X

History, Legend, Religion

THE six primitive parishes of Guernsey belonged to a single lord, Néel, viscount of Cotentin, conquered at the battle of the Dunes in 1047. At this time, says Dumaresq, there was a volcano in the Channel Islands. The date of the twelve parishes of Jersey is inscribed in the Black Book of the cathedral at Coutances. The Sire de Briquebec went by the title of Baron of Guernsey. Alderney belonged to Henri l'Artisan. Jersey has submitted to two robbers, Cæsar and Rollo.

Haro is a salute to the Duke (Ha! Rollo!), unless it comes from the Saxon *haran*, to shout. The cry *Haro!* is repeated three times while kneeling on the main road, and all work ceases in the place where the cry has been uttered, until justice is done.

Before Rollo, duke of the Normans, Salomon, king of the Bretons, had been in the archipelago. This is the reason that Jersey is so much like Normandy and Guernsey so closely resembles Brittany. Nature reflects history. Jersey possesses more meadow land and Guernsey more rocks; Jersey is greener and Guernsey rougher.

Gentlemen's houses covered the islands. The Count of Essex left a ruin at Alderney, Essex Castle. Jersey possesses Montorgeuil, Guernsey has Cornet Castle. Cornet Castle is built on a rock which was formerly a Holm, or Helmet. This metaphor is found again in the Casquets, Casques. Cornet Castle was besieged by a pirate from Picardy, named Eustache, and Montorgeuil by Duguesclin. Fortresses, like women, boast of their besiegers when they are distinguished.

A pope in the fifteenth century declared that Jersey and Guernsey were neutral ground. He thought of war and not of schism. Calvinism was preached in Jersey by Pierre Morice and in Guernsey by Nicholas Baudoin. It made its entry into the Norman Archipelago in 1562. Calvin's doctrines prospered there, as well as those of Luther, very much hampered to-day by Methodism, an outgrowth of Protestantism, which contains the future of England.

Churches abound in the archipelago. This is a noticeable fact. There are temples everywhere. Catholic devotion is outdone. A corner of land in Jersey, or in Guernsey, possesses more chapels than any portion of Spanish or Italian soil of the same dimensions. Methodists, Primitive Methodists, United Methodists, Independent Methodists, Baptists, Presbyterians, Millenaries, Quakers, Bible Christians, Plymouth Brethren, Nonsectarians, etc.; add also the English Episcopal Church and the English Roman Papist. There is a Mormon chapel in Jersey. The orthodox Bibles can be distinguished by their spelling of Satan without a capital letter: *satan*. That is right.

Speaking of Satan, they hate Voltaire. The word Voltaire is, it seems, one of the varieties of the name of Satan. When Voltaire is talked about, all differences vanish; the Mormon agrees with the Anglican, united by anger, and all sects have but one hatred. The anathema of Voltaire is the point of intersection of every variety of Protestantism. It is a remarkable fact that Catholicism detests Voltaire and that Protestantism execrates him.

Geneva exceeds Rome. There is an ascending scale in malediction. Calas, Sirvin, so many eloquent pages against the dragonnades[1] are of no avail. Voltaire denied dogma; that is enough. He defended Protestants, but he wounded Protestantism. The Protestants pursue him with an orthodox ingratitude. Someone who was about to speak in public, in Saint-Hélier, to beg for a collection, was warned that if he named Voltaire in his speech the collection would be a failure. As long as the past has breath enough to make itself heard, Voltaire will be rejected. Listen to all these opinions: He has neither genius, nor talent, nor wit. When old he was insulted; when dead he was outlawed. He is everlastingly "discussed"; in that his glory consists. Is it possible to speak of Voltaire with calmness and justice? When a man rules an age and embodies progress, he is no longer subject of criticism, but of hatred.

XI

The Old Haunts and the Old Saints

THE Cyclades describe a circle; the Norman Archipelago outlines a triangle. On looking at the Channel Islands on a map, which is a man's bird's-eye view, a triangular segment of sea is seen between these three culminating points: Alderney, which marks the northern point; Guernsey, which marks the western point; Jersey, which marks the southern point. Each one of these three mother islands is surrounded by what might be called her young chicken islets. Near Alderney are Burhou, Ortach and the Casquets; near Guernsey, Herm, Jethou,

1. The series of persecutions of the French Protestants under Louis XIV.

and Lihou. On its French side Jersey opens the curve of its Bay of Saint-Aubin, toward which the two groups, scattered but distinct, of the Grelets and the Minquiers seem, in the blue of the water, which is, like the air, azure, to descend like two swarms toward the door of a bee-hive. In the centre of the archipelago, Sark, near which are Bréchou and Goat's Island, is the connecting link between Guernsey and Jersey. The comparison of the Cyclades to the Channel Islands would certainly have attracted the attention of the mystical and mythical school which, under the Restoration, attached itself to the doctrines of de Maistre advocated by d'Eckstein, and would have given him material for a symbol: the rounded Grecian Archipelago, *ore rotundo*; the Channel Archipelago, sharp, rough, surly, angular; one the emblem of harmony; the other, of dispute. It is not without reason that one is Greek and the other Norman.

Formerly, in pre-historic times, these isles of the Channel were wild. The first islanders were probably primitive men, whose type is found at Moulin-Guignon, and who belong to the race with retreating jaw-bones. One-half of the year they lived on fish and shell-fish, and the other half on what they could pick up from wrecks. To pillage their coasts was their main expedient. They knew only two seasons—*the season of fishing and the season of shipwreck*; like the Greenlanders, who call summer *the hunt for reindeer* and winter *the hunt for seals.* All these islands, which at a later period belonged to Normandy, were covered with thistles, brakes, and brambles, lairs of wild beasts, the abode of pirates. An old local chronicler said, energetically: "Rat traps and pirate traps." The Romans came there, and were only able to make a slight advance toward honesty; they crucified pirates and celebrated the *Furinales*—that is to say, the festival of thieves. This festival is still celebrated in some of our villages on the 25th of July, and in our cities all the year round.

Jersey, Sark, and Guernsey were formerly called Ange, Sarge, and Bissarge. Alderney is Redanæ, unless it is Thanet. A legend affirms that in Rat Island (*insula rattorum*), the promiscuous association of male rabbits and female rats produces the *cochon d'Inde* (guinea-pig), according to Furetière, Abbot of Chalivoy, the same who reproached La Fontaine with being ignorant of the difference between wood with the bark on and ornamental wood. It was a long time before France recognized Alderney on its shores. Alderney, in fact, only had an imperceptible place in the history of Normandy. Rabelais, however, was acquainted with the Norman Archipelago. He mentions Herm, and Sark, which he calls Cerq: "I assure you that this land is the same that I have formerly seen called the isles of Cerq and Herm, between Britanny and England." (Edition of 1558, Lyon, p. 423.)

The Casquets are dreaded on account of shipwrecks. The English, two hundred years ago, made a business of fishing up cannon there. One of these cannon, covered with oysters and mussels, is in the museum of Valognes.

Herm is a solitary; St. Tugdual, the friend of St. Sampson, prayed in Herm, the same as St. Magloire did in Sark. On all these pointed rocks have dwelt sainted hermits. Hélier prayed in Jersey, and Marcouf among the rocks of Calvados. It was the period when the hermit Eparchias became St. Cybard in the cavern of Angloulême, and where the anchorite Crescentius, in the depths of the forest of Trèves, caused the temple of Diana to crumble by looking fixedly at it for five years. It was at Sark, which was his sanctuary, his "jonad naomk," that Magloire composed the hymn for All Saints' Day, rewritten by Santeuil, *Cælo quos eadem gloria consecrat.* From thence he also threw stones at the Saxons, whose pillaging ships on two occasions disturbed him while at prayer. At this time the archipelago was also somewhat troubled by the amwarydour, chief of the Celtic colony. From time to time Magloire crossed the water and consulted with the Mactierne of Guernsey, Nivou, who was a prophet. One day Magloire, having worked a miracle, made a vow never to eat fish again. Also, to take care of the manners of the dogs and to preserve the monks from guilty thoughts, he banished female dogs from the island of Sark, a law which still exists. St. Magloire rendered several other services to the archipelago. He went to Jersey to put some sense into the populace, who on Christmas day had the bad habit of transforming themselves into all kinds of beasts in honor of Mithras. St. Magloire stopped this bad custom. His relics were stolen in the reign of Nominoë, the feudatory of Charles the Bald, by the monks of Lehon-lez-Dinan. All these facts are proven by the Bollandists, *Acta Sancti Marculphi*, etc., and by the *Ecclesiastical History* of the the Abbé Trigan. Victrice of Rouen, the friend of Martin of Tours, had his grotto in Sark, which, in the eleventh century, was under the orders of the Abbey of Montebourg. At present Sark is a fief divided among forty tenants.

XII
Local Circumstances

EACH island has its own currency, its own dialect, its own government, its special prejudices. Jersey is uneasy about a French proprietor. What if he should buy all the island! In Jersey strangers are forbidden to buy land; in Guernsey it is permitted. On the other hand, religious austerity is carried to less excess in the first island than in the second; the Jersey Sunday is a freer day than the Guernsey Sunday. The Bible is more obeyed at Saint-Pierre-Port than at Saint-Hélier. The purchase of Guernsey property is accompanied by a singular peril for the uninformed stranger; the buyer gives security on his purchase for twenty years, that the commercial and financial position of the seller shall be the same as it was at the very time in which the sale took place.

Other confusions grow out of the currency and the measures. The shilling, our old *ascalin* or *chelin*, is worth twenty-five sous in England, twenty-six sous in Jersey, and twenty-four sous in Guernsey. The *poids de la Reine* also varies; the Guernsey pound is not the Jersey pound, which, in its turn, is not the English pound. In Guernsey the fields are measured by square roods and the square rood by perches. This measurement is different in Jersey. In Guernsey only French money is used, called by English names. A franc is called a "ten-pence." The absence of symmetry is carried to such an extent that there are more women than men in the archipelago—six women to five men.

Guernsey has had many nicknames, some of them archæological; the savants call it Granosia, and the loyal, "Little England." In fact, its geometrical form resembles England; Sark would be her Ireland, but an island at the east. In the waters of Guernsey are found two hundred varieties of shellfish and forty kinds of sponges. The Romans dedicated the island to Saturn, but the Celts to Gwyn; it did not gain much by the change, for Gwyn is, like Saturn, a devourer of children. It possesses an old code of French laws which dates from 1331, and is called *le Précepte d'Assize*. Jersey, in its turn, possesses three or four old Norman tables: the court of inheritance, from whence are derived the fiefs; the *cour de Catel*, which is a criminal court; the *cour du Billet*, a commercial tribunal, and the Saturday court, a police court. Guernsey exports vinegar, cattle, and fruit, but above all, she exports herself: her principal commerce is in gypsum and granite. Guernsey contains three hundred and five uninhabited houses. Why? The answer in regard to some, at least, is told in one of the chapters of this book. The Russians who were housed in Jersey at the beginning of this century have left their mark in the horses. The Jersey horse is a singular mixture of the Norman horse and the Cossack horse; he is an admirable runner and a powerful walker; he could carry Tancred and drag Mazeppa.

In the seventeenth century there was a civil war between Guernsey and Cornet Castle, Cornet Castle being for Stuart and Guernsey for Cromwell. It is the same as though the Île Saint-Louis should declare war against the Quai des Ormes. In Jersey two factions exist, the Rose and the Laurel, diminutives of the Whigs and the Tories. Division, hierarchy, caste, compartments, please the islanders of this archipelago, so appropriately called "the unknown Normandy." The Guernsians, in particular, are so fond of islands that they count them in the population; at the head of this small social order, sixty families, the *sixty*, live apart; half-way up the social scale, forty families, the *forty*, form another group, equally isolated; around them are the people. As to the authority, which is at the same time local and English, it is divided thus: ten parishes, ten rectors, twenty constables, a hundred and sixty douzeniers, a royal court with a prosecutor and a controller, a parliament called the *States*, twelve judges called jurats, a bailiff. *Balnivus et coronator*, say the old charters. In law they follow the customs of Normandy. The prosecutor is appointed by commission and the bailiff by patent, a very serious English distinction. Besides the bailiff, who represents the civil authority, there is the dean, who rules over the spiritual welfare, and the governor, who commands the military. The other offices are outlined in the "list of gentlemen who occupy the first positions in the island."

XIII
The Work of Civilization in the Archipelago

JERSEY is the seventh port of England. In 1845 the archipelago possessed four hundred and forty vessels with a capacity of forty-two thousand tons; in its port there was a traffic of sixty thousand tons entering and of fifty-four thousand tons leaving, on twelve hundred and sixty-five vessels of all nations, of which one hundred and forty-two were steamers. These figures have more than tripled in twenty years.

Paper money is used on a large scale in the islands, and with excellent results. In Jersey, anyone who wishes can issue bank-notes; if these bank-notes are honored when they fall due, the bank is established. The bank-note of the archipelago invariably represents a pound sterling. The day when the note bearing interest shall be understood by the Anglo-Normans, they will, no doubt, make use of it, and this curious spectacle can then be seen, of the same thing in the state of Utopia in Europe and of accomplished progress in the Channel Islands. The financial revolution would be microscopically accomplished in this little corner of the world.

A firm, living, alert, and quick intelligence characterizes the Jerseymen, who could, if they wished, be excellent Frenchmen. The Guernsians, though quite as clear-sighted and reliable, are slower.

These are strong and brave people, more enlightened than is generally supposed, and among whom there is much that is astonishing. Newspapers, both English and French, are numerous here; six in Jersey, four in Guernsey; very large and very good journals. Such is the powerful and irreducible English instinct. Suppose a desert island; the day after his arrival, Robinson Crusoe publishes a newspaper, and his man Friday subscribes to it.

To complement it, there is the placard; limitless and colossal bill-posting; sheets of all colors and sizes, capital letters, pictures, illustrated texts, in the open air; on all the walls of Guernsey one vast vignette, representing a man six feet high with a bell in his hand sounding an alarm. Guernsey now contains more posters than all France.

This publicity promotes life, energy of thought, very often with unexpected results, leveling the population by the habit of reading, which produces dignity of manners. On the road to Saint-Hélier or Saint-Pierre-Port you talk with an unexceptionable man, dressed in a black coat closely buttoned, with very white linen, speaking to you of John Brown, and informing himself about Garibaldi. Is he a reverend? Not at all. He is a drover. A contemporary writer visits Jersey, enters a grocery store,[1] and,

1. Charles Asplet, Beresford street.

in a magnificent parlor communicating with the store, behind a glass case, he perceives his complete works bound and arranged in a high and large bookcase surmounted by a bust of Homer.

XIV
Other Peculiarities

THE people between one isle and another fraternize; they also laugh amiably at each other. Alderney, subordinate to Guernsey, is sometimes vexed at this, and would like to attract the traffic to herself and make Guernsey her satellite. Guernsey replies good-naturedly with this popular jest:

Hale, Pier', hale, Jean,
L'Guernesey vian.

These islanders, being an ocean family, are sometimes bitter with each other, but never really angry. Anyone who attributes grossness to them, misunderstands them. We do not attach any weight to the pretended proverbial dialogue between Jersey and Guernsey: "You are asses," replied to by "You are toads." The inhabitants of the Norman Archipelago are incapable of making such salutations. We will not admit that Vadius and Trissotin[1] have become two isles in the ocean.

Besides, Alderney has its relative importance. Alderney is the London of the Casquets. The daughter of the lighthouse keeper, Houguer, born in the Casquets, when twenty years old made the voyage to Alderney. She was

1. The pedant and the poet in Molière's *Les Femmes Savantes*.

distracted by the tumult and wished for her own native rocks again. She had never seen oxen. On seeing a horse, she exclaimed: "What a large dog!"

In these Norman Isles people grow old early, not in reality, but because it is customary for them to consider themselves old.

Two persons, meeting, converse thus: "The good man who used to pass here every day is dead." "How old was he?" "Well, at least thirty-six."

Are the women of this insular Normandy to be blamed or praised that they find it so difficult to become servants? Two in the same house find it difficult to agree. Neither one will make any concession; hence follows a very difficult, irregular, and highly spasmodic type of service. They take but moderate interest in their master, without bearing a grudge against him. He gets along as he can. In 1852 a French family, in the course of events, landed in Jersey, and took in their service a cook, native of Saint-Brelade, and a chambermaid, born in Bouley Bay. One morning in December the master of the house, having risen early, found the front door wide open, and no servants. These two women had been unable to come to an understanding, and after a quarrel, having besides taken into consideration that their wages had been paid, had packed up their belongings and left; each one went her own way, in the middle of the night, leaving their employers asleep and the door open. One had said to the other: "I will not stay with a drunkard," and the other had replied: "I will not stay with a thief."

Always the two on the ten, is an old proverb of the country. What does it mean? That if you have a workman or serving-woman, never allow your two eyes to leave off looking at their ten fingers. Advice of a hard master; it's old distrust that shows up old idleness. Diderot relates that to mend a broken pane of glass in his window in Holland, five workmen came. One carried the new pane of glass, another the putty, another the pail of water, another the trowel, and still another the sponge. It took these five men two days to replace the window-pane.

Let us attribute this to the old Gothic slowness born of servitude, as Creole indolence is born of slavery, vices shared by every nation, but which, in our day, are vanishing under the friction of progress; are disappearing in every land, in the Channel Islands as well, and perhaps even more rapidly there than elsewhere. In these industrious island communities, energy, associated with honesty, becomes more and more the law of labor.

In the Norman Archipelago certain things belonging to the past may still be seen. This, for example: COURT OF FIEF, held in the parish of Saint-Ouen, in M. Malzard's house, Monday, the 22nd of May, 1854, at the hour of noon. The court is presided over by the seneschal; on his right is the provost, and on his left the bailiff. Present at the hearing, the noble squire, Lord of Morville, and also of other places, who possesses a part of the village in vassalage. The seneschal required an oath from the provost, the purport of which is as follows: "You swear and promise by your faith in God, that you will both well and faithfully perform the duties of provost of the court of fief and the manor of Morville, and will preserve the right of the lord." And the said provost, having raised his hand and saluted the lord, said: "I swear it."

French is spoken in the Norman Archipelago, with some variations, as one will see: *Paroisse* (parish) is pronounced *paresse*. One has *un mâ à la gambe qui n'est pas commua* (one has a pain in the leg that is unusual). "How do you do?" *Petitement. Moyennement. Tout à l'aisi*; these three words mean badly, not badly, well. To be sad is "to have low spirits." To feel badly is to have *un mauvais sent*. To make mischief is *faire du ménage*. To sweep the room, to wash the dishes, etc. is *picher son fait*. The bucket, often filled with refuse, is *le bouquet*. One is not drunk, one is *bragi*; not wet, but *mucre*. To be hypochondriacal is to have *des fixes*. A girl is a *hardelle*; an apron, a *devantier*; a tablecloth, a *doublier*; a gown is a *dress*; a pocket, a *pouque*; a drawer, a *haleur*; a cabbage, a *caboche*; a closet, a *press*; a coffin, a *coffre à mort*. Christmas boxes or New Year's gifts are *irvières*; the causeway is the *cauchie*; a mask is a *visagier*; pills are *boulets*; soon is *bien dupartant*. The market-place contains but little, provisions are scarce, fish and vegetables are *écarts*. Early potatoes are *temprunes* in Guernsey, *heurives* in Jersey. To go to law, to build, to travel, to keep house, to keep open table, to entertain, is *coûtageux* (in Belgium, and in French Flanders, *frayeux*). A girl doesn't let herself be kissed for fear of returning to her parents' home *bouquie* (in disarray, or with her hair undone). *Noble* is one of the words most frequently used in this French locality. Everything which succeeds is a *noble train*. A cook brings from market *un noble quartier de veau*. A well-fed duck is a *noble pirot*. A fat goose is a *noble picot*. Judicial and legal terms are also tinged with a soupçon of Norman law. A law document, a petition, a law bill are "lodged at the record-office." A father who gives his daughter in marriage owes her nothing, *pendant qu'elle est couverte de mari*.

According to the Norman custom, an unmarried woman who is pregnant, points out the father of her child from among the population. She sometimes makes her own choice. This occasions some inconvenient consequences.

The French spoken by the old inhabitants of the archipelago is, perhaps, not altogether their fault.

Fifteen years ago many French came to Jersey; we have already mentioned this fact. (Let us say, in passing, that it was not well understood why they left their country; some of the inhabitants called them *ces biaux révoltés*.) One of these Frenchmen received visits from an old professor of the French language who said he had been established in the country for some time. He was an Alsatian, accompanied by his wife. He showed little reverence for the Norman French which is the Channel idiom. On entering, he said in his own strongly tinged accent: *"J'ai pien te la beine à leur abrendre le vranzais. On barle ici badois* (I have much trouble in teaching them French, they speak *patois* here)."

"How, *badois*?"

"Yes, *badois*."

"Ah! *patois*?"

"So it is, *badois*."

The professor continued his complaints about the Norman *badois*. His wife having spoken to him, he turned toward her and said: *"Ne me vaites pas ici de zènes gonchicales* (Don't make any conjugal scenes here)."

XV
Antiquities and Antiques; Customs, Laws, and Manners

LET us acknowledge that to-day each of the Norman isles possesses its college and many schools, also excellent professors; some of them French, others natives of Guernsey and Jersey.

As to the *patois* denounced by the Alsatian professor, it is a real language, in no way contemptible. This *patois* is a complete idiom, very rich and quite singular. By its obscure but profound light it elucidates the origin of the French language. This *patois* was the language of many learned men, among whom we must mention the one who translated the Bible into the Guernsey language. M. Métivier is to the Celtic-Norman tongue what the Abbé Eliçagaray was to the language of the Basque provinces of Spain.

In the Isle of Guernsey there are an eighteenth-century chapel with a stone roof, and a Gallic statue of the sixth century, which serves as a jamb to the door of a cemetery; probably unique specimens. Another unique specimen is a descendant of Rollo, a very worthy gentleman, who peaceably dwells in the archipelago. He consents to consider Queen Victoria his cousin.

The pedigree is apparently proven, and is not at all improbable.

In this island the people value their coats-of-arms highly. We have heard M. make this reproach to D.: "They have taken our escutcheons and placed them on their tombs."

A countryman says: "My ancestors."

Fleurs-de-lys are abundant; England willingly wears fashions which France has discarded. There are few citizens of the middle classes who are without a fence ornamented by fleurs-de-lys.

They are very touchy about misalliances. In—I did not remember which of the islands—Alderney, I think, the son of a very old family of wine merchants, having married the daughter of a recent hatter, the indignation was universal; all the island blamed the son, and a venerable dame exclaimed: "Is that a cup to give parents to drink from?" The Princess Palatine was not more tragically exasperated when she reproached one of her cousins, married to the Prince of Tingre, with having lowered herself to a Montmorency.

At Guernsey, to offer your arm to a lady means betrothal. A bride, during the eight days following her wedding, goes out only to church. A taste of prison seasons the honeymoon. Besides, a certain modesty is appropriate. Marriage requires so few formalities that it is easily concealed. Cahaigne, when in Jersey, heard this exchange of questions and answers between a mother, an old woman, and her daughter, forty years old: "Why do you not marry this Stevens?" "Do you wish, then, mother, that I should be married twice?" "How so?" "We have now been married four months."

At Guernsey, in October 1863, a girl was imprisoned for six months "for having annoyed her father."

XVI
Continuation of Peculiarities

THE Channel Islands have as yet but two statues, one at Guernsey, the Prince Consort, the other at Jersey, called "the Gilded King": they call it by that name because they do not know whom it represents and cannot tell whom it immortalizes. It stands in the centre of the large square of Saint-Hélier. An anonymous statue is still a statue, and that flatters the self-esteem of the population; it is probably erected to the glory of someone. Nothing is quarried more slowly than a statue, and nothing grows faster. When it is not the oak, it is the mushroom. Shakespeare waits everlastingly for his statue in England, Beccaria is still waiting for his in Italy, but it appears that M. Dupin is going to have his in France. It is gratifying to see these public evidences of respect given to the men who have been an honor to their country, as in London, for example, where the enthusiasm, admiration, regret, and the crowd in mourning grew visibly at the three respective funerals of Wellington, Palmerston, and the boxer, Tom Sayers.

Jersey has a Hangman's Hill, which is lacking in Guernsey. Sixty years ago a man was hanged in Jersey for having stolen twelve sous out of a drawer; it is true that about the same time a child of thirteen was hanged in England for stealing cakes and in France the innocent Lesurques was guillotined. These are the beauties of capital punishment.

Jersey, more advanced than London, would not now tolerate the gallows. Here the death penalty is tacitly abolished.

In prison the inmates' reading is carefully watched. A prisoner is allowed to read the Bible only. In 1830 a Frenchman named Béasse, condemned to death, was allowed to read the tragedies of Voltaire while awaiting his execution. This atrocity would not now be tolerated. Béasse was the next to the last man hanged in Jersey. Tapner is, and will be, let us hope, the last.

Until 1825 the bailiff of Guernsey received for his fee the thirty Tours pounds, about fifty francs, that were given him in the time of Edward III. Now he receives three hundred pounds sterling. In Jersey the royal court is called the *cohue* (mob). A woman who undertakes a lawsuit is called the *actrice*. In Guernsey people are condemned to be whipped; in Jersey the accused is put in an iron cage. The people laugh at the relics of the saints, but they venerate the old boots of Charles II. They are respectfully preserved in the manor of Saint-Ouen. Tithes are collected. On walks one notices the shops of the tithe-collectors. *Jambage* is abolished, but *poulage* is strictly enforced.[1] The writer of these lines gives two hens a year to the Queen of England.

The tax is rather oddly based on the entire fortune, real or surmised, of the tax-payer. The result is that great consumers are not attracted to the island. M. de Rothschild, if he lived in Guernsey in some pretty cottage worth about twenty thousand francs, would pay fifteen hundred thousand francs a year. Let us add that if he resided here only five months in the year, he would pay nothing. It is the sixth month that is to be dreaded.

As for climate, it is an extended spring. Winter there may be; summer there is, without doubt, but not in extreme; never as in Senegal or Siberia. The Channel Islands are to England what the isles of Hyères are to France. People with delicate lungs are sent there from Albino. Such a parish in Guernsey as Saint-Martin, for example, resembles a little Nice. No Tempe, no Gémenos, no Val-Suzon surpasses the valley of Vaux in Jersey and the valley of Talbots in Guernsey.

Looking only at the southern slopes, nothing could be greener, milder, and fresher than this archipelago. "High

1. The tributes, respectively, of hams and poultry.

life" can exist there. These little islands have their stylish people. French is spoken here; we have just recollected that the upper circles say: *"Elle a-z-une rose à son chapeau* (She has a rose in her hat)." In this style they carry on charming conversations.

Jersey admires General Don; Guernsey, General Doyle. These were two old governors who flourished at the beginning of the century. Don street is in Jersey and Doyle road in Guernsey. Besides, Guernsey has built and dedicated to her general a great column which overlooks the sea, and which can be seen from the Casquets; and Jersey has honored General Don with a cromlech. This cromlech was near Saint-Hélier; it was on the hill where Fort Regent now stands. General Don accepted the cromlech, and ordered it carted, block by block, to the shore, placed it on a frigate, and carried it off. This monument was the marvel of the Channel Islands; it was the only circular cromlech of the archipelago; it had looked down on the Cimmerians, who remembered Tubal-Cain, in the same way that the Esquimaux remember Frobisher; it had looked down upon the Celts, whose brain, in comparison to the brain of the present day, is in the proportion of thirteen to eighteen; it had looked down into those strange wooden donjons in which bodies are found in sepulchral mounds, and which make one hesitate between du Cange's etymology of *domgio* and Barleycourt's of *domi-junctae*; it had looked down on the flint tomahawk and the Druid hatchet; it had seen the great willow Teutates; it had existed before the Roman wall; it embodied four thousand years of history. At night the sailors perceived, afar off in the moonlight, this enormous crown of straight rocks situated on the high Jersey cliffs. To-day it is a heap of stones in some corner of Yorkshire.

XVII
Compatibility of Extremes

THE law of primogeniture exists; also tithes, the parish, and the lord; there is the lord of fief, the lord of manor; the clamor of *haro* (hue and cry); "the cause in the clamor of *haro* between Nicolle, squire, and Godfrey, lord of Mélèches, has been called before the justices, after the opening of the court, by the usual prayer." (Jersey, 1864). The pound of Tours, also the law of seizin and ouster, the right of forfeiture, the feudal tenure, the law of redemption exist, the past exists. One may be messire. There are bailiff and seneschal, also *centeniers, vingteniers*, and *douzeniers*. There are the *vingtaine* at Saint-Sauveur, and the *cueillette* at Saint-Ouen. The canonical hours are in the forenoon. Christmas, Easter, Midsummer, and Michaelmas are the days when legal payments fall due. Real estate is not sold, it is granted. Dialogues such as these may be heard before the authorities: "Provost, is this the day, the place, and the hour for which the proceedings of the courts of feuds and seigniory have been published?" "Yes." "Amen." "Amen." The case "of the citizen denying that his holding is in enclaves" is provided for. There are "contingencies, treasure trove, weddings, etc., from which the lord may profit." There is the "lord's enjoyment as protector until a capable party presents himself." Also summons and confession, record and double record; besides the superior courts, enfeoffments, confiscations, freeholds, and royal rights.

In the midst of the Middle Ages, do you say? No; say rather in the midst of liberty. Come, live, breathe freely.

Go where you please, do what you like, be what you wish; no one has the right to know your name. If you have a god of your own, preach him. If you have a flag of your own, erect it. Where? In the street. If it is white, let it be white; if it is blue, all right; if it is red, why red is a color. If you wish to denounce the government, mount a stone and make a speech. If you wish to assemble together publicly, assemble. How many? As many as you wish. What is the limit? No limit. If you wish to assemble the people, do so. In what place? In the public square. I may attack royalty? That is nothing to us. If I wish to post notices, there are the walls. One can think, speak, write, print, and harangue without interference.

To hear everything and to read everything implies, on the other side, to speak everything and to write everything. Thence absolute freedom of word and press. The printer has his opinions and the apostle his, but it is the pope only who can carry out his opinions. It only depends upon you to be pope. You have only to invent a religion. Imagine a new form of god, of whom you will constitute yourself the prophet. No one makes any objection to it. If need be, the policemen will help you. There are no hindrances. Entire liberty; a grand sight. Things already decided are rediscussed. After the same style they preach to the priest and judge the judge. The papers print: "Yesterday the court passed an iniquitous sentence." An astonishing thing! Possible judicial error has no claim to respect. Human justice is given over to disputation as well as divine revelations. Individual independence could with difficulty have more scope. Everyone is his own ruler, not by law, but by custom. Sovereignty is so complete and so intermingled with life that it is, so to speak, no longer perceived. Justice can be breathed; it is colorless, imperceptible, and as necessary as the air. At the same time one is "loyal." These are citizens who are proud of being subjects. To sum up, the nineteenth century rules and governs; it penetrates through all the windows of the Middle Ages left standing. A vein of liberty runs through the old Norman laws. This ruin is penetrated by the light of liberty. Never was an anachronism so accommodating. History calls this archipelago Gothic; as far as industry and intelligence are concerned, it belongs to the present day. The simple pleasure of breathing prevents the people from being inert. This does not prevent one from being lord of Mélèches. Legally, a form of feudalism, actually a republic. Such is this phenomenon.

To this liberty there is one exception—one only. We have already hinted at it. There is a tyrant in England. The tyrant of the English is known by the same name as the creditor of Don Juan, it is Sunday. The English say, "time is money"; the tyrant Sunday reduces the business week to six days; in other words, deprives England of the seventh of her capital. And it is not possible to make any resistance. Sunday reigns by custom, which is more despotic than law. Sunday, this king of England, has Low Spirits for his Prince of Wales. He has the right of boredom. He closes the workshops, the laboratories, the libraries, the museums, the theatres, almost the gardens and the woods. However, let us insist upon it, the English Sunday oppresses Jersey less than Guernsey. At Guernsey a poor Frenchwoman who keeps a tavern, pours out a glass of beer for someone; it is Sunday; fifteen days in prison. An exile, a bootmaker, wishes to work on Sunday to gain wherewith to feed his wife and children. He closes his shutters so that his hammer cannot be heard; if it is heard, a fine. One Sunday, an artist, just arrived from Paris, stops on the road to draw a tree; an officer speaks to him and directs him to cease this offence, and through leniency does not bring him before the recorder. A Southampton barber shaves someone on Sunday; for penalty he pays three pounds sterling to the public treasury. The reason is quite simple; God rested on this day.

Moreover, the people are happy who are free six days out of seven. Sunday being the symbol of servitude, we know nations whose week contains seven Sundays.

Sooner or later these last fetters will disappear. Without doubt the spirit of orthodoxy is tenacious. Without doubt, for example, the action brought against Bishop Colenso is serious. Think, however, of the advance that England has made toward liberty since the time when Elliot was brought before the court of assizes for having declared that the sun was inhabited.

There is an autumn for the fall of prejudices. It is the time of the decline of monarchies. This time has arrived.

The civilization of the Norman Archipelago is going onward and will not stop. This civilization is indigenous, which does not prevent it from being hospitable and cosmopolitan. In the seventeenth century it underwent the reaction of the English Revolution, and in the nineteenth the rebound of the French Revolution. Twice it has experienced the deep agitation independence.

Besides, all archipelagoes are free countries. Mysterious work of the sea and the wind.

XVIII
Asylums

THESE islands, formerly to be dreaded, have become milder. They were composed of rocks, they are now places of refuge. These abodes of distress have become points of rescue. All those who escape disaster emerge there. All those who are shipwrecked, either by tempests or revolutions, come there. These men, the sailor and the exile, wet with different kinds of foam, dry themselves at the same time in this warm sunlight. Chateaubriand, young, poor, obscure, without a country, seated himself on a stone of the old wharf at Guernsey. A good woman said to him in French: "What do you want, my friend?" It is very sweet to the banished Frenchman, and almost a mysterious alleviation, to find once more in the Channel Islands this idiom, which is civilization itself; these accents of our provinces; these clamors of our ports; these refrains of our streets and of our fields. *Reminiscitur Argos*. In the midst of this ancient Norman population Louis XIV cast a useful number of brave

Frenchmen speaking pure French; the revocation of the Edict of Nantes revitalized the French language in these islands. The French banished from France gladly spend their time in this Channel archipelago; they walk about among the rocks and dream the reveries of men who wait; this choice is explained because of the charm of finding their native tongue spoken there. The Marquis de Rivière, the same person to whom Charles X said: "By the way, I have forgotten to tell thee that I have made thee a duke," wept when he saw the apple trees of Jersey, and preferred the Pier' road of Saint-Hélier to Oxford street in London. It is on this Pier' road that the Duke d'Anville dwelt, who was also called Rohan and La Rochefoucauld. One day when M. d'Anville, who owned an old hunting dog, was obliged to consult a physician of Saint-Hélier about his health, he thought it would be well to consult him also about his dog. He asked the Jersey physician for a prescription for his terrier. The dog was not even sick; it was a joke on the part of the great lord. The doctor gave his advice. The next day the duke received a bill from the doctor, written as follows:—

Two consultations:
1. For the duke, one louis.
2. For his dog, ten louis.

These islands have been places of refuge for the unfortunate. Every form of misfortune has passed through them, from Charles II fleeing from Cromwell to the Duc de Berry on his way to Louvel. Two thousand years ago Cæsar, who was promised to Brutus, went there. From the seventeenth century to date these islands have extended a welcome to the whole world; their hospitality is their pride. They have the impartiality which belongs to asylums.

Royalists, they receive the conquered republic; Huguenots, they admit the Catholic exile. They even show him the politeness, as we have remarked, of hating Voltaire as much as he does. And as, according to many people, and especially according to the religions of State, to hate our enemies is the best way of loving us, Catholicism ought to find itself very much loved in the Channel Islands.

For the newcomer, escaped from shipwreck, and living there a phase in his unknown destiny, the pressure of this solitude is sometimes overwhelming; there is despair in the air, and suddenly one feels a soothing caress in it; a breath passes and lifts one up again. What is this breath? A note, a word, a sigh; nothing. This nothing is sufficient. Who in this world has not felt the power of this: a nothing!

Ten or twelve years ago a Frenchman, who had lately landed in Guernsey, was wandering about on one of the western beaches, alone, sad, bitter, thinking of his lost country. In Paris the people saunter, in Guernsey they roam. This island appeared dismal to him. A fog covered everything; the shore resounded under the force of the breakers; the sea tossed immense explosions of foam over the rocks; even the heavens were threatening and black. It was, nevertheless, spring; but spring by the sea has a wild sound; it is called the equinox. It is more like a hurricane than a zephyr; one day in May can be remembered when the foam under this blast leaped twenty feet higher than the top of the signal mast, which is on the highest platform of Cornet Castle. This Frenchman felt as though he was in England; he did not know a word of English; he saw an old Union Jack, torn by the wind, floating from a ruined tower at the end of a bleak cape; two or three cottages were there; in the distance all was sand and heath, waste land, thorny furze; some horizontal batteries, with large embrasures, showed their angles; the stones cut by man partook of the same sadness as the rocks hewn by the sea; the Frenchman felt within him the depth of inward sadness which is the beginning of homesickness; he looked, he listened; not a ray; cormorants in pursuit, clouds in flight; everywhere on the horizon a leaden weight; a vast black and blue curtain falling from the zenith; the ghost of melancholy in the shroud of the storm; nowhere anything that betokened hope, and nothing which resembled his native land; the Frenchman brooded, more and more cast down; suddenly he raised his head; a voice reached him from one of the half-opened cottages—a voice, clear, fresh, delicate—a child's voice, and this voice sang:

The key of the fields, the key of the woods,
The key of the loving hearts.

XIX

ALL these reminiscences of France in the archipelago are not equally happy. We know someone who, in the charming island of Sark, one Sunday, heard in a farmyard this verse of an old French Huguenot song, very solemnly sung in chorus by religious voices having the grave Calvinistic accent:

Everybody stinks, stinks, stinks,
Like a carcass;
Nothing, nothing, nothing, but my kind Jesus,
Who has a sweet perfume.

It is melancholy and almost sad to think that people have died in Cévennes hearing these same words. This verse, involuntarily high comic, is tragic. People laugh at it; they should cry over it. At this verse Bossuet, one of the forty members of the French Academy, cried "Kill! kill!"

Moreover, as for fanaticism, hideous when it persecutes and touching when it is persecuted, the outward hymn is nothing. It has its great and sad inner hymn, which it chants mysteriously in its soul beneath the words. It penetrates even the grotesque with sublimity, and whatever may be the poetry and the prose of its priests, it transfigures this prose and this poetry by the immense latent harmony of its faith. It corrects the deformity of formulæ by the grandeur of trials nobly borne and punishments endured. Where poetry is wanting, it substitutes conscience. The libretto of the martyr may be insipid, but what does that matter if the martyr is noble.

XX
Homo Edax

IN time the configuration of an island changes. An island is formed by the ocean. Matter is eternal, not its appearance. Everything on the earth is perpetually moulded by death, even the extrahuman monuments, even granite. Everything changes shape, even the shapeless. Edifices built by the sea crumble like the rest.

The sea, which has raised them, overthrows them.

In fifteen hundred years, between the mouth of the Elbe and the mouth of the Rhine alone, seven islands out of twenty-three have disappeared. Look for them at the bottom of the sea. It was in the thirteenth century that the sea formed the Zuyder Zee; in the fifteenth it created the Bay of Bier-Bosch by submerging twenty-two villages; in the sixteenth it improvised the Gulf of Dollart by swallowing Torum. A hundred years ago, before Bourgdault, now cut perpendicularly on the Norman cliff, the bell of the old Bourgdault could still be seen submerged under the sea. It is said that at Ecréhou, sometimes, at low tide, can be seen trees, now submarine, of the druid forest which was drowned in the eighth century. Formerly Guernsey was joined to Herm, Herm to Sark, Sark to Jersey, and Jersey to France. Between France and Jersey a child could stride across the strait. A fagot was thrown there when the bishop of Coutances passed by, in order that he need not wet his feet.

The ocean builds up and demolishes; and man assists the sea, not by building up, but by destroying.

Of all the teeth of time, the most industrious is the pick-axe of man. Man is a gnawing creature. He modifies and alters everything subject to him, whether for better or worse. Here he disfigures, there he transfigures. The Breach of Roland is not so fabulous as it appears to be; the mark of man is imprinted on nature. The scar of human work is visible on the divine work. It seems that a certain power of achievement is given to man. He appropriates creation to human needs. Such is his function. He has the audacity necessary to accomplish it; one might also say the impiety. The collaboration is something offensive. Man, this short-lived being, this creature always surrounded by death, undertakes the infinite. To all these ebbs and flows of nature, to element which shows affinity with element, to surrounding phenomena, to the vast traveling of forces in the depths, man declares his blockade. He too states his, "Thou shalt go no farther." He has his idea of fitness; the universe must accept it. Besides, has he not a universe of his own? He expects to make of it what seems to him good. A universe is raw material. The world, work of God, is man's canvas.

Everything restrains man, but nothing stops him. He overcomes limits by jumping over them. The impossible is a perpetually receding frontier.

A geological formation, having at its base the mud of the deluge and at its summit the eternal snow, is, for man, a wall like any other; he pierces it, and passes through. He divides an isthmus, subdues a volcano, cuts away a cliff, mines minerals, cuts a promontory to pieces. Formerly he took all this trouble for Xerxes; to-day, less foolish, he takes the trouble for himself. This diminution of stupidity is called progress. Man works at his house, and his house is the earth. He disarranges, displaces, suppresses, knocks down, levels, mines, undermines, digs pits, breaks, crushes, effaces that, abolishes this, and reconstructs with the materials he has thus procured. Nothing makes him hesitate; no bulk, no obstruction, no consideration of splendid material, no majesty of nature. If the immensities of nature are within his reach he batters them down. This side of God which can be ruined, tempts him; and he undertakes to assault immensity, carrying his hammer in his hand. The future will, perhaps, witness the demolition of the Alps. Globe, let thine ant alone.

The child breaking his plaything seems to be seeking its soul. Man also seems to be looking for the soul of the earth.

Let us not, however, exaggerate our power; notwithstanding what man may do, the grand lines of creation remain; the supreme mass does not depend upon man. He can produce an effect upon portions, not upon the whole. And it is well that it is so. Everything is providential. These laws are higher than we. What we do does not extend beyond the surface. Man clothes or strips the earth; the clearing away of a forest only deprives the earth of a vestment. But to cause the earth to revolve more slowly on its axis, hasten the course of the globe in its orbit, add to or subtract a fathom from the allotted seven hundred and eighteen thousand leagues daily traveled by the earth around the sun, to modify the precession of the equinoxes, to suppress one drop of rain—never! What is on high remains on high. Man may change the climate, not the season. Let him cause the moon to revolve in other than the ecliptic!

Dreamers, some of them illustrious, have dreamed of restoring perpetual spring to the earth. The extreme seasons, summer and winter, are produced by the excess of the inclination of the earth's axis on the plane of this ecliptic of which we have just spoken. In order to suppress these seasons all that would be necessary would be to straighten this axis. Nothing more simple. In the pole, plant a stake reaching to the centre of the earth, attach a chain to it, beyond the earth find a roadway, have ten teams of ten billion horses each, make them pull, the axis will straighten, and you will have spring. You see, it is not much to accomplish.

Let us look elsewhere for Eden. Spring is good; liberty and justice are better. Eden is allegorical, not material.

To be free and just depends upon us.

Serenity is within. Our perpetual spring is found within us.

XXI

Power of the Stone-Breakers

GUERNSEY is a triangle. The queen of triangles is Sicily. Sicily was sacred to Neptune, and each of its three angles was dedicated to one of the points of the trident. On the three capes were three temples—one consecrated to Dextra, another to Dubia, and the other to Sinistra. Dextra was the river cape, Sinistra the ocean cape, Dubia the rainy cape. Whatever Pharaoh Psammosteus may have said when he threatened Thrasydaeus, king of Agrigentum, with making Sicily "as round as a disc," this triangle will not be remodeled by man; it will keep its three promontories until the deluge which produced them, coming again, shall destroy them. Sicily will always have its Cape Faro pointing toward Italy, its Cape Passero looking toward Greece, and its Cape Boeo projecting toward Africa; and Guernsey will always possess its Point of Ancresse in the north, its Point Plainmont in the southwest, and its Point Jerbourg in the southeast.

The island of Guernsey is almost in a state of demolition. Its granite is good; who wants it? The whole cliff is put up at auction. The inhabitants sell the island piece by piece. The curious Roque-au-Diable has been sold lately for several pounds sterling; when the vast quarry of the Ville-Baudue is exhausted, they will pass on to another.

All over England this stone is in demand. Merely for the embankments which are being constructed on the Thames, two hundred thousand tons will be required. Loyal folk, who are particular about the solidity of royal statues, have very much regretted that the pedestal of the bronze statue of Albert is of Cheesering granite instead of the good Guernsey stone. However that may be, the coasts of Guernsey are falling under the pickaxe. At Saint-Pierre-Port, under the windows of the inhabitants of la Falue, a mountain of stone has disappeared in four years.

And the same demolition is taking place in America as in Europe. At this very time, Valparaiso is selling to the highest bidder the magnificent and venerable hills which caused it to be named "Vale of Paradise."

Old Guernsians would no longer recognize their island. They would be tempted to say, "They have changed my native place." Wellington remarked it of Waterloo, which was his native place. Add to this the fact that Guernsey, which formerly spoke French, now speaks English; another demolition.

Until the year 1805 Guernsey was divided into two islands. An inlet crossed it from side to side, from East Mount Crevel to West Mount Crevel. This inlet opens on the west opposite the Fruguiers and the two Sauts-Roquiers; bays projected quite a distance inland, one even as far as Salterns; this arm of the sea was called the Braye du Valle. In the last century Saint-Sampson was an anchorage for vessels on both sides of an ocean lane—a narrow and winding street. In the same way that the Dutch have dried up the Sea of Haarlem, making it an ugly plain, the Guernsians have filled up the Braye du Valle, now a meadow. Of the street they have made a blind alley; this blind alley is the port of Saint-Sampson.

XXII
Kind-Heartedness of the Inhabitants of the Islands

WHOEVER has seen the Norman Archipelago loves it; whoever has lived there esteems it.

They are a noble little people with large souls. They possess the spirit of the sea. These men of the Channel Islands are a peculiar race. They assume a certain supremacy over *la grand' terre*, the mainland. They look down upon the English, who in their turn, are sometimes disposed to disdain "those three or four flower pots in that bit of sea." Jersey and Guernsey reply: "We are the Normans, and it is we who conquered England." We may smile at this, but we also cannot fail to admire it.

The day will come when Paris will make the fortune of these islands by making them the fashion; and they deserve it. A constantly increasing prosperity awaits them as soon as they are known. They have the singular attraction of combining a climate conducive to idleness with a strong, industrious population. This rural spot is a workyard. The Norman Archipelago is not so sunny as the Cyclades, but it is greener; it has as much verdure as the Orkneys, and more sun. It does not possess the temple of Astypalaea, but it has the cromlechs. It does not have Fingal's Cave, but it has Sark. The Huet mill is equal to Tréport; the beach of Azette is as good as that of Trouville; Plémont equals Étretat. The country is beautiful, the people are good, history is proud of them. The strength of their character is majestic. The archipelago possesses an apostle, Hélier; a poet, Robert

Wace; a hero, Pierson; also, many of the best generals and best admirals of England were born in the archipelago. These poor fishermen are magnificent in an emergency; to aid the subscriptions gotten up for those who were suffering from the inundations at Lyons, and for the starving people of Manchester, Jersey and Guernsey gave more in proportion to their population than either France or England.

These people are very fond of risk and danger, a remnant of their old life of former days as smugglers. They go everywhere. They swarm. The Norman Archipelago colonizes to-day as did the archipelago of Greece in olden days. There is glory in that. One finds Jerseymen and Guernsians in Australia, in California, and in Ceylon. North America contains its New Jersey and its Guernsey, which is in Ohio. These Anglo-Normans, although a little stiff-necked in regard to their religious sects, possess an unalterable aptitude for progress. Every form of superstition, so be it, but all of reason, too. Has not France been a robber? Has not England been cannibalistic? Let us be modest and remember our tattooed ancestors.

Where robbers used to prosper, commerce now rules. Superb transformation. Without doubt, the work of the ages, but of mankind also. The magnanimous example of this is given by this microscopic archipelago. Small nations such as these are the proof of civilization. Let us love them and venerate them. These microcosms reflect in miniature, in all its phases, the great structure of humanity. Jersey, Guernsey, and Alderney, haunts of wild animals in former times, workshops now. Reefs once, now ports.

For one who observes that series of avatars called history, there is no more touching spectacle than to see these nocturnal sea-people mount by slow degrees until they ascend to the sunshine of civilization. The man of shadows turns and faces the dawn. Nothing is greater, nothing more pathetic. Once a pirate, now a workman; once savage, now a citizen; once a wolf, now a man. Has he less daring than formerly? No. Only this audacity moves toward the light. What splendid contrast there is between the present honest and fraternal system of navigation, coastal, inland, and commercial, and the old ill-shapen *dromond*, having for its motto, *Homo homini monstrum*. The barrier has given place to the bridge. Obstacles have been turned to good account. Where these people used to be pirates they are now pilots. And they are more enterprising, more courageous than ever. This country has remained the country of adventure at the same time as it has become the abode of honesty. The lower the point from which progress starts, the more we are touched by the ascent. The dung of the nest on the egg-shell causes one to admire the wing-span of the bird. We think good-naturedly of the old piracy of the Norman Archipelago. In the presence of all these charming and placid sails, triumphantly guided across the labyrinths of waves and rocks by the lenticular lighthouse and the electric lighthouse, one thinks—with the satisfied conscience inherent in obvious progress—of those old-time stealthy and fierce sailors who once sailed in sloops without compasses, on dark waters lividly lighted from afar, from promontory to promontory, by old-fashioned braziers with their fitful flames which, in iron cages, were tormented by the tremendous winds of the deep.

PART I

SIEUR CLUBIN

BOOK FIRST
WHAT A BAD REPUTATION IS COMPOSED OF

I
A Word Written on a Blank Page

THE CHRISTMAS of 182– was remarkable in Guernsey. It snowed on that day. In the Channel Islands, a winter where it freezes to the point of forming ice is memorable, and snow is an event.

On the morning of that Christmas day, the road which skirts the sea coast from Saint Peter Port to le Valle was perfectly white. It had been snowing from midnight until dawn. About nine o'clock, a little after sunrise, the road was almost deserted, as it was not yet time for the Anglicans to go to the church of Saint-Sampson, or for the Wesleyans to go to the Eldad chapel. In the portion of the road which separates the first tower from the second tower, there were but three passers-by,—a child, a man, and a woman. These three wayfarers, walking at a distance from each other, had evidently no connection with each other.

The child, aged about eight years, halted, and looked at the snow with curiosity. The man followed the woman at an interval of a hundred paces. He, as well as she, was proceeding in the direction of Saint-Sampson. The man, who was still young, seemed something like a working-man or a sailor. He wore his everyday clothes,—a jacket of coarse brown cloth, and trousers with tarred leggings,—which seemed to indicate that, notwithstanding the festival, he was not on his way to any chapel. His thick shoes of undressed leather, their soles garnished with big nails, left upon the snow an imprint more resembling the lock of a prison than the foot of a man.

The woman wayfarer already had on, evidently, her church toilet; she wore a large wadded mantle of black corded silk, beneath which she was very coquettishly attired in a gown of Irish poplin in alternate stripes of pink and white, and, but for her red stockings, she might have been taken for a Parisienne. She advanced with a light, free vivacity, and one divined that she was a young girl from that walk which had, as yet, borne no burden of life. She had that fugitive grace of bearing which marks the most delicate of transitions, youth, the two twilights mingled, the beginning of womanhood, the end of childhood. The man did not notice her.

All at once, near a clump of green oaks standing at the corner of a small garden, at the spot called Basses-Maisons, she turned around, and this movement made the man look at her. She halted, seemed to reflect for a moment, then stooped down, and the man thought that she wrote something on the snow with her finger. She straightened herself up, set out on her way again, and redoubled her pace; turned once more, this time with a laugh, and disappeared on the left of the road, in the path bordered by hedges which leads to the Château of Lievre. When she turned for the second time, the man recognized Déruchette, a bewitching girl of the neighborhood.

He felt no desire to hasten his steps, and a few minutes later he found himself near the group of oaks, at the corner of the garden. He was no longer thinking of the pedestrian who had disappeared, and it is probable that if, at that moment, some porpoise had leaped out of the sea or some redbreast appeared on the bushes, this man would have passed on his way, with his eyes fixed on the porpoise or the redbreast.

Chance ordained that he should have his eyes cast down. His glance fell mechanically on the place where the young girl had paused. Two tiny feet were imprinted there, and beside them he read this word, traced by her in the snow—

Gilliatt

That word was his name.

He was called Gilliatt.

He remained for a long time motionless, gazing at that name, at those little footprints, at the snow, then he pursued his way pensively.

II

The Bu de la Rue

GILLIATT dwelt in the parish of Saint-Sampson. He was not beloved. There were reasons for this:—

In the first place, he lived in a "haunted" house. It sometimes happens that in Jersey or in Guernsey, in the country or even in the city, in passing through some deserted nook, or in a street full of inhabitants, you will meet with a house whose entrance is barricaded; holly obstructs the door; plasters of planks, well nailed on, close up the windows of the ground floor; the windows of the upper stories are both open and shut: all the sashes are barred, but all the panes are broken. If there be a paddock, a yard, the grass is growing there; the encircling parapet is crumbling; if there be a garden, it is all nettles, brambles, and hemlock, and strange insects may be there espied. The chimneys are cracked, the roof is falling in; what can be seen of the interior of the rooms is dismantled; the wood is rotten, the stone is damp. On the old walls there is paper which is peeling off. Thereon you can study the old fashions of wall-paper: the griffins of the Empire, the crescent-shaped draperies of the Directory, the balusters and small columns of Louis XVI. The thickness of the webs, full of flies, denotes the profound peace enjoyed by the spiders. Sometimes one perceives a broken jug on a shelf. That is a "haunted" house. The devil comes thither at night.

A house, like a man, can become a corpse. A superstition suffices to kill it. Then it is terrible. These dead houses are not uncommon in the Channel Islands.

Rustic and maritime populations are not at ease on the score of the devil. Those of the channel, an English archipelago on a French sea coast, hold very well-defined ideas with regard to him. The devil has envoys all over the earth. It is certain that Belphegor is the ambassador of hell in France, Hutgin in Italy, Belial in Turkey, Thamuz in Spain, Martinet in Switzerland, and Mammon in England. Satan is an emperor, like any other. Satan Cæsar. His household is very well appointed: Dagon is grand seneschal; Succor Benoth is head of the eunuchs; Asmodeus, banker of the gaming-table; Kobal, director of his theatre; and Verdelet, grand master of ceremonies; Nybbas is the buffoon. Wiérus, a learned man, and a good authority on witches and demons, calls Nybbas the "great parodist."

The Norman fishermen in the channel have to take many a precaution when they are on the sea, because of the illusions which the devil creates. It was long thought that Saint-Maclou dwelt on the great square rock of Ortach, which lies in the open sea between Alderney and Casquets, and many old sailors were wont to affirm in former days that they had very often seen him, from a distance, sitting there and reading a book. Hence mariners, as they passed, made many a genuflection before the rock of Ortach, until one day the fable was destroyed to make way for the truth. It was discovered and it is known at the present day, that the inhabitant of the rock of Ortach is not a saint, but a devil. This devil, a certain Jochmus, had the audacity to pass himself off for several centuries as Saint-Maclou. However, the church herself falls into these mistakes. The devils, Raguhel, Oribel, and Tobiel, were saints until 745, when Pope Zachary, having scented them out, expelled them. One must be very learned in demonology in order to effect these expulsions, which are certainly very useful.

The old people of these parts relate—but these facts

belong to the past—that the Catholic population of the Norman archipelago was, in former days, and in spite of itself, in closer communication with the demon than the Huguenot population. Why? We know not. One thing is certain, that this minority was formerly much annoyed by the devil. He had conceived an affection for the Catholics, and sought their society, which would lead one to suppose that the devil is Catholic rather than Protestant. One of his most unendurable familiarities was to make nocturnal visits to the conjugal beds of Catholics, when the husband was wholly, and the wife half asleep. Hence misunderstandings.

Ratouillet thought that this was the manner of Voltaire's birth. There is nothing improbable about it. Moreover, this case is fully known and described in the formulæ of exorcism under the heading:— *De erroribus nocturnis et de semine diabolorum.* At Saint-Hélier it raged with special violence towards the end of the last century, probably as a punishment for the crimes of the revolution. The consequences of excesses of the revolution are incalculable. However that may be, this possible advent of the demon at night, when one does not see clearly, when one is asleep, troubled many orthodox women. There is nothing agreeable about giving birth to a Voltaire.

One of them, being troubled in her mind, consulted her confessor on the means of clearing up this equivocal situation in season. The confessor replied, "In order to assure yourself whether you have to do with the devil or your husband, feel his forehead; if you find horns there you may be sure . . ." "Of what?" asked the woman.

The house wherein Gilliatt dwelt had been haunted, but was so no longer. It was, therefore, all the more suspected. No one is ignorant of the fact that when a sorcerer installs himself in a haunted dwelling the devil considers that house sufficiently well guarded, and shows the sorcerer the politeness of not returning thither unless invited like a doctor.

This house was called the Bû de la Rue, the end of the street. It was situated at the point of a tongue of land, or rather rock, which formed a tiny separate anchorage in the inlet of Houmet-Paradis. The water is deep there. This house stood completely alone on this point, almost outside the island, with just enough land for a tiny garden. High tides sometimes flooded the garden. Between the port of Saint-Sampson and the inlet of Houmet-Paradis, rises the large hill surmounted by the group of towers and ivy called the Château du Valle, or of the Archangel, so that, from Saint-Sampson, the Bû de la Rue was not visible.

Nothing is more common than sorcerers in Guernsey. They exercise their profession in certain parishes, and the nineteenth century affects it not in the least. They indulge in regular criminal practices. They boil gold. They gather herbs at midnight. They cast the evil eye upon people's cattle. People consult them, they cause the "water of sick people" to be brought to them, and they are heard to say in a low tone, "the water appears to be very cloudy." One day in 1857, one of them discovered the presence of seven devils in "the water" of a sick person. They are feared and formidable. One of them recently bewitched a baker, "as well as his oven." Another one has the wickedness to close and seal with the greatest care "envelopes with nothing in them." Another, still, even indulges so far as to keep in his house, on a shelf, three bottles labelled B. These monstrous facts have been proved.

Some sorcerers are obliging, and take your maladies upon themselves for two or three guineas. In this case, they writhe on their beds, giving vent to cries. While they are writhing you say: "Stay, there is no longer anything the matter with me." Others cure you of all complaints by knotting a kerchief round your body. The means is so simple that one marvels that no one has already hit upon it. In the last century, the royal court of Guernsey put them on a pile of fagots and burned them alive. In our day it condemns them to eight weeks in prison on bread and water, and four weeks in close confinement, alternately. *Amant alterna catenæ.*

The last burning of sorcerers in Guernsey took place in 1747. The city utilized for that purpose one of its squares, the Carrefour du Bordage. The Square du Bordage beheld eleven sorcerers burned between 1565 and

1700. As a rule, the culprits confessed. They were aided to their confession by torture. The Carrefour du Bordage has rendered other services also to society and religion. Heretics were burned there. Under Mary Tudor, a mother and her two daughters were burned: the mother's name was Perrotine Massy. One of the daughters was with child. She brought forth the child in the coals of the pile of fagots. The chronicle says: "Her belly burst." A living child came forth; the new-born infant rolled out of the fiery furnace; a man by the name of House picked it up. Bailiff Hélier Gosselin caused the child to be flung back into the fire.

III

"For Your Wife, When You Marry

LET us return to Gilliatt.

It was said in the countryside that a woman, having with her a little child, had come to dwell in Guernsey towards the close of the Revolution. She was English, unless she was French. She bore some name or other, which Guernsey pronunciation and peasant orthography converted into Gilliatt. She lived alone with the child who was, according to some, her nephew, according to others, her son, according to others, her grandson, according to others still, no relation at all to her. She had a little money, on which she lived in a poor way. She bought a bit of meadow land at la Sergentée, and a piece at Roque-Crespel, near Rocquaine. At that epoch, the house at the Bû de la Rue was haunted. No one lived in it for thirty years. It was falling into ruins. The garden, too frequently visited by the sea, could produce nothing. Besides the nocturnal sounds and lights, the house had this peculiarly alarming feature about it, that if one left a ball of worsted on the chimney-piece, in the evening with needles and a full plate of soup, one found the soup eaten the next morning, the plate empty, and a pair of mittens knitted. This old house was offered for sale, together with the demon who was in it, for a few pounds sterling. This woman purchased it, evidently tempted by the devil—or by the low price.

She did more than buy it, she lived in it with her child; and from that moment the house quieted down. "That house has what it wants," said the people of the country. It ceased to be haunted. Cries were no longer heard there at daybreak. There was no longer any light, except the tallow candle burned in the evening by the good woman. The candle of a witch is equivalent to the torch of the devil. This explanation satisfied the public.

This woman turned to account the few roods of land which she possessed. She had a good cow that furnished yellow butter. She harvested white beans, cabbages, and "golden drop" potatoes. She sold, like everybody else, "parsnips by the barrel, onions by the hundred, and beans by the denerel." She did not go to the market, but had her harvest sold by Guilbert Falliot, at the Abreuveurs of Saint-Sampson. Falliot's register shows that he once sold for her as much as twelve bushels of "potatoes called three-months, of the earliest variety."

The house had been wretchedly repaired, just sufficiently to admit of living in it. It only rained into the rooms in very hard storms. It was composed of a ground floor and an attic. The ground floor was divided into three rooms, two for sleeping and one where they ate. The attic was reached by a ladder. The woman did the cooking and taught the child to read. She did not go to any of the churches, which caused her to be regarded, on due consideration, as a Frenchwoman. Not to go "to any place" is serious.

In short, they were enigmatical people.

It is probable that she was French. Volcanoes cast forth stones, and revolutions cast forth men. Families are thus sent to great distances, destinies are expatriated; groups are dispersed and crumbled to pieces: people fall from the clouds, some in Germany, some in England, some in America. They astonish the natives of the country.

Whence come these strangers?

That Vesuvius smoking yonder has spit them out. Names are conferred on these aërolites, on these expelled and lost individuals, on these people eliminated by fate; they are called emigrés, refugees, adventurers. If they remain, they are tolerated; if they take their departure, people are relieved.

Sometimes they are absolutely inoffensive individuals, strangers—the women at least—to the events which have driven them forth, cherishing neither hatred nor resentment, greatly astonished and involuntary projectiles. They take root again as best they may. They have harmed no one, and do not understand what has happened to them. I have seen a poor tuft of grass dashed wildly into the air by an explosion in a mine. The French revolution, more than any other explosion, was characterized by these distant projections.

The woman who was called "la Gilliatt" in Guernsey was, perchance, such a tuft of grass.

The woman grew old, the child became a youth. They lived alone and were avoided. They were sufficient for each other. "The she-wolf and her cub lick each other in turn." This is one of the proverbs which the kindliness environing them applied to them. The youth became a man, and then, since the old and withered barks of life must always fall, the mother died. She bequeathed him the meadow of the Sergentée, the jaonnière of the Roque-Crespel, the house of the Bû de la Rue, besides, as the official inventory says, "one hundred golden guineas, *dans le pid d'une cauche*," that is to say, in the foot of a stocking. The house was sufficiently furnished with two oaken coffers, two beds, six chairs, and one table, with the requisite utensils. On a shelf were several books, and in one corner a trunk which was not in the least mysterious, and which had to be opened for the inventory. This trunk was of tawny leather with arabesque patterns in copper nails and pewter stars, and contained a woman's outfit, new and complete, in handsome Dunkirk linen, shifts and petticoats, and silk gowns in the piece, with a paper on which they read the following, written by the hand of the dead woman:—

"For your wife, when you marry."

This death was an overwhelming blow for the survivor. He had been shy, he became wild. The solitude around him was complete. It was not alone isolation, but a blank. As long as there are two, life is possible. Alone, it seems as though one could no longer drag it. One ceases to pull. This is the first form of despair. Later on, one comprehends that duty consists in a series of submissions. One looks at death, one looks at life, and one accepts. But it is a submission which makes the heart bleed.

Gilliatt being young, his wound healed over. At that age, the flesh of the heart unites again. His sadness, effaced little by little, mingled with the nature about him, became a sort of charm, attracted him toward things and away from men, and amalgamated this soul ever more and more with solitude.

IV

Unpopularity

GILLIATT, as we have said, was not beloved in the parish. Nothing more natural than this antipathy. Motives abounded. In the first place, the house in which he lived, as has just been explained.

Next, his origin. Who was that woman? And why that child? The country folk do not like enigmas connected with strangers. Then, his dress, which was that of a working-man, while he had enough, although not rich, to live upon without doing anything. Next, his garden, which he succeeded in cultivating, and from which he produced potatoes, in spite of equinoctial gales. Next, the big books which lay on his shelf and which he read.

There were still other reasons. Why did he live a solitary life? The Bû de la Rue was a sort of lazar-house; Gilliatt was kept in quarantine; that is why it was very simple that people should be amazed at his isolation and should hold him responsible for the solitude which they created around him.

He never went to chapel. He often went out by night. He talked to sorcerers. Once he had been seen seated on the grass with an astonished look on his face. He haunted the dolmen of Ancresse and the fairy stones which lie here and there about the country. People felt sure of having seen him salute the Singing Rock politely. He bought all the birds that were brought to him and set them at liberty. He was civil to people in the streets of Saint-Sampson, but he made a circuit to avoid passing through it. He often went fishing and always came home with fish. He worked in his garden on Sunday. He had a bagpipe purchased of some Scotch soldiers passing through Guernsey, and which he played among the rocks on the seashore at nightfall. He made gestures like a sower. What treatment can be expected for a man like that?

As for the books which came from the dead woman, and which he read, they were suspicious. The Reverend Jaquemin Hérode, Rector of Saint-Sampson, when he entered the house for the funeral of the woman, had read on the backs of the books such titles as these: "Rosier's Dictionary"; "Candide," by Voltaire; "Advice to the Public with regard to Health," by Tissot. A French emigrant gentleman, who had retired to Saint-Sampson, had said: "This must be the Tissot who carried the head of the Princess de Lamballe."

The reverend gentleman had noticed upon one of the books this really crabbed and ill-sounding title: "De Rhubarbaro."

Let us say, however, that the work being written in Latin, as the title indicates, it is doubtful whether Gilliatt, who did not know Latin, read this book.

But it is just those books which a man does not read which condemn him the most. The Spanish Inquisition passed judgment on this point and placed it beyond a doubt.

However, this was only Doctor Tillingius's treatise on rhubarb, published in Germany, in 1679.

People were not sure that Gilliatt did not make charms, philtres, and "distilled waters." He had phials.

Why did he go to walk in the evening, and sometimes even until midnight on the downs? Evidently, with the object of conversing with the evil spirits who are to be found by night in the mists along the seashore.

Once he helped the sorceress of Torteval—an old woman named Moutonne Gahy—to extricate her wagon from the mud.

On being interrogated as to his profession, during a census taken in the island, he replied: "Fisherman—when there are any fish to catch." Put yourself in the place of these people—such replies are not liked.

Wealth and poverty are comparative terms. Gilliatt had meadows and a house, and, compared with those who have nothing at all, he was not poor. One day, in order to try him and perhaps with the object of making advances to him, for there are women who would marry the devil if he were rich, a girl said to Gilliatt: "When are you going to take a wife?" He replied: "I will take a wife when the Singing Rock takes a husband."

This Singing Rock is a huge, erect stone, planted upright in a garden near M. Manézurier de Fry. This stone requires much watching. No one knows why it is there. A cock which is not seen, can be heard crowing there, an extremely disagreeable thing. And then, it is averred that it was placed in that garden by sarregousets, which are the same thing as *sins*.

At night, when it thunders, if one sees men flying through the red of the clouds and through the quivering of the air, they are sarregousets. A woman who lives at Grand-Mielles knows them. One evening when there were sarregousets in a public square, this woman cried to a carter who did not know which road to take: "Ask your way of them; they are well-disposed folk, and very civil to strangers." One might lay a heavy wager that this woman was a sorceress.

That learned and judicious king, James I, had women

of this sort boiled alive, tasted the broth, and decided from the taste of the broth, "She was a witch," or "She was not one."

It is to be regretted that the kings of the present day do not possess these talents, which make one comprehend the utility of the institution.

It was not without serious cause that Gilliatt lived in the odor of witchcraft. Being at sea at midnight during a storm, alone in a bark near the Sleeper (Sommeilleuse), Gilliatt was heard to inquire,—

"Is there room to pass?"

A voice cried from the summit of the rocks,—

"Certainly! Courage!"

To whom was he speaking, if not to some one who replied to him? This seems to us a proof.

On another stormy evening, so dark that nothing could be seen, quite close to the Catiau-Roque, which is a double row of rocks where sorcerers, goats, and hobgoblins go on Friday to dance, people were certain that they had recognized Gilliatt's voice, mingled in the following terrible conversation,—

"How is Vésin Brovard?" (This was a mason who had fallen from a roof.)

"He is recovering."

"True God! he fell from a higher spot than that great beam. It is a miracle that he broke no bones."

"The people had fine weather for a seaweed last week."

"Better than to-day."

"Certainly! There will not be much fish in the market."

"The wind is too high."

"They will not be able to lower their nets."

"How goes it with Catherine?"

"To a charm."

"Catherine" was evidently a sarregousette.

Gilliatt, to all appearances, was dealing in deeds of darkness. At least, no one doubted it.

He was sometimes seen pouring water on the earth from a jug which he had. Now, water cast on the ground takes the shape of a devil.

There exist on the road to Saint-Sampson, opposite

Martello-tower number one, three stones arranged in the form of a staircase. They formerly sustained on their platform, now empty, a cross—unless they upheld a gibbet. These stones are very malign.

Very good and wise men and absolutely trustworthy persons affirmed that they had seen Gilliatt in conversation with a toad near these stones. Now, there are no toads in Guernsey; Guernsey has all the snakes, and Jersey has all the toads. This toad must have swum from Jersey to talk with Gilliatt. The conversation was friendly.

These facts were demonstrated; and the proof is that the three stones are still there. People who doubt can go and see them, and at a little distance there is even a house on whose corner this sign may be read: "Dealer in cattle, dead and alive, old cordage, iron, bones, and chewing tobacco; is prompt in payment and in his attention."

A person must needs be very incredulous to dispute the presence of these stones and of this house. All this injured Gilliatt.

The ignorant alone are ignorant of the fact that the greatest danger of the Channel Seas is the king of the Auxcriniers. No marine personage is more to be feared. Any one who sees him is shipwrecked between one Saint-Michel and the other. Being a dwarf, he is small, and being a king, he is deaf. He knows the names of all those who have died in the sea, and the spot where they are. He knows that cemetery, the ocean, thoroughly.

A head massive below and narrow above, a thickset body, a deformed and viscous belly, warty knots upon his skull, short legs, long arms, fins instead of feet, claws in place of hands, a large, green face,—such is this king. His claws are webbed, his fins provided with nails. Let the reader imagine a spectral fish with the face of a man.

To get rid of him, it is necessary to exorcise him or to fish him up from the sea. In the meanwhile, he is sinister. Nothing is more frightful than a sight of him. Above the surges and the billows, behind the denseness of the fog, one catches sight of an outline which is a being; a low brow, a flat nose, flattened ears, a huge mouth lacking teeth, a glaucous grin, eyebrows in the shape of chevrons, big, merry eyes. He is ruddy when the lightning is livid, and pallid when the lightning is crimson. He has a stiff, dripping beard, which spreads out, cut square, on a membrane in the shape of a shoulder cape, which is ornamented with fourteen shells, seven in front and seven behind. These shells are extraordinary for those who are well posted in shells.

The king of the Auxcriniers is visible only when the sea is violent. He is the lugubrious juggler of the tempest. His form is seen, roughly outlined in the mist, in a squall, in the rain. His navel is hideous. An armor of scales covers his sides like a waistcoat. He stands erect on the crest of those rolling waves which gush forth beneath the pressure of the gusts, and writhe like shavings from the joiner's plane. He rears himself fully out of the foam, and if there are, on the horizon, ships in distress, he dances, livid in the gloom, his face lighted up by a vague smile, with a mad and terrible air. It is an evil thing to encounter.

At the time when Gilliatt formed one of the preoccupations of Saint-Sampson, the last persons who had beheld the king of the Auxcriniers declared that his cape now had but thirteen shells. Thirteen; nothing can be more dangerous. But what had become of the fourteenth? Had he given it to any one? And to whom had he given it? No one could say, and people confined themselves to conjectures. One thing is certain, that M. Lupin-Mabier, of the Place of les Godaines, a man possessed of land, a proprietor taxed at eighty quarters, was ready to take his oath that he had once seen in Gilliatt's hands a very singular shell.

It was no rare thing to hear such dialogues as the following between two peasants,—

"Have I not a fine ox yonder, neighbor?"

"He's bloated, neighbor."

"Well, 'tis true all the same!"

"He's better as tallow than as meat."

"Good heavens!"

"Are you sure that Gilliatt has not looked at him?"

Gilliatt would pause at the edge of the fields near the laborers, and at the borders of gardens near the gardeners, and he sometimes uttered mysterious words:

"When the devil's bit thrives, reap the winter rye."

(Parenthesis: the devil's bit is scabious.)

"The ash is in leaf, there will be no more frost."

"Summer solstice, thistle in flower."

"If it rain not in June, the wheat will turn white. Fear the mildew."

"The wild cherry tree is forming its clusters; beware of the full moon."

"If the weather on the sixth day of the moon is like that of the fourth day or of the fifth day, it will be the same nine times out of twelve in the first case, and eleven times out of twelve in the second, during that entire moon."

"Have an eye on the neighbors at law with you. Beware of malice. A pig to whom one has given warm milk, bursts. A cow whose teeth have been rubbed with a leek, will eat no more."

"The smelt is milting, beware of fevers."

"The frog is showing himself, sow melons."

"The hepatica is in flower, sow barley."

"The linden is in bloom, mow the meadows."

"The white poplar flowers, open the forcing-frames."

"The tobacco is in blossom, close the hot-houses."

And, terrible to relate, if they followed his advice, they found it of advantage.

One night in June, as he was playing the bagpipe on the downs, in the direction of Denire de Fontenelle, the mackerel fishing proved a failure.

One evening, at low tide, on the strand opposite his house, Bû de la Rue, a cart, loaded with seaweed, was upset. He was probably afraid of being brought before the courts, for he took a great deal of trouble to help lift the cart, and he reloaded it himself.

A little girl in the neighborhood being troubled with lice, he went to Saint-Pierre-Port, returned with an ointment and rubbed the child with it; Gilliatt had freed her from her lice, which signified that Gilliatt had given them to her.

Every one knows that there is a charm for giving lice to people.

Gilliatt was reputed to look at wells, which is dangerous when the glance is evil, and it is a fact that one day at Arculons, near Saint-Pierre-Port, the water in a well became unwholesome. The good woman to whom the well belonged, said to Gilliatt: "Look at this water." And she showed him a glassful of it. Gilliatt admitted it. "The water is thick, it is true," he said. The good woman, who was suspicious of him, said: "Cure it for me." Gilliatt questioned her whether she had a stable?—whether the stable had a drain?—whether the stream from the drain did not pass quite close to the well? The good dame said "yes." Gilliatt entered the stable, worked at the drain, turned the stream aside, and the water became good once more. In the countryside, people thought what they pleased. A well does not become bad, then good again, without a cause; the trouble with this well was not considered natural at all, and it is, in fact, not difficult to believe that Gilliatt had cast a spell on that water.

Once, when he went to Jersey, it was noticed that he lodged in the Rue des Alleurs, at Saint-Clement. Alleurs are ghosts.

In villages, signs concerning a man are picked up; these signs are put together; the total forms a reputation.

It chanced that Gilliatt was caught suffering with a nosebleed. This seemed serious. The skipper of a bark, who had nearly made the circuit of the globe, affirmed that among the Tungus all sorcerers bleed at the nose. When one sees a man bleeding at the nose, one knows with whom one has to deal. Nevertheless, reasonable people pointed out that what characterizes sorcerers in Tungusia may not, to the same degree, characterize sorcerers in Guernsey.

In the vicinity of Saint-Michel, he was seen to halt in a meadow belonging to the gardens of the Huriaux, bordering the highway of the Videclins. He whistled in the meadow, and a moment later, there was a cow there; a moment later still, a magpie. The fact was attested by a notable man who was afterwards a douzenier[1] of the Dozen authorized to make a new survey and register of Perchage of the Fief le Roi.

At Hamel, in the vingtaine[2] of the Epine, there were

1. A member of the administrative council in Jersey and Alderney.
2. A division of the parish in the Norman Isles.

old women who were positive that they had heard swallows calling Gilliatt one morning at daybreak.

Add to this that he was not of a good disposition.

One morning, a poor man was beating an ass. The ass would not go on. The man kicked him in the belly, and the ass fell. Gilliatt ran to raise the ass, the ass was dead. Gilliatt boxed the man's ears.

Another day, seeing a boy descending from a tree with a brood of young woodpeckers, featherless and unfledged, Gilliatt took the brood from this boy, and carried his malice to such an extent as to put them back in the tree.

Some passers-by reproached him for this, he confined himself to pointing to the old birds screaming above the tree, and who returned to their brood. He had a weakness for birds. This is a sign by which magicians are generally recognizable.

Children delight in searching out the nests of gulls, and seabirds in the cliffs. They bring back quantities of blue, yellow, and green eggs, with which to make circular ornaments for the fronts of chimneys. As the cliffs are perpendicular, their foot sometimes slips, they fall and are killed. Nothing is so pretty as screens decorated with the eggs of sea-birds. Gilliatt knew not how to invent anything except what was bad. At the peril of his life he climbed down the abrupt faces of the rocks on the shore, and hung up trusses of hay, old hats, and all sorts of scarecrows, in order to prevent the birds from making their nests there, and, consequently, the children from going there.

This is why Gilliatt was almost hated by his neighbors.

V

Other Suspicious Things About Gilliatt

OPINION was not thoroughly settled in regard to Gilliatt.

He was generally believed to be a "marcou," some even went so far as to think him a "cambion." A cambion is the son of a woman and the devil.

When a woman has, by one husband, seven male children in succession, the seventh is a "marcou." But no female child must interrupt the series of boys.

The marcou has a natural fleur-de-lis imprinted on some portion of his body, which gives him the power of healing scrofula, equally with the kings of France. There are marcous almost everywhere in France, particularly in the Orléanais. Each village of the Gâtinais has its marcou. In order to cure the sick, it is only necessary for the marcou to breathe upon their sores, or to let them touch his fleur-de-lis. The experiment is chiefly successful on the night of Good Friday. Ten years ago, the marcou of Ormes, in Gâtinais, surnamed "The Handsome Marcou," and consulted by all Beauce, was a cooper named Foulon, who had a horse and a carriage. The gendarmerie had to be brought out, in order to prevent his miracles. He had the fleur-de-lis under his left breast. Other marcous have it elsewhere.

There are marcous in Jersey, in Alderney, and in Guernsey. This arises, no doubt, from the rights which France holds over the Duchy of Normandy. Otherwise, to what purpose the fleur-de-lis?

There are also scrofulous persons in the Channel Islands, which renders marcous necessary.

Several persons who were present on one occasion when Gilliatt was bathing in the sea, thought they saw the fleur-de-lis on him. Being questioned on that subject, he merely burst out laughing. For, like other men, he sometimes laughed. From that time forth, no one ever saw him bathe; he bathed only in solitary and perilous places. Probably at night, by moonlight; a suspicious circumstance, as the reader must admit.

Those who persisted in believing him to be a cambion, that is to say a son of the devil, were evidently mistaken. They should have known that there are no cambions except in Germany. But fifty years ago, le Valle and Saint-Sampson were regions of ignorance.

It is manifestly absurd to believe that any one in Guernsey is a son of the Devil.

Gilliatt was consulted simply because he made people uneasy. Peasants came with fear and trembling, to tell him about their maladies. This fear begets confidence: and, in the country, the more the physician is suspected of magical powers, the more efficacious the remedy. Gilliatt had prescriptions of his own, which he had inherited from the old dead woman; he bestowed them on those who asked, and would take no pay. He cured whitlow by the application of herbs, the liquor from one of his phials cut short the course of a fever; the chemist of Saint-Sampson, whom we should call a *pharmacien* in France, thought that it was probably a decoction of cinchona. The most ill-disposed willingly acknowledged that Gilliatt was a very good fellow for sick people where his ordinary remedies were concerned; but he would hear nothing as to being a marcou; if a scrofulous person asked leave to touch his fleur-de-lis, his only reply was to shut the door in his face; he absolutely refused to perform miracles, which is ridiculous in a sorcerer. Do not be a sorcerer; but, if you are one, fulfil your profession.

There were one or two exceptions to the universal antipathy. Sieur Landoys du Clos-Landès was clerk of the parish of Saint-Pierre-Port, custodian of the documents and guardian of the register of births, marriages, and deaths. This clerk Landoys was proud of being descended from the Treasurer of Bretagne, Pierre Landais, hung in 1485. One day, Sieur Landoys, while bathing, ventured too far out into the sea and came near drowning. Gilliatt plunged into the water, came near drowning also, and saved Landoys. From that day forth, Landoys said no more evil words of Gilliatt. To those who expressed surprise at this, he replied,—

"Why do you wish me to detest a man who has done me no harm, and who has rendered me a service?"

The clerk-registrar even came to admit Gilliatt to a certain friendship. This registrar was a man devoid of prejudices. He did not believe in sorcerers. He laughed at those who were afraid of ghosts. As for himself, he had a boat in which during his leisure hours he fished for amusement, and he had never seen anything extraordinary, unless occasionally a white woman leaping over the water in the moonlight, and even of that he was not quite sure. Moutonne Gahy, the witch of Torteval, had given him a little bag to fasten under his cravat, as a protection against evil spirits; he jeered at this bag and did not know what it contained; nevertheless, he wore it, feeling himself more secure when he had that charm on his neck.

Some bold persons ventured to follow the example of the Sieur Landoys, and to admit some attenuating circumstances in Gilliatt's favor, some appearances of good qualities, his sobriety, his abstinence from gin and tobacco, and they sometimes even went so far as to bestow upon him this fine encomium: "He neither drinks, nor smokes, nor chews, nor takes snuff."

But sobriety is a good quality only when one possesses other virtues.

Public aversion rested upon Gilliatt.

At all events, Gilliatt, being a marcou, could render service. On a certain Good Friday, at midnight, the day and hour employed in that sort of cures, all the scrofulous persons in the island, through inspiration, or by appointment among themselves, came in a mass to the Bû de la Rue, with clasped hands and pitiable sores, to ask Gilliatt to cure them. He refused. In this his malevolence was recognizable.

VI
THE PAUNCH BOAT

SUCH was Gilliatt.

He was not ugly. He was, possibly, handsome. There was a certain antique, barbarian grace in his profile. In repose, he resembled a Dacian of the column of Trajan. His ear was small, delicate, without any lobe, and of an admirable form for hearing. Between his eyebrows was that proud, vertical wrinkle which indicates the bold and persevering man. The corners of his mouth dropped, which denotes bitterness; his brow had a certain serene and noble curve, his frank eye looked at one steadily, although troubled by that contraction of the lids which fishermen acquire, from the reflection of the waves. His laugh was youthful and charming. No ivory was whiter than his teeth. But the sun had burned him almost as black as a Negro. One cannot meddle with impunity with the ocean, the tempest, and the night; at thirty years of age he appeared forty-five. He wore the sombre mask of the winds and of the sea.

He had received the nickname of Gilliatt the Crafty.

An Indian fable says: "One day Brahma asked force, 'Who is stronger than you?' She replied, 'Adroitness.' " A Chinese proverb says, "What could not the lion do, if he were a monkey!"

Gilliatt was neither a lion nor a monkey, but the things that he did confirmed the Chinese proverb and the Hindoo fable. Of ordinary stature and ordinary strength, he was able (so inventive and powerful was his dexterity) to lift the burdens of a giant, and to perform the prodigies of an athlete.

There was something of the gymnast about him; he used with equal facility his right hand or his left.

He did not hunt, but he fished. He spared birds, but not fish. Woe to the dumb.

He was an excellent swimmer.

Solitude creates men of talent or idiots. Gilliatt presented himself under both aspects. At times he was seen with the "astonished air," of which we have spoken, and one would have taken him for a brute. At other moments, he had an indescribably deep glance. Ancient Chaldæa had men like this; at certain hours the dulness of the shepherd became transparent and allowed the mage to be seen.

In short, he was only a poor man who knew how to read and write. It is probable that he stood on the boundary line between the dreamer and the thinker. The thinker wills, the dreamer is passive. Solitude adds to the simple and modifies them to a certain extent. They become permeated, unconsciously, with a kind of sacred awe. The gloom in which Gilliatt's mind dwelt was composed in almost equal quantities of two elements, both dark, but very different. Within him, ignorance, weakness; outside of him, mystery, immensity.

By dint of climbing the rocks, scaling the cliffs, going and coming in the archipelago in all weathers, of managing the first boat which presented itself, of risking himself day and night in the most difficult passages, he had come to be a surprising seaman, but without drawing any advantage from it, and for his own whim and pleasure.

He was a born pilot. The true pilot is the mariner who navigates the bottom of the sea even more than its surface. The waves are an external problem, continually complicated by the submarine configuration of the places through which the vessel's course is directed. It seemed when one beheld Gilliatt sailing across the shallows and reefs of the Norman archipelago, as though he possessed, beneath the arch of his cranium, a chart of the bottom of the sea. He knew all and braved all.

He knew the buoys in the channels better than the cormorants who perched upon them. The imperceptible differences which distinguish the four upright buoys of the Creux, Alligande, the Trémies, and the Sardrette from each other, were perfectly distinct and clear to him, even in a fog. He neither hesitated over the stake with an oval ball at Anfré, nor the triple lance-iron of le Rousse, nor the white ball of la Corbette, nor the black ball of Longue-Pierre, and there was no fear of his confounding the Cross of Goubeau with the sword planted in the earth at la Platte, nor the hammer buoy of the Barbées, and the swallow-tailed buoy of the Moulinet.

His rare science as a mariner was demonstrated with especial brilliancy one day when there was at Guernsey one of those sorts of maritime jousts called regattas. The problem was as follows: to navigate alone a boat with four sails, from Saint-Sampson to the Isle of Herm, which is one league distant, and to bring it back to Saint-Sampson. There is no fisherman who cannot manœuvre a boat with four sails, and the difficulty does not seem to be great, but this is what increased it.

In the first place, the boat itself, which was one of those large and heavy deep-bellied boats of the Rotterdam pattern, which the sailors of the last centuries called "Dutch Paunches." This ancient Holland lighter, low-lying and broad in the beam, with lee-boards on the starboard and port sides which are let go, sometimes on one side, sometimes on the other, according to the wind, and which take the place of a keel, are still to be met with occasionally at sea.

In the second place, the return from Herm was rendered more difficult by a heavy ballast of stone. They were to go out empty and return loaded. The prize of the contest was the "Paunch." It was given in advance to the winner. This paunch had served as a pilot boat; the pilot who had commanded and sailed it for twenty years was one of the most robust mariners of the channel; at his death, no one could be found to sail her, and it was decided to make it the prize of a regatta. Though not decked over, she had good qualities, and might tempt a skilful seaman. The mast was placed on the bow, which increased the drawing power of the sails. Another advantage, the mast did not interfere with the cargo. It had a solid hull; heavy but roomy, and kept the open sea well; a really serviceable boat.

There was much eagerness in the contest; the task was

a hard one, but the prize was fine. Seven or eight fishermen, the most vigorous on the island, presented themselves. They tried in turn; not one of them could get as far as Herm. The last who contended was noted for having rowed, in rough weather, across the redoubtable gut which lies between Sark and Brecq-Hou. Dripping with perspiration, he brought back the boat and said: "It is impossible."

Then Gilliatt stepped into the craft, first seized the oar, next the main sheet, and stood out to the open sea. Then without making fast the sheet, which would have been imprudent, and without letting go of it, which kept the sail under his control, he allowed the sheet to run along the traveller at the will of the wind, without falling to leeward, and grasped the helm with his left hand. In three quarters of an hour, he was at Herm.

Three hours later, although a strong south wind had risen and was blowing across the roadstead, he returned to Saint-Sampson with his cargo of stones. By way of luxury and bravado he had added to the cargo the little bronze cannon of Herm, which the people of that isle fired every year on the fifth of November, in sign of rejoicing over the death of Guy Fawkes.

Guy Fawkes has been dead, we may remark in passing, two hundred and sixty years; 'tis a very long period of joy.

Gilliatt, thus overloaded and encumbered, steered back, one might say brought back, the boat to Saint-Sampson, although he had the Guy Fawkes cannon on board besides.

On seeing this, Mess Lethierry exclaimed: "Here's a bold sailor!"

And he offered his hand to Gilliatt.

We shall speak of Mess Lethierry again.

The paunch was adjudged to Gilliatt.

This adventure did not injure his nickname of The Crafty.

Some persons declared that there was nothing astonishing about the thing, since Gilliatt had concealed a branch of wild mélier in his boat. But this could not be proved.

From that day forth, Gilliatt had no other vessel but

the paunch. In that heavy craft he went fishing. He moored it in the very good little anchorage which he had for his private use under the very wall of his house of the Bû de la Rue. At nightfall, he threw his nets over his shoulder, crossed his garden, climbed over the parapet of dry stones, sprang from one rock to another, and leaped into the boat. Thence to sea.

He caught many fish, but it was affirmed that the branch of mélier was always attached to his boat. The mélier is the medlar tree. No one had seen the branch, but every one believed in it.

What fish he had more than he needed, he did not sell, but gave away.

The poor accepted his fish, but cherished a grudge against him, notwithstanding, on account of that branch of medlar tree. Such things should not be done. One should not trick the sea.

He was a fisherman, but he was not that alone. From instinct, and in order to direct his mind, he had learned three or four trades. He was a joiner, a blacksmith, a cartwright, a caulker, and even a bit of a machinist. No one could mend a wheel better than he. He fabricated all his fishing implements in a manner peculiar to himself. In one corner of the Bû de la Rue, he had a little forge and an anvil, and, as the paunch had but one anchor, he had himself and alone made a second for it. This anchor was an excellent one; the ring was of the proper strength, and Gilliatt, without any one having told him, discovered the exact dimensions which the stock must have to prevent the anchor from tripping.

He had patiently replaced all the nails in the planking of the paunch by tree-nails, which rendered rust-holes impossible.

In this manner he had greatly improved the good sea qualities of the paunch. He took advantage of it to go from time to time, to spend a month or two in some solitary islet, like Chousey or the Casquets. People said,—

"Stay, Gilliatt is gone away." This caused no one any regret.

VII
For a Haunted House, a Visionary Inhabitant

GILLIATT was a man of dreams. Hence his audacity, hence, also, his timidity. He had ideas on many things peculiarly his own.

There was, perhaps, in Gilliatt, something of the man of hallucinations and visions. Hallucination haunts a peasant like Martin, as well as a king like Henri IV. The Unknown sometimes gives the spirit of man surprises. An abrupt rent in the gloom suddenly permits a glimpse of the invisible, then closes again. These visions are sometimes transfiguring; they convert a camel-driver into Mahomet, and a goatherd into Jeanne d'Arc. Solitude generates a certain quantity of sublime exaltation. 'Tis the smoke of the burning bush. The result is a mysterious lucidity of mind which converts the student into a seer, and the poet into a prophet; the result is Horeb, Kedron, Ombos, the intoxication of the laurels of Castalia chewed, the revelations of the month Busion; it results in Peleïa at Dodona, Phemonaë at Delphi, Trophonius at Lebadea, Ezechiel on the Chebar, Jerome in the Thebaid.

Generally, the visionary state overwhelms the man and stupefies him. There is such a thing as sacred brutalization. The fakir's vision is a burden to him, as his goitre is to the cretin.

Luther, speaking to the devils in the attic at Wittenberg; Pascal, masking hell with the screen in his cabinet; the Negro, Obi, conversing with the white-faced god

Bassum—present the same phenomenon differently interpreted by the brains which it traverses, according to their force and dimensions. Luther and Pascal were and remain great; the Obi is imbecile.

Gilliatt was neither so high nor so low. He was a dreamer. Nothing more.

He looked on nature a little strangely.

As he had often happened to find in perfectly limpid sea water tolerably large animals, of strange and various shapes, of the species medusa, which, out of water, resembled soft crystal, and which thrown back into the water blended with their surroundings in transparency and color, he drew the conclusion that since living transparencies inhabit the water, other transparencies, equally living, might also inhabit the air.

Birds are not inhabitants of the air; they are amphibious. Gilliatt did not believe that the air was deserted.

He said: Since the sea is filled, why should the atmosphere be empty? Creatures of the color of the air would be effaced in the light, and would elude our vision; who can prove to us that there are none such? Analogy indicates that the air must have its fish, as well as the sea; these fish of the air would be diaphanous, a mercy of creating providence for us as well as for them; allowing the light to pass through their forms, casting no shadow, and possessing no outline, they would remain unknown to us, and beyond our grasp. Gilliatt imagined that if the earth could be drained of atmosphere, and that if one could fish in the air as in a pond, one would find a multitude of surprising beings; and, he added, in his revery, many things would be explained.

Reverie, which is thought in a nebulous state, borders closely on sleep, and is bounded by it, as its frontier. The air inhabited by living transparencies would be the beginning of the unknown; but beyond, the vast opening of the possible presents itself. There other beings, there other facts. No supernatural sin; but the occult continuation of infinite nature. Gilliatt, in that laborious idleness which constituted his existence, was a close observer. He even went so far as to include sleep in the domain of his observations. Sleep is in contact with the possible, which we call also the improbable. The nocturnal world has an existence of its own. Night, as night, is a universe in itself. The material human organism on which weighs an atmospheric column fifteen leagues in height, is fatigued at night, it is sinking with lassitude, it lies down, it rests; the eyes of the flesh close; then, in that sleeping head, less inert than is generally believed, other eyes open: the Unknown makes its appearance. The sombre things of the unknown world become the neighbors of man, either because there is actual communication or because the distant vistas of the abyss gain a visionary exaggeration; it seems as though the indistinct inhabitants of space come to look at us, and that they have a curiosity about us, the inhabitants of earth; a phantom creation ascends or descends toward us, and envelops us in a twilight; before our spectral contemplation, another life than ours assembles and disperses, composed of ourselves and of something else; and the sleeper, not fully aware nor fully unconscious, catches a glimpse of these strange animals, these extraordinary vegetations, these terrible or smiling lividnesses, these larvæ, these masks, these figures, these hydras, these confusions, this moonlight without a moon, these obscure decompositions of the marvellous, these augmentations and diminutions in a troubled thickness, these floatings of forms in the shadows, all that mystery which we call dreams, and which is nothing but the approach of an invisible reality. Dreams are the aquarium of night.

So thought Gilliatt.

VIII

The Chair of Gild-Holm- Ur

ONE might search in vain to-day in the inlet of Houmet for Gilliatt's house, garden, and the creek in which he sheltered the paunch. The Bû de la Rue no longer exists. The little peninsula where stood this house has fallen beneath the picks of the quarrymen, and has been carried away, cartload by cartload, on the vessels of the dealers in rocks and of granite. It has become a quay, a church, and a palace in the capital. That whole crest of reefs has long since been conveyed to London.

These projections of rocks into the sea, with their chasms and crevices, are miniature mountain chains; on looking at them, one receives the same impression that a giant would have from looking at the Cordilleras. The local dialect calls them "Banques." These banks have various shapes. Some resemble a dorsel spine, each rock is a vertebra; others, the skeleton of a fish; others, a crocodile drinking.

At the extremity of the Banque of the Bû de la Rue, there was a great rock which the fishermen of Houmet called the Beast's Horn. This rock, though less lofty, resembled the Pinnacle in Jersey. At high tide, the water separated it from the bank, and the Horn was isolated. At low tide, it could be reached by an isthmus of rocks. The curious feature about this rock was, that on the side toward the sea there was a sort of natural chair, hollowed out by the sea and polished by the rain. This chair was treacherous. One was insensibly attracted thither by the beauty of the view; one paused there "for love of the prospect," as they say in Guernsey; something detained you there; there is a charm in vast horizons. This chair offered itself to you; it formed a sort of niche in the perpendicular face of the cliff; it was easy to climb into that niche; the sea, which had hewn it out of the rock had also arranged beneath it a sort of staircase of flat stones; the abyss indulges in these attentions of politeness; distrust its politeness; the chair tempted one to ascend thither; there one felt at ease; for seat, the granite worn and rounded by the foam; for arms, two hollows which seemed made expressly; for back, the whole high, vertical wall of the rock above one's head, which one admired without thinking of saying to one's self that it was impossible to scale it; nothing more simple than to forget one's self in this arm-chair; one beheld the whole sea laid before one, one saw in the offing, vessels arriving or departing, one could follow a ship with the eyes until it sank beyond the Casquets, below the curve of the ocean, one marvelled, gazed, enjoyed, one felt the caress of the breeze and the waves; there exists in Cayenne a bat which lulls you to sleep in the shade with a gentle waving of its dusky wings; the wind is this invisible bat; when it is not engaged in ravaging, it is engaged in lulling to sleep. One gazed at the sea, one listened to the wind, or yielded to the drowsiness of ecstasy. When the eyes are filled with an excess of beauty and light, it is luxury to close them. All at once, one roused one's self. It was too late. The sea had risen little by little. The water surrounded the rock.

One was lost.

What a terrible thing was this rock in the rising sea.

The tide rises imperceptibly at first, then violently. On arriving at the rocks, it is seized with anger, it foams. Swimming is not always successful among the breakers. Excellent swimmers have been drowned at the Horn of the Bû de la Rue.

In certain places, at certain hours, gazing at the sea is dangerous. It is what looking at a woman sometimes is.

The very old inhabitants of Guernsey formerly called this niche fashioned in the rock by the sea, the "Chair Gild-Holm-'Ur," or *"Kidormur."* A Celtic word, it is said, which those who know Celtic do not understand and which those who know French understand. *"Qui-*

dort-meurt"—"he who sleeps, dies." Such is the peasant translation.

Readers are free to choose between this translation, "he who sleeps, dies," and the one given in 1819, I think, in the *Armoricain* by M. Athénas. According to this learned Celtic scholar, Gild-Holm-'Ur signifies the "halting-place of flocks of birds."

Another chair of this sort exists in Alderney, which is called the monk's chair, so well made by the sea and with a projecting point of rock so aptly adjusted that one might say that the sea is so amiable as to place a stool under your feet.

At high water, when the ride was full, the chair of Gild-Holm-'Ur was no longer visible. The water covered it completely.

The chair of Gild-Holm-'Ur was the neighbor of the Bû de la Rue. Gilliatt knew it well and sat in it. He often went there. Did he meditate? No. We have just described it—he dreamed. He did not, however, allow himself to be caught by the tide.

BOOK SECOND
MESS LETHIERRY

I
A Restless Life and a Quiet Conscience

MESS LETHIERRY, the notable man of Saint-Sampson, was a redoubtable sailor. He had navigated a great deal. He had been cabin-boy, sailmaker, top-man, helmsman, boatswain's mate, boatswain, pilot, and captain. He was now a shipowner. No one knew the seas as he did. He was intrepid in assisting ships in distress. In bad weather, he strolled along the strand and watched the horizon.

What is that yonder? Some one is in trouble. It might be a Weymouth lugger, or an Alderney cutter, a bisquine from Courseulle, the yacht of a lord, an Englishman, a Frenchman, a poor man, a rich man, the devil himself, it mattered not; he sprang into a boat, called two or three brave men or dispensed with them as might be, constituted himself the entire crew, unfastened the moorings, seized the oar, pushed out to sea, mounted, descended, and mounted once again on the rolling waves, plunged into the hurricane, went to meet danger. He could be seen far away in the storm, erect in his boat, dripping with rain, blended with the flashes of lightning, with the face of a lion, and covered with a mane of foam. He sometimes passed his whole day thus in danger, amid the waves, amid the hail, in the wind, lying alongside vessels in distress, saving men, saving cargoes, fighting the tempest. In the evening he returned home and knit a pair of stockings.

This life he had led for fifty years, from the age of ten to that of sixty; so long as he was young. At sixty he perceived that he could no longer lift the great anvil at the forge of Varchin with one arm; this anvil weighed three hundred pounds; and all at once, he was made a prisoner by the rheumatism. He was obliged to give up the sea. Then he passed from the heroic to the patriarchal age. He was no longer anything but a worthy man.

His rheumatism came to him about the time when he had gotten into easy circumstances. These two products of labor are fond of keeping one another company. At the moment when one becomes rich, one is paralyzed. This crowns life.

People say to themselves: "Now let us enjoy ourselves."

In islands like Guernsey, the population is composed of men who have passed their lives in making the circuit of their field, and of men who have passed their life in sailing around the world. They constitute two sorts of laborers, the tillers of the soil and the toilers of the sea. Mess Lethierry belonged to the second category, though he knew the land. He had led the hard life of a toiler. He had travelled on the continent; he had been for a while a ship's carpenter at Rochefort, then at Cette. We have just alluded to the tour of the globe; he had accomplished his tour of France as journeyman carpenter. He had toiled at the apparatus for draining the salt works in Franche-Comté. This honest man had led a life of adventure.

In France, he had learned to read, to think, to will. He had done a little of everything, and in everything he had maintained his integrity. At the foundation of his nature, however, he was simply a sailor. The water belonged to him. He was accustomed to say: "The fishes are in my house." In short, his whole existence, with the exception of two or three years, had been devoted to the ocean; "thrown into the water," as he expressed it. He had navigated the great seas, the Atlantic and the Pacific, but he preferred the Channel. He was wont to exclaim with affection: "That is the fierce one!" He had been born at sea, and there he wished to die. After having made the circuit of the globe once or twice, and being in a condition to judge, he had returned to Guernsey and had not stirred from thence since. Henceforth, the extent of his voyages was Granville and Saint-Malo.

Mess Lethierry was a Guernsian, that is to say, Norman, that is to say, English, that is to say, French. Within him, this quadruple country was submerged and drowned, as it were, in his greater country, the ocean.

During all his life, and wherever he went, he retained the habits of a Norman fisherman.

This did not prevent his opening some old volume now and then, from taking pleasure in a book, from knowing the names of philosophers and poets, and from jabbering a little in all languages.

II
A Taste That He Had

GILLIATT had something of the savage in his nature. Mess Lethierry had similar characteristics.

This savage had, however, certain refinements in his nature. He was fastidious in regard to the hands of women. In his youth, when he was still almost a child, between cabin-boy and sailor, he had heard Admiral de Suffren exclaim: "Yonder is a pretty girl, but what horrible, great, red hands!" The word of an admiral is a command in all matters. Above an oracle there stands an order. The exclamation of the Bailli de Suffren rendered Lethierry dainty and exacting on the point of small, white hands. His own hand, a large, mahogany-colored spatula, was a battle club in lightness, and a pair of pincers for a friendly grasp, and smashed a paving-stone when it fell, clenched, upon it. He had never married. Either the wish or the opportunity had been lacking. The reason may possibly be discovered in the fact that this sailor was inexorable in his demand for hands like a duchess's, and it is rare to find the fisher girls of Portbail with hands like those.

Nevertheless, it was said at Rochefort en Charente that he had, in earlier days, discovered a coquettish grisette who realized his ideal. She was a pretty girl with pretty hands. She was spiteful and scratched. Woe to any one who attacked her. Capable of being used as claws when required, and exquisitely neat, her nails were without fear and without reproach. These charming nails had first enchanted Lethierry and then disturbed him; and, fearing that the day might come when he should no longer be the master of his mistress, he decided not to take this love affair before monsieur the mayor.

On another occasion, in Alderney, a girl pleased him. He was thinking of marriage, when an inhabitant said to him: "I congratulate you, you will have a fine *bouselière* in her." He obtained an explanation of this commendation. In Alderney a certain custom prevails. They take a cow-dung and fling it against the wall. When it is dry, it falls, and is used for fuel. These pieces of dried dung are called *coipiaux.* An Alderney girl has no chance of being married unless she is a good hand at making these. This talent put Lethierry to flight.

However, he possessed in the matter of love or liaison a kind of coarse peasant philosophy, the wisdom of a sailor always captivated, but never enslaved, and he was wont to boast of having been, in his youth, easily conquered by a *"cotillon."* What is now called a crinoline was then called a *cotillon.* This signifies both more and less than a wife.

These rough mariners of the Norman archipelago are gifted with wit. Nearly all of them can read and write. On Sundays, little cabin-boys eight years of age may be seen seated on a coil of rope with book in hand. These Norman sailors have always been sarcastic, and have, as the saying goes, made "mots." It was one of them, bold pilot Quéripel, who tossed at Montgomery, when he had taken refuge in Jersey after his unlucky lance-thrust at

Henri II, this sarcasm: "A mad head hath broken an empty head." It was another, Touzeau, skipper at Saint-Brelade, who made this philosophical pun, wrongly attributed to Archbishop Cannes: "After death, popes become butterflies and lords become mites."[1]

III

The Ancient Dialect of the Sea

THESE mariners of the Channel Islands are veritable old Gauls. These islands, which at the present day are becoming rapidly anglicized, remained for a long time aboriginal. The peasant of Sark speaks the language of Louis XIV.

Forty years ago, the classic dialect of the sea was to be found in the mouths of the sailors of Jersey and Alderney. One would have supposed one's self in the midst of the sea life of the seventeenth century. A philological specialist might have gone thither to study the ancient dialect of seaman and of battle shouted by Jean Bart through that speaking trumpet which terrified Admiral Hidde. The maritime vocabulary of our fathers, today almost completely changed, was still in use in Guernsey towards 1820.

A vessel which worked well to windward was a "good plyer"; a vessel which veered to the wind almost of itself, in spite of its foresails and its helm, was "an ardent vessel." To get under way was "to take *aire*"; to close-reef, was "*capeyer*"; to make fast the end of a running rope was "*faire dormant*"; to get the weather gage was "*faire chapelle*"; to ride firm at anchor was "*faire teste*";

1. Après la mort, les papes deviennent papillons, et les sires deviennent cirons.

to be in disorder on board was "*être en pantenne*"; to have the wind in the sails was "*porter-plain.*"

Not one of these expressions is any longer in use.

To-day they say, "*louvoyer*" (to beat to windward), then they said, "*leauvoyer*"; now "*naviguer*" (to sail), then they said, "*naviger*"; they say, "*virer vent devant*" (to tack), they used to say, "*donner vent devant*"; they say "*aller de l'avant*" (to have headway), they said, "*tailler de l'avant*"; they say, "*tirez d'accord*" (pull together), they used to say, "*halez d'accord*"; they say, "*dérapez*" (trip the anchor), they formerly said, "*déplantez*"; they say, "*embraquez*" (haul taut), they said: "*abraquez*"; they say, "*taquets*" (cleats), they said, "*bittons*"; they say, "*burins,*" they said, "*tappes*"; they say, "*balancines*" (halliards), they said, "*valencines*"; they say "*tribord*" (starboard), they said "*stribord*"; they say "*les hommes de quart à bâbord*" (the men of the larboard watch), they said, "*les basbourdis*"; Tourville wrote to Hocquincourt, "*nous avons single*" (we have sailed), instead of *cinglé.*

Instead of "*la rafale*" (the squall), "*le raffal*"; instead of "*bossoir*" (cat-head), "*boussoir*"; instead of "*drosse*" (tackle), "*drousse*"; instead of "*loffer*" (luff), "*faire une olofée*"; instead of "*élonger*" (lay alongside), "*alonger*"; instead of "*forte brise*" (stiff breeze), "*survent*"; instead of "*jouai*" (stock), "*jas*"; instead of "*soute*" (magazine), "*fosse.*"

Such was the nautical tongue in the Channel Islands, at the beginning of this century.

Ango would have been touched to hear a Jersey pilot speak. While everywhere else sails "*faseyaient*" (shivered), in the Channel Islands they "*barbeyaient.*" A "*saute-de-vent*" (sudden shift in the wind) was a "*follevente.*" Nowhere else were the two Gothic modes of mooring in use, the "*valture,*" and the "*portugaise.*" Only there could the old commands be heard: "*Tour-et-choque*!" (belay and slack); "*Bosse-et-bitte!*" (stopper and bite).

A Granville sailor would say, "*le clan*" (sheavehole), while a sailor of Saint-Aubin or Saint-Sampson still said "*le canal de pouliot.*" What was "*bout d'alonge*" (flukes) at Saint-Malo, was "*oreille d'âne*" at Saint-Hélier.

Mess Lethierry, precisely like the Duc de Vivonne, called the concave curve of decks, "the shear," and the caulker's chisel, "*la patarasse*."

It was with this uncouth dialect between his teeth that Duquesne beat Ruyter, that Duguay-Trouin beat Wasnaer, and that Tourville brought the first galley which bombarded Algiers, broadside on, in full daylight, in 1681. To-day it is a dead language. The idiom of the sea is entirely different at the present time. Duperré would not understand Suffren.

The language of signals has been no less transformed; and it is a long way from the four pennants, red, white, blue, and yellow, of La Bourdonnais to the eighteen flags of the present day which, hauled up by twos, by threes, and by fours, offer to the necessities of distant communication seventy thousand combinations, are never at a loss, and so to speak, foresee the unforeseen.

IV
One Is Vulnerable Through What One Loves

MESS LETHIERRY wore his heart on his hand; a large hand and a great heart. His defect consisted in this admirable quality,—confidence. He had a way peculiar to himself, of entering into an engagement; it was solemn. He said: "I give my word of honor on it to the good God." That said, he went through to the end. He believed in the good God, not in the rest. What little church-going he did, was done out of politeness. At sea he was superstitious.

Nevertheless, bad weather had never made him retreat; this was because he was but little accessible to opposition. He no more tolerated it from the ocean than from any one else. He meant to be obeyed; so much the worse for the sea if it resisted; it must take the consequences. Mess Lethierry did not yield.

An angry wave had no more power to stop him than a disputatious neighbor. What he said was said, what he planned was done. He bent neither before objection nor before tempest. *No* did not exist for him; neither in the mouth of a man nor in the thunder of a cloud. He went his way. He did not permit any one to refuse him. Hence his obstinacy in life, and his intrepidity on the ocean.

He liked to season his fish soup, knowing the exact dose of pepper, salt, and herbs which it required, and he took as much pleasure in cooking it as in eating it. A being who is transfigured by a pea jacket, and brutalized by a coat; who resembles, with his hair flying in the breeze, Jean Bart, and, in a round hat, Jocrisse; awkward in the town, strange and formidable at sea; the back of a porter; no oaths, very rarely wrath, a soft, very gentle tone which becomes thunder through a speaking-trumpet; a peasant who has read the Encyclopedia; a Guernsey man who has seen the Revolution; a very learned ignoramus, no bigotry, but all sorts of visions, more faith in the White Lady than in the Holy Virgin; the form of Polyphemus; the logic of the weathervane; the will of Christopher Columbus; something of the bull and something of the child in his nature; a nose almost flat, large cheeks, a mouth with all its teeth perfect, a frown all over his face, a face that looked as though it had been jumbled together by the billows, and on which the compass has turned for forty years, an air of storm on his brow, a carnation of rock in the open sea;—now add to this a good-tempered smile on that harsh face, and you will have before you Mess Lethierry.

Mess Lethierry had two loves, Durande and Déruchette.

BOOK THIRD
DURANDE AND DÉRUCHETTE

I
CHATTER AND SMOKE

THE HUMAN BODY might well be regarded as only an appearance. It hides our reality. It lies thick over our light, or our shadow. The reality is our soul. To speak absolutely, the human visage is a mask. The true man is that which is beneath man. If one could perceive that man crouching and hidden behind that illusion which is called the flesh, one would have more than one surprise. The common error consists in taking the external being for the real being. Such and such a maiden, for example, would appear a bird if one could see her as she is.

A bird with the form of a maiden, what more exquisite! Imagine that you have her with you. That would be Déruchette. The delicious creature! One would be tempted to say to her, "Good-day, Mademoiselle Goldfinch." One beholds no wings, but one hears the chirping. Sometimes she sings. By her chatter, she is below man; by her singing, above him. There is mystery in that song; a virgin is the envelope of an angel. When womanhood begins, the angel departs; later on she returns, bringing a little one to the mother. While awaiting life, she who will one day be a mother is for a long time a child, the little girl lingers in the maiden, and is a linnet. One thinks as one looks at her: "How amiable of her not to fly away!" The sweet, familiar being follows its own pleasure about the house, flits from branch to branch, that is to say, from room to room, enters, goes out, approaches, plumes its feathers or combs its hair, makes all sorts of little gentle noises, murmurs one knows not what ineffable thing in your ears. It questions and is answered; one interrogates it, it chirps in reply. One chatters with it. To chatter refreshes one after serious talk. This being has heaven in it. It is a celestial thought mingled with your black thought. You feel grateful to it for being so light, so fleeting, so fugitive, so intangible, and for having the goodness not to be invisible, when it might, so it seems, be impalpable. Here below, the beautiful is a necessity.

There are on earth few more important functions than this: to be charming. The forest would be in despair without the humming-bird. To scatter joy, to beam with happiness, to possess amid sombre things an exhalation of light, to be the gilding of destiny, to be harmony, to be grace, to be prettiness, is to render a service. Beauty does one good by being beautiful. This creature has the fairy quality of being an enchantment for all who surround her; sometimes she knows nothing of it herself, and then it is but the more sovereign; her presence lights, her approach warms; she passes by, one is content; she halts, one is happy; to look at her is to love; she is the dawn with a human face; she need do nothing but simply exist there, that suffices; she makes an Eden of the house, it breaks forth from every pore; she communicates this ecstasy to all, without giving herself any other trouble than to breathe beside them. To have a smile which, one knows not how, lightens the weight of the monstrous chain dragged by all living beings in common, is, what would you have me say,—divine.

This smile Déruchette had. We will say more, Déruchette was that smile. There is something which resembles us more than our face, and that is our physiognomy; and there is something which resembles us more than our physiognomy, and that is our smile; Déruchette smiling, was Déruchette.

The Jersey and Guernsey race are peculiarly attractive. The women, especially the young girls, possess a florid and charming beauty. There the Saxon fairness and Norman freshness are combined. Rosy cheeks and blue eyes. The star is lacking in these glances. The English education subdues it. Those limpid eyes will be irresistible whenever the Parisian depth shall appear in them. Paris, happily, has not yet made its entrance into Englishwomen.

Déruchette was not a Parisienne, but neither was she a Guernsian. She was born at Saint-Pierre-Port, but Mess Lethierry had brought her up. He had trained her to be a dainty creature; and so she was.

Déruchette had an indolent, and at the same time, an aggressive look, without being aware of it. Perhaps she did not know the meaning of the word love, and she liked to make people fall in love with her. But with no bad intentions. She never dreamed of marriage. The old emigrant gentleman who had taken root in Saint-Sampson said; "That little girl makes powder flirtation."

Déruchette had the prettiest little hands in the world, and feet to match them. She had kindness and sweetness, in all her person; her family and riches were Mess Lethierry, her uncle; her occupation was to enjoy life; her talent, a few songs; her knowledge, beauty; her wit, innocence; her heart, ignorance; she had the graceful repose of the Creole, a mixture of giddiness and vivacity, the teasing gayety of childhood, with an inclination to melancholy; toilets which were rather insular, elegant but incorrect, bonnets with flowers all the year round; an innocent brow, a supple and graceful neck, chestnut hair, a white skin slightly freckled in summer, a large mouth, and on that mouth the adorable and dangerous brightness of a smile. This was Déruchette.

Sometimes in the evening, after sunset, at the moment when night is blending with the sea, at the hour when the twilight lends a sort of terror to the waves, there could be seen entering the channel of Saint-Sampson, on the sinister swell of the billows, an indescribable shapeless mass, a monstrous silhouette which whistled and spat, a horrible thing which roared like a beast and smoked like a volcano, a sort of hydra on the foam, and dragging after it a fog, and flinging itself towards the city with a frightful beating of paddles and a throat from which spouted flames. This was Durande.

II
The Eternal History of Utopia

A STEAMBOAT was a prodigious novelty in the waters of the channel in 182–. The whole Norman coast was long terrified by it. To-day, ten or twelve steamers crossing each other's course in various directions, on one marine horizon, make no one even lift his eyes; at the most, they occupy for a moment the special expert who can distinguish by the color of their smoke whether this one burns Welsh coal, and that one, Newcastle coal. They pass, 'tis well. Welcome, if they are arriving; a prosperous voyage, if they are departing.

People were less calm on the subject of those inventions during the first quarter of this century, and these mechanisms and their smoke were viewed with special disfavor among the islanders of the channel. In this puritan archipelago, where the Queen of England has been blamed for violating the Bible,[1] because she gave birth while under the influence of chloroform, the first success won by the steamboat was to be christened the Devil-boat. To these good fisher folk, formerly Catholics, now Calvinists, always bigots, it seemed to be hell afloat. A local preacher treated this question: "Have we the right to make fire and water work together, when God has separated them?"[2] Did not this beast of fire and iron resemble Leviathan? Was not this reconstituting chaos, in the measure possible to human beings? This is not the first time that progress has been described as a return to chaos.

1. Genesis, iii. 16: "In sorrow thou shalt bring forth children."
2. Genesis, i. 4.

"Mad idea, gross error, absurdity;" such had been the verdict of the academy of sciences when consulted by Napoleon at the beginning of this century as to the steamboat; the fishermen of Saint-Sampson are excusable for being in a scientific matter, on a level with the geometricians of Paris, and in the matter of religion, a little island like Guernsey is not compelled to possess more light than a great continent like America. In 1807, when Fulton's first steamboat, commanded by Livingston, provided with Watt's engine sent from England, and managed besides the ordinary crew, by only two Frenchmen, André Michaux and another, when this first steamboat made its first trip from New York to Albany, it chanced to be the seventeenth of August. Thereupon, Methodism took up the word, and in all the chapels the preachers cursed that machine, declaring that *seventeen* was the total of the ten horns and the seven heads of the beasts of the Apocalypse. In America, the beast of the Apocalypse was invoked against the steamship; and in Europe, the beast of Genesis. Therein lay the whole difference.

The wise men had rejected the steamboat as impossible; the priests, in their turn, rejected it as impious. Science had condemned, religion anathematized. Fulton was a species of Lucifer. The simple folk of shore and country clung to this reprobation because of the discomfort which this novelty gave them. In the presence of the steamboat, the religious point of view was as follows: fire and water are a divorce. This divorce is ordained by God. One should not put asunder what God has joined together; one must not unite what he has put asunder. The peasants' point of view was this: It frightens me.

Nothing less than Mess Lethierry was required in order to engage in such an undertaking as a steamboat from Guernsey to Saint-Malo at that distant epoch. He alone could conceive it as a freethinker, and realize it as a bold mariner. His French side conceived the idea, his English side executed it.

How it came about we will tell.

III
Rantaine

ABOUT forty years before the period at which the events we are here relating took place, in the suburbs of Paris, near the circumscribing wall, between the Fosse-aux-Lions and the Tombe Issoire, there stood a suspicious house. It was an isolated hovel, a resort for cut-throats when needful. There, with his wife and his child, dwelt a sort of *bourgeois* ruffian, a former clerk to the procurator of the Châtelet, who had become a thief pure and simple. He figured later on in the Court of Assizes.

This family was named Rantaine.

Two flowered porcelain cups were to be seen on a mahogany chest of drawers in the wretched hovel; on one could be read in gilt letters: "Souvenir of friendship," and on the other: "Token of esteem." The child was in the den, pell-mell with crime. The father and mother having belonged to the *demi-bourgeoisie,* the child was taught to read; he was brought up after a fashion. The mother pale, almost in rags, mechanically "gave an education" to her little one, making him spell, and breaking off to help her husband in some evil desire or to sell herself to a passer-by. Meanwhile, the "Cross of Jesus" remained open on the table at the place where they had stopped, and the child beside it, in thought.

The father and mother, caught in the very act of committing some crime, disappeared in penal obscurity. The child also disappeared.

Lethierry in his wanderings encountered another adventurer like himself, rescued him from some predicament, rendered him a service, for which he was grateful, took a liking to him, befriended him, brought him to Guernsey, found him intelligent at the coasting business, and made him his partner. This man was little Rantaine grown up.

Rantaine, like Lethierry, had a robust neck, a large and powerful space for carrying burdens between his shoulders, and the loins of the Farnese Hercules. Lethierry and he had the same gait and the same build; Rantaine was the taller of the two. Those who saw their backs as they walked along the port, side by side, said,—

"Yonder are the two brothers."

From the front it was another matter. All that was open in Lethierry's countenance was reserved and cautious in Rantaine. Rantaine was circumspect, Rantaine was a master of fencing, played the harmonica, snuffed a candle with a bullet at twenty paces, dealt a magnificent blow of the fist, recited verses from *La Henriade,* and interpreted dreams. He knew by heart Treneuil's *"Les Tombeaux de Saint-Denis."* He affirmed that he had been connected with the Sultan of Calicut, "whom the Portuguese call the Zamorin."

If any one could have turned over the little notebook which he carried on his person, one would have found, among other notes, jottings like the following: "At Lyons, in one of the fissures of the wall of one of the dungeons of Saint-Joseph, there is a file hidden."

He spoke with grave deliberation. He said that he was the son of a chevalier of Saint-Louis. His linen was mismatched and marked with different letters; no one was more sensitive than he on the score of honor; he fought and killed his man, there was something of the mother of an actress in his watchful glance for an insult, strength serving to envelop subtlety—that was Rantaine.

The force of his blow, applied in a fair, upon a "Moor's head," had forever won the heart of Lethierry.

His adventures were wholly unknown in Guernsey. They were checkered. If destinies have a wardrobe, Rantaine's destiny must have been clad as a harlequin. He had seen the world and made life. He was a circumnavigator. His trades formed a scale. He had been cook in Madagascar, bird-raiser in Sumatra, a general in Honolulu, an editor of a religious journal in the Galápagos islands, a poet at Oomrawuttee, a Freemason in Haiti. In this last quality, he had pronounced at Grand-Goâve a funeral oration of which the local journals have preserved this fragment,—

"Farewell then, beautiful soul! In the azure vault of the heavens whither thou now takest thy flight, thou wilt, no doubt, meet good Abbé Léandre Crameau of Petit-Goâve! Tell him that, thanks to ten years of glorious efforts, thou has completed the church of l'Anse-à-Veau! Farewell, transcendant genius, model man!"

It will be seen that his Freemason's mask did not prevent his wearing the false nose of a Catholic. The first won him the good opinion of the men of progress; the second, of the men of order. He declared himself a pure-blooded white. He hated the blacks; nevertheless, he certainly admired Soulouque.

In Bordeaux, in 1815, he had been a royalist (*verdet*). At that epoch, the fumes of his royalism sprang from his brow in the form of an immense white plume. He had passed his life in making eclipses,—appearing, disappearing, reappearing. He was a revolving-light rascal. He knew some Turkish; instead of guillotine, he said *"néboïssé."* He had been a slave in Tripoli to a thaleb, and he had there learned Turkish to an accompaniment of blows; his duties had consisted in going at evening to the doors of the mosques, and there reading aloud before the faithful, the Koran, written on small bits of board, or on the shoulder blades of camels. He was probably a renegade.

He was capable of everything and something worse.

He burst with laughter and frowned at the same time. He said; "In politics I esteem only those men who are inaccessible to influence." He said: "I advocate morals." He was gay and cordial rather than otherwise. The shape of his mouth belied the sense of his words. His nostrils might have passed for the nostrils of a horse. At the corners of his eyes there were crossroads of wrinkles, where all sorts of dark thoughts met together. The secret of his physiognomy could only be deciphered there. His crows'-feet were the talons of a vulture. His skull was low at the top, and broad at the temples. His ears, ill-shapen and encumbered with hairy thickets, seemed to say: "Do not speak to the beast which is in this cave."

One fine day, no one at Guernsey knew what had become of Rantaine.

Lethierry's partner had "slipped his cable," leaving the partnership cash box empty.

There was money of Rantaine's in that cash box, no doubt, but there were also fifty thousand francs belonging to Lethierry.

Lethierry, in his business of coaster and ship carpenter, had saved one hundred thousand francs, in the course of forty years of industry and probity. Rantaine had carried off half of it.

Lethierry, half ruined, did not flinch, and cast about instantly for some means to retrieve his fortune. The fortunes of men of spirit may be ruined, but not their courage. People were then beginning to talk about the steamboat. The idea occurred to Lethierry to try Fulton's machine, whose merits were so contested, and to connect the Norman Archipelago and France by steamer. He played his last trump on that idea. He devoted to it the remainder of his fortune. Six months after Rantaine's flight, a vessel with smoke was seen to issue from the stupefied port of Saint-Sampson, which produced the effect of a fire at sea, the first steamer which navigated the channel.

This boat, on which the hatred and contempt of all immediately bestowed the sobriquet of "Lethierry's galiot," was announced to make regular trips from Guernsey to Saint-Malo.

IV

Continuation of the History of Utopia

AT first, as the reader will of course understand, the thing did not prosper. All the owners of coasters who made the trip to the Isle of Guernsey, from the French side, were loud in their outcries. They denounced this attack on Holy Scripture and their monopoly. The chapels fulminated against it. One reverend gentleman, named Elihu, described the steamboat as "irreligious." The sailing-vessel was declared orthodox. They distinctly saw the devil's horns on the heads of the oxen which the steamer brought and landed.

This protest lasted for a considerably long time. Nevertheless, little by little, they came to see that the cattle arrived in a less fatigued state, and sold better, that the meat was better, that the risks of the sea were less for men also; that this passage, besides being less costly, was quicker and more sure; that one set out at a fixed hour, and arrived at a fixed hour; that fish, thus travelling more rapidly, were fresher, and that they could now pour upon the French markets the surplus of the large catches of fish which are so frequent in Guernsey; that the butter from the admirable Jersey cows made the transit more rapidly in the "Devil-boat" than in the sailing sloops, and no longer lost some of its good quality, so that Dinan called for it, and Saint-Brieuc demanded it, and Rennes wanted it; that there was, in short, thanks to what was called "Lethierry's galiot," security of transit, regularity of communication, a prompt and easy method of going back and forth, an increase of circulation, a multiplication of outlets, extension of commerce, and that, in short, they must make up their minds to this "Devil-boat," which violated the Bible and enriched the island. Some strong minds ventured to approve in a certain measure. Sieur Landoys, the clerk, granted the boat his esteem. Moreover, this was impartiality on his part, for he did not love Lethierry; in the first place, because Lethierry was Mess and he was only Sieur. Next, because although registrar at Saint-Pierre-Port, Landoys was a parishioner of Saint-Sampson; now, there were but two men in the parish who had not prejudices,—Lethierry and himself; the least that they could do was to detest each other. To belong on board the same ship drives men apart.

Nevertheless, Sieur Landoys was honest enough to approve of the steamboat. Others joined Sieur Landoys. The affair rose imperceptibly; affairs have their tide; and in course of time, with continued and increasing success, with the evidence of service rendered, the improvement in the general welfare of all being proved, there came a day when, with the exception of a few wiseacres, every one admired "Lethierry's galiot."

It would be less admired at the present day. This steamer of forty years ago would make our present constructors smile. This marvel was misshapen, this prodigy was infirm.

There is no less distance between our great transatlantic steamers of the present time, and the boat with wheels and fire with which Denis Papin manœvred on the Fulde in 1707, than between the three-decker *Montebello,* two hundred feet long, fifty wide, with a mainmast one hundred and fifteen feet high, displacing a weight of three thousand tons, carrying eleven hundred men, a hundred and twenty cannon, ten thousand cannon-balls, and a hundred and sixty packets of grape-shot, belching forth on each broadside, when in action, thirty-three hundred pounds of iron, and spreading to the wind, when it sails, five thousand six hundred square metres of canvas, and the Danish galley of the second century, found full of stone axes, bows, and battle clubs, in the marine marshes of Wester-Satrup, and deposited in the town hall of Flensburg.

An interval of precisely one hundred years, 1707–1807,

separates Papin's first boat from Fulton's first boat. "Lethierry's galiot" was certainly an advance upon those two rough sketches, but it was itself a rough sketch. This did not prevent its being a masterpiece. Every embryo of science presents this double aspect; a monster as a fœtus; a marvel as a germ.

V
THE DEVIL-BOAT

"LETHIERRY'S GALIOT" was not rigged to the best advantage for sailing, and this was no defect, since it is one of the laws of naval architecture; besides, as the vessel had fire for its motive power, sails were only accessories. Let us add that a side-wheel steamer is scarcely affected by any sails which may be applied to it. The galiot was too short, too round, too squat, it had too much beam, too much quarter; boldness of invention had not been carried so far as to make it light; the galiot had some of the defects, and some of the good qualities of the paunch. She pitched but little, but she rolled a great deal. The paddle boxes were too high. She had too much beam for her length. The engine was massive and encumbered her, and in order to render the vessel fit for a heavy cargo, they had been obliged to heighten the bulwarks out of all proportion, which gave to the galiot nearly the same defect as the old seventy-fours, a bastard model and which ought to be cut down, in order to render them fit for fighting or sailing. Being short, she should have turned quickly, the time employed in an evolution being in proportion to the length of vessels, but the weight deprived her of the advantage gained by her shortness.

Her midship-frame was too large, which slackened her speed, the resistance of the water being in proportion to the greatest section submerged, and to the square of the speed of the vessel. The stern was vertical, which would not be a fault nowadays, but at that time the invariable custom was to give it a slope of forty-five degrees. All the curves of the hull were harmonious, but not sufficiently long for the obliquity, and, above all, for the parallelism of the prism of water displaced, which should never be thrown back otherwise than laterally.

In heavy weather, she shipped too much water, sometimes at the bow, sometimes at the stern, which indicated an error in placing the centre of gravity. As the cargo was not where it should have been, owing to the weight of the engine, the centre of gravity often shifted behind the mainmast, and then they were obliged to trust to steam and distrust the mainsail, for the effect of the mainsail in that case was to make the vessel fall off, instead of keeping her near the wind. The remedy was, when they were very near the wind, to let go the mainsheet; in this way the wind was fixed on the bow by the tack jib, and the mainsail no longer produced the effect of a stern sail. This manœuvre was difficult. The helm was the old-fashioned tiller, not a wheel as at the present day, but with a bar, turning on its hinges, fixed in the stern-posts, and moved by a horizontal beam passing above the stern frame.

Two small boats were suspended from the davits. The vessel had four anchors, the sheet anchor, the second anchor, or working anchor, and two small bower anchors. These four anchors, which were bent by chains, were worked, as occasion demanded, by the great capstan at the stern, or the little capstan at the bow.

At that epoch the hydraulic capstan had not yet replaced the intermittent efforts of the handspike. As the vessel had but two bower anchors, one on the starboard and the other on the port, the vessel could not be moored in a tideway, which placed it rather at a disadvantage in certain winds. However, in such cases, it could make shift with the second anchor. The buoys were of the ordinary kind, and so constructed as to bear up the weight of the buoy ropes while remaining afloat. The longboat was of useful dimensions; it was the main dependence of the vessel, and was large enough to raise the sheet anchor.

One novelty in this vessel was that it was partly rigged with chains, which deprived the running ropes of none of their freedom of movement nor the standing rigging of its tension. The masts, though of secondary importance, were well proportioned; the top-rigging, drawn taut, looked light. The timbers were solid but coarse, since steam does not require so much delicacy of wood as canvas. This boat had a speed of two leagues an hour. When lying-to, she rode well. Such as she was, "Lethierry's galiot" was a good sea boat, but she lacked sharpness wherewith to cut the water, and one could not say that she worked easily. One felt that in danger, on a reef, or in a waterspout, she would be hard to handle. She creaked like a misshapen thing. As she rolled on the waves, she made a noise like that of a new shoe.

This vessel was above all things a carrier, and like all vessels fitted out for commerce rather than for war, was designed exclusively for the stowage of cargo. She accommodated but few passengers. The transportation of cattle rendered stowage difficult and very peculiar. Cattle were then stowed in the hold, which was another complication. At the present time they are carried on the forward deck. The paddle boxes of Lethierry's Devil-boat were painted white, the hull, to the water line, red, and all the rest of the vessel black, in accordance with the ugly fashion of this century.

When empty, she drew seven feet of water, and when loaded, fourteen.

The engine was powerful. The power was one horse for every three tons burden, which is nearly equal to that of a tug-boat. The paddles were well placed, a little ahead of the vessel's centre of gravity. The engine had a maximum pressure of two atmospheres. It consumed a great deal of coal, though it was a condensing and expanding engine. It had no fly-wheel, owing to the instability of its point of support, and this was remedied, as at the present day, by a double apparatus which caused two cranks fixed at the extremities of the shaft to alternate, and were so arranged that one was always at right angle or quarter turn, while the other was at its dead centre. The whole engine rested on a single cast-iron plate; so that, even in the case of serious injury, no blow of the waves could deprive it of its equilibrium, and the hull, crushed out of shape, could not put the engine out of order. To render the engine still more solid, the principal connecting-rod had been placed near the cylinder, which transferred the centre of oscillation from the middle to the end of the walking beam. Since then, oscillating cylinders have been invented which do away with connecting-rods; but at that epoch, the connecting-rod near the cylinder seemed the final word in machinery. The boiler was divided by partitions, and provided with a brine pump. The paddles were very large, which diminished the loss of power, and the smokestack was very tall, which increased the draught of the furnace; but the size of the wheels exposed them to the waves, and the height of the stack offered resistance to the wind. Wooden floats, iron hooks, cramps, cast-iron hubs, such were the paddle wheels, well constructed and, surprising to say, capable of being taken apart. There were always three floats submerged. The speed of the centre of the floats only exceeded by one-sixth, the speed of the vessel; therein lay the defect in the wheels.

Moreover, the end of the cranks was too long, and the slide-valve distributed the steam in the cylinder with too much friction. At that period, this engine seemed and was admirable.

This engine had been made in France, at the foundry of Bercy. Mess Lethierry had devised it himself, to some extent; the mechanic who had built it on his model was dead; so that this engine was unique and it was impossible to replace it. The designer remained, but the builder was gone.

The engine cost forty thousand francs.

Lethierry himself had made the galiot under the great covered ship shed which stands beside the first tower between Saint-Pierre-Port and Saint-Sampson. He had gone to Bremen to buy the timber. On this structure, he had exhausted all his knowledge as a ship's carpenter, and his talent was to be recognized in the planking, whose seams were narrow and even, and covered with sarangousti, an Indian mastic which is better than pitch.

The sheathing was well fastened. Lethierry smeared the keel with galgal.

In order to correct the curve of the hull he had adjusted the jib-boom to the bowsprit, which allowed him to add a flying-jib to the jib. On the day when it was launched, he said: "There, I am afloat."

The galiot was, in fact, a success, as the reader has seen.

Accidentally or intentionally, it was launched on the fourteenth of July. On that day Lethierry, standing on the deck between the two paddle boxes, gazed intently at the sea and exclaimed: " 'Tis thy turn! The Parisians took the Bastille; now we take thee!"

"Lethierry's galiot" made the trip from Guernsey to Saint-Malo once a week. She set out on Tuesday morning and returned on Friday evening, the eve of market day, which is Saturday. It was of much larger tonnage than the largest coasting sloops in all the archipelago, and its capacity being in proportion to its dimensions, a single one of these voyages was equal, for the voyage out and return, to four voyages of an ordinary cutter. Hence, decided advantages.

The reputation of a vessel depends on its stowage, and Lethierry was a good stevedore. When he could no longer work on the sea himself, he trained a sailor to take his place as a stower of the cargo. At the end of two years, the steamer brought in a net income of seven hundred and fifty pounds sterling a year; that is to say, eighteen thousand francs. The pound sterling of Guernsey is worth twenty-four francs; that of England, twenty-five; and that of Jersey, twenty-six. This trifling difference is less trifling than it appears; the banks find a profit in it.

VI
ENTRANCE OF LETHIERRY INTO GLORY

THE galiot prospered. Mess Lethierry beheld the moment drawing near when he would become monsieur. At Guernsey one does not become monsieur at one bound. Between the man and the gentleman there is a whole ladder to be climbed; to begin with, first rung, the name, alone, Pierre, I will assume it to be; next, second rung, Vésin (neighbor) Pierre; next, third rung, Father Pierre; then, fourth rung, Sieur Pierre; next, fifth rung, Mess Pierre; then, at the top, Monsieur Pierre.

This ladder which starts from the ground, continues into the blue sky. The whole hierarchy of England enters into it, and is graded in it. Here are the rungs, ever more and more luminous; above the gentleman there is the esquire, above the esquire, the knight ("sir"); then, still ascending, the baronet (a hereditary "sir"); then the lord, "laird" in Scotland; then the baron, then the viscount, then the earl ("jarl" in Norway), then the marquis, then the duke, then the peer of England, then the prince of the blood royal, then the king. This ladder rises from the people to the middle classes (*bourgeoisie*), from the middle classes to the baronetage, from the baronetage to the peerage, from the peerage to royalty.

Thanks to his rash but successful deed, thanks to steam, thanks to his engine, thanks to the Devil-boat, Mess Lethierry had become a personage. In order to construct the galiot he had been obliged to borrow money; he had run into debt in Bremen, he had run into debt at Saint-Malo; but each year he diminished his indebtedness.

He had purchased in addition, on credit, at the very entrance to the port of Saint-Sampson, a pretty stone house, perfectly new, situated between the sea and a garden, on whose corner this name was to be read: "les Bravées." The mansion of les Bravées, whose front formed a part of the very wall of the port, was remarkable for a double row of windows opening on the north on an enclosure full of flowers, on the south towards the ocean; so that the house had two fronts, one towards tempests, the other towards roses.

These fronts seemed made expressly for the two inhabitants, Mess Lethierry and Miss Déruchette.

The house of les Bravées was popular in Saint-Sampson, for Mess Lethierry had at length become popular. This popularity sprang a little from his kindness, his devotion, his courage, a little from the quantity of men whom he had saved, in great part from his success, and because he had given to the port of Saint-Sampson the privilege of the arrival and departure of the steamboat.

On perceiving that the Devil-boat was a decidedly good thing, Saint-Pierre, the capital, had claimed it for its port, but Lethierry had stood firm for Saint-Sampson. It was his birthplace,— "That is where I was launched," he was wont to say.—Hence a lively local popularity. His quality of a taxpaying proprietor constituted him what is called in Guernsey, a "habitant." He had been appointed douzenier. This poor sailor had climbed five out of the six rounds of the social ladder of Guernsey; he was a mess; he was on the brink of monsieur, and who knows whether he would not even succeed in passing the boundary to monsieur? Who knows whether one day, they would not read in the Almanac of Guernsey, in the chapter "Gentry and Nobility," this superb and unprecedented inscription: "Lethierry, Esq?"

But Mess Lethierry disdained or rather ignored the side of things which produce vanity. He felt himself to be useful; therein lay his joy. Being popular touched him less than being necessary. As we have said, he had but two loves, and consequently but two ambitions, Durande and Déruchette.

At all events, he had invested in the lottery of the sea and had won the grand prize.

This grand prize was the Durande, afloat and sailing.

VII
The Same Godfather and the Same Protectress

AFTER creating this steamer, Lethierry had christened it. He had named it Durande,—La Durande; we shall never call it otherwise. We must also be permitted, typographical usage to the contrary notwithstanding, not to italicize this name Durande, in this, conforming to the thought of Mess Lethierry, for whom the Durande was almost a person.

Durande and Déruchette are the same name. Déruchette is the diminutive. This diminutive is very much used in the west of France.

Saints in country places often bear their name with all its diminutives and all its augmentatives. One would suppose that there were many persons, where there is in reality but one. This identity of patron saints, male and female, under different names, is not of rare occurrence. Lise, Lisette, Lisa, Elisa, Isabelle, Lisbeth, Betsy,—the whole multitude represent Elisabeth. It is probable that Mahout, Maclou, Malo, and Magloire are the same saint. However, we do not insist on this point.

Sainte-Durande is a saint of Angoumois and Charente. Is she authentic? is a question for the Bollandists. Correct or not, she is the patron saint of numerous chapels.

Lethierry, being at Rochefort when a young sailor, had made the acquaintance of this saint, probably in the person of some pretty Charente maid, perhaps the grisette with the handsome nails. He had retained a sufficient recollection of her to bestow this name on the two things which he loved: Durande on the galiot, Déruchette on the girl.

He was the father of the one, and the uncle of the other.

Déruchette was the daughter of his deceased brother. She had no longer either father or mother. He had adopted her. He took the place of father and mother.

Déruchette was not only his niece, she was his goddaughter as well. It was he who had held her over the baptismal font. It was he who had found her that patroness, Sainte-Durande, and that Christian name, Déruchette.

Déruchette had been born, as we have said, at Saint-Pierre-Port. Her name was inscribed at its proper date, on the parish register.

As long as the niece was a child, and as long as the uncle was poor, no one paid any heed to that appellation, "Déruchette"; but when the little girl became a Miss, and when the sailor became a gentleman, "Déruchette" shocked people. They were astonished at it. They asked Mess Lethierry: "Why Déruchette?"

He replied, "That's the way the name is." They made many attempts to have it changed. He did not lend his countenance to this.

One day a fine lady belonging to the "high life" of Saint-Sampson, the wife of a retired wealthy blacksmith, said to Mess Lethierry,—

"Henceforth, I shall call your daughter 'Nancy.' "

"Why not Lons-le-Saulnier?" said he.

The fine lady did not yield her point, and said to him on the following day:—"I have found a pretty name for your daughter,—'Marianne.' "

"A pretty name in sooth," replied Mess Lethierry, "but composed of two villainous beasts,—a husband (*mari*), and an ass (*âne*)."

He stuck to Déruchette.

The reader will be mistaken if he concludes from the above remark that Mess Lethierry did not wish to give his niece in marriage. He did wish to marry her off, certainly, but after his own fashion; he meant her to have a husband after his own sort, who should work much while she did but little. He liked black hands on a man and white hands on a woman. In order that Déruchette might not spoil her pretty hands, he had directed her to the ways of a young lady. He had given her a music master, a piano, a little library, and also a little thread and some needles in a work-basket. She read more than she sewed, and was more of a musician than a reader. This was what Mess Lethierry wished for her to be. Charming, that was all that he desired. He had brought her up to be a flower rather than a woman. Any one who has studied sailors will understand this. Roughness loves delicacy. In order that the niece might realize the uncle's ideal, it was requisite that she should be rich. Mess Lethierry meant that she should be. His big steamboat was toiling to that end. He had charged Durande with providing Déruchette's dowry.

VIII
"Bonny Dundee

DÉRUCHETTE occupied the prettiest chamber of les Bravées, with two windows, furnished in veined mahogany, adorned with a bed, whose curtains were checkered green and white, and having a view of the garden and of the lofty hill on which stands the château of le Valle. It was on the other side of this hill that the Bû de la Rue was situated.

In this chamber, Déruchette had her music and her piano. She accompanied herself on this piano when singing her favorite air, the melancholy Scotch melody, "Bonny Dundee"; all of evening lies in that air, all of the dawn lay in her voice; this formed a pleasantly surprising contrast; people said: "Miss Déruchette is at her piano"; and the passers-by at the foot of the hill sometimes paused before the garden wall of the Bravées, to listen to the fresh singing and the sad ballad.

Déruchette was joy itself going and coming in the house. She created a perpetual springtime there. She was beautiful, but more pretty than beautiful, and more graceful than pretty. She reminded the good old pilots, Mess Lethierry's friends, of that princess in a ballad of soldiers and sailors who was so beautiful "that she passed for such in the regiment." Mess Lethierry said, "She has a cable of hair."

She had been of remarkable beauty from her very infancy. They had long feared for her nose, but the little girl, probably determined to be pretty, had held her own; her growth had played her no ill turn; her nose had grown neither too long nor too short; as she grew up she remained charming.

She never called her uncle anything but "father."

He tolerated in her some gardening and housekeeping talents. She herself watered her beds of hollyhocks, purple foxgloves, perennial phlox, and scarlet bennet; she cultivated pink crépis and pink oxalis. She took advantage of the climate of that Island of Guernsey, which is so hospitable to flowers. Like every one else, she had aloes in open ground, and, what is more difficult, she was successful with Nepal cinquefoil. Her little kitchen garden was skilfully arranged; she made spinach follow radishes, and peas succeed spinach; she knew how to plant Dutch cauliflower and Brussels sprouts, which she planted in July, and turnips for August, curled chicory for September, round parsnips for the autumn, and rampion for winter. Mess Lethierry allowed her to pursue her course, provided that she did not use the spade and rake too much herself, and, above all, that she did not personally apply the dressing.

He had given her two servants, named, the one, Grâce, and the other, Douce, which are two Guernsey names. Grâce and Douce did the work of the house and garden, and they had a right to red hands.

As for Mess Lethierry, he had for a chamber a little

den looking on the port, and adjoining the large room on the ground floor, where the entrance door was situated, and where all the various staircases of the house ended. His chamber was furnished with his hammock, his chronometer, and his pipe. There were also a table and a chair. The raftered ceiling had been whitewashed, as well as the four walls. On the right of the door was nailed the Archipelago of the Channel Islands, a fine marine chart, bearing this inscription: "W. Faden, 5 Charing Cross, Geographer to His Majesty"; and on the right, other nails held outspread on the wall one of those huge cotton handkerchiefs on which are figured in colors the signals of all the navies on the globe, having at the four corners the standards of France, Russia, Spain, and the United States of America, and in the centre the English Union Jack.

Douce and Grâce were two creatures of a certain kind, in the good sense of the word. Douce was not ill-disposed, and Grâce was not ugly. These dangerous names had not turned out badly. Douce, unmarried, had a "gallant." In the Channel Islands this word is in use, the thing also. These two maids had what may be called the Creole style of service, a sort of slowness peculiar to Norman domesticity in the archipelago. Grâce, coquettish and pretty, gazed incessantly at the horizon with the uneasiness of a cat. This was caused by the fact, that having, like Douce, a gallant, she had also, so it was said, a sailor husband whose return she feared. But that does not concern us.

The contrast between Grâce and Douce is, that in a less austere and less innocent household, Douce would have remained the servant, while Grâce would have become the lady's maid. Grâce's possible talents were wasted with a candid girl like Déruchette. Besides, the love affairs of Douce and Grâce were latent. Nothing reached Mess Lethierry in regard to them, and nothing of them was reflected on Déruchette.

The room on the ground floor, a hall with a fireplace, surrounded by tables and chairs had, in the last century, served as a place of assembly for a conventicle of French Protestant refugees. The bare stone wall had, for its sole luxury, a frame of black wood, wherein was outstretched a placard of parchment ornamented with the feats of Bénigne Bossuet, Bishop of Meaux. Some of the poor diocesans of that eagle, persecuted by him at the time of the revocation of the Edict of Nantes, and who had taken shelter in Guernsey, had affixed this frame to the wall to bear it witness. There one could read, if one succeeded in deciphering a heavy writing and yellow ink, such little-known facts as the following,—

"Oct. 29, 1685, demolition of the temples of Morcef and of Nanteuil, demanded of the king by M. the Bishop of Meaux."

"April 2, 1686, arrest of Cochard, father and son, for their religion, at the request of M. the Bishop of Meaux. Released; the Cochards having abjured."

"Oct. 28, 1699, M. the Bishop of Meaux sends to Ponchartrain a petition of remonstrance that it will be necessary to place the demoiselles de Chalardes and de Neuville, who are of the reformed religion, in the house of the new Catholics of Paris."

"July 7, 1703, was executed the order requested of the king by M. the Bishop of Meaux, to cause to be shut up in the hospital a certain Baudoin and his wife, *bad Catholics* of Fublaines."

At the end of the room, near the door of Mess Lethierry's chamber, a little niche of boards which had formed the Huguenot pulpit had become, thanks to a grating with an aperture, the "office" of the steamer; that is to say, the office of the Durande, kept by Mess Lethierry in person. On the old oak pulpit, a register, with its pages lettered debit and credit, replaced the Bible.

IX
THE MAN WHO HAD SEEN THROUGH RANTAINE

As long as Mess Lethierry had been able to navigate, he had run the Durande himself, and he had had no other pilot, no other captain than himself; but the hour had come, as we have already said, when Mess Lethierry had been obliged to find a substitute. For this he had chosen Sieur Clubin, of Torteval, a silent man. Sieur Clubin enjoyed along the whole coast a name for severe probity. He was the *alter ego,* the double of Mess Lethierry.

Sieur Clubin, though he had the air of a notary rather than of a sailor, was a skilful and capable mariner. He possessed all the talents which risk, perpetually undergoing transformations, demands. He was a clever stower of cargo, a handy man aloft, a careful and able boatswain, a robust helmsman, an experienced pilot, and a bold captain. He was prudent, and he sometimes pushed prudence even to daring, which is a great quality at sea. His fear of the probable was tempered by his instinct of the possible. He was one of those mariners who face danger in a proportion known to themselves, and who know how to extract success from every adventure. All the certitude which the sea can leave a man he had. Sieur Clubin was, in addition, a renowned swimmer; he belonged to that race of men inured to the gymnastics of the billows who remain in the water as long as desired, who, at Jersey, set out from Havre-des-Pas, turn the Cotelette, make the tour of the Hermitage and of Château

Elizabeth, and return to their starting point at the expiration of two hours. He came from Torteval, and he was reputed to have often made the dreaded passage, swimming, from the Hanois to the point of Plainmont.

One of the things which had most commended Sieur Clubin to Mess Lethierry was that, knowing or seeing through Rantaine, he had pointed out the man's lack of probity to him, and had said to him: "Rantaine will rob you." This had been verified. More than once, in unimportant matters it is true, Mess Lethierry had put the probity of Sieur Clubin, pushed even to scruple, to the proof, and he confided much of his business to him. Mess Lethierry said: "All conscience deserves all confidence."

X

Tales of Long Voyages

MESS LETHIERRY, for the sake of his own ease, always wore his sea clothes and his tarpaulin overcoat, rather than his pilot jacket. This made Déruchette's little nose wrinkle. Nothing is so pretty as a pouting beauty. She scolded and laughed. "Good father," she cried, "phew! you smell of tar!" And she gave him a little tap on his big shoulder.

This good old hero of the sea had brought back surprising tales from his voyages.

He had seen in Madagascar, bird's feathers, three of which sufficed to form the roof of a house.

He had seen in India, stalks of sorrel nine feet high.

He had seen in New Holland, flocks of turkeys and geese led and guarded by a shepherd dog which is a bird, and which is called the agami.

He had seen cemeteries of elephants.

In Africa, he had seen gorillas, a sort of man-tiger, seven feet in height. He knew the ways of all monkeys, from the savage baboon, which he called the *macaco bravo,* to the howling baboon, which he called the *macaco barbado.*

In Chile, he had seen a monkey soften the hunters by showing them her little one.

In California, he had seen the trunk of a hollow tree which had fallen on the ground, in whose interior a man on horseback could ride fifty paces.

In Morocco, he had seen the Mozabites and the Biskris fight with matraks and bars of iron; the Biskris because they had been treated as *kelb,* that is to say, as dogs, the Mozabites because of having been treated as *khamsi,* which means people of the fifth sect.

In China, he had seen the pirate Chanh-thong-quan-lark-Quoi chopped into little pieces for having assassinated the âp of a village.

At Thun-daû-Môt, he had seen a lion carry off an old woman from the midst of a market in a village.

He had been present at the arrival of a great serpent, coming from Canton to Saigon, to celebrate in the pagoda of Cholen the festival of Quan-nam, goddess of navigators. He had contemplated among the Moï the grand Quan-Sû.

At Rio de Janeiro, he had seen Brazilian ladies place in their hair little spheres of gauze, each containing a *vagalumes,* a beautiful phosphorescent fly, so that they had a headdress of stars.

He had fought ant hills in Uruguay, and spiders in Paraguay, hairy and as large as a child's head, covering with their claws a diameter of a third of a yard, and attacking man, against whom they launch their hairs, which sink into the flesh like darts, and there raise swellings.

On the river Arinos, an affluent of the Tocantins, in the virgin forests to the north of Diamantina, he had verified the existence of the terrible bat people, the murcilagos, men who are born with white hair and red eyes, dwell in the gloom of the woods, sleep by day, wake by night, and fish and hunt in the dark, seeing better when there is no moon.

Near Beirut, in the camp of an expedition of which he was a member, a pluviometer having been stolen from a tent, a sorcerer clad in two or three narrow strips of leather, and resembling a man dressed in his suspenders, had rung a bell attached to the tip of a horn so furiously that a hyæna had come and brought back the pluviometer. This hyæna was the thief.

These true stories resembled fairy tales so closely that they amused Déruchette.

The "doll" of the Durande was the bond between the boat and the girl. In the Norman isles, the figure-head carved at the prow, a statue of wood almost sculptured, is called the "doll." Hence, the local locution for "navigating" is: "to be between poop and *poupée*" (doll).

The "doll" of the Durande was particularly dear to Mess Lethierry.

He had ordered the carver to make it like Déruchette. It bore as little resemblance to her as if it had been done with an axe. It was a log of wood trying to be a pretty girl.

This unshapely block was an object of illusion to Mess Lethierry. He contemplated it with the faith of a believer. His faith was complete in the presence of this figure. He recognized Déruchette in it perfectly. It is a little the way in which the dogma resembles truth; and the idol, deity.

Mess Lethierry had two great joys every week; one joy on Tuesday, the other on Friday. The first joy consisted in seeing the Durande take her departure; the second joy in seeing her return. He leaned on his elbows at his window, gazed upon his work and was happy. There is something of this in Genesis. *Et vidit quod esset bonum,*—and he saw that it was good. On Friday, the presence of Mess Lethierry, at his window, was equivalent to a signal. When people beheld him lighting his pipe at the casement of les Bravées, they said, "Ah! the steamboat is on the horizon." One kind of smoke announced the other.

The Durande, on entering port, made her cables fast to a large iron ring, under Mess Lethierry's windows, fixed in the base of the Bravées. On these nights, Lethierry enjoyed an admirable sleep in his hammock, conscious that Déruchette was asleep on one side of him, and the Durande anchored on the other.

The anchorage of the Durande was close to the bell of the port. There was a small bit of the quay there in front of the Bravées.

This quay, the Bravées, the house, the garden, the tiny streets bordered with hedges, the greater part of the surrounding houses even, do not exist at the present day. The trade in Guernsey granite has caused these lands to be sold. This whole place is occupied at the present moment by the sheds of stonecutters.

XI
A Glance at Possible Husbands

DÉRUCHETTE grew up, and was not yet married. Mess Lethierry, in making of her a girl with white hands, had also rendered her somewhat difficult to suit. Such educations turn against you later on.

Besides, he was still more fastidious himself. The husband whom he imagined for Déruchette was also something of a husband for Durande. He would have liked to provide for his two daughters at the same time. He would have liked to have the commander of one, the pilot of the other.

What is a husband?

He is the captain on the voyage of matrimony. Why not the same skipper for girl and boat? A household obeys the tides. He who knows how to handle a bark knows how to guide a woman. Both are subjects of the moon and the wind.

As Sieur Clubin was only fifteen years younger than Mess Lethierry, he could be for Durande only a temporary skipper; a young pilot was needed, a permanent captain, a true successor to the founder, the inventor, the creator. The definitive pilot of Durande would be in some measure the son-in-law of Mess Lethierry. Why not blend the two sons-in-law in one? He cherished this idea. He also beheld a lover appear in his dreams. A powerful topman, sunburned and tawny, an athlete of the sea, that was his ideal. It was not, however, exactly that of Déruchette. She had a more rosy dream.

At all events, uncle and niece seemed to be agreed that there was no haste. When people had come to regard Déruchette as a probable heiress, throngs of suitors had presented themselves. Such eagerness is not always of good quality. Mess Lethierry felt it. He growled, "a girl of gold, a suitor of brass." And he dismissed the applicants. He waited, so did she.

One singular thing was that he did not set much store by the aristocracy. On that point, Mess Lethierry was not altogether an Englishman. One would find it difficult to believe that he had refused for Déruchette a Ganduel of Jersey, a Bugnet-Nicolin of Sark. People do not hesitate to affirm, though we doubt the possibility of this, that he had not accepted overtures coming from the aristocracy of Alderney, and that he had declined the propositions of a member of the family of Édou, which is evidently descended from *Édou-ard* the Confessor.

XII
An Exception in the Character of Lethierry

MESS LETHIERRY had one defect—a great one. He hated a priest; not as an individual, but as an institution. One day, as he was reading—for he sometimes read—Voltaire,—for he now and then read Voltaire,—these words, "Priests are cats," he laid down the book, and was heard to mutter in a low tone, "I feel that I am a dog."

It must be remembered that the priests, Lutherans and Calvinists as well as Catholics, had vigorously combated and persecuted him in the creation of his local Devil-boat.

To be a revolutionist in navigation, to try to adapt a spirit of progress to the Norman archipelago, to make the poor little island of Guernsey undergo the first trial of a new invention, was damnable temerity, and we have not concealed the fact. Hence, they had condemned him loudly. Let it not be forgotten that we are speaking here of the ancient clergy, very different men from the present clergy, who, in almost all the local churches, have a liberal tendency towards progress. They had interfered with Lethierry; the total amount of obstacle which could be contained in sermons and preachings had been opposed to him. Detested by the churchmen, he detested them. Their hatred of him was the extenuating circumstance of his towards them.

But, let us state, his aversion for priests was a peculiarity of his nature. There was no necessity for his hating them or being hated by them. As he had said, he was the dog among these cats. He was against them in idea, and what is more unconquerable, by instinct. He felt their secret claws, and he showed his teeth. Somewhat haphazard, we must admit, and not always appropriately. Not to make distinctions is a mistake. There is no good hatred in the mass. The Savoyard vicar would have found no mercy in his sight. It is not certain that such a thing as a good priest was possible in Mess Lethierry's eyes. By virtue of being a philosopher, he lacked somewhat in wisdom. The intolerance of the tolerant exists, as well as the rage of the moderates. But Lethierry was so kindly by nature that he could not be really a good hater. He repulsed, rather than attacked. He kept the churchmen at a distance. They had done him harm, he confined himself to not wishing them well. The shade of difference between their hatred and his lay in the fact that theirs was animosity, and his was antipathy.

Guernsey, small as is the island, has room for two religions. It contains the Catholic religion and the Protestant religion. Let us add that it does not place the two religions in the same church. Each form of worship has its own temple or chapel. In Germany, at Heidelberg, for instance, they do not stand so much on ceremony; they cut the church in two, one half for Saint Peter, the other half for Calvin; between the two a partition to prevent fisticuffs; equal shares to each; the Catholics have three altars, the Huguenots have three altars; as the hours for service are the same, the single bell rings for both at once. It summons at the same time to God and the devil, a very simple arrangement. The phlegmatic German accommodates himself to these customs. But at Guernsey each religion has a home of its own. There is the orthodox parish, and there is the heretic parish. One may choose between them. Neither the one nor the other,—such had been the choice of Mess Lethierry.

This sailor, this workman, this philosopher, this upstart of labor, while very simple in appearance, was by no means simple at bottom. He had his contradictions and his obstinacies. As to the priest, he was not to be shaken. He could have given points to Montlosier.

He permitted himself to indulge in very disrespectful

railleries. He said things peculiar to himself, eccentric, but sensible. Going to confession he called, "combing one's conscience." The small knowledge of letters which he possessed, a certain amount of reading picked up at sea between squalls, was impaired by faults of spelling. He had also faults of pronunciation, but they were always naïve. When peace was made by Waterloo, between the France of Louis XVIII and the England of Wellington, Mess Lethierry said: "Bourmont has been the traitor of union between the two camps."[1] Once, he wrote *papauté, pape ôté.*[2]

We do not think that this was done intentionally.

His antipapacy did not conciliate the Anglicans in his behalf. He was no more beloved by the Protestant rectors than by the Catholic curés. In the presence of the gravest dogmas, his irreligion burst forth almost without restraint. Chance having led him to hear a sermon on hell by the Reverend Jaquemin Hérode, a magnificent sermon filled from one end to the other with sacred texts proving eternal pains, punishment, torments, damnations, inexorable chastisements, endless burnings, inextinguishable curses, the wrath of the Omnipotent, celestial furies, divine vengeances, incontestable facts, he was heard to say gently, as he was coming out with one of the faithful: "You see I have such a queer idea, I imagine that God is good."

This leaven of atheism came from his residence in France.

Although a Guernsey man, and of tolerably pure race, he was called "the Frenchman" in the island, because of his improper mind. He made no secret of the fact that he was impregnated with subversive ideas. His persistence in constructing that steamer, that Devil-boat, had proved it. He said: "I was suckled by '89." That is not a good sort of milk.

Moreover, he was guilty of inconsistencies. It is very difficult to remain by one's self in small countries. In France to keep up appearances, and in England to be respectable—a peaceable life is to be had only at this

1. *Traître d'union,* instead of *trait d'union,* point of union, hyphen.
2. Papacy; pope taken away.

price. Being respectable implies a multitude of observances, from Sunday well sanctified, to a cravat properly tied. "Don't get yourself pointed at," that is the terrible law. To be pointed at is the diminutive of the anathema. Little towns, hotbeds of gossips, excel in this isolating malignity, which is a curse viewed through the small end of the telescope. The most valiant fear this ordeal. A man faces grapeshot, he faces the hurricane, but beats a retreat before Madame Pimbêche.

Mess Lethierry was more tenacious than logical, but beneath this pressure even his obstinacy gave away. He "put water in his wine"—another phrase full of latent concessions and sometimes of such as cannot be acknowledged. He held aloof from members of the clergy, but he did not close his door resolutely against them. On official occasions, and at the stated times for pastoral visits, he received in a proper manner the Lutheran rector or the Papist chaplain, whichever it might be.

At distant intervals, he accompanied Déruchette to the Anglican parish church, while the latter, as we have said, only went herself on the four great festivals of the year.

In short, these compromises, which cost him an effort, irritated him, and, far from inclining him towards churchmen, increased his inward resistance. He indemnified himself by more raillery. This man, being devoid of bitterness, had no acidity in his nature, except in that direction. There was, however, no way of amending him.

In fact and absolutely, such was his temperament, and people had to accept it.

All the clergy were distasteful to him. He possessed the irreverence of the revolution. He made little distinction in the form of worship. He did not even do justice to this great progress of ideas: the cessation of belief in the real presence. His shortsightedness in these matters went so far that he could not see any difference between a minister and an abbé. He confounded a reverend doctor with a reverend father. He said: "Wesley is no better than Loyola." When he saw a pastor go by with his wife, he turned aside. "Married priest!" he said, with the absurd accent which those two words had in France at that time. He was wont to relate that, on his last trip to

London, he had seen "the bishopess of London." His disgust at this sort of union went as far as anger. "Gown and gown cannot wed," he cried. The priesthood, in his eyes, was equivalent to a distinct sex. He would naturally have said: "Neither man nor woman; only a priest." He applied, with bad taste, to the Anglican clergy and to the Papal clergy, the same disdainful epithets; he included the two "cassocks" in the same phraseology; he did not trouble himself to vary the soldier's metonymies in use at that period for any priest, no matter what they were, Catholic or Lutheran. He said to Déruchette: "Marry whom you will, provided it is not a priest."

XIII

Heedlessness Adds New Grace to Beauty

WHEN Mess Lethierry had once said a thing, he remembered it; when Déruchette had once said a thing, she forgot it. Therein lay the difference between uncle and niece.

Déruchette, brought up as the reader has seen, was accustomed to but little responsibility. We insist upon it that more than one latent peril is contained in an education not taken with sufficient seriousness. It is, perhaps, unwise to wish to make one's child happy too soon.

Déruchette believed that, provided she was content, all was well. Besides, she was also conscious that her uncle was happy when he saw her so. She held nearly the same ideas as Mess Lethierry. Her religion was satisfied with going to church four times a year. The reader has seen her in her Christmas toilet. She was wholly ignorant of life. She possessed all the qualities necessary to render her one day mad with love. In the meantime, she was gay.

She sang and chattered at haphazard, took life as it came, tossed a word and passed on, did a thing and fled, was charming. Add to this, English liberty. In England, the children go about alone, the young girls are their own mistresses, youth has free rein. Such are the customs. Later on, these free girls make slaves of wives. We use the two words here in their best sense: free in growth and development, but slaves to duty.

Déruchette awoke each morning with little thought of her actions of the preceding day. She would have been greatly embarrassed had she been asked how she had spent her time the previous week. This did not prevent her having at certain hours, troubles, a mysterious discomfort, and a sombre feeling passing over her brightness and her joy. These azure depths have such clouds, but these clouds passed away quickly. She came forth from them with a burst of laughter, not knowing why she had been sad, nor why she was serene. She played with every one. Her roguery delighted in teasing the passers-by. She played tantalizing little jokes upon the young men; if she had encountered the devil she would have had no mercy on him, she would have played a trick on him. She was pretty and at the same time so innocent that she presumed upon it. She gave a smile as a kitten gives a scratch with its claw. So much the worse for the person scratched. She thought no more of it. Yesterday had no existence for her; she lived in the plentitude of to-day. This is to have too much happiness. With Déruchette, the memory of a thing vanished as snow melts.

BOOK FOURTH
THE BAGPIPE

I
THE FIRST RED GLEAMS OF DAWN, OR A CONFLAGRATION

GILLIATT had never spoken to Déruchette. He knew her through having seen her at a distance, as one knows the morning star.

At the time when Déruchette had met Gilliatt on the road from Saint-Pierre-Port to le Valle, and had surprised him by writing his name in the snow, she was sixteen. It was only the evening before that Mess Lethierry had said to her: "Play no more childish tricks. You are grown up now."

That name, "Gilliatt," written by that child, had fallen into unknown depths.

What were women to Gilliatt? He himself could not have told. When he met one, he alarmed her, and he was afraid of her. He never spoke to a woman except from urgent necessity. He had never been a "gallant" of any of the country maidens. When he was alone in the road and beheld a woman coming towards him, he climbed over the wall of a garden, or hid himself in a thicket and fled. He even avoided old women.

He had seen one Parisian lady in the course of his life. A travelling Parisienne, a strange event for Guernsey at that distant epoch. And Gilliatt had heard the Parisienne narrate her griefs in these words: "I am greatly annoyed, I have just got some drops of rain on my hat; it is apricot, and that is a color which stains." Having found, later on, between the leaves of a book, an ancient fashion plate, representing "a lady of the Chaussée d'Antin," in full toilette, he had pasted it upon his wall in memory of that apparition.

On summer evenings, he hid behind the rocks of the Houmet-Paradis inlet, to watch the peasant maids bathe in the sea in their shifts. One day he had watched, through a hedge the witch of Torteval put on her garter. He was probably spotless.

On that Christmas morning when he encountered Déruchette, and when she laughingly wrote his name in the snow, he returned home, no longer knowing why he had gone out. Night came, he did not sleep. He thought of a thousand things;—that it would be well to cultivate black radishes in his garden; that the exhibition was good,—that he had not seen the boat from Sark pass by; had something happened to it?—that he had seen some white stonecrop in flower, a rare thing at that season.

He had never exactly known what relationship the old woman who was dead bore to him; he said to himself decidedly that she must be his mother, and he thought of her with redoubled tenderness. He thought of the woman's clothing, which lay in the leather trunk. He thought that the Reverend Jaquemin Hérode would probably some day be appointed dean of Saint-Pierre-Port, surrogate of the bishop, and that the rectorship of Saint-Sampson would become vacant. He thought that the day after Christmas would be the twenty-seventh day of the moon, and that, consequently, high water would come at twenty-one minutes past three, half ebb at fifteen minutes past seven, and low tide at thirty-three minutes past nine, and half flood again at thirty-nine minutes past twelve.

He recalled the minutest details in the costume of the highlander who had sold him his bagpipe: his bonnet, ornamented with a thistle; his claymore; his tight coat, with short, square lappets; his skirt, the kilt or philabeg, ornamented with the sporran purse and the smushing-mull, a horn snuff-box; his pin made of a Scotch stone; his two girdles, the sashwise and the belt; his sword; his cutlass, the dirk; and his skene dhu, a black knife with a black handle ornamented with two cairngorums,[1] and

1. Most of the Scottish words are given as Hugo wrote them, except that the spelling has been corrected.

the bare knees of the soldier, his stockings, his plaid gaiters, and his shoes with buckles. This equipment became a spectre, pursued him, gave him a fever, lulled him to sleep. When he awoke it was broad daylight, and his first thought was Déruchette.

On the following day he slept, but all night long he saw the Scotch soldier again. He said to himself in his sleep that the sittings of the superior court after Christmas would be held on the twenty-first of January. He also dreamed of old rector Jaquemin Hérode. When he awoke, he thought of Déruchette, and felt violent anger against her; he regretted that he was no longer a small boy, because then he could go and fling stones at her windows.

Then he reflected that if he were a small boy, he would have his mother, and he began to weep.

He formed a project of going to pass three months at Chousy, or the Minquiers. But he did not go.

He did not set foot again on the road from Saint-Pierre-Port to le Valle.

He fancied that his name, Gilliatt, remained graven there on the earth, and that all the passers-by must be looking at it.

II

An Entrance, Step by Step, into the Unknown

ON the other hand, he saw les Bravées every day. He did not do it intentionally, but he went in that direction. It chanced that his road always lay along the path which skirted Déruchette's garden wall.

One morning as he was on this path, a market woman

who was coming from les Bravées said to another, "Miss Lethierry likes sea-kale."

He made a trench for sea-kale in his garden at the Bû de la Rue. Sea-kale is a sort of cabbage which has the flavor of asparagus.

The garden wall of les Bravées was very low, one could easily climb over it. The idea of climbing over it would have seemed terrible to him. But he was not prohibited from hearing as he passed, like all the rest of the world, the voices of persons who were talking in the chambers or in the garden. He did not listen but he heard. Once, he heard the two servants, Douce and Grâce, quarrelling. That was one of the noises of the house. That quarrel lingered in his ear like music.

On another occasion, he distinguished a voice which was not like that of the others, and which, as it seemed to him, must be the voice of Déruchette. He took to flight.

The words which that voice had pronounced remained forever graven in his memory. He repeated them to himself every moment. These words were,—

"Will you please to give me the broom?"

By degrees he became bolder. He dared to stay awhile. It once happened that Déruchette, whom it was impossible to see from the outside, although her window was open, was at her piano and singing. She was singing her air: "Bonny Dundee." He turned very pale, but he summoned up his courage so far as to listen.

Spring arrived. One day, Gilliatt had a vision, heaven opened. Gilliatt saw Déruchette watering her lettuce.

Soon he did more than pause. He observed her habits. He noticed her hours, he waited to see her.

He took good care not to show himself.

Little by little, at the same time that the shrubbery was becoming filled with butterflies and roses, he became accustomed to see Déruchette in the garden, as he stood motionless and mute for hours together, hidden behind that wall, seen by no one, holding his breath. One becomes gradually accustomed to poison.

From his hiding-place he often heard Déruchette conversing with Mess Lethierry under a thick arch of yoke-elms, where there was a seat. Their words reached him distinctly.

How much progress he had made! He had now come to spying and eavesdropping. Alas! there is a spy in every human heart.

There was another seat visible and quite close, at the edge of an alley. Déruchette sat on it sometimes.

From the flowers which he saw Déruchette pluck and smell, he had divined her tastes in the matter of perfumes. The convolvulus was the odor which she preferred, next the pink, then the honeysuckle, then jasmine. The rose came only fifth. She looked at the lily, but she did not smell of it.

From her choice of perfumes, Gilliatt imagined her character in his thoughts. To each odor he attached some perfection.

The mere idea of speaking to Déruchette made his hair stand on end.

A good, old peddler woman, whose wandering industry brought her from time to time into the lane which skirted the enclosure of les Bravées, finally began to notice, in a confused way, Gilliatt's assiduity near this wall, and his devotion to this deserted place. Did she connect the presence of this man in front of that wall with the possibility of a woman behind it? Did she perceive that vague, invisible thread? Had she, in her beggared decrepitude, remained sufficiently young to recall something of her happier days, and did she still know, amid her winter and her night, what the dawn was? We know not, but it appears that once, as she passed near Gilliatt, "standing on guard," she cast in his direction the nearest approach to a smile of which she was still capable, and muttered between her toothless gums: "That warms one."

Gilliatt heard this word, he was struck by it, he murmured with an inward interrogation point: "That warms one? What does the old woman mean?" He repeated this saying mechanically all day, but he did not understand it.

One evening, when he was at his window at the Bû de la Rue, five or six young girls of Ancresse, came, as a pleasure excursion, to bathe in the inlet of Houmet.

They played very innocently in the water, a hundred paces away from him. He closed his window violently. He perceived that a nude woman caused him horror.

III

The Air Bonny Dundee Finds an Echo on the Hill

BEHIND the enclosure of the garden of les Bravées was an angle of the wall covered with holly and ivy, with nettles, with a wild tree-mallow, and a large mullein sprouting amid the blocks of granite: it was in this nook that he passed nearly the whole of his summer. He stood there in an indescribably pensive mood. The lizards, accustomed to him, warmed themselves on the same stones.

The summer was bright and full of dreamy indolence. Gilliatt had above his head the flitting clouds. He sat on the grass. Everything was full of the sounds of birds. He clasped his brow in his hands and asked himself: "But why did she write my name in the snow?" The sea breeze came in great puffs from the distance. At intervals in the quarries of la Vandue, the horn of the miners sounded abruptly, warning passers-by to stand aside, and that a charge was about to be exploded. The port of Saint-Sampson was not visible; but the tips of the masts could be seen above the trees. Stray gulls were flying about. Gilliatt had heard his mother say that women could be in love with men, that such things did happen sometimes. He answered himself: "That is it. I understand. Déruchette is in love with me."

He felt profoundly sad. He said to himself: "But she also, she, on her part, is thinking of me; it is well." He reflected that Déruchette was rich, and that he was poor. He then thought that the steamboat was an execrable invention. He could never remember the day of the month. He watched, in a vague way, the big, black bumble-bees, with their yellow thighs and short wings, as they plunged noisily into the holes in the wall.

One evening, Déruchette retired to her room to go to bed. She approached her window to close it. The night was dark. All at once, Déruchette began to listen; somewhere in the dark shadow there was music. Some one who was probably on the slope of the hill or at the foot of the towers of the Château du Valle, or perhaps even still farther away, was playing an air upon an instrument. Déruchette recognized her favorite melody, "Bonny Dundee," played on the bagpipe. She could not understand it at all.

From that time forth, this music was repeated from time to time, at the same hour, particularly on very dark nights.

Déruchette did not like this very much.

IV

A Nocturnal Serenade

Pour l'oncle et le tuteur, bonshommes taciturnes,
Les sérénades sont tapages nocturnes.[1]

FOUR years passed away.

Déruchette was approaching twenty-one, and was still unmarried.

1. "For the uncle and the guardian, taciturn men, serenades are nocturnal uproars." Couplet from an unpublished comedy.

Some writer has said: "A fixed idea is a gimlet. Every year it sinks in one turn. If any one desires to extract it for us the first year, it would pull out our hair; the second year it would tear our skin; the third year it would break our bones; the fourth year it would tear out our brain."

Gilliatt had reached the fourth year of it.

He had not yet spoken a word to Déruchette. He dreamed of that charming girl, that was all.

It once happened that, being by chance at Saint-Sampson, he had seen Déruchette talking with Mess Lethierry in front of the door of les Bravées, which opened on the road to the Port. Gilliatt ventured to approach very near. He was quite sure that she had smiled as he passed. There was nothing impossible about that.

Déruchette still heard the bagpipe from time to time.

Mess Lethierry also heard that bagpipe. He had at last noticed the persistency of that music beneath Déruchette's windows. Tender music, an aggravating circumstance. A nocturnal gallant was not to his taste. He wished Déruchette to marry when the day arrived, when she should desire it, and when he should desire it, purely and simply, without romance, and without music. Provoked, he lay in wait, and he thought that he had caught a glimpse of Gilliatt. He had thrust his fingers into his whiskers, a sign of wrath, and had muttered: "What does that fellow mean by his piping? He loves Déruchette, that is clear. You are wasting your time. He who wants Déruchette must apply to me, and not by playing the flute."

An event of considerable importance, long foreseen, had taken place. It was announced that the Reverend Jaquemin Hérode was appointed surrogate to the Bishop of Winchester, Dean of the Island, and receiver of Saint-Pierre-Port, and that he would take his departure from Saint-Sampson for Saint-Pierre, immediately after his successor was installed.

The new rector must soon arrive. This priest was a gentleman of Norman origin, Monsieur Joë Ebenezer Caudray, anglicized into Cawdry. Some facts were known concerning the future rector which kindliness and malice interpreted in an inverse sense. He was said to be young and poor, but in his youth was tempered with much learning, and his poverty by many expectations. In the special language created for inheritance and wealth, death is called expectations. He was the nephew and heir of the old and opulent Dean of Saint-Asaph. At the death of this dean, he would be rich. M. Ebenezer Caudray had distinguished connections; he had almost the right to the title of Honorable.

As for his doctrine, it was variously judged. It was Anglican but, according to the expression of Bishop Tillotson, "very free"; that is to say, very severe. He repudiated phariseeism; he held by the presbytery rather than by the episcopacy. He dreamed of the primitive church, when Adam had the right to choose Eve, and when Frumartinus, Bishop of Hierapolis, abducted a maiden for the purpose of making her his wife, saying to her parents,—

"She wishes it and I wish it. You are no longer her father, and you are no longer her mother; I am the angel of Hierapolis, and she is my wife. God is the father."

If what was said was to be believed, M. Ebenezer Caudray subordinated the text: "Honor thy father and thy mother," to the text, of greater authority in his view, "The woman is the flesh of the man. The woman shall leave her father and her mother to cleave to her husband."

Moreover, this tendency to circumscribe paternal authority and religiously to favor all modes of forming the conjugal union, is peculiar to all Protestantism, particularly in England and *singularly* so in America.

V
Well-Merited Success Is Always Hated

MESS LETHIERRY'S affairs at that moment were as follows: The Durande had fulfilled all that she had promised. Mess Lethierry had paid his debts, repaired the breaches in his fortune, cancelled his indebtedness at Bremen, and met his bills of exchange at maturity in Saint-Malo. He had cleared the house of les Bravées of the mortgages with which it was burdened; he had bought in all the little local charges inscribed against the property.

He was the possessor of a great productive capital—the Durande. The net revenue from the vessel was now a thousand pounds sterling, and continued to increase. Properly speaking, the Durande constituted his entire fortune.

She was also the fortune of the island. The most profitable part of her business was the transportation of cattle, and, in order to improve the stowing capacity and to facilitate the entrance and exit of the animals, they had been obliged to dispense with the quarter boats and the yawls. This was, possibly, an imprudence. The Durande had but one boat remaining—the long-boat. It was, however, an excellent boat.

Ten years had elapsed since Rantaine's theft.

This prosperity of the Durande had one weak side; it was that it did not inspire confidence; it was believed to be chance. Mess Lethierry's situation was only looked upon as exceptional. He was regarded as having committed a fortunate folly. Some one who had imitated him at Cowes, in the Isle of Wight, had not been successful. The attempt had ruined his stockholders. Lethierry said,—

" 'Twas because the engine was badly constructed."

But people shook their heads. Novelties have this to their disadvantage—that every one bears them a grudge; the slightest false step compromises them. One of the commercial oracles in the Norman Archipelago, Jauge the banker from Paris, on being consulted as to a speculation in steamers, answered, it is said, turning his back on the speaker. "You are proposing a *conversion* to me: the conversion of money into smoke."

On the other hand, sailing-vessels found as many people to invest in their stock as they wished. The captains obstinately preferred canvas to the boiler.

In Guernsey, the Durande was a fact, but steam was not an established principle. Such is the unrelenting animosity of conservatism in the presence of progress. It was said of Lethierry, "That is good, but he could not do it again"; far from being an encouragement, his example frightened people. No one would have dared to risk a second Durande.

VI

The Luck of a Shipwrecked Crew in Meeting a Sloop

THE equinox begins early in the Channel. The sea is narrow and compresses the wind and irritates it. West winds begin in the month of February, and the waves are shaken up in every direction.

Navigation becomes an anxious matter; the people of the coast watch the signal pole, they are engrossed with the thought of ships which may be in distress.

The sea appears like an ambush; an invisible clarion sounds the alarm for war; vast and furious blasts overwhelm the horizon; there is a terrible wind. The night whistles and howls. In the depths of the clouds, the black face of the tempest puffs out his cheeks.

The wind is one danger, the fog is another.

Fogs have always been the dread of navigators. In certain fogs, microscopic prisms of ice are held in suspension, to which Mariotte attributes halos, mock suns, and mock moons. Storm fogs are composite; different vapors of unequal specific gravity there combine with watery vapors, and are superposed one upon another in an order which divides the mist into zones, and makes of the fog a veritable formation; iodine is at the bottom, sulphur above the iodine, bromine above the sulphur, phosphorus above the bromine.

This, in a certain measure, by playing the part of electric and magnetic tension, explains many phenomena, Saint-Elmo's fire, the fires of Columbus and of Magellan, the flying stars mingled with the ships, of which Seneca speaks, the Castor and Pollux twin flames of which Plutarch speaks, the Roman legion whose javelins Cæsar thought he saw take fire, the peak of the castle of Duino in Friuli, which the soldier of the guard caused to give forth sparks, by touching it with the iron of his lance, and perhaps, even, those lightnings from below which the ancients called "the terrestrial lightnings of Saturn."

At the equator, an immense permanent fog seems to encircle the world. The function of the cloud ring is to cool the tropics, just as the function of the Gulf Stream is to warm the Pole. Under the cloud ring, the fog is fatal. These are the horse latitudes; there the navigators of former centuries were accustomed to throw their horses into the sea, in time of storm, in order to lighten their vessels, and, in time of calm, to economize their stock of fresh water.

Columbus said, *"Nube abaxo es muerte"*—death lurks under the cloud.

The Etruscans, who are in meteorology what the Chaldæans are in astronomy, had two high priests, the high priest of thunder and the high priest of the cloud; the fulgurators observed the lightning, and the aquilegers observed the clouds. The college of the priest-augurs of Tarquinii was consulted by the Tyrians, the Phœnicians, the Pelasgians, and all the primitive navigators of the ancient Mare Internum.

The mode of generation of tempests was seen to some extent even at that time; it is intimately connected with the mode of generation of fogs, and it is, properly speaking, the same phenomenon. There exist on the ocean three regions of fogs, one equatorial, two polar; mariners give them but a single name, "The Black Pot."

Along all coasts, and especially in the Channel, equinoctial fogs are dangerous. They produce sudden night on the sea. One of the perils of the fog, even when it is not very thick, is that it prevents the recognition of the change of depth by the change of color in the water; the result is a dangerous concealment of the approach of breakers and shoals. One runs on a reef without warning. Fogs often leave a vessel no other resource than to heave to or anchor. There are as many shipwrecks caused by fog as by wind.

Nevertheless, after a very violent hurricane which followed one of these foggy days, the mail boat, *Cashmere,* arrived safely from England. It entered Saint-Pierre-Port as the first ray of dawn appeared on the sea, and at the very moment when the cannon of the Château Cornet announced the sunrise. The sky had cleared up. The sloop *Cashmere* was expected, as it was to bring the new rector of Saint-Sampson.

Shortly after the arrival of the sloop, the rumor spread through the town that she had been hailed, during the night, by a long-boat containing a shipwrecked crew.

VII
The Luck of an Idler in Being Seen by a Fisherman

THAT night, Gilliatt, at the moment when the wind had slackened, had gone out to fish, but without taking his paunch too far from the coast.

As he was returning on the flood tide, about two o'clock in the afternoon, in fine, sunny weather, and passing before the Beast's Horn in order to make the bight of the Bû de la Rue, it seemed to him that he saw a shadow cast in the projection of the chair Gild-Holm-'Ur, which was not that of the rock. He ran the paunch in that direction and saw that a man was seated in the chair Gild-Holm-'Ur. The tide was already very high, the rock was encircled by the waves, return was no longer possible. Gilliatt made signs to the man, but he remained motionless. Gilliatt drew nearer.

The man was asleep.

He was dressed in black. "He looks like a priest," said Gilliatt to himself. He approached still nearer and beheld the face of a young man.

The features were unknown to him.

Fortunately, the cliff was perpendicular, the water was very deep, Gilliatt tacked and succeeded in running close to the wall. The tide raised the boat enough to allow Gilliatt, by mounting on the gunwale of the paunch, to reach the man's feet. He mounted the rail and raised his hands. If he had fallen at that moment, it is doubtful whether he would have reappeared on the surface of the water. The sea was heaving in, and he would inevitably have been crushed between the paunch and the rock.

He pulled the foot of the sleeping man.

"Ho! what are you doing there?"

The man awoke.

"I was looking about," said he.

He was now fully awakened and continued,—

"I have just arrived in this part of the country, I came here on a pleasure trip, I passed the night at sea, I found it beautiful here, I was fatigued, and I fell asleep."

"In ten minutes more you would have been drowned," said Gilliatt.

"Bah!"

"Jump into my boat."

Gilliatt kept the boat in position with his foot, clung with one hand to the rock and offered the other hand to the man in black, who leaped quickly into the boat.

He was a very handsome young man.

Gilliatt seized the oar, and in two minutes the paunch had reached the inlet of the Bû de la Rue.

The young man wore a round hat and a white cravat. His long, black coat was buttoned up to his cravat. He had light hair, *en couronne,* a feminine face, a clear eye, a grave manner.

In the meanwhile, the paunch had touched the shore. Gilliatt passed the cable through the mooring ring, then turned and beheld the very white hand of the young man holding out to him a gold sovereign.

Gilliatt gently pushed the hand aside.

A silence ensued which was broken by the young man.

"You have saved my life."

"Perhaps," replied Gilliatt.

The moorings were made fast. They stepped out of the boat.

The young man repeated.

"I owe you my life, monsieur."

"What of that?"

This reply from Gilliatt was followed by another silence.

"Do you belong to this parish?" asked the young man.

"No," replied Gilliatt.

"Of what parish are you?"

Gilliatt raised his right hand, pointed to the sky and said,—

"Of that one."

The young man bowed to him and departed.

After taking a few steps, the young man paused, searched in his pocket, drew forth a book and returned towards Gilliatt, holding out the book to him.

"Permit me to offer you this."

Gilliatt took the book.

It was a Bible.

An instant later, Gilliatt, with his elbows resting on the parapet, was watching the young man turn the corner of the path which leads to Saint-Sampson.

Little by little he dropped his head, forgot this newcomer, no longer knew whether the chair of Gild-Holm-'Ur existed, and everything disappeared for him in the fathomless depths of reverie. Gilliatt had an abyss,—Déruchette.

A voice calling to him roused him from this gloom.

"Hé, Gilliatt!"

He recognized the voice and raised his eyes.

"What is it, Sieur Landoys?"

It was, in fact, Sieur Landoys who was passing along the road a hundred paces from the Bû de la Rue, in his phaeton, drawn by his little horse. He had halted to hail Gilliatt, but seemed busy and in haste.

"There is some news, Gilliatt."

"Where?"

"At les Bravées."

"What is it?"

"I am too far away to tell you."

Gilliatt shuddered.

"Is Miss Déruchette about to be married?"

"No, far from it."

"What do you mean?"

"Go to les Bravées, you will find out."

And Sieur Landoys whipped up his horse.

BOOK FIFTH
THE REVOLVER

I
THE CONVERSATIONS AT THE JEAN TAVERN

SIEUR CLUBIN was a man who waits his opportunity.

He was short and yellow with the strength of a bull. The sea had not succeeded in tanning his skin. His flesh resembled wax. He was the color of a candle, and he had the candle's discreet light in his eyes. His memory was peculiarly retentive. For him to see a man once was to have him registered as if in a note-book. His eye took an impression of a face and kept it; in vain did the visage grow old. Sieur Clubin knew it again. Impossible to throw this tenacious memory off the track.

Sieur Clubin was curt, sober, cold; never a gesture. His air of candor won at first sight. Many people considered him artless; he had in the corner of his eye a wrinkle astonishingly expressive of simplicity. There was no better sailor than he, as we have said; there was no one like him for hauling in sheets or for keeping the sails well trimmed. No reputation for religion and integrity stood higher than his. Any one who suspected him would himself have been regarded with suspicion. He was a friend of M. Rébuchet, money-changer in Saint-Malo, Rue Saint-Vincent, beside the armorer's, and M. Rébuchet was wont to say: "I would give Clubin my shop to keep."

Sieur Clubin was a widower. His wife, like himself, had been strictly honest. She had died with the reputation of unsullied virtue. If the *bailli* had paid court to her, she would have gone and told the king; and if the Deity had been in love with her, she would have told the curé. This couple, Sieur and Dame Clubin, had realized in Torteval the ideal of the English term "respectable." Dame Clubin was the swan; Sieur Clubin was the ermine. A stain would have been fatal to him. He could not have found a pin without searching for the owner. He would have sent the town-crier round with a box of matches. One day he entered a wine-shop in Saint-Servan and said to the proprietor: "I breakfasted here three years ago. You made a mistake in the bill," and he returned him sixty-five centimes. His was a great probity, accompanied by a certain contraction of the lips.

He seemed to be on the watch. For whom? Probably for rascals.

Every Tuesday he took the Durande from Guernsey to Saint-Malo. He reached Saint-Malo on Tuesday evening, remained two days to load, and set out for Guernsey again on Friday morning.

There was a little tavern in Saint-Malo at that time, near the port, which was called the Jean Tavern.

The construction of the present quays has demolished this inn. At that epoch the sea came up to the Saint-Vincent and Dinan gates. Saint-Malo and Saint-Servan were put in communication at low tide, by carrioles and maringottes[1] rolling and circulating among the vessels lying high and dry, avoiding the buoys, the anchors, and cordage, and sometimes running the risk of breaking their leather hoods on a lowered yard or the end of a jibboom. Between tides, the coachmen lashed their horses across this sand, where six hours later the wind lashed the waves. On this same strand, in former days, roamed the four and twenty watch-dogs of Saint-Malo, who ate a naval officer in 1770. This excessive zeal led to their suppression. To-day, nocturnal barking is no longer heard between the little Tallard and the grand Tallard.

1. A small carriage, furnished with rails on the sides and ends, the seats being movable.

Sieur Clubin put up at the Jean Tavern. The French office of the Durande was located at that place.

The custom-house men and coastguards came to take their meals and to drink at the Jean Tavern. They had their separate table. The custom-house officers of Binic met the officers of Saint-Malo there, for the good of the service.

The skippers of vessels also came there, but ate at another table.

Sieur Clubin sat sometimes at the one, sometimes at the other, preferring the table of the custom-house officials, however, to that of the skippers. He was welcome at both.

These tables were well served. There were supplies of foreign beverages for mariners far from home. A dandified sailor from Bilbao would have found an *helada* there. Stout was drunk, as at Greenwich, and brown *gueuse,* as at Antwerp.

Captains on long voyages and ships' chandlers sometimes were seen at the skippers' table. There they exchanged news.

"How are sugars?"

"That kind goes only in small lots. But raw sugars sell; three thousand sacks of Bombay and five hundred hogsheads of Sagua."

"You will see that the duty will result in overturning Villèle."

"And indigo?"

"Only seven Guatemala surons have been handled."

"The *Nanine-Julia* has come into the roads. A pretty three-master from Bretagne."

"The two cities of La Plata are quarrelling again."

"When Montevideo grows fat, Buenos Aires grows lean."

"They have had to reship the cargo of the *Regina-Cœli,* condemned at Callao."

"Cocoa is rising, sacks from Caracas are quoted at two hundred and thirty-four, and Trinidad sacks at seventy-three."

"It appears that at the review on the Champ de Mars, people shouted, 'Down with the ministers!' "

"Salted green hides from Saladeros are selling, ox-hides at sixty francs, cow-hides at forty-eight."

"Have they passed the Balkans? What is Diebitsch doing?"

"At San Francisco, the supply of anise-seed is short. Plagniol olive oil is quiet. Gruyère cheese in tins, thirty-two francs the quintal."

"Well, is Leo XII dead?" etc., etc.

These things were shouted out and noisily commented upon. At the table of the custom-house officers and coastguards, they talked less loudly.

Matters connected with the coast police and revenue require less publicity and less distinctness in conversation.

The skippers' table was presided over by an old foreign captain, M. Gertrais-Gaboureau. M. Gertrais-Gaboureau was not a man, he was a barometer. His familiarity with the sea had given him a surprising infallibility of prognostication. He decreed the weather for the following day. He auscultated the wind, he felt the pulse of the tide. He said to the cloud: "Show me your tongue." That is to say, the lightning. He was the doctor of the waves, the breeze, the squall. The ocean was his patient. He had made the tour of the world as one takes a clinical course, examining every climate in both good and bad health; he knew the pathology of the seasons to the very last details. He was heard to announce facts like the following,—

"The barometer once went down, in 1796, to three lines below tempest."

He was a sailor from love of the profession. He hated England as much as he loved the sea. He had studied the English navy carefully, in order to get at its weak points. He explained in what respect the *Sovereign* of 1637 differed from the *Royal William* of 1670, and from the *Victory* of 1755. He compared their upper works. He regretted the towers on deck and the funnel-shaped tops of the *Great Harry* of 1514, probably from the point of view of the French cannon ball, which lodged so well in these surfaces. For him nations existed only in their marine institutions, and odd synonyms were peculiar to him. He liked to designate England by "Trinity House,"

Scotland by "Northern Commissioners," and Ireland by "Ballast-board."

He abounded in information, he was alphabet and almanac, low-water mark and tariff. He knew by heart the tolls of the lighthouses, especially of the English—a penny a ton for passing by this one, and a farthing for passing by that one.

He would say to you: "The lighthouse on Small's Rock, which used to consume only two hundred gallons of oil, now burns fifteen hundred gallons."

One day, on board ship, in the course of a serious illness, he was thought to be dead, the crew surrounded his hammock, he interrupted the hiccoughs of his death agony to say to the master carpenter: "It would be a good idea to make a mortise in the masthead caps, on each side, and put in a cast-iron sheave, to reeve the top-ropes through."

This habit of command gave him an expression of authority.

It was rare that the subject of conversation, though, was the same at the table of the skippers as at that of the custom-house officials. This case presented itself, however, in the early days of that month of February to which we have now brought the story we are relating. The three-master *Tamaulipas,* Captain Zuela, coming from Chile and about to return thither, attracted the attention of both messes. At the skippers' table they talked of her cargo; at the custom-house table, of the set of her sails.

Captain Zuela, of Copiago, was a Chilean, and a bit of a Colombian. He had fought independently in the war for independence, holding now with Bolivar and again with Morillo, according as he saw his advantage. He had become rich by dint of being of service to every one. There was no man more Bourbonist, more Bonapartist, more absolutist, more liberal, more atheist, and more Catholic. He belonged to that great party which may be called the Lucrative party. He made his appearance in France from time to time, on business; and, judging from what was said, he willingly gave passage on his vessel to people taking flight, bankrupts or political outlaws, it mattered little to whom, so long as they paid. His process of embarkation was simple. The fugitive waited on a desert point of the shore, and at the moment of setting sail, Zuela despatched a boat to fetch him. He had in this way, on his preceding voyage, aided in the escape of a contumacious person connected with the Berton trial, and this time he intended, it was said, to carry off some men who had been compromised in the Bidassoa affair. The police, having been warned, had an eye upon him.

This was a period of flights. The Restoration was a reaction; now, revolutions bring about emigrations, and restorations produce banishments.

During the first seven or eight years after the return of the Bourbons, panic reigned everywhere, in finance, in industry, in commerce, which felt the earth trembling, and in which failures abounded. There was a desperate scramble in politics. Lavallette had taken flight, Lefebvre-Desnouettes had taken flight, Delon had taken flight. The courts of exception were more crowded than Trestaillon.

People shunned the bridge of Saumur, the esplanade de la Réole, the wall of the observatory of Paris, the tower of Taurias d'Avignon, landmarks in history, which reaction has marked, and where one still distinguishes at the present day that bloody hand. In London, the Thistlewood trial, branching into France, in Paris the Trogoff trial, with branches in Belgium, Switzerland, and Italy, had multiplied the causes for uneasiness and flight, and augmented that mysterious underground rout which created so many gaps even in the highest ranks of the social system of the day.

To place one's self in safety—that was men's sole care. To be compromised was to be lost. The spirit of the military courts had survived their institution. Condemnations were matters of favor. People fled to Texas, to the Rocky Mountains, to Peru, to Mexico. The men of the Loire, traitors then, patriots to-day, had founded the *champ d'asile.* A song of Béranger says, "Savages, we are Frenchmen; take pity on our glory."

To expatriate one's self was the only resource. But nothing is less simple than flight; that monosyllable contains abysses. Everything is an obstacle to the man who is fleeing. Stealing away implies disguising one's self. Important and even illustrious characters were reduced to the expedients of malefactors. And even then they succeeded badly. They were not practical. Their habits of freedom of action rendered their slipping through the meshes of authority difficult.

A pickpocket who had forfeited his ticket of probation was more correct, in the eyes of the police, than a general. Can one imagine innocence constrained to paint its face, virtue assuming a false voice, glory hiding under a mask? Such and such a passer-by with a suspicious air, was a person of renown in quest of a false passport. The equivocal course of a man making his escape did not prove that he was not a hero. Fugitive and characteristic traits of the time, which so-called standard history neglects, and which the true painters of the century should bring out clearly. Behind these flights of honest people, had slipped in the flights of thieves, less watched and less suspected. A scamp, forced to disappear, profited by the confusion, formed one of a number of exiles, and often, as we have said, thanks to more art, seemed, in that twilight, more of an honest man than the honest man.

Nothing is more awkward than probity in the clutches of justice. It understands nothing of the matter, and is sure to commit itself. A counterfeiter could escape more easily than a conventionary. Strange to say, one could almost affirm, particularly in the case of dishonest people, that flight led to everything. The amount of civilization which a rascal brought from Paris or from London served him in lieu of capital in primitive or barbarous countries, was a recommendation for him, and installed him as an initiator. There was nothing impossible in the adventure of escaping from the criminal code here and arriving at the priesthood abroad. There was something fantastic in the disappearance, and more than one flight had results like a dream.

A flight of this description led to the unknown and the chimerical. A bankrupt who absconded from Europe, reappeared twenty years later as Grand Vizier to the Mogul, or king of Tasmania.

Assisting fugitives became an industry, and, in view of

the frequency of the fact, an immensely profitable industry. This speculation was eked out by certain kinds of commerce. Any one who wished to make his escape to England applied to the smugglers; he who wished to flee to America betook himself to sea captains, like Zuela.

II

Clubin Perceives Some One

ZUELA sometimes came to eat at the Jean Tavern. Sieur Clubin knew him by sight.

Moreover, Sieur Clubin was not proud; he did not disdain to know rascals by sight. He even went so far sometimes as to know them in deed, giving them his hand in the open street, and bidding them good-day. He talked English to the smuggler, and jabbered Spanish with the *contrabandista.*

He had some sayings on this point: "One can derive good from a knowledge of evil."

"It is useful for the gamekeeper to converse with the poacher."

"The pilot should sound the pirate, the pirate being a reef."

"I taste a rascal as a physician tastes poison."

There was no reply to this. Every one acknowledged that Captain Clubin was right. He was approved for not being ridiculously dainty. Who would have dared to speak ill of him? All that he did was done "for the good of the service." Everything was quite simple, coming from him. Nothing could compromise him. If crystal were to try to spot itself, it could not. This confidence was the just reward of long honesty, and therein lies the excellence of well-established reputations. Whatever

Clubin did or seemed to do, no one suspected any harm on the score of virtue; he had acquired a state of impeccability; moreover, he was very circumspect, so it was said; and from an intimacy which would have been suspicious in any other person, his probity extricated itself with additional reputation for cleverness. This reputation for cleverness combined harmoniously with his renown for simplicity, without either contradiction or trouble. Such a thing as a clever and unassuming man does exist. This is one of the varieties of the honest man, and one most appreciated.

Sieur Clubin was one of the men who, when encountered in conversation with a sharper or a bandit, are accepted, understood, and respected all the more, and who possess in their favor the satisfied confidence of public esteem.

The *Tamaulipas* had completed her lading. She was ready for sea, and would soon set sail.

On Tuesday evening the Durande arrived at Saint-Malo when it was still broad daylight. Sieur Clubin, as he stood on the bridge and superintended the manœuvres of making a landing, perceived near the Petit-Bey, on the sandy beach, between two rocks, in a very secluded spot, two men talking together. He looked at them with his marine glass, and recognized one of the men. It was Captain Zuela. He thought that he recognized the other, also.

The other was a man of lofty stature, and rather gray. He wore the broad-brimmed hat and sober garments of the Friends. He was probably a Quaker. He kept his eyes modestly lowered.

On arriving at the Jean Tavern, Sieur Clubin learned that the *Tamaulipas* intended to sail in a fortnight.

It was afterwards learned that he had already made some inquiries on other points.

That night he entered the shop of the gunsmith in the Rue Saint-Vincent, and said to him,—

"Do you know what a revolver is?"

"Yes," replied the gunsmith, "it is an American weapon."

"It is a pistol which begins the conversation over again."

"In fact, it has in itself question and reply."

"And retort also."

"Quite true, Monsieur Clubin. A revolving barrel."

"And five or six bullets."

The gunsmith opened the corner of his lips a little, and gave vent to that click of the tongue which, accompanied by a shake of the head, expresses admiration.

"The weapon is good, Monsieur Clubin. I think it will make its way."

"I should like a six-chambered revolver."

"I have none."

"How is that, when you are a gunsmith?"

"I have not the article as yet. You see, it is a novelty. It is just out. Only pistols are made in France so far."

"The devil!"

"It is not on sale yet."

"The devil!"

"I have excellent pistols."

"I want a revolver."

"I admit that it is more advantageous. But wait a moment, Monsieur Clubin."

"What?"

"I think that there is one of the things in Saint-Malo at the present moment, a second-hand one."

"A revolver "

"Yes."

"For sale?"

"Yes."

"Where?"

"I think I know where. I will inquire."

"When can you give me an answer?"

"Second-hand, but good."

"When shall I return?"

"If I procure you a revolver, it will be good."

"When will you give me an answer?"

"After your next trip."

"Do not say that it is for me," said Clubin.

III

Clubin Carries Away and Does Not Bring Back

SIEUR CLUBIN completed the lading of the Durande, took on board a number of cattle and several passengers, and quitted Saint-Malo for Guernsey on Friday morning, as usual.

On that same Friday, when the vessel was in the open sea, which permits the captain to absent himself from the bridge for a few moments, Clubin entered his cabin, locked the door, took a travelling-bag which he had, put some garments in the elastic compartment, biscuits, some boxes of preserve, a few pounds of cocoa in sticks, a chronometer, and a marine glass in the solid compartment, locked the bag, and through the handles ran a rope, all ready to haul it up at need. Then he descended into the hold, entered the chainlocker, and was seen to come up again with one of those knotted ropes under his arm, which are provided with a hook and which are used by caulkers at sea, and by thieves on shore. These ropes facilitate climbing.

On arriving at Guernsey, Clubin went to Torteval. There he remained for thirty-six hours. He took with him the valise and the knotted rope, and did not bring them back.

Let us state, once for all, that the Guernsey which is treated in this book is the ancient Guernsey, which no longer exists, and which it would be impossible to find today anywhere except in country places. There it is still alive, but it is dead in the towns. The remark which we make concerning Guernsey should also apply to Jersey. Saint-Hélier is equal to Dieppe; Saint-Pierre-Port is the same as Lorient. Thanks to progress, thanks to the admirable spirit of enterprise of this brave little insular people, everything has been transformed within the last forty years in the Channel archipelago. Where there was darkness, there is light. Having made this observation, let us pass on.

In those times, which have already become historical, smuggling was very active in the channel. Contraband vessels abounded, particularly on the west coast of Guernsey. Persons fully informed as to the smallest details of what took place half a century ago even go so far as to cite the names of many of these vessels, nearly all Asturian and Guipuzcoan. There is no doubt of the fact that hardly a week passed without the arrival of one or two of them in the Bai des Saints or at Plainmont. It had all the appearances of a regular service. One ocean cave at Sark was, and is still, called "the shops," because people came to this grotto to purchase merchandise of the smugglers. To meet the requirements of this kind of traffic, a sort of contraband language, now forgotten, and which was to Spanish what the "Levantine" is to Italian, was spoken in the Channel.

At many points on the French and English shores, smuggling had a cordial, but secret understanding with legitimate and protected commerce; it had the right of entrance to more than one financier in high position, by a private door, it is true; and it was slyly interfused in commercial circulation and in the whole arterial system of trade. Merchant in front, smuggler at the rear; that was the history of many a fortune. Séguin said it of Bourgain; Bourgain said it of Séguin. We do not vouch for their statements. Perhaps they slandered each other. However that may be, smuggling, hunted down by the laws, incontestably had very good connections in finance. It had an understanding "with the best society." The cavern, where Mandrin formerly elbowed the Comte de Charolais, was honest on the exterior and had an irreproachable façade turned towards society; gable end to the street.

Hence much connivance, necessarily disguised. These

mysteries demanded impenetrable secrecy. A smuggler knew many things, and was forced to hold his peace; an inviolable and rigid good faith was his law. A smuggler's chief quality was loyalty. Without discretion, no smuggling. There are the secrets of fraud, as there are the secrets of the confessional.

These secrets were faithfully guarded. The smuggler swore to maintain silence about everything, and he kept his word. There was no one in whom one could so well confide as in a smuggler.

The judge-alcade of Oyarzun one day caught a smuggler, and put him to the torture, in order to name his secret capitalist. The smuggler did not reveal the name. This capitalist was the judge-alcade himself. Of these two accomplices, the judge and the smuggler, one had been obliged, in order to comply with the law in the sight of all, to apply torture, to which the other had submitted rather than to violate his oath.

The two most famous smugglers who haunted Plainmont at that epoch, were Blasco and Blasquito. They were *Tocayos*. It is a sort of Spanish and Catholic relationship which consists in having the same patron saint in Paradise; a thing not less worthy of consideration, it must be admitted, than having the same father on earth.

When one was very nearly initiated into the furtive itinerary of smuggling, nothing was easier, and at the same time more difficult than to have dealings with these men. It was only necessary to have no fear of night excursions, to go to Plainmont, and confront the mysterious interrogation point which stands there.

IV
Plainmont

PLAINMONT, near Torteval, is one of the three angles of Guernsey. At the extremity of the cape, there is a lofty, turfy ridge which overlooks the sea.

This summit is a lonely place.

It is all the more lonely because a single house is visible there.

This house adds terror to the solitude.

It is said to be haunted.

Haunted or not, its aspect is singular.

This house, built of granite, and one story high, stands in the midst of the grass. It is in good condition, and can be made perfectly habitable. The walls are thick and the roof is solid. Not a stone is out of position in the walls: not a tile is lacking in the roof. A brick chimney buttresses the angle of the roof. This house turns its back on the sea. The side towards the ocean is merely a blank wall. On examining the wall attentively, a bricked-up window is to be perceived. The two gables have three windows. The door is walled up. The two windows of the ground-floor are also walled up. On the first floor,—and this is what strikes one first on approaching,—there are two open windows. Their opening renders them dark in broad daylight. They have no panes, not even sashes. They open upon the gloom within. One would say that they were the empty sockets from whence two eyes had been torn. There is nothing in this house. One perceives from the yawning apertures the dilapidation within. No wainscoting, no woodwork, naked stone. One fancies that one beholds a sepulchre with windows, which permits the spectres to gaze out. The rain undermines it on the side towards the sea. A few nettles shaken by the breeze caress the base of the walls. No other human habitation on all the horizon. This house is an empty thing wherein dwells silence. Nevertheless, if one halts and lays one's ear to the wall, one hears, confusedly, at times, the flutter of frightened wings. Above the walled-up door, on the stone which forms the architrave, are engraved these letters: "ELM-PBILG," and this date: "1780."

At night, the melancholy moon finds entrance here.

The sea surrounds this house. Its situation is magnificent, and for this reason the aspect is more gloomy. The beauty of the place becomes an enigma. Why does no human family inhabit this dwelling? The place is beautiful, the house is good. Whence comes this abandonment? These questions suggested by reverie succeed others of the reason. This field is cultivatable, why is it not cultivated? No master. The door walled up. What, then, is the matter with the place? Why has man fled from it! What is going on here? If nothing is going on, why is there no one here? When all are asleep, is there some one awake?

The dark squall, the wind, the birds of prey, the hidden beasts, unknown beings, appear to the thought and mingle with that house. To what wayfarers is it the hostelry? One pictures to one's self showers of rain and of hail beating in at the windows. The vague drippings of tempests have left their traces on the inner wall. These walled and open chambers are visited by the hurricane?

Has a crime been committed here? It seems that this house, given over to gloom, must call for help at night. Does it remain silent? Do voices come from it? With whom has it dealings in this solitude? The mystery of the hours of darkness is secure here. This house disquiets one at midday; what is it at midnight? In looking at it one looks at a secret. One asks one's self, since reverie has its logic, and the possible has its bent, what takes place at this house between the twilight of evening and the twilight of morning. Can it be that the immense dispersion of extra-human life has, on that deserted summit, a point of intersection which stops it and which forces it to descend and to become visible? Does the scattered come to eddy here? Does the impalpable become condensed, to the extent of assuming form?

Enigmas.

Holy awe lies in these stones. The gloom which broods over these forbidden chambers is more than gloom; it belongs to the unknown.

After sundown, the fishing boats will return, the birds will become silent, the goatherd behind the rocks will depart with his goats, the crevices of the stones will give passage to the first glidings of reassured reptiles; the stars will begin to peep out, the breeze will blow, night will come on, those yawning windows will be there. They offer entrance to dreams, and it is by apparitions, by the faces of phantoms, vaguely distinct, by masks in flashes of light, by mysterious tumults of souls and shades, that popular belief, at once both stupid and profound, translates this dwelling's sombre intimacies with the world of darkness.

The house was "haunted"; this word explains everything.

Credulous minds have their explanation; but positive minds have theirs also. Nothing more simple, say they, than this house. It is an ancient post of observation, dating from the days of the Revolution, and the Empire, and smuggling. It was built there for that purpose. The war finished, the post was abandoned. The house was not demolished, because it might prove useful again. The door and windows have been walled up on the ground floor, as a protection against intruders, and so that no one could enter; the windows on the three sides facing the sea have been walled up because of the south and west winds. That is all.

The ignorant and credulous insist: In the first place, that the house was not built at the time of the war of the Revolution. It bears a date—1780—anterior to the Revolution. Next, that it was not built to serve as a military post; it bears the letters "ELM-PBILG," which contain the double monograms of the two families, and which indicate, in accordance with usage, that the house was built for the establishment of a newly married pair. Hence it had been inhabited. Why is it no longer so? If the door and the casements have been walled up to prevent any one from making his way into the house, why were two windows left open? All should have been walled up, or none. Why no shutters? Why no sashes? Why no glass? Why wall up the windows on one side if they are not walled up on the other? The rain is prevented from entering on the south, but allowed to enter on the north.

The credulous are wrong, no doubt, but the positive are certainly not right. The problem remains unsolved.

One thing is certain, that the house bears the reputation of having been more useful than injurious to the smugglers.

The exaggeration of fright deprives facts of their true proportions. Without doubt, many nocturnal phenomena among those which compose the "haunting" of the house, might be explained by obscure and furtive visits, by brief sojourns of men who immediately re-embarked, sometimes by the precautions, sometimes by the audacity of certain suspicious gentry of trade, hiding themselves for the purpose of committing evil, and allowing themselves to be seen for the purpose of awakening fear.

At that already distant period, many audacious deeds were possible. The police, particularly in that little country, was not what it is to-day.

Let us add that if the house was, as it was said, convenient for smugglers, their meetings must have had plenty of elbow room up to a certain point, precisely because the house was superstitiously avoided. Its ghostly reputation prevented its being denounced. It is not to customhouse officials and policemen that one applies against spectres. Superstitious persons make signs of the cross, not legal complaints. They see or think they see, and hold their tongues. There exists a tacit connivance, involuntary, it may be, but real, between those who inspire fear and those by whom it is experienced. The frightened are conscious that they do wrong to be frightened, they imagine that they have stumbled upon a secret, they have a fear, which is mysterious to themselves, of aggravating their position, and of irritating the apparitions. This renders them discreet. And, even setting aside this calculation, the instinct of credulous people is towards silence; there is dumbness in fear, the terrified speak little; it seems as though horror said to them: "Hush!"

It must be borne in mind that this goes back to the time when the Guernsey peasants believed that the mystery of the manger was repeated every year by the oxen and asses, on a certain day; a period at which no one would have dared to enter a stable on Christmas night for fear of finding the animals on their knees.

If local legends are to be believed, and the tales of the persons whom one meets, superstition was formerly carried to the point of suspending from the walls of that house of Plainmont, from nails which are still to be seen here and there, rats minus their paws, bats minus their wings, carcasses of dead beasts, toads crushed between the leaves of a Bible, sprigs of yellow lupin, strange votive offerings, hung there by imprudent nocturnal passers-by, who thought that they had seen something, and who hoped, by these gifts, to obtain their pardon, and to conjure away the bad humor of the witches, spectres, and sorcerers.

There have always been people,—and even some in very high positions,—who have believed in *abacas* and witches' Sabbaths. Cæsar consulted Sagana; and Napoleon, Mademoiselle Lenormand. There are consciences so uneasy that they try to obtain indulgences even from the Devil. "May God do, and may Satan not undo," was one of the prayers of Charles V. Others are still more timorous. They even go so far as to persuade themselves that one can be in the wrong towards evil. To be irreproachable so far as the demon is concerned, is one of their anxieties.

Hence religious practices turned towards this immense but unknown power of evil. It is a form of bigotry as well as any other. Crimes against the demon exist in certain diseased imaginations; it tortures eccentric casuists of ignorance to have violated the laws of the nether world; they have scruples on the side of the darkness. To believe in the efficacy of devotion to the mysteries of the Brocken and Armuyr, to imagine that one has sinned against hell, to have recourse because of chimerical infractions to chimerical penitences, to confess the truth with the spirit of a lie, to make one's *mea culpa* before the father of the fault, to confess in inverse sense,—all this exists or has existed. The reasons of trials for magic and witchcraft prove this on every page. Human dreams go as far as that. When man takes to getting frightened he does not stop. One dreams of imaginary faults, of imaginary purifications, cleans one's conscience by the shadow of the witches' broom.

At all events, if that house has secrets, that is its affair; setting aside a few chances and exceptions, no one goes there to see it, it is left alone; it suits no one's taste to run the risk of infernal encounters.

Thanks to the terror which guards it, and which wards off any one who might observe and bear testimony, it has always been easy to enter this house at night by means of a rope ladder, or even simply of the first ladder at hand, taken from the neighboring gardens. A supply of provisions and clothing would permit one to await there in perfect security opportunity and the proper time for a furtive embarkation.

Tradition relates that forty years ago, a fugitive, from politics according to some, from commerce, according to others, remained for some time concealed in the haunted house of Plainmont, whence he succeeded in embarking on a fishing boat for England. From England one easily reaches America.

This same tradition affirms that provisions deposited in this house remain there untouched, Lucifer, as well as the smugglers, having an interest in getting the person who has placed them there to return.

From the height on which this house was situated, one perceived in the southwest, a mile from the shore, the Hanway Rock.

This reef is celebrated. It had committed all the bad actions of which a reef can be guilty. It was one of the most redoubtable assassins of the sea. It lay in wait for vessels at night, like a traitor. It had enlarged the cemeteries of Torteval and of la Rocquaine.

In 1862, a lighthouse was placed on that reef.

To-day, the Hanway reef lights the navigation which it was wont to lead astray, the ambush holds a torch in its hand. That rock which was formerly avoided as a malefactor is now sought on the horizon as a protector and guide. Then Hanway reassures those vast nocturnal spaces which it terrified in former days. It is something like a brigand turned gendarme.

There are three Hanways, Great Hanway, Little Hanway, and la Mauve (the gull). It is on Little Hanway that the "Red Light" beacon stands to-day.

This reef forms a part of a group of points, some of them submarine, some projecting from the sea. It towers above them. It has, like a fortress, its outworks: on the side of the high seas, a cordon of thirteen rocks; on the north, two breakwaters, the Hautes-Fourquies, the Aiguillons, and a sand bank, the Hérouée; on the south, three rocks, Cat Rock, Pierced Rock, and Roque Herpin, plus two sand banks, the South Boue and the Boue du Monet, and also, in front of Plainmont, level with the surface of the water, the Tas de Pois d'Aval.[1]

It is difficult but not impossible for a swimmer to swim across the strait from Hanways to Plainmont. It will be remembered that this was one of Sieur Clubin's feats. The swimmer who knows these shoals has two points where he can rest, Round Rock and, further on, a little to the left, in an oblique line, the Red Rock.

V
The Bird-Nesters

It was near the same time of the day on that Saturday spent by Sieur Clubin at Torteval, that a singular incident occurred, which was not extensively noised abroad at first in the country, and which was only made known long afterwards. For many things, as we have just re-

1. The Heap of Peas Below.

marked, remain unknown, because of the fright which they cause in those who have witnessed them.

On the night between Saturday and Sunday—we mention the date with precision and we think it is exact—three children climbed over the heights of Plainmont. These children were returning to the village. They came from the sea. They were what is called in the local idiom *"déniquoiseaux."* Read: *Déniche-oiseaux*—"Bird-nesters." Wherever there are cliffs and holes in the rocks above the sea, young bird-nesters abound. We have said a few words on this point already. The reader will remember that Gilliatt took an interest in it, because of the birds and of the children.

The bird-nesters are a sort of sea gamin, not very timid.

The night was very dark. Thick masses of clouds piled upon each other concealed the horizon. Three o'clock in the morning had just sounded from the church tower of Torteval, which is round and pointed and resembles a magician's cap.

Why were these children returning so late? Nothing more simple. They had been on a hunt for sea-gulls' nests in the Tas de Pois d'Aval. The season having been very mild, the pairing of the sea birds had begun very early. These children, in watching the conduct of the males and females around their nests, and absorbed in the eagerness of this pursuit, had forgotten the hour. The flood tide had surrounded them; they had not been able to regain in season the little inlet where they had moored their boat, and they had been obliged to wait on one of the points of the Tas de Pois until the ebb tide. Hence their late return. These returns are awaited with feverish anxiety by mothers who, on finding them safe, manifest their joy in anger, and relieve their tears by administering punches on the head. They were accordingly in haste, and decidedly uneasy. Their haste was of that kind which willingly tarries, and which includes a reluctance to arrive. They had in prospect a kiss, to be followed with cuffs on the ear.

Only one of those children had nothing to fear; he was an orphan. This boy was French, without either father or mother, and quite content at that moment to have no mother. As no one took any interest in him, he would not receive a beating. The other two were Guernsey lads, and of that same parish of Torteval.

The lofty ridge of rocks scaled, the three bird-nesters arrived on the plateau whereon stands the haunted house.

They began by being afraid, which is the duty of every passer-by, and above all of every child, at that hour and in that spot.

They were very anxious to run away at full speed, and they were very anxious to stop and look.

They paused.

They gazed at the house.

It was all dark and formidable.

It was an obscure block in the midst of the deserted plateau; a symmetrical, but hideous, excrescence; a lofty, square mass with right-angled corners, somewhat similar to an immense altar of darkness.

The children's first thought had been to run, their second was to approach it. They had never seen this house at that hour. There is such a thing as the curiosity of fear. They had a little French lad with them, which emboldened them to approach. It is well known that the French fear nothing.

Besides, to be many in a danger is reassuring; to share fear among three is encouraging. And then, they are hunters, they are children; all three of them together do not number thirty years; they are on a quest, they are rummaging, they are spying out hidden things; can they stop on the road? they thrust their heads into this hole; how can they avoid advancing into that hole? He who is on a hunting expedition allows himself to be carried away with the excitement of the chase; he who goes on an excursion for discovery, is caught in a set of gearing wheels. Having gazed so much into the nests of birds gives one a taste for looking a little into a nest of spectres. Pry about a bit in the infernal regions? Why not?

From prey to prey, one comes to the demon. After sparrows, hobgoblins. The boys proceeded to investigate the real state of the case with regard to all the fears which their parents had instilled in their minds. Nothing is more seductive than to be on the track of hobgoblin tales. The idea of knowing as much about them as the good wives is tempting.

All this mixture of ideas, in a state of half confusion and half instinct in the minds of these Guernsey bird-nesters, had their temerity as a result. They went towards the house.

And the small boy who served as their mainstay in this bit of daring was worthy of the position. He was a resolute lad, an apprentice to a ship caulker; one of those children who are already men. He slept at the shipyard under a shed, on straw, earned his own living, had a loud voice, liked to climb walls and trees, cherishing no prejudice against apples that came within his reach. He had worked at repairing war vessels, the son of chance, a child of luck, a gay orphan, born in France, no one knew where, two reasons for being bold, thinking nothing of giving a penny to a poor woman, very mischievous, but good-hearted, sandy-haired, and one who had talked with Parisians. At that time, he was earning a shilling a day at caulking fishing vessels under repair at the Pêqueries.

When the fancy seized him, he allowed himself a holiday and went bird-nesting. Such was the little French boy.

The solitude of the place had something indescribably funereal about it. They felt conscious of its threatening aspect. It was wild and savage. This plateau, silent and bare, terminated in a precipice at a very short distance from its steep slope. The sea below was still. There was no wind. Not a blade of grass stirred.

The little bird-nesters advanced slowly, the French lad at their head, staring at the house the while.

One of them afterwards, in narrating the story, or as much of it as he still remembered, added: "It said nothing."

They approached, holding their breath, as one might approach a wild animal.

They had climbed the steep hill which lies behind the house and which ends on the side of the sea in a little isthmus of rocks almost inaccessible; they had come quite close to the building; but they saw only the south front, which is all walled up; they did not dare to turn to the left, which would have exposed to them the other front where there are the two terrible windows.

Nevertheless, they grew bolder, the caulker's apprentice having said to them: "Let's veer to larboard; that's the fine side. We must see the black windows."

They veered to larboard, and reached the other side of the house.

The two windows were lighted up.

The boys fled.

When they were some distance away, the little French lad turned round.

"Stay," said he. "The lights have disappeared."

In fact, there was no longer any light in the windows. The silhouette of the house was outlined against the vague lividness of the sky, as though stamped out with a punch.

Fear did not vanish, but curiosity came back. The bird-nesters approached once more.

All at once, the light reappeared simultaneously at both windows. The two Torteval boys took to their heels and fled. The little imp of a French lad did not advance, neither did he retreat.

The light vanished, then flashed forth again. Nothing could be more horrible. The reflection made a vague streak of light on the grass wet with the dew. At one time, the light cast upon the inner wall of the house great black profiles which moved, and shadows of enormous heads.

However, as the house had neither partitions nor ceiling, having no longer anything but the four walls and the roof, one window could not be lighted without the other being lighted also.

Perceiving that the caulker's apprentice remained, the other two bird-nesters returned, step by step, one following the other, trembling and curious. The caulker's apprentice said to them, in a low voice,—

"There are ghosts in the house. I saw the nose of one of them."

The two little fellows from Torteval hid behind the French lad, and raised on tiptoe, over his shoulder, sheltered by him, using him as a shield, opposing him to the thing, reassured by having him between them and the vision, gazed likewise.

The house seemed to be gazing at them in its turn. In that vast, mute darkness, it had two red eyeballs. They were the windows. The light vanished, reappeared, vanished again, as such lights do. These sinister intermissions are probably caused by the opening and shutting of hell. The vent hole of the sepulchre produces effects like those of a dark lantern.

All at once, a very opaque blackness in human form rose past one of the windows as though it came from outside, then plunged into the interior of the house. It seemed as though some one had just entered.

It is the habit of ghosts to enter through the window.

The light was more brilliant for a moment, then it was extinguished, and did not again reappear. Then noises were heard there. These noises resembled voices. It is always like that. When one sees, one does not hear; when one hears, one does not see.

Night on the sea has a peculiar silence. The stillness is more profound there than elsewhere. Then there is neither wind nor surge, in that moving expanse. Where, ordinarily, the flight of eagles could not be heard, one can hear the movements of a fly. This sepulchral quiet lent a sombre relief to the sounds which proceeded from the building.

"Let us see," said the little French boy.

And he took a step towards the house.

The other two were so afraid that they decided to follow him. They dared not run away alone.

Just as they had passed a large pile of fagots which, in some inexplicable manner, reassured them in this solitude, a sparrow-owl flew out of a bush. This rustled the branches. Sparrow-owls have an awkward way of flying, with a suspicious sidelong swoop. The bird passed in a slanting direction close to the children, fixing its round clear eyes upon them through the darkness.

There was no little trembling in the group behind the little Frenchman.

He said to the bird,—

"Sparrow, you come too late. I want to see."

And he advanced.

The creaking of his coarse, hobnailed shoes on the gorse did not prevent their hearing the noises, which rose and fell with the calm accentuation and continuity of a dialogue.

A moment later he added,—

"Besides, only fools believe in ghosts."

Insolence in the midst of danger rallies cowards and urges them forward.

The two Torteval boys resumed their march, treading in the footsteps of the caulker's apprentice.

The haunted house seemed to them to increase immensely in size. In this optical illusion of fear there was some reality. The house actually did grow larger, because they were approaching it.

In the meantime, the voices inside the house became more and more distinct. The children listened. The ear also has its power of exaggeration. It was something different from a murmur, more than a whisper, less than an uproar. At times, a word or two, clearly articulated, was detached from the rest. These words, which it was impossible to understand, sounded strangely. The boys halted, listened, then began their advance again.

" 'Tis the ghosts talking," muttered the caulker's apprentice, "but I don't believe in ghosts."

The Torteval children were greatly tempted to fall back behind the pile of fagots; but they were already a long way from it, and their friend, the caulker, continued to walk towards the house. They trembled at remaining with him, and they dared not leave him.

Step by step, and in perplexity, they followed him.

The caulker's apprentice turned towards them and said,—

"You know that it is not true. There are none."

The house grew higher and higher. The voices became more and more distinct.

They drew nearer.

As they approached, they perceived that there was something like a muffled light in the house. It was a very vague light, like one of those dark-lantern effects just mentioned, and which are common in the illumination of witches' meetings.

When they were very close they halted.

One of the two Torteval boys ventured this remark,—

"They are not ghosts; they are the ladies in white."

"What's that dangling from the window?" asked the other.

"It appears to be a rope."

"It is a snake."

" 'Tis the hangman's rope," said the French lad, authoritatively. "That suits them. But I don't believe it."

And in three bounds rather than in three steps, he reached the base of the wall of the building. There was something feverish about this boldness.

The other two imitated him shivering, and placed themselves very close to him, one pressing his right side, the other, his left. The boys applied their ears to the wall. The talking in the house continued.

This is what the phantoms were saying,[1]—

"So 'tis settled?"

"Settled."

" 'Tis said?"

"Yes, said."

"A man is to wait here, and he will be able to go to England with Blasquito?"

"By paying for it."

"By paying for it."

"Blasquito will take the man in his bark."

"Without seeking to learn from what country he comes?"

"That does not concern us."

"Without inquiring his name?"

"We ask no names; we weigh purses."

"Good. The man will wait in this house."

"He must have something to eat."

"He shall have it."

"Where?"

"In this bag which I have brought."

"Very good."

"Can I leave the bag here?"

"Smugglers are not thieves."

"And when do the rest of you set out?"

"To-morrow morning. If your man were ready he might come with us."

1. The whole conversation was in Spanish.

"He is not ready."

"That's his affair."

"How many days will he have to wait in this house?"

"Two, three, four days, more or less."

"Is it certain that Blasquito will come?"

"Certain."

"Here? To Plainmont?"

"To Plainmont."

"What week?"

"Next week."

"What day?"

"Friday, Saturday, or Sunday."

"He cannot fail?"

"He is my Tocayo."

"Will he come in any weather?"

"At any time. He knows no fear. I am Blasco, he is Blasquito."

"So he cannot fail to come to Guernsey?"

"I come one month; he comes the next month."

"I understand."

"Counting from Saturday next, a week from to-day, five days will not pass before Blasquito arrives."

"But if the sea be very rough?"

"Egurraldia gaïztoa?"[1]

"Yes."

"Blasquito will not come so quickly, but he will come."

"Where is he coming from?"

"From Bilbao."

"Where is he going?"

"To Portland."

"That is well."

"Or to Torbay."

"That is better."

"Your man may rest easy."

"Blasquito will not betray him?"

"Cowards are traitors. We are brave men. The sea is the church of winter. Treachery is the church of hell."

"No one can hear what we are saying?"

"It is impossible to hear or to see us. Fear creates a desert here."

1. Basque. Bad weather.

"I know it."

"Who would dare to run the risk of listening to us?"

"That is true."

"Besides, if any one were to listen, he would not understand. We are speaking a wild language of our own which no one here knows. Since you speak it, it means that you are one of us."

"I have only come to make arrangements with you."

"That is well."

"Now I am going."

"So be it."

"Tell me—what if the passenger should wish Blasquito to take him elsewhere than to Portland or to Torbay?"

"Let him bring doubloons."

"Will Blasquito do what the man wishes?"

"Blasquito will do what the doubloons command."

"Does it take much time to go to Torbay?"

"As it pleases the wind."

"Eight hours?"

"More or less."

"Will Blasquito obey his passenger?"

"If the sea obeys Blasquito."

"He will be well paid."

"Gold is gold. The wind is the wind."

"That is true."

"Man with gold can do what he will. God does what He will with the wind."

"The man who counts on going with Blasquito will be here on Friday."

"Good."

"At what time will Blasquito arrive?"

"At night. He arrives at night. He departs at night. We have a wife whose name is the Sea, and a sister whose name is Night. The wife sometimes deceives; the sister, never."

"All is settled. Farewell, men."

"Good night. A drop of brandy?"

"Thanks."

" 'Tis better than syrup."

"I have your word."

"My name is Point of Honor."

"Farewell."

"You are a gentleman and I am a caballero."

It was clear that devils alone could talk thus. The children listened no longer, and this time took to flight for good, the little Frenchman, convinced at last, running even faster than the others.

On the Tuesday which followed this Saturday, Sieur Clubin was again in Saint-Malo, with the Durande.

The *Tamaulipas* was still lying in the roadstead.

Sieur Clubin asked the innkeeper of the Jean Tavern, between two whiffs of his pipe,—

"Well, and when does that *Tamaulipas* sail?"

"Day after to-morrow, Thursday," replied the innkeeper.

That evening, Clubin supped at the table of the coast guardsmen, and, contrary to his custom, he went out after supper. The result of this absence was that he could not attend to the Durande's office, and almost lost his cargo. This was noticed in so punctual a man.

It appeared that he conversed for a few minutes with his friend the money-changer.

He returned two hours after Noquette had sounded the curfew. The Brazilian bell rings at ten o'clock. Hence, it was midnight.

VI
The Jacressarde

FORTY years ago, Saint-Malo had an alley called la Ruelle Coutanchez. This alley no longer exists, having been absorbed in improvements.

It consisted of a double row of wooden houses leaning towards each other, and leaving between them sufficient space for a narrow rivulet, which was called the street. People walked with their legs far apart on both sides of the water, knocking their heads or their elbows against the houses on the right and the left.

These old barracks of the Norman Middle Ages have almost human profiles. From ruined houses to ghosts is not a long step. Their receding stories, their overhanging walls, their bowed penthouses, and their thickets of iron-work resemble lips, chin, noses, and eyebrows. The garret window is the eye of a one-eyed man. The wall is the cheek, wrinkled and covered with blotches. Their foreheads touch, as though they were plotting some evil deed. All those words of ancient civilization,—slit-weazen, slash-face, cut-throat,—are closely connected with that architecture.

One of the houses in Coutanchez alley, the largest, the most famous, or the most notorious, was called the Jacressarde.

The Jacressarde was the lodging-house for those who have no lodging. In all towns, and particularly in seaports, there is a residuum beneath the population. People without avowed employment, to such a degree that even justice itself cannot succeed in forcing an avowal from them; rovers seeking adventures, hunters after expedients, chemists of the sharper species, always putting life back into the crucible, people in rags of every shape and all manners of wearing them, the withered fruits of dishonesty, bankrupt existences, consciences which have defaulted, those who have failed in the house-breaking trade (for great masters in breaking and entering move in a higher sphere), workers in evil trades, both male and female, scamps of both sexes, tattered and ragged elbows, rascals who have ended in indigence, scoundrels who have missed the wages of sin, the vanquished in the social duel, the hungry who have been devoured, the knife-grinders of crime, blackguards in every sense of the word. Human intelligence is there, but bestial. It is the dung heap of souls. It collects in a corner, over which passes, from time to time, that cleansing touch of the broom which is called the police.

In Saint-Malo, la Jacressarde was that corner.

It is not the great criminals, bandits, assassins, thieves, the great products of ignorance and indigence, who are found in such dens. If murder is represented there, it is by some brutal drunkard; theft does not go beyond the pickpocket. It is rather the spittle of society than its vomit. The vagabond, yes; the highwayman, no. Nevertheless, one could not trust to it. This last stage of Bohemians may contain villainous extremes. Once, in casting the net over l'Épi-scié, which was to Paris what the Jacressarde was to Saint-Malo, the police caught Lacenaire.

These dens admit everything. Falls have a levelling tendency. Sometimes tattered honesty descends here. Virtue and probity have been known to have strange experiences. One must neither esteem the Louvre nor despise the galleys by appearances. Public respect, as well as universal reprobation, requires weeding. One meets surprises. An angel in the brothel, a pearl in the dung heap, such gloomy and dazzling discoveries are possible.

The Jacressarde was a courtyard, rather than a house; and a well, rather than a courtyard. It had no story looking on the street. A lofty wall pierced by a low door formed its façade. On raising the latch and opening the door, you found yourself in a courtyard.

In the middle of this court, one beheld a round hole, surrounded by a stone curb on a level with the soil. It was a well. A pavement framed the curb.

The court, which was square, was built up on three sides. On the street side, on the wall, but facing the door of the gateway, and to the right and the left, stood the house.

If you entered there after nightfall, somewhat at your own risk and peril, you heard a confused sound of breathing, and if there was sufficient moonlight or starlight to give form to the obscure lineaments which you had before your eyes, this is what you beheld:—

The courtyard, the well; around the court, opposite the door, a shed, in the shape of a sort of a horseshoe with square corners, a wormeaten gallery, entirely open, with a rafted ceiling, supported by stone pillars unequally spaced; in the centre, the well; around the well, a litter of straw; and, like a circular chaplet, upright soles, the bottoms of boots trodden at the heels, toes peeping through the holes in shoes, and many bare heels, the feet of sleeping men, women, and children.

Beyond these feet, as the eye penetrated into the shadow of the shed, it distinguished bodies, forms, sleeping heads, inert outstretched forms, rags of both sexes, promiscuousness in a dung heap, an indescribable and sinister layer of humanity. This sleeping-room was open to every one. The charge was two sous a week. The feet touched the well. On stormy nights, the rain fell on those feet; on winter nights, it snowed on those bodies.

Who were these people? The unknown. They came at night, and they went away in the morning. The social order is made up in part of these spectres. Some glided in for a night and did not pay. The majority of them had eaten nothing during the day. Every kind of vice, and abjectness, all sorts of infection and distress; the same sleep of exhaustion on the same bed of filth. The dreams of all these souls kept each other company. A gloomy meeting, wherein moved and blended in the same miasma, weariness, weakness, the heavy slumber of drunkenness, the walking to and fro of a day without a morsel of bread, and without a good thought, pallor with closed eyelids, remorse, covetousness, hair mingled with filth, faces bearing the look of death, perhaps kisses from mouths of darkness. This human putridity fermented in this vat. They had been cast into this shelter by fate, by a journey, by the arrival on the preceding evening of a vessel, by a release from prison, by chance, by the night. Here destiny emptied its basket every day. He entered who wished, he slept who could, he spoke who dared, for it was a place of whispers. They hastened to crowd together. They tried to forget themselves in sleep, since one cannot find oblivion in darkness. They snatched from death what they could. They closed their eyes in this confused agony, which began anew every evening. Whence came they? from society, since they were wretched; from the sea, since they were scum.

Not every one who wished could get straw. More than one naked form lay on the bare pavement; they lay down exhausted, they rose up paralyzed. The well, lacking both curb or cover, always yawning open, was thirty feet deep. The rain fell into it; filth oozed into it, all the drippings of the court filtered into it. The bucket for drawing water stood beside it. They who were thirsty drank from it. Whoever was disheartened drowned himself in it. From sleep on the dung heap, men glided into that final sleep. In 1819, a boy of fourteen years was drawn out of it.

In order not to incur danger in that house, one had to be of the "right kind." The uninitiated were not viewed with a friendly eye there.

Did these beings know each other? no. They scented each other out by instinct. The head of the house was a woman, young, tolerably pretty, who wore a cap with ribbons, was now and then washed with water from the well. She had a wooden leg.

The court became empty at daybreak, its regular lodgers fled.

In the courtyard there was a cock and some hens, which scratched in the dung heap all day. The court was traversed by a horizontal beam, on posts, in the form of a gallows, which was not so very much out of place there. A silk gown, wet and muddy, which belonged to the woman with the wooden leg, would frequently be seen on the day after a rain, hanging out to dry on that beam.

Above the shed, and like it encircling the court, there was a story, and above the story a loft. A rotten, wooden staircase piercing the ceiling of the shed, led upstairs; a tottering staircase noisily ascended by the staggering woman.

The transient lodgers, by the week or by the night, occupied the courtyard; the steady lodgers occupied the house.

Windows, without a single pane of glass; jambs, without a door; chimneys, without a hearth,—such was the house. The passage from one room to another was made either through a hole, of an oblong shape, which had been the doorway, or through a triangular aperture, which formed the intermediate space between the timbers of the partition. The plastering had fallen down and littered the floor. No one knew how the house held together. The wind shook it. They mounted as best they could on the slippery steps of the staircase. All was open.

Winter entered the hovel as water is absorbed by a sponge. The abundance of spiders reassured one against its immediate downfall. No furniture. Two or three straw pallets in the corners, yawning widely, showing more dust than straw within. Here and there a jug and an earthen pan, serving various purposes. A close and hideous odor.

From the windows one looked out upon the courtyard. This view resembled the top of a scavenger's cart. The things, not to speak of the men, which lay rotting, rusting, and mouldering there, were indescribable. The fragments fraternized together; some fell from the walls, some from the living creatures. The rubbish was sown with rags and tatters.

Besides its floating population, quartered in the court, la Jacressarde had three lodgers, a charcoal dealer, a ragpicker and a "maker of gold." The charcoal man and the ragpicker occupied two straw pallets on the first floor; the "maker of gold," a chemist, lodged in the loft, which was called, no one knew why, an attic. No one knew in what corner the woman lodged. The maker of gold was something of a poet. He inhabited a chamber next the roof, under the tiles, which had a narrow dormer window and a large stone fireplace, which made a gulf wherein the wind howled. As the window had no sash, he had nailed across it a bit of iron sheathing, which had come from the wreck of a vessel. This sheet iron let in a little light and a great deal of air. The charcoal man paid with a sack of coals, from time to time; the ragpicker paid with a measure of grain, for the chickens, a week; the maker of gold paid nothing. Meanwhile, he burned the house. He had torn away what little woodwork there was, and every now and then he pulled from the wall or the roof a lath, wherewith to heat the crucible. On the partition, above the ragpicker's pallet, there could be seen two columns of figures in chalk, made by the ragpicker, from week to week, one column of threes and one of fives, according as the measure of grain had cost him three farthings or five centimes. The gold pot of the "chemist" was an old, broken bomb, promoted by him to the dignity of a crucible, in which he combined his ingredients. Transmutation of metals absorbed him.

Sometimes he spoke to the tatterdemalions in the courtyard, who laughed at him. He said, "Those people are full of prejudices." He was resolved not to die until he had flung the philosopher's stone at the windows of science. His furnace ate up a great deal of wood. The railing of the staircase had disappeared into it. The whole house was on its way thither, bit by bit. The landlady said to him, "You will leave me nothing but the shell." He pacified her by making verses to her.

Such was la Jacressarde.

A boy, with a broom in his hand, who was, perhaps, a dwarf, twelve years of age or sixty, with a goitre on his neck, was the servant.

The regular frequenters entered by the door to the court; the public entered through the shop.

What was this shop?

The lofty wall facing the street and to the right of the entrance to the court was pierced by a square opening, serving at once as a door and a window, with shutter and sash, the only shutter in the whole house which had hinges and a bolt. Behind this aperture, opening on the street, there was a little chamber, a compartment stolen from the sleeping shed. Over the street door this inscription was written in charcoal: "Curiosities sold here." The word was already in use at that time. On three boards fastened against the window like shelves, several china jars without ears were visible, a Chinese parasol in goldbeater's skin, with figures, cracked here and there, impossible to open and shut, shapeless fragments of iron or crockery, dilapidated hats and bonnets, three or four conch shells, several packages of old bone and brass buttons, a snuff-box with a portrait of Marie-Antoinette, and a tattered copy of Boisbertrand's algebra.

This was the shop. This assortment constituted the "curiosities." The shop communicated, by a rear door, with the court in which the well was situated. It contained a table and a chair. The woman with the wooden leg was the shopkeeper.

VII
Nocturnal Purchases and a Shady Vendor

CLUBIN had been absent from the Jean Tavern the whole of Tuesday evening; he was absent again on Wednesday evening.

That evening at dusk, two men entered Coutanchez alley; they halted in front of la Jacressarde. One of them knocked at the window. The shop door opened. They entered. The woman with the wooden leg bestowed on them the smile reserved for respectable citizens. A candle stood on the table.

These men were, in fact, two respectable citizens.

The one who had knocked said: "Good evening, my good woman. I have come for that affair."

The woman with the wooden leg smiled once more, and went out through the door opening on the courtyard with the well.

A moment later, the rear door opened again, and a man presented himself in the opening. This man wore a cap and a blouse, and under his blouse appeared the shape of some object. There were bits of straw in his blouse, and he had the look of a man just awakened.

He advanced. They exchanged glances. The man in the blouse had a confused but cunning air. He said,—

"Are you the gunsmith?"

The man who had knocked replied,—

"Yes. Are you the Parisian?"

"Called Peaurouge (Red skin). Yes."

"Show it."

"Here it is."

The man drew from beneath his blouse a weapon which was very rare in Europe at that period, a revolver.

This revolver was new and bright. The two citizens examined it. The one who seemed to be acquainted with the house, and whom the man in the blouse had called "the gunsmith," tried the mechanism. He passed it to the other man, who appeared to be more of a stranger and who kept his back turned to the light.

The gunsmith resumed,—

"How much?"

The man in the blouse replied,—

"I have just come from America with it. Some people bring monkeys, parrots, and animals, as though the French were savages. I have brought this. It is a useful invention."

"How much?" repeated the gunsmith.

"It is a pistol which turns round like a mill-wheel."

"How much?"

"Bang, one shot. Bang, a second shot. Bang, a hail-storm. That does some execution."

"How much?"

"There are six chambers."

"Well, how much?"

"Six chambers, that makes six louis."

"Will you take five louis?"

"Impossible, one louis a bullet. That's the price."

"Shall we make a trade? Be reasonable."

"I have named a fair price. Examine it, monsieur gunsmith."

"I have examined it."

"The chamber turns like Monsieur Talleyrand. That chamber might be put in the dictionary of weathervanes. 'Tis a jewel."

"I have seen it."

"As for the barrel, 'tis of Spanish forging."

"I have noticed it."

"It is twisted. This is the way this twisting is done. The basket of an old junk man is emptied into the forge. They fill it full of old iron scraps, old blacksmith's nails, broken horseshoes"—

"And old scythe blades."

"I was going to mention that, monsieur gunsmith. They give all these scraps a good welding heat, and that makes a magnificent iron.—"

"Yes, but it may have cracks, flaws, cross breaks."

"Pardieu! But the cross breaks are remedied by little dovetails, just as the risk of defects in soldering is avoided by hard pounding. The material is flattened out with the big hammer, it is then subjected to two welding heats; if the iron has been overheated, it is retempered by plunging it into melted fat, and with light blows. Then the stuff is drawn out, well rolled, and with that iron, fichtre! such barrels as this are made."

"So you belong to that craft?"

"I am of all crafts."

"The barrel is water color."

"'Tis a beauty, monsieur gunsmith. It is produced with butter of antimony."

"We will say, then, that we are to pay you five louis for that."

"Allow me to call monsieur's attention to the fact that I had the honor to say six louis."

The gunsmith lowered his voice,—

"Listen, Parisian. Take advantage of the opportunity. Get rid of this. A weapon like this is of no good to such men as you. It directs attention to a man."

"In fact," said the Parisian, "it is a little conspicuous. 'Tis better for a respectable citizen."

"Will you take five louis?"

"No, six. One for each hole."

"Well, six napoleons."

"I want six louis."

"You are not a Bonapartist, then? You prefer a louis to a napoleon?"

The Parisian called Peaurouge smiled.

"Napoleon is greater," said he, "but Louis is worth more."

"Six napoleons."

"Six louis. It makes a difference of twenty-four francs to me."

"In that case, no trade."

"So be it. I keep the toy."

"Keep it."

"Beating me down! the idea! It shall not be said that I parted like that with a thing which is a new discovery."

"Good evening, then."

"It is an improvement on the pistol which the Chesapeake Indians call Nortay-u-Hah."

"Five louis ready money, that means gold."

"Nortay-u-Hah, that means 'short gun.' A great many people do not know that."

"Will you take five louis and a silver crown thrown in."

"Citizen, I have said six."

The man who stood with his back turned to the candle and who had not yet spoken, was making the mechanism work during this dialogue. He bent down to the gunsmith's ear and whispered to him,—

"Is the article good?"

"Excellent."

"I will give the six louis."

Five minutes later, while the Parisian, surnamed Redskin, was thrusting the six louis d'or which he had just received, into a secret slit under the armpit of his blouse, the gunsmith and the purchaser, the latter bearing off the revolver in his trousers pocket, quitted the Ruelle Coutanchez.

VIII

The Red Ball and the Black Ball Carom

On the following day, which was Thursday, something tragic took place at a short distance from Saint-Malo, near the Point du Décollé, at a spot where the cliff is lofty and where the sea is deep.

A tongue of rocks in the form of a lance head, which

is connected with the land by a narrow isthmus, runs out into the water, and there ends abruptly in a great, perpendicular reef; nothing is of more frequent occurrence in the architecture of the sea. In order to reach the plateau of the perpendicular rock from the shore, one follows an inclined plane, the slope of which is sometimes decidedly steep.

On a plateau of this description, about four o'clock in the afternoon, stood a man enveloped in a large military cloak, and probably armed beneath it, a fact easily recognized from the angular folds of his mantle. The peak on which this man stood was a tolerably extensive platform, dotted with great cubes of rock like immense paving stones, which left narrow passages between them. This platform, on which grew short, thick turf, ended, on the side towards the sea, in an open space, terminating in a vertical escarpment. This escarpment, elevated sixty feet above high water, seemed as though cut by the plummet. Its angle was broken on the left, however, and presented one of those natural staircases peculiar to granite cliffs, whose very inconvenient steps sometimes require the strides of giants, or the leaps of clowns. This fall of rocks descended perpendicularly to the sea, and plunged into it. It was almost a breakneck angle. Nevertheless, in case of necessity, one could embark there under the very wall of the cliff.

The breeze was blowing. The man, muffled in his cloak, firm on his legs, with his left hand clasping his right elbow, was closing one eye, and applying the other to a telescope. He seemed to be absorbed in intent scrutiny. He had approached the brink of the precipice, and stood there motionless, his glance fixed immovably on the horizon. The tide was high. The waves beat against the base of the cliff below him.

The object which this man was observing was a vessel in the offing, which was, in truth, behaving strangely.

This vessel, which had left the port of Saint-Malo hardly an hour before, had come to a stop behind the Banquetiers. She was a three-master. She had not cast anchor, perhaps because the bottom would only permit her to swing on the edge of the cable, and because the vessel would have strained on her anchor under the cut-water. She had contented herself with lying to.

The man, who was a coastguard, as was evident from his uniform cape, was watching all the manœuvres of the three-master, and seemed to be taking mental notes of them. The vessel had heaved to, with her head-sheets hauled to windward, which was indicated by the fore-topsail being laid aback, and the wind left in the main topsail; she had hauled aft the mizzen-sail and trimmed the mizzen-topsail as close as possible, so as to offset the sails by each other, and make but little headway or leeway. She did not care to present too much sail to the wind, because she had only braced the fore-topsail so that it hung perpendicular to the keel. In this manner, lying to, she did not sag to leeward more than half a league an hour.

It was still broad daylight, especially on the open sea and on the crest of the cliff. The lower part of the coast was becoming dark.

The coastguard, wholly absorbed in his duty, and carefully keeping a watch on the offing, had not thought of scrutinizing the rock beside and below him. His back was turned towards the sort of hardly practicable staircase which placed the plateau of the cliff in communication with the sea. He had not observed that something was moving there. On that staircase, behind a projecting point, there was some one, a man, hidden there, to all appearances, before the arrival of the coastguard. From time to time, a head emerged from the shadow beneath the rock, looked up and watched the watcher. The head, covered with a large American hat, was that of the Quaker-looking man, who had been talking among the stones of the Petit-Bey, with Captain Zuela, ten days previously.

All at once the coastguard's attention appeared to redouble. He rapidly wiped the glass of his telescope with his sleeve, and pointed it intently at the three-master.

A black spot had just detached itself from her side.

This black spot, resembling an insect on the sea, was a boat.

The boat seemed desirous of reaching the shore. It was manned by several sailors, who were rowing vigorously.

It veered off little by little, and directed its course towards the Point du Décollé.

The coastguard had reached the point of most intense scrutiny. He had approached still closer to the extreme edge of the cliff.

At that moment, a man of lofty stature, the Quaker, rose behind the coastguard at the top of the staircase. The watcher did not see him.

This man paused for a moment, with arms at his side and fists clenched, and with the eye of a sportsman taking aim, he gazed at the back of the coastguard.

Only four paces separated him from the coastguard; he placed one foot in front, then halted; he took a second step and paused again; he made no other movement than walking; all the rest of his body was like a statue; his foot trod the turf noiselessly; he took the third step, and paused; he almost touched the coastguard, who was still motionless with his telescope. The man slowly brought his two clenched fists on a level with his collar bone, then his forearms abruptly descended, and his two fists struck the coastguard on the shoulders as though fired from a cannon. The shock was fatal. The coastguard had not time to utter a cry. He fell head foremost from the cliff into the sea. The soles of his shoes were visible during the space of a flash of lightning. It was like the fall of a stone. The sea closed again.

Two or three great circles formed on the dark water.

Nothing remained but the telescope, which had escaped from the coastguard's hand and had fallen on the grass.

The Quaker bent over the brink of the precipice, watched the circles disappear in the waves, waited a few minutes, then straightened himself up, humming between his teeth,—

Monsieur d'la Police est mort
En perdant la vie.[1]

He bent over a second time. Nothing made its appearance. Only, at the spot where the coastguard had been

1. "Monsieur of the Police died by losing his life," a pun on a popular ballad about a certain Seigneur de la Palice.

engulfed, a sort of reddish-brown thickness had formed, which spread over the undulations of the waves. It is probable that the coastguard had fractured his skull on some submarine rock. His blood rose up and formed a stain on the foam. As the Quaker watched this reddish spot, he resumed,—

Un quart d'heure avant sa mort
Il était encore . . .[1]

He did not finish.

He heard a very soft voice say behind him,—

"Here you are, Rantaine, good day. You have just killed a man."

He turned round, and beheld, fifteen paces behind him, at the mouth of one of the small passages between the rocks, a little man with a revolver in his hand.

He replied,—

"As you see. Good day, Sieur Clubin."

The little man started.

"You recognize me?"

"You recognized me," retorted Rantaine.

In the meantime, they could hear the sound of oars on the water. It was the boat observed by the coastguard, which was approaching.

Sieur Clubin said in a low voice, as though speaking to himself,—

"That was quickly done."

"What can I do for you?" asked Rantaine.

"Not much. It is just ten years since I have seen you. You must have prospered in your affairs. How are you?"

"Well," said Rantaine. "And you?"

"Very well," replied Sieur Clubin.

Rantaine took a step towards Clubin.

A small, sharp noise struck his ear. It was Sieur Clubin cocking his revolver.

"Rantaine, we are fifteen paces apart. That's a good distance. Remain where you are."

"Ah!" ejaculated Rantaine. "What do you want with me?"

1. "A quarter of an hour before his death he was still [quite alive]."

"I have come to have a talk with you."

Rantaine did not stir. Sieur Clubin went on,—

"You have just assassinated a coastguard."

Rantaine cocked the brim of his hat and replied,—

"You have already done me the honor to tell me so."

"In less precise terms. I said, 'A man'; I now say 'a coastguard.' That coastguard was number six hundred and nineteen. He was the father of a family. He leaves a wife and five children."

"That's as it should be," said Rantaine.

A momentary pause ensued.

"These are picked men, these coastguards," pursued Clubin, "nearly all of them old sailors."

"I have noticed," said Rantaine, "that these men generally do leave a wife and five children."

Sieur Clubin continued,—

"Guess how much this revolver cost me."

" 'Tis a fine weapon," replied Rantaine.

"What do you value it at?"

"I value it highly."

"It cost me a hundred and forty-four francs."

"You must have bought it," said Rantaine, "at the shop for weapons in the Ruelle Coutanchez."

Clubin resumed,—

"He did not utter a cry. A fall cuts short the voice."

"Sieur Clubin, there will be a breeze to-night."

"I am the only one in the secret."

"Do you still stop at the Jean Tavern?" asked Rantaine.

"Yes, one is not badly off there."

"I remember having eaten good sauerkraut there."

"You must be excessively strong, Rantaine. Such shoulders as you have! I should not like to get a rap from you. When I came into the world, I was so puny-looking that they did not know whether they would succeed in raising me."

"They did succeed, luckily."

"Yes, I still stop at that old Jean Tavern."

"Do you know, Sieur Clubin, how I recognized you? Because you recognized me. I said to myself: 'No one but Clubin could do that.' "

And he advanced a step.

"Stand back where you were, Rantaine."

Rantaine retreated, and indulged in this aside,—

"One becomes a child before such a machine as that."

Sieur Clubin continued,—

"This is the situation; we have on our right, in the direction of Saint-Énogat, three hundred paces from here, another coastguard, number six hundred and eighteen, who is alive; and on our left, in the direction of Saint-Lunaire, a custom-house station. That makes seven armed men who can arrive here in five minutes. The rock will be surrounded. The pass will be guarded. Impossible to escape. There is a corpse at the foot of the cliff."

Rantaine cast a sidelong glance at the revolver.

"As you say, Rantaine, it is a pretty weapon. Perhaps it is only loaded with powder. But what of that? One shot will suffice to bring an armed force. I can fire six."

The alternate splash of the oars was becoming very distinct. The boat was not very far away.

The big man looked at the little man in a strange way. Sieur Clubin spoke in a voice that was more and more tranquil and gentle.

"Rantaine, the men in the boat which is approaching, on learning what you have just done here, would lend armed assistance and aid in arresting you. You pay ten thousand francs to Captain Zuela for your passage. By the way, you would have found it cheaper with the smugglers of Plainmont; but they would only have taken you to England; and, besides, you cannot run the risk of going to Guernsey, where people have the honor of knowing you. I return to the situation. If I fire, you are arrested. You pay to Zuela for your flight, ten thousand francs. You have given him five thousand in advance. Zuela will keep the five thousand francs and will go off with them. There you have it. Rantaine, you are well disguised. That hat, that queer coat, and your gaiters change you. You have forgotten the spectacles. You have done well to let your whiskers grow."

Rantaine forced a smile which bore close resemblance to a gnashing of teeth. Clubin continued,—

"Rantaine, you have on a pair of American breeches, with double fobs. In one is your watch. Keep it."

"Thanks, Sieur Clubin."

"In the other, there is a small box of wrought iron, which opens and shuts with a spring. It is an old sailor's snuff-box. Pull it out of your fob, and toss it to me."

"But this is robbery!"

"You are free to call the guard."

And Clubin gazed steadily at Rantaine.

"Stay, Mess Clubin,—" said Rantaine, advancing a step and holding out his open palm.

"Mess" was a piece of flattery.

"Remain where you are, Rantaine."

"Mess Clubin, let us come to an understanding. I offer you half."

Clubin folded his arms, from which peeped the muzzle of the revolver.

"Rantaine, for whom do you take me? I am an honest man."

And he added after a pause,—

"I must have all."

Rantaine muttered between his teeth: "This fellow is made on a stiff model."

Meanwhile, Clubin's eye had begun to flash. His voice became as clear and trenchant as steel. He exclaimed,—

"I see that you mistake me. What you call robbery, I call restitution. Listen, Rantaine. Ten years ago, you quitted Guernsey by night, taking with you from the treasury of a concern fifty thousand francs which belonged to you, and forgetting to leave there fifty thousand francs which belonged to another man. Those fifty thousand francs, stolen by you from your partner, excellent and worthy Mess Lethierry, amount, with compound interest for ten years, to eighty thousand eight hundred and sixty-six francs, sixty-six centimes. Yesterday, you entered a money-changer's office. I will tell you his name: Rébuchet, Rue Saint-Vincent. You counted out to him seventy-six thousand francs in bank notes, for which he gave you three English bank notes of a thousand pounds each, plus the odd change. You placed those bank bills in the iron snuff-box in your right-hand fob. These three thousand pounds sterling make seventy-five thousand francs. In the name of Mess Lethierry, I will content myself with that. I set out to-morrow for Guernsey, and I mean to carry them back to him. Rantaine, the three-master which is lying to yonder is the *Tamaulipas*. You had your trunks put aboard her last night, mixed with the bags and the hammocks of the crew. You wish to quit France. You have your own reasons for so doing. You are going to Arequipa. The boat is coming to take you off. You are waiting for it here. It is coming. It can be heard in the water. It depends upon me to let you go or to force you to remain. Enough said. Throw me that iron snuff-box."

Rantaine opened his fob, pulled out a little box, and threw it to Clubin. It was the snuff-box. It rolled to Clubin's feet.

Clubin bent without lowering his head, picked up the snuff-box with his left hand, keeping his two eyes and the six barrels of the revolver directed towards Rantaine.

Then he exclaimed,—

"Turn your back, my friend."

Rantaine turned his back.

Sieur Clubin placed his revolver under his arm, and pressed the spring of the snuff-box. The box opened.

It contained four bank notes, three of a thousand pounds each and one of ten pounds.

He folded up the three bank notes of a thousand pounds again, replaced them in the iron snuff-box, shut the box once more, and put it in his pocket.

Then he picked up a pebble from the ground. He wrapped this pebble in the ten-pound note and said,—

"Turn round again."

Rantaine turned round.

Sieur Clubin continued,—

"I told you that I would be content with the three thousand pounds. Here are ten pounds which I return to you."

And he flung the bill, weighted with the pebble, to Rantaine.

Rantaine sent the pebble and the bank note into the sea with a kick.

"As you please," ejaculated Clubin. "Come, you must be rich. I am satisfied."

The sound of oars which had been constantly approaching, during this dialogue, ceased. This indicated that the boat was at the foot of the cliff.

"Your carriage is below. You may go, Rantaine."

Rantaine stepped toward the staircase, and disappeared.

Clubin advanced cautiously to the brink of the precipice, and, thrusting his head over, watched him descend.

The boat had stopped near the bottommost step of the crag, at the very place where the coastguardsman fell.

As he watched Rantaine going down, Clubin muttered,—

"Six hundred and nineteen is a good number! He thought that he was alone. Rantaine thought that there were only two of them. I alone knew that there were three of us."

He caught sight, on the grass at his feet, of the telescope which the coastguard had dropped; he picked it up.

The sound of oars began again. Rantaine had just leaped into the boat, and she was putting out to sea.

When Rantaine was in the boat, after the first stroke of the oars, and the cliff was beginning to recede behind him, he suddenly rose erect, his face became convulsed, he pointed downward with his fist, and shouted,—

"Ha! he is the devil himself, a low-lived scoundrel."

A few seconds later, Clubin, as he stood on the summit of the cliff, and pointed the telescope at the boat, distinctly heard these words articulated by a loud voice amid the noise of the waves,—

"Sieur Clubin, you are an honest man; but you will not mind my writing to Lethierry to acquaint him with the facts, and here in the boat is a Guernsey sailor, who belongs to the crew of the *Tamaulipas,* named Ahier-Tostevin; he will return to Saint-Malo on Zuela's next voyage, and will bear witness that I have delivered to you on behalf of Mess Lethierry, the sum of three thousand pounds sterling."

It was the voice of Rantaine.

Clubin was a man who did things thoroughly. Motionless as the coastguard had been, and on the same spot, with his eye at the telescope, he did not remove his gaze from the boat for a moment. He saw it grow less among the billows, disappear, reappear, and approach the vessel which was lying to, and board it; and he could recognize Rantaine's tall form on the deck of the *Tamaulipas*.

When the boat had been taken on board, and hung at the davits, the *Tamaulipas* set sail. The breeze was blowing off shore, she spread all her sails. Clubin's telescope remained fixed upon her outline, growing more and more indistinct, and, half an hour later, the *Tamaulipas* was no longer anything but a black speck, diminishing on the horizon against the pallid twilight of the sky.

IX
Information Useful to Persons Who Await or Who Fear Letters from Across the Sea

ON that evening, Sieur Clubin once more returned late.

One of the causes of his delay was that before returning he had gone as far as the Dinan gate, where there were drinking shops. In one of these shops, where he was not known, he had bought a bottle of brandy, which he had placed in the large pocket of his pilot coat, as though with the design of concealing it; then, as the Durande was to sail on the morrow, he had taken a turn on board to assure himself that everything was in order.

When Sieur Clubin re-entered the Jean Tavern, there was no one in the taproom but the old sea captain, M. Gertrais-Gaboureau, who was drinking his glass and smoking his pipe.

M. Gertrais-Gaboureau saluted Sieur Clubin between a whiff and a draught.

"Good evening, Captain Clubin."

"Good evening, Captain Gertrais."

"Well, the *Tamaulipas* has sailed."

"Ah!" said Clubin, "I had not noticed it."

Captain Gertrais-Gaboureau spat, and said,—

"Zuela has cut stick."

"When?"

"This evening."

"Where is he going?"

"To the devil."

"No doubt; but where?"

"To Arequipa."

"I knew nothing about it," said Clubin.

He added,—

"I'm going to bed."

He lighted his candle, walked towards the door, and came back.

"Have you ever been to Arequipa, Captain Gertrais?"

"Yes. Years ago."

"What ports do you put into?"

"Pretty nearly everywhere. But this *Tamaulipas* won't put into any port."

M. Gertrais-Gaboureau emptied the ashes from his pipe on the edge of a plate, and continued,—

"You know the lugger *Cheval-de-Troie,* and that fine three-master the *Trente-Mouzin,* which sailed for Cardiff. I did not approve of their sailing, because of the weather. They have come back in a pretty condition. The lugger was loaded with turpentine; she sprung a leak, and in pumping out the water she pumped out her whole cargo. As for the three-master she suffered mostly in her upper works; the cut-water, the headsail, the stanchions, the stock of the larboard anchor, all broken. The jibboom broken off close to the cap. The bowsprit shrouds and bobstays—well, go see how they look. The mizzen-mast is all right; but it got a severe strain. All the iron of the bowsprit is gone, and, incredible to state, the bowsprit is not scratched but it is completely stripped. The vessel's sheathing is open for three good square feet on the larboard. That's what comes of not listening to people."

Clubin had placed his candle on the table, and had begun to stick in afresh a row of pins which he had in the collar of his rough overcoat. He began again,—

"Didn't you say, Captain Gertrais, that the *Tamaulipas* will not put in at any port?"

"She will not. She is going straight to Chile."

"In that case, she cannot send any news of herself while on the passage."

"Pardon me, Captain Clubin. In the first place, she can send her despatches by any vessel which she meets bound for Europe."

"That is true."

"Then there is the ocean letter-box."

"What do you call the ocean letter-box?"

"Don't you know about that, Captain Clubin?"

"No."

"When one is passing through the straits of Magellan—"

"Well?"

"Snow everywhere, bad weather always, abominably bad winds and heavy seas."

"What then?"

"When you have doubled Cape Monmouth—"

"Well, what then?"

"Then you double Cape Valentine."

"Well, what next?"

"Next you double Cape Isidore."

"And then?"

"You double Point Anna."

"Good. But what do you call the ocean letter-box?"

"We are coming to that. Mountains on the right, mountains on the left. Penguins everywhere, and stormy-petrels. A terrible place. Ah! a thousand saints, a thousand monkeys! What a rattletrap and how it knocks about! The storm does not need any help. That is where one watches the sheer rail! That is where one takes in sail! That is where you replace your mainsail with the main-staysail, and the main-staysail with the fore-staysail. Gust on gust. And then sometimes four, five, six days of lying to. Often you have nothing but lint left of a new set of sails. What a dance! Squalls fit to make a three-master skip like a flea. I have seen on an English brig, the *True Blue,* a cabin boy, busy on the jibboom, carried off to all the five hundred thousand millions of God's thunders, and the jibboom with him. You are swept into the air like butterflies! I have seen the boatswain's mate of the *Revenue,* a pretty schooner, snatched from above the forecrosstrees and killed instantly. I have had my rails stove in, and my water-ways smashed to a jelly. One comes out of there with all one's canvas in ribbons. Frigates of fifty guns leak like baskets. And what a wretched devil of a coast! Nothing can be worse. Rocks slashed up as though in child's play. You approach Port Famine. There it is worse than worst. The roughest sea I ever saw in my life. Hellish coasts. All at once you see two words, 'Post-office,' painted in red."

"What do you mean, Captain Gertrais?"

"I mean, Captain Clubin, that immediately after having doubled Point Anna, you behold on a rock a hundred feet high, a pole. It is a pole with a barrel round its neck. This barrel is the letter-box. The English must needs write 'Post-office' on it. Why did they meddle? 'Tis the letter-box of the ocean; it does not belong to that honorable gentleman the King of England. This letter-box is common property. It belongs to all flags. 'Post-office,' 'tis perfect Chinese! it produces on you the effect of a cup of tea suddenly offered you by the devil. This is the way the service is performed. Every ship which passes sends a boat to the pole with its despatches. The officer in command of the boat deposits your packet in the barrel, and takes the packet which he finds there. You take charge of these letters; the vessel which comes after you will take charge of yours. As we are sailing in different directions, the continent from which you are coming is the one to which I am going. I carry your letters, you carry mine. The barrel is bitted to the post with a chain. And it rains! And it snows! And it hails! A deuce of a sea! The little imps fly from all quarters. The *Tamaulipas* will pass there. The barrel has a good cover on hinges, but no lock or padlock. You see that one can write to one's friends. Letters reach their destination."

"That's very odd," muttered Clubin, thoughtfully.

Captain Gertrais-Gaboureau turned to his glass.

"Suppose, for instance, that rascal of a Zuela were to write to me, the scamp tosses his scrawl into the barrel at Magellan, and in four months' time I receive the villain's scribbling. Ah, by the way, Captain Clubin, do you sail to-morrow?"

Clubin, absorbed in a sort of somnambulism, did not hear. Captain Gertrais repeated his question.

Clubin came to himself.

"Certainly, Captain Gertrais. It is my day. I must start to-morrow morning."

"If it were my case, I should not start, Captain Clubin; the hair of the dog's coat feels damp. The sea birds have been flying round the lantern of the lighthouse these two nights past. A bad sign. I have a storm glass which is cutting capers. We are in the second quarter of the moon; it is the maximum of dampness. I have just seen some pimpernels with their leaves shut, and a field of clover whose stalks were perfectly upright. The earthworms are coming out, the flies are biting, the bees are keeping close to their hives, the sparrows are holding consultations. The sound of bells is clearly heard from a distance. This evening, I heard the angelus from Saint-Lunaire. And then the sunset was dirty. There will be a heavy fog to-morrow. I advise you not to start. I fear a fog more than a tornado. The fog is treacherous."

BOOK SIXTH
THE DRUNKEN HELMSMAN AND THE SOBER CAPTAIN

I
THE DOUVRES ROCKS

ABOUT FIVE LEAGUES out on the open sea, to the south of Guernsey, opposite the Point of Plainmont, between the Channel Islands and Saint-Malo, lies a group of rocks called the Douvres. This spot is dangerous.

This title, Douvre, Dover, belongs to many rocks and cliffs. There is, especially near the Côtes-du-Nord, a Douvre rock on which a lighthouse is now in process of construction, a dangerous reef, but which must not be confounded with this one.

The point of France nearest to the Douvres is Cape Bréhat. The Douvres lie a little farther from the coast of France than from the first island of the Norman archipelago. The distance of that reef from Jersey is pretty nearly measured by the extreme length of Jersey. If the island of Jersey were turned upon la Corbière as upon a hinge, Point Saint-Catherine would almost strike the Douvres. This makes a distance of more than four leagues.

In these civilized seas, the most savage rocks are rarely desert places. Smugglers are to be met with at Hagot, custom-house officers at Binic, Celts at Bréhat, oyster dredgers at Cancale, rabbit hunters at Césambre (Cæsar's island), crab catchers at Bréchou, trawlers at the Minquiers, wreckers at Ecréhou. At the Douvres, no one.

There the sea birds alone are at home.

No place is more dreaded. The Casquets, where, it is said, the *Blanche-Nef* was lost, the bank of Calvados, the Needles of the Isle of Wight, the Ronesse, which renders the coast of Beaulieu so dangerous, the shallows of Préel, which block the entrance to Merquel, and which compel the placing of the red-painted beacon at twenty fathoms of water, the treacherous approach to the Etables and Plouha, the two granite Druids on the south of Guernsey, old Anderlo and little Anderlo, the Corbière, the Hanways, the Isle of Ras, connected with terror by this proverb,—

Si jamais tu passes le Ras,
Si tu ne meurs tu trembleras,[1]

the Mortes-Femmes, the passage of the Boue and the Frouquil, the Déroute between Guernsey and Jersey, the Hardent between the Minquiers and Chausey, the Mauvais Cheval between Boulay Bay and Barneville, all have a less evil reputation. It would be better to face all these reefs one after the other than the Douvres a single time.

In that perilous sea of the Channel, which is the Ægean Sea of the West, the Douvres have no equal in terror except the Pater-Noster reef between Guernsey and Sark.

And again, from the Pater-Noster one can make a signal; a vessel in distress there can obtain assistance. To the north, Point Dicard or d'Icare is visible; and to the south, Gros-Nez. From the Douvres, nothing is to be seen.

Storm, water, cloud, the limitless, the uninhabited. Nothing goes there except when astray. The granite cliffs are of enormous and hideous size—precipices everywhere, stern, inhospitable abyss.

It is in the open sea. The water is very deep there. A reef absolutely isolated like the Douvres attracts and shelters animals who require to be far away from man.

1. If ever you pass the Ras, if you do not die you will tremble.

It is a sort of vast, submarine madrepore. It is a sunken labyrinth. There, at a depth reached only with difficulty by divers, are caverns, dens, lairs, the crossings of dark streets. Monstrous creatures swarm there. They devour one another. The crabs eat the fish, and are in turn eaten themselves. Terrible living forms, not made to be seen by human eyes, wander through this gloom. Vague lineaments of antennæ, tentacles, gills, fins, yawning jaws, scales, claws, nippers, float there, quiver, grow huge, decompose, and are effaced in the fatal transparency. Frightful swimming swarms prowl about, doing their work. It is a hive of hydras.

The horrible is there, the imaginary.

Imagine, if you can, a nest of holothurians.

To look into the depths of a sea is to behold the imagination of the Unknown. It is to see it from the terrible side. The gulf is analogous to the night. There also there is sleep,—apparent sleep, at least,—of the conscience of creation. There, in full security, are accomplished the crimes of the irresponsible. There, in a frightful peace, the rough draughts of life, almost phantoms, wholly demons, fulfil the fierce occupations of darkness.

Forty years ago, two rocks of singular form indicated the Douvres reef to passers-by on the ocean. These were two vertical points, sharp and curving, whose tips almost touched each other. One might fancy them to be the tusks of a submerged elephant, rising out of the sea. Only, they were the tusks, tall as towers, of an elephant as large as a mountain. These two natural towers of the obscure city of monsters, left between them only a narrow passage through which the waters dashed. This tortuous passage, with many crooked turns in its length, resembled a section of street between two walls. These twin rocks were called the Douvres. There was the great Douvre and the little Douvre; one was sixty feet high, the other, forty. The action of the water finally sawed into the base towers, and the violent equinoctial storm of the twenty-sixth of October, 1859, overthrew one of them. The one which remains, the small one, is truncated and worn.

One of the strangest rocks of the Douvres group is called "the Man." This still exists. During the last century, some fishermen who lost their way amid these breakers, found a corpse on the summit of this rock. Beside the body lay a quantity of empty shells. A man had been shipwrecked on this rock, had taken refuge there, and had subsisted for some time on shell-fish, and had died there. Hence this name, "the Man."

The solitudes of the sea are mournful. It is tumult and silence. What takes place there no longer concerns the human race. It is of unknown utility. Such is the isolation of the Douvres. All about, as far as the eye can reach, is the immense ferment of the waves.

II

Unexpected Brandy

On Friday morning, the day after the departure of the *Tamaulipas,* the Durande set out for Guernsey. She left Saint-Malo at nine o'clock.

The weather was clear, there was no mist; old Captain Gertrais-Gaboureau seemed to have been talking nonsense.

The preoccupation of Sieur Clubin had, decidedly, almost made him miss his cargo. He had taken on board only a few bales of goods from Paris for the fancy stores at Saint-Pierre-Port, three cases for the Guernsey hospital, one of yellow soap, another of candles, the third of French sole leather and choice Cordovan leather. He was bringing back of his former cargo a case of crushed sugar and three cases of Congo tea which the French custom-house had refused to admit. Sieur Clubin had taken but few cattle on board, only a few oxen. These oxen were rather carelessly stored in the hold.

There were six passengers on board; one Guernsey

man, two cattle dealers from Saint-Malo; a "tourist," as the expression ran even at that period, a demi-bourgeois Parisian probably a commercial traveller; and an American who was travelling for the purpose of distributing Bibles.

The Durande carried a crew of seven men, not counting Captain Clubin; a helmsman, a coal-heaver, a carpenter, a cook, who served as a seaman at need, two firemen, and a cabin-boy. One of the firemen was also the engineer. This fireman-engineer, a very brave and intelligent Dutch Negro, who had escaped from the sugar plantations of Surinam, was named Imbrancam. The Negro Imbrancam understood and worked the engine admirably. At first, as he appeared perfectly black in his engine-room, he had contributed not a little in imparting a diabolical name to the Durande.

The helmsman, a Jerseyman by birth, and a Cotentin by origin, was named Tangrouille. The Tangrouilles belonged to the high nobility.

This was literally true.

The Channel Islands are, like England, an aristocratic country. Castes still exist there. Castes have their own ideas, which serve as their safeguard. These ideas of caste are everywhere the same, in India as in Germany. Nobility is won by the sword and lost by labor. It is preserved by idleness. To do nothing is to live nobly; whoever does not work is honored. A trade involves loss of rank. In France there was formerly no exception made, save for glass workers. As emptying bottles constituted, to a certain extent, the glory of gentlemen, the making of bottles did not dishonor them. In the Channel archipelago, as well as in Great Britain, he who wishes to remain noble must remain rich. A workman cannot be a gentleman. If he has been one, he is so no longer. Such and such a sailor is descended from knights banneret, and he is only a sailor. Thirty years ago, a real Gorges at Alderney, who would have had a right to the seigniory of Gorges, confiscated by Philip Augustus, gathered seaweed, barefooted in the sea. A Carteret is a carter in Sark. There are a draper at Jersey and a shoemaker at Guernsey named Gruchy, who declare that they are Grouchys and cousins to the Marshal of Waterloo.

The ancient records of the benefices of the diocese of Coutances make mention of a seigniory of Tangroville, an evident relation of Tancarville on the Basse-Seine, which is Montmorency. In the fifteenth century, Johan de Hérondville, archer and squire of the Sire of Tangroville, bore behind him "his corselet and other harness." In May, 1371, at Pontorson, at the review of Bertrand du Guesclin, "Monsieur de Tangroville did his duty as knight bachelor." In the Norman Isles, if poverty overtakes a man, he is speedily eliminated from the nobility. A change of pronunciation suffices. Tangroville becomes "Tangrouille," and it is done.

This is what happened with the helmsman of the Durande.

At Saint-Pierre-Port, at the Bordage, there is a dealer in old iron, named Ingrouille, which is probably Ingroville. Under Louis le Gros, the Ingrovilles possessed three parishes in the Court of Assessors of Valogne. An Abbé Trigan has written the *Ecclesiastical History of Normandy*. This chronicler Trigan was curate of the Seigniory of Digoville. If the Lord of Digoville had descended to the plebeian state, he would have been called "Digouille."

Tangrouille, that Tancarville, and that possible Montmorency, had this ancient quality of a gentleman, a grave defect in a helmsman: he was in the habit of getting intoxicated.

Sieur Clubin had persisted in keeping him. He had made himself responsible for him to Mess Lethierry.

Helmsman Tangrouille never left the vessel, and slept on board.

On the eve of departure, when Sieur Clubin arrived, at a tolerably late hour in the evening, to pay a visit to the ship, Tangrouille was asleep in his hammock.

In the course of the night, Tangrouille woke up. It was his nightly custom. Every drunkard, who is not his own master, has his hiding-place. Tangrouille had his, which he called his storeroom. Tangrouille's storeroom was in the water-hold. He had located it there to disarm suspicion. He thought he was sure that this hiding-place was known only to himself.

Sieur Clubin being sober, was severe. The little rum and gin which the helmsman could conceal from the captain's vigilant eye, he kept in reserve in a mysterious nook of the water-hold, at the bottom of a sounding bucket, and almost every night he had an amorous rendezvous with his storeroom. The surveillance was rigid, the orgy was a poor one, and Tangrouille's nightly excesses were confined to two or three mouthfuls swallowed on the sly. Sometimes, even the storeroom was empty.

That night Tangrouille had found an unexpected bottle of brandy. His joy had been great and his amazement still greater. From what cloud had that bottle fallen? He could recall neither how nor when he had brought it on board the ship. He had drunk it immediately,—partly out of prudence, for fear the brandy might be discovered and seized. He had flung the bottle into the sea. On the following day, when he took the helm, Tangrouille staggered a little.

Nevertheless, he steered nearly as usual.

As for Clubin, he had returned to sleep at the Jean Tavern, as the reader knows.

Clubin always wore under his shirt a leather travelling belt, in which he kept, in case of emergencies, a score of guineas, and which he only took off at night. Inside this belt was his name, "Sieur Clubin," written by himself on the rough leather with thick, lithographic ink, which is indelible.

On rising, before sailing, he placed in this belt the iron box containing the seventy-five thousand francs in bank notes; then he buckled the belt round his body as usual.

III
Interrupted Conversations

THE departure was made pleasantly. As soon as their valises and portmanteaus had been disposed of under and upon the benches, the passengers indulged themselves in that never-failing survey of the boat which seems obligatory, so habitual is it.

Two of the travellers, the tourist and the Parisian, had never seen a steamboat before, and from the very first stroke of the paddle-wheels they admired the foam. Then they admired the smoke. They examined, piece by piece and almost strand by strand, as they lay upon the deck and lower deck, all the maritime apparatus of rings, hooks, clamps, bolts, which, in virtue of their precision and adjustment, are a sort of colossal jewelry,—iron jewelry gilded with rust by the tempest. They made the circuit of the little signal gun lashed on the deck, "chained up like a watch-dog," remarked the tourist, and "covered with a blouse of tarred canvas to prevent it from taking cold," added the Parisian. As they left the land, they exchanged the usual observations on the view of Saint-Malo; one passenger enunciated the axiom that approaches from the sea are deceptive, and that at a distance of a league no coast so closely resembles Ostend as Dunkirk. He completed what he had to say on Dunkirk by this remark, that its two light-ships painted red were called: one, the *Ruytingen,* the other, the *Mardyck.*

Saint-Malo grew smaller in the distance, then disappeared.

The sea was perfectly calm. The wake which stretched

out behind the ship, almost without a curve, as far as the eye could reach, formed a long street fringed with foam.

Guernsey is in the middle of a straight line drawn from Saint-Malo in France to Exeter in England. A straight course at sea is not always practical. Nevertheless, steamers have it within their power, to a certain extent, to follow the straight course which is denied to sailing vessels.

The sea, complicated by the wind, is a combination of forces. A vessel is a combination of machinery. Forces are infinite machines, machines are limited forces. It is between these two organisms, the one inexhaustible, the other intelligent, that the combat called navigation is waged.

A will in a mechanism furnishes a counterbalance to the infinite. The infinite also contains a mechanism. The elements know what they do and whither they go. No force is blind. Man must watch these forces, and seek to discover their laws.

Until the law is found, the struggle continues; and in this struggle, steam navigation is a sort of perpetual victory won by the human race, every hour in the day, at all points on the sea. Steam navigation has this admirable point about it, that it disciplines the ship. It lessens the obedience demanded by the winds and increases their obedience to man.

Never had the Durande worked better at sea than on that day. She behaved admirably.

Towards eleven o'clock, with a fresh breeze from the nor'–nor'west, the Durande was in the open sea off the Minquiers, under little steam, sailing to the west, on the starboard tack, and as near the wind as possible. The weather was still fine and clear. But the trawlers were coming inshore.

Little by little, the sea was cleared of vessels, as though every one were thinking of regaining port.

It could not be said that the Durande held exactly her accustomed course. The crew thought nothing of it; their confidence in the captain was absolute; still, through the helmsman's fault, perhaps, there was a little deviation from the course. The Durande appeared to be steering towards Jersey rather than towards Guernsey. A little after eleven o'clock, the captain rectified the course, and they steered straight for Guernsey. Only a little time had been lost. In short days, lost time has its inconveniences. There was a fine February sun.

Tangrouille, in his present state, was no longer very steady on his feet, nor very strong in the arm. The result was that the worthy helmsman frequently got off the course, which slackened the speed.

The wind had almost died out.

The Guernsey passenger, who had a telescope, pointed it from time to time at a little tuft of grayish mist slowly borne by the wind along the extreme western horizon, and which resembled dusty wool.

Captain Clubin wore his usual austere, puritanical expression. He appeared to redouble his watchfulness.

All was peaceful and almost joyous on board the Durande, and the passengers chatted. By shutting one's eyes during a sea voyage, one can judge of the state of the sea by the *tremolo* of the conversation. Full freedom of mind on the part of the passengers corresponds to perfect tranquillity of the water.

It is impossible, for example, that a conversation like the following should take place under any other conditions than a very calm sea.

"Do look, monsieur, at that pretty green and red fly."

"It is lost at sea, and is resting on the vessel."

"A fly does not soon get fatigued."

"In truth, it is so light. The wind carries it."

"An ounce of flies has been weighed, sir, and afterwards counted, and there were found to be six thousand two hundred and sixty-eight."

The Guernsey man with the telescope had approached the Saint-Malo cattle dealers, and their chat was something in this style,—

"The Aubrac ox has a round, thickset body, short legs, and tawny hide. He works slowly, because of the shortness of his limbs."

"In that respect, the Salers ox is worth more than the Aubrac."

"Monsieur, I have seen two fine oxen in the course of my life. The first had short legs, a thick forepart, a full rump, large haunches, a good length from the nape of his neck to his tail, a good height to his shoulder, easy movements and a loose skin. The second showed all the signs of judicious fattening. A thickset body, strong neck and shoulders, slender legs, a white and red coat, a sloping rump."

"That's the Cotentin breed."

"Yes, but having some connection with the Angus or the Suffolk bull."

"Believe me if you will, sir, but in the South they have competitive donkey shows."

"Of donkeys?"

"Of donkeys, as I have had the honor of telling you. And it is the ugly ones which are considered handsome."

"Then it is as with the mules. The ugly ones are the good ones."

"Precisely. The Poitevin mare. Big belly, coarse limbs."

"The best she-mule known is a barrel on four poles."

"Beauty in beasts is not the same thing as beauty in men."

"And above all, in women."

"That is true."

"For my part, I hold that a woman should be pretty."

"I maintain that she should be well dressed."

"Yes, neat, clean, with care, with some style."

"With a perfectly new look. A young girl should always seem to be just from the jeweller's shop."

"To return to my oxen. I saw those two oxen sold at the market of Thouars."

"I know the market of Thouars. The Bonneaux of la Rochelle and the Babus, the wheat dealers of Marans,—I do not know whether you have heard them mentioned,—must go to that market."

The tourist and the Parisian were talking with the American colporteur. Here also, the conversation was "on fair-weather topics."

"Sir," the tourist was saying, "the following is the floating tonnage of the civilized world: France, seven hundred and sixteen thousand tons, Germany one million tons; the United States, five millions; England, five millions five hundred thousand. Add the contingent of the secondary powers. Total: twelve millions, nine hundred and four thousand tons, distributed among one hundred and forty-five thousand ships scattered over the waters of the globe."

The American interrupted,—

"It is the United States, sir, which have five millions, five hundred thousand."

"I agree to that," said the tourist. "You are an American?"

"Yes, sir."

"I agree again."

A silence ensued; the American missionary asked himself whether this was a case for offering a Bible.

"Sir," began the tourist again, "is it true that you have such a taste for nicknames in America that you disguise all your celebrated men in them, and that you call your famous Missouri banker, Thomas Benton, 'Old Ingot'?"[1]

"The same as we call Zachary Taylor, 'Old Zach.' "

"And General Harrison, 'Old Tip,' do you not? and General Jackson 'Old Hickory'?"

"Because Jackson is as hard as hickory wood, and because Harrison whipped the Red Skins at Tippecanoe."

"That is a Byzantine fashion that you have."

"It is our way. We call Van Buren 'The Little Wizard'; Seward, who introduced fractional currency, 'Billy the Little'; and Douglas, the Democratic Senator from Illinois, who is four feet high and very eloquent, 'The Little Giant.' You may travel from Texas to Maine, and you will not find a person who will speak the name 'Cass,' they say 'The Great Michigander'; nor the name 'Clay,' they say 'The miller's boy with the scar.'[2] Clay is the son of a miller."

"I should prefer to say Clay or Cass," remarked the Parisian; "it is shorter."

"You would be out of fashion. We call Corwin, who is Secretary of the Treasury, 'The wagoner's boy.' Daniel Webster is 'Black Dan.' As for Winfield Scott, as his first thought after having beaten the English at Chippeway, was to seat himself at table, we call him, 'Quick, a plate of soup!' "[3]

1. "Old Bullion."
2. "The Mill Boy of the Slashes."
3. "A Hasty Plate of Soup."

The tuft of mist in the distance had grown larger. It now occupied on the horizon a segment of about fifteen degrees. One would have thought it a cloud, which for lack of wind was dragging along on the water. There was hardly any breeze now. The sea was smooth. Although it was not yet noon, the sun had grown pale. It lighted but no longer warmed.

"I think we are going to have a change of weather," said the tourist.

"Perhaps we shall have rain," said the Parisian.

"Or fog," added the American.

"In Italy," said the tourist, "the least rain falls at Molfetta, and the most at Tolmezzo."

At noon, the bell rang for dinner, according to the usage of the archipelago. Any one dined who wished. Some passengers carried their provisions with them, and ate gayly on deck. Clubin did not dine.

As they ate, the conversations continued.

The Guernsey man, having a scent for Bibles, approached the American. The American said to him,—

"Do you know this sea?"

"Certainly. I belong here."

"So do I," said one of the Saint-Malo men.

The Guernsey man signified his assent with a nod, and continued,—

"We are in the open sea now, but I should not have liked the fog while we were off the Minquiers."

The American said to the Saint-Malo man,—

"The islanders are more at home on the sea than the people of the coast."

"That is true; we coast people only have half a dip in the salt water."

"What are the Minquiers?" continued the American.

The Saint-Maloan replied,—

"They are very ugly rocks."

"There are also the Grelets," remarked the Guernsey man.

"Parbleu!" replied the Saint-Maloan.

"And the Chouas," added the Guernsey man.

The man from Saint-Malo burst out laughing.

"So far as that goes," said he, "there are also the Sauvages."

"And the Monks," observed the Guernsey man.

"And the Duck," exclaimed the Saint-Maloan.

"Monsieur," rejoined the Guernsey man, politely, "you have a reply for everything."

"*Malouin malin!*—Saint-Malo men are cunning."

Having made this repartee, the Saint-Malo man winked.

The tourist interposed a question.

"Must we pass all that collection of rocks?"

"Not at all. We have left it at the sou'-sou'west. It lies behind us."

And the Guernsey man went on,—

"Taking big rocks and small, the Grelets have fifty-seven points."

"And the Minquiers forty-eight," said the Saint-Maloan.

Here the dialogue was confined to the Saint-Malo man and the Guernsey man.

"It seems to me, Monsieur de Saint-Malo, that there are three rocks which you have not included."

"I am reckoning them all."

"The Dérée at Maître Island?"

"Yes."

"And the Maisons?"

"Which are seven rocks in the middle of the Minquiers? Yes."

"I see that you know those rocks."

"If I did not know rocks I should not belong to Saint-Malo."

"It is pleasing to hear the arguments of Frenchmen."

The Saint-Malo man saluted in his turn, and said,—

"The Savages are three rocks."

"And the Monks two."

"And the Duck one."

"The Duck indicates that it is only one."

"No, for the Suarde is four rocks."

"What do you call the Suarde?" asked the Guernsey man.

"What you call the Chouas, we call the Suarde."

"It is not safe to pass between the Chouas and the Duck."

"That is possible only to birds."

"And to fish."

"Not too easily. In heavy weather, they get knocked against the walls."

"There is sand in the Minquiers."

"Around the Maisons (houses)."

"They are eight rocks which are visible from Jersey."

"From the beach of Azette, 'tis true. Not eight, only seven."

"At low tide, one can walk about among the Minquiers."

"No doubt, there is land left bare."

"And the Dirouilles?"

"The Dirouilles have nothing in common with the Minquiers."

"I mean to say that they are dangerous."

"They lie in the direction of Granville."

"It is evident that you men of Saint-Malo, like us, are fond of navigating in these seas."

"Yes," replied the Saint-Malo man, "with this difference, that we say: 'we have a habit of,' and you say: 'we are fond of.' "

"You are good sailors."

"I am a cattle dealer."

"Who was that famous man from Saint-Malo?"

"Surcouf."

"What other?"

"Duguay-Trouin."

Here the Parisian commercial traveller intervened.

"Duguay-Trouin? He was taken by the English. He was as amiable as he was brave. He managed to please a young Englishwoman. It was she who procured his liberty."

At that moment, a voice of thunder shouted,—

"Thou art drunk!"

IV

In Which Captain Clubin Displays All His Qualities

EVERY one turned round.

It was the captain addressing the helmsman.

Sieur Clubin was not in the habit of calling any one "thou." For him to hurl such an apostrophe at helmsman Tangrouille, Clubin must have been very angry, or he must have desired to appear so. An outburst of wrath at the proper time relieves one of responsibility, and sometimes transfers it.

The captain, standing on the bridge, between the two paddle boxes, was gazing steadily at the helmsman. He repeated between his teeth,—"Drunkard!"

Worthy Tangrouille hung his head.

The fog bank had grown larger. It now occupied nearly half of the horizon. It was advancing in every direction at once; there is something of the nature of a drop of oil in fog. This fog spread insensibly. The wind bore it on without haste, without noise. It was gradually taking possession of the ocean. It came from the north-west, and the vessel had it on the bows. It was like a vast, vague, moving cliff. It was cut out upon the sea like a wall. There was a definite point where the immense expanse of water entered beneath the fog and disappeared.

This point of entrance into the fog was still about half a league distant. If the wind changed, they might be able to avoid entering the fog; but it must change at once. The half-league interval was filling up and decreasing visibly; the Durande was moving forward, the fog was also advancing. It was coming towards the ship, and the ship was going towards it.

Clubin ordered them to put on more steam and sheer off to the east.

In this manner they skirted the fog for a while, but it continued to advance. Nevertheless, the ship was still in the full sunlight.

Time was lost in these manœuvres which could hardly prove successful. Night comes on quickly in February.

Thc Guernsey man watched the fog. He said to the Saint-Malo man,—

"That's an ugly fog."

"A nasty thing at sea," observed one of the Saint-Malo men.

The other Saint-Malo man added,—

"That's what spoils a trip."

The Guernsey man approached Clubin.

"Captain Clubin, I am afraid that we shall get caught in the fog."

Clubin replied,—

"I wanted to remain at Saint-Malo, but I was advised to sail."

"Who advised you?"

"Some of the old sailors."

"In fact," resumed the Guernsey man, "you did right to sail. Who knows whether there will not be a tempest to-morrow? At this season, one may wait and only find it worse."

A few minutes later, the Durande entered the fog bank.

It was a singular instant. All at once those who were at the stern could not see those who were at the bow. A soft, gray partition cut the boat in two.

Then the whole vessel plunged into the fog. The sun was no longer anything but a sort of exaggerated moon. Every one suddenly began to shiver with the cold. The passengers put on their overcoats, and the sailors their pea-jackets. The sea, which was almost without a ripple, had the cold menace of tranquillity. It seems as though there were something to be apprehended from this excess of calm. All was wan and pallid. The black smokestack and the black smoke contended with the livid mist which enshrouded the vessel.

Deviation to the east was henceforth useless, and the captain directed the ship's head towards Guernsey, and put on more steam.

The Guernsey passenger, as he prowled around the engine-room, heard the Negro Imbrancam talking to his mate the fireman. The passenger listened. The Negro was saying,—

"This morning, in the sunlight, we went slowly; now, in the fog, we are going fast."

The Guernsey man went back to Sieur Clubin.

"Captain Clubin, there is no cause for anxiety; but are we not carrying too much steam?"

"What would you have, sir? We must certainly make up for the time lost by that drunkard of a helmsman."

"That is true, Captain Clubin."

And Clubin added,—

"I am in haste to arrive. The fog is enough, night would be too much."

The Guernsey man rejoined the Saint-Malo passengers, and said to them,—

"We have an excellent captain."

At intervals, great surges of fog, which one would have said had been carded, shut down heavily and concealed the sun. Then it reappeared, paler and as though ailing. The little which could be seen of the heavens resembled the strips of painted sky, dirty and spotted with oil, of old theatrical stage scenery.

The Durande passed close to a cutter which had prudently cast anchor. It was the *Shealtiel* of Guernsey. The skipper of the cutter noticed the Durande's high rate of speed. It also struck him that she was not in her exact course. She seemed to be bearing too much to the west. This ship under full speed in the fog astonished him.

Towards two o'clock, the fog was so thick that the captain was forced to quit the bridge and get nearer the helmsman. The sun had vanished, all was fog. A sort of white obscurity reigned on board the Durande. She sailed in diffused pallor. The sky was no longer visible, neither was the sea.

There was not a breath of wind.

The can of turpentine suspended under the foot bridge between the paddle boxes, did not even oscillate.

The passengers had become silent.

Still the Parisian hummed between his teeth Béranger's song, "*Un jour le bon Dieu s'éveillant.* One day the good God waking."

One of the Saint-Malo passengers addressed him.

"Monsieur comes from Paris?"

"Yes, monsieur. '*Il mit la tête à la fenêtre.* He thrust his head out of the window.' "

"What are they doing in Paris now?"

" '*Leur planète a péri peut-être.* Their planet may have perished.' Monsieur, in Paris everything is going at sixes and sevens."

"Then it is on land as it is on the sea."

" 'Tis true that we have an infernal fog here."

"And one which may cause disasters."

The Parisian exclaimed,—

"But why disasters? in what way disasters? What purpose do disasters serve? 'Tis like the conflagration at the Odéon. That reduced whole families to beggary. Is that just? Stay, sir, I do not know what your religion is, but I am not satisfied."

"Neither am I," said the Saint-Malo man.

"All that happens here below seems to be out of gear. I have an idea that the good God is not in it."

The Saint-Malo man scratched the top of his head, like some one making an effort to understand.

The Parisian continued,—

"The good God is absent. There ought to be a decree to force God to take up his permanent residence here. He is at his country house, and does not trouble himself about us. So everything goes wrong. It is evident, my dear sir, that the good God is no longer at the seat of government, that he is on a vacation, and that the vicar, some seminary angel, some idiot with the wings of a sparrow, is conducting affairs."

Moineau (sparrow) was mispronounced *moigneau,* after the manner of a street arab.

Captain Clubin, who had stepped up to the two talkers, laid his hand on the Parisian's shoulder.

"Hush!" said he! "Take heed to your words, sir. We are at sea."

No one uttered another word.

At the expiration of five minutes, the Guernsey man, who had heard all, muttered in the ear of the Saint-Malo man,—

"And a religious captain!"

It was not raining, but their clothing felt damp. They were only sensible of the progress they made through an increase of discomfort. They seemed to be entering into sadness. Fog causes silence on the ocean; it lulls the waves to sleep, and stifles the wind.

Amid that silence, there was something indescribably uneasy and plaintive about the hoarse breathing of the Durande.

They no longer met any vessels. If, in the distance, either in the direction of Guernsey or of Saint-Malo, there were still any ships on the sea outside of the fog, the Durande, submerged in the fog, was not visible to them, and its long trail of smoke, attached to nothing, produced the effect of a black comet in a white sky.

All at once, Clubin exclaimed,—

"Scoundrel! you have just steered wrong. You want to ruin us. You deserve to be put in irons! Begone, you drunken rascal!"

And he seized the helm.

The humiliated helmsman took refuge among the sailors forward.

The Guernsey man said,—

"We are saved."

They continued to advance rapidly.

Towards three o'clock, the under part of the fog began to lift, and they saw the sea once more.

"I don't like the looks of that," said the Guernsey man.

The fog could, in fact, be lifted only by the sun or the wind. If by the sun, it is well; by the wind, it is not so well. Now, it was too late for the sun. The sun grows weak at three o'clock in February. A rise in the wind, at that critical point in the day, is not desirable. It is often the forerunner of a tempest.

However, if there was any breeze, it was hardly perceptible.

Clubin, with his eye on the binnacle, grasping the helm and steering, was muttering between his teeth such words as the following, which reached the passengers' ears,—

"No time to lose. That drunkard has delayed us."

But his countenance was utterly devoid of expression.

The sea was less calm beneath the fog. Several waves were visible. Patches of glassy light floated by on the water. These patches of light on the waves cause mariners anxiety. They indicate holes pierced by the wind in the ceiling of the fog above. The fog lifted, and closed in again, more dense than ever. At times, the density was complete. The vessel was caught in a regular floe of fog. At intervals, this redoubtable circle opened part way, like a claw, allowed a small view of the horizon, then closed again.

The Guernsey man, armed with his telescope, stood sentinel on the bow of the vessel.

A clearing came, then closed.

The Guernsey man wheeled round thoroughly frightened,—

"Captain Clubin!"

"What's the matter?"

"We are steering straight for the Hanways."

"You are mistaken," said Clubin, coldly.

The Guernsey man persisted,—

"I am sure of it."

"Impossible."

"I just saw the rocks on the horizon."

"Where?"

"Yonder."

"That is the open sea. Impossible."

And Clubin kept the vessel directed towards the point indicated by the passenger.

The Guernsey man seized his telescope again. A moment later he ran to the stern.

"Captain!"

"Well?"

"Tack ship."

"Why?"

"I am sure that I have seen a rock, very high and very near. It is the Great Hanway."

"You must have seen some thicker fog bank."

"It is the Great Hanway. Tack ship, in the name of heaven!" Clubin gave the helm a turn.

V

Clubin Puts the Finishing Touch to Admiration

A CRASH was heard. The splitting of a vessel's side on a reef in the open sea is one of the most melancholy sounds conceivable. The Durande came to a dead halt. Several passengers were thrown down by the shock, and rolled along the deck.

The Guernsey man raised his hands to heaven.

"On the Hanway! I predicted it."

A long-drawn cry broke out on the vessel.

"We are lost!"

Clubin's voice, dry and curt, dominated the cry.

"No one is lost! Silence!"

Imbrancam's black form, bare to the waist, came up the hatchway leading to the engine-room.

The Negro said calmly,—

"Captain, the water is coming into the hold. The fire will soon be out."

It was a frightful moment.

The shock had resembled a suicide. It could not have been more terrible had it been done intentionally. The Durande had dashed upon the rock as though attacking it. One point of rock had penetrated the ship like a nail. More than six feet square of her planking had been crushed, the stern was broken, the bow stove in, the open hull drank in the water with a horrible boiling sound. It was a wound through which shipwreck entered. The rebound had broken the pendants of the rudder, which hung loose and beat about. The keel had been stove in by the reef, and around the vessel nothing was visible but the thick, compact fog, now almost black. Night was fast drawing on.

The Durande made a plunge forward. She was like the horse which has the bull's horn in his bowels. She was dead.

The hour of half high tide made itself felt on the sea.

Tangrouille was sobered; no one is drunk during a shipwreck; he went down between decks, came up again, and said,—

"Captain, the water is gaining on the hold. In ten minutes, it will be even with the scuppers."

The passengers rushed about the deck in a bewildered manner, wringing their hands, leaning over the rail, staring at the machinery, making all the useless movements of terror. The tourist had fainted away.

Clubin made a sign with his hand, every one became silent. He questioned Imbrancam.

"How much longer can the engine work?"

"Five or six minutes."

Then he questioned the Guernsey passenger.

"I was at the helm. You saw the rock. On which bank of the Hanway are we?"

"On the Mauve. Just now, when it lighted up, I recognized the Mauve perfectly."

"As we are on the Mauve," continued Clubin, "we have the great Hanway on our port side, and the little Hanway on the starboard. We are a mile from the shore."

The crew and passengers listened, quivering with anxiety and attention, their eyes riveted on the captain.

There was no object in lightening the vessel, and, besides, it was impossible. In order to throw the cargo into the sea, they would have been obliged to open the portholes and increase the chances for the water to enter. It would have been useless to cast anchor; they were nailed fast. Moreover, on this bottom, which would have made it impossible to trip the anchor, the chain would probably have parted. As the engine was not injured and could be worked while the fire was not extinguished, that is to say, for a few minutes longer, they could use the whole force of wheels and steam to move backward and tear themselves from the reef. In that case, they would sink immediately. The rock stopped up the leak to a certain extent, and obstructed the passage of the water. It presented an obstacle. The opening freed, it would be impossible to stop the leaks and free her with pumps. He who withdraws the dagger from a wound in the heart, kills the wounded man on the spot. To disengage themselves from the rock was simply to founder.

The cattle, on being reached by the water in the hold, began to bellow.

Clubin gave the command,—

"Launch the long-boat."

Imbrancam and Tangrouille rushed forward and cast off the lashings. The rest of the crew looked on, petrified.

"All hands to the ropes," shouted Clubin.

This time all obeyed.

Clubin, impassive, continued, in that ancient language of command which the sailors of the present day would not understand.

"Haul taut! Take a turn if the capstan is clogged! Stop heaving! Slack! Don't let the blocks of the davit tackle get fouled! Lower away! Slack away both ends together, sharp! Together! Look out that it doesn't go down end first! There's too much strain! Hold on to the lanyards of the davits! Stand by there!"

The long-boat was now on the water.

At the same instant, the wheels of the Durande stopped, the smoke ceased, the engine was submerged!

The passengers, gliding down the ladder or hanging to the rigging, let themselves drop into the boat rather than descended into it. Imbrancam picked up the fainting tourist, carried him into the boat, then climbed back upon the vessel.

The sailors rushed forward in the rear of the passengers. The cabin-boy had fallen under their feet, and they were trampling over him.

Imbrancam barred the passage.

"No one before the lad," said he.

He brushed aside the sailors with his black arms, seized the cabin-boy and handed him to the Guernsey passenger, who stood up in the boat to receive him.

The cabin-boy saved, Imbrancam stood aside and said to the others,—

"Pass on."

In the meantime, Captain Clubin had gone to his cabin and had made up a package of the papers and instruments belonging on board. He removed the compass from the binnacle. He handed the papers and instruments to Imbrancam, and the compass to Tangrouille, and said to them: "Get into the boat."

They obeyed. The crew had preceded them. The long-boat was full, the water was on a level with the gunwales.

"Now," shouted Clubin, "give way."

A cry arose from the long-boat.

"And you, captain?"

"I remain here."

Shipwrecked men have but little time for deliberation, and still less for becoming affected. Still, those who were in the boat and in comparative safety, felt an emotion which was not altogether selfish. All voices insisted simultaneously,—

"Come with us, captain."

"I remain."

The Guernsey man, who was used to the sea, replied,—

"Listen, captain. You have run around on the Hanway. You only need to swim a mile to gain Plainmont. But with a boat one cannot land short of la Rocquaine, and that is two miles. There are breakers, and there is the fog. This long-boat will not reach la Rocquaine for two hours to come. It will be a dark night. The sea is rising, the wind is freshening. A storm is at hand. We ask no better than to come back for you, but if heavy weather comes on, we shall not be able. You are lost if you remain. Come with us."

The Parisian interposed,—

"The long-boat is full, and over full, it is true, and one man more would be one man too many. But there are thirteen of us, which is bad for the boat, and it is better to overload it with another man than with an unlucky number. Come, captain."

Tangrouille added,—

"It is wholly my fault, and not yours. It is not right that you should remain."

"I stay," said Clubin. "The vessel will be torn in pieces tonight by the tempest. I shall not leave it. When the ship is lost, the captain is dead. It will be said of me: 'He did his duty to the end.' Tangrouille, I forgive you."

And folding his arms, he shouted,—

"Obey orders. Cast off the ropes. Give way."

The boat began to move. Imbrancam had seized the helm. All hands which were not rowing were raised towards the captain. All mouths shouted: "Hurrah for Captain Clubin!"

"That's an admirable man," said the American.

"Monsieur," replied the Guernsey man, "he's the most honest sailor afloat."

Tangrouille wept.

"If I had had any courage," he muttered, "I should have remained with him."

The long-boat entered the fog and disappeared.

Nothing more was visible.

The splash of the oars decreased and died away.

Clubin remained alone.

VI

The Interior of an Abyss Illuminated

WHEN this man found himself on that rock, beneath that cloud, in the midst of that water, far from all human contact, left for dead, alone between the rising sea and the approaching night, he felt a profound satisfaction.

He had succeeded.

He had realized his dream. The bill of exchange at long date, which he had drawn upon destiny, had been paid over to him.

For him, abandonment meant deliverance. He was on the Hanway, a mile from land; he had seventy-five thousand francs. Never had a more clever shipwreck been accomplished. Nothing had gone wrong; it is true that everything had been foreseen. Clubin, from his youth up, had cherished one idea; to put honesty as his stake on the gaming table of life; to pass for an upright man, and starting from that point to await his chancc, let the stakes swell, hit on the best way, divine the moment; not to grope, but to seize; to make one blow, and only one, to end by a sweepstake, to leave imbeciles behind him. His intention was to succeed once where stupid sharpers fail twenty times in succession, and, while they end on the gallows, to end in a fortune himself. Rantaine once met, had been his illuminating flash. He had immediately mapped out his plan. To force Rantaine to disgorge; to render the latter's possible revelations null and void by disappearing; to pass for dead, the best of all ways of disappearing; to that end was to wreck the Durande. This wreck was necessary. Moreover, to go away leaving a good reputation behind him at his departure, which rendered his whole existence a masterpiece. Any one who had seen Clubin amid this shipwreck would have thought he beheld a demon, and a happy one.

He had lived all his life for that moment.

His whole person expressed these words: "At last!" A frightful serenity rendered that obscure brow pallid. His dull eye, whose depths seemed to be impenetrable, became clear and terrible. The inward fires of that soul were reflected there.

The interior tribunal has its electric phenomena, like external nature. An idea is a meteor; at the moment of success, the accumulated meditations which have preceded it open a little, and a spark flashes forth from it; to possess within one's self the talons of evil and to feel one's prey therein is a happiness which has a radiance of its own; an evil thought triumphing illuminates the face; certain combinations which have been successful, certain objects attained, certain fierce felicities cause lugubrious expansions of light to appear and disappear in the eyes of men. It is a joyful storm, it is a menacing dawn. It proceeds from the conscience which has become a shadow and a cloud.

It lighted up the eyes of this man.

This lightning resembled nothing which is to be seen flashing on high or here below.

The repressed rascality which existed in Clubin was breaking forth.

Clubin gazed at the immense obscurity, and could not restrain a burst of low and sinister laughter.

He was free! he was rich!

His unknown had freed itself at last. He had solved his problem.

Clubin had plenty of time before him. The sea was rising, and consequently it upheld the Durande, which it would finally lift. The vessel remained firmly on the reef; there was no danger of her foundering. Moreover, he must allow the long-boat time to get away, to be lost, perhaps. Clubin hoped so.

Erect on the shipwrecked Durande, he folded his arms, enjoying this abandonment in the dark.

Hypocrisy had weighed upon this man for thirty years. He was evil and had coupled himself with probity. He hated probity with the hatred of a man unhappily mated. He had always cherished a rascally intention; since he had attained the age of manhood, he had worn the rigid armor of appearances.

Beneath, he was a monster; he lived in the skin of an honest man with the heart of a bandit. He was a fair-spoken pirate. He was the prisoner of honesty; he was shut up in the mummy-case of innocence, he had worn the wings of an angel, which are so wearisome to a scoundrel. He was overburdened with public esteem. It is hard to pass for an honest man, to think evil and to speak well and to keep all these in equilibrium! He had been the phantom of uprightness, while he was the spectre of crime. This contradiction had been his fate. He had been obliged to assume a plausible countenance, to remain always presentable, to froth in secret, to smile instead of gnashing his teeth. Virtue was for him a stifling thing. He had passed his life in a desire to bite the hand which was laid upon his mouth.

But while wishing to bite it, he had been obliged to kiss it.

To have lied is to have suffered. To be hypocrite is to be patient in the double sense of the word; he calculates a triumph and undergoes a torture. The indefinite premeditating on an evil deed, accompanied by and dosed with austerity; inward infamy seasoned with an excellent reputation, the constant putting of people on the wrong scent, never being one's self, creating an illusion, is fatiguing. To produce candor out of all the black stuff which one grinds over in one's brain, to desire to devour those who venerate you, to be caressing, to hold yourself in, to repress yourself, to be always on the alert, to watch yourself incessantly, to put a fair face on your latent crime, to make your deformity appear beautiful, to fabricate a perfection out of your wickedness, to tickle with the dagger, to put sugar in the poison, to keep a guard over your gestures and over the music of your voice, not to wear your own look, nothing is more difficult, nothing is more torturing. The odiousness of hypocrisy is obscurely felt by the hypocrite. It is nauseating to drink one's own imposture continually. The sweetness communicated by craft to wickedness, disgusts the wicked man, forced to have this mixture constantly in his mouth, and there are moments of upheaval when hypocrisy is on the point of vomiting forth its secret thought. To be obliged to swallow down that saliva again is horrible. Add to this a deep-seated pride. There are strange moments when the hypocrite esteems himself. There is a huge *I* in the scoundrel. The worm crawls in the same manner as the dragon, and has the same manner of rearing to strike. The traitor is only the despot under constraint, who cannot accomplish his will otherwise than by resigning himself to a secondary part. It is littleness capable of enormity. The hypocrite is a dwarfed Titan.

Clubin imagined, in good faith, that he had been ill-used. By what right had not he been born rich? He would have asked no better than to have inherited a hundred thousand livres income from his father and mother. Why had he not inherited it? It was no fault of his. Why had he been deprived of all the enjoyments of life, and forced to toil, that is to say, to deceive, to betray, to destroy? Why, by this means, had they condemned him to this torture of flattering, of crawling, of humoring, of making himself beloved and respected, and of wearing, night and day, another face than his own? To dissimulate is a violence restrained. One hates the person to whom one lies. At last the hour had struck. Clubin was taking his revenge.

On whom? On all, and for everything.

Lethierry had done him nothing but good; a grievance the more; he was avenging himself on Lethierry.

He was taking his revenge on all those before whom he had restrained himself. He was taking his revenge. Whoever had thought well of him was his enemy. He had been the captive of that man.

Clubin was at liberty. His exit was made. He stood outside of men. What they took for his death was his life. It was about to begin. The true Clubin had stripped off the false Clubin. With one blow he had broken every tie. He had kicked Rantaine into space, Lethierry into ruin, human justice into the darkness, opinion into error, all humanity away from himself. He had just eliminated the world.

As for God, that word of three letters troubled him but little.

He had passed for a religious man. Well, what next?

There are caverns in the hypocrite, or to speak more truly, the entire hypocrite is a cavern.

When Clubin found himself alone, his cavern opened. Then came a moment of delight for him, he aired his soul.

He breathed in his crime to the full extent of his lungs.

The very depths of evil were manifested in that visage. Clubin blossomed out. At that moment, Rantaine's look, compared to his, would have seemed like that of a newborn infant.

What a deliverance was that rending away of the mask! His conscience rejoiced at beholding itself hideously naked, and taking without restraint its ignoble bath in evil. The long constraint of human respect ends by inspiring a mad taste for indecency. One comes to a certain lascivious enjoyment in crime. There exists in these frightful moral abysses, so seldom sounded, an atrocious and strangely fascinating revelation, which is the obscenity of crime. The insipidity of false good repute awakens an appetite for shame. Such a person disdains men so much that he would like to be despised by them. He becomes weary of being esteemed. He admires the first jostling of degradation. He gazes enviously at turpitude, which is so much at ease in ignominy. Eyes lowered under obligation often have these stealthy glances. Nothing is nearer Messalina than Marie Alacoque. Look at la Cadière, and the nun of Louviers. Clubin, also, had lived under the veil. Effrontery had always been his ambition. He envied the prostitute and the brazen front of accepted opprobrium; he felt himself more of an outcast than she, and had a disgust for passing as immaculate. He had been the Tantalus of cynicism. At last, on this rock, in this solitude, he could be frank; and he was. What voluptuousness to feel himself sincerely abominable! All the ecstasies possible to hell, Clubin experienced at that moment, the arrearages of dissimulation had been paid over to him; hypocrisy is an advance payment; Satan had reimbursed it. Clubin indulged himself in the intoxication of being shameless, since men had disappeared and there was nothing but heaven left. He said to himself: "I am a scoundrel!" and he was satisfied.

Nothing like it had ever taken place in a human conscience.

The irruption of a hypocrite,—no outbreak of a crater is comparable to that.

He was delighted that no one was there, and yet he would not have been displeased if some one had been there. He would have rejoiced in being monstrous before a witness.

He would have been happy to tell the human race to its face: "You are an idiot."

The absence of men assured his triumph, but diminished it.

He had only himself as a spectator of his glory.

Being in the pillory has a certain charm of its own: all the world knows that you are infamous.

To force the crowd to look at you is to exercise an act of power. A convict standing on a platform in a public square, with the iron collar about his neck, is the despot of all the looks which he forces to turn towards him. There is a pedestal on yonder scaffold. What finer triumph than to be the centre of universal attention? To force the public eye to look is one of the forms of supremacy. To those to whom evil is the ideal, opprobrium in an aureole. From that point they dominate. They are on the top of something. They display themselves in sovereign fashion. A post which the universe beholds is not without some analogy to a throne.

To be exposed is to be contemplated.

An evil reign has, evidently, some of the joys of the pillory. Nero burning Rome, Louis XIV treacherously seizing the Palatinate, the Regent George slowly killing Napoleon, Nicholas assassinating Poland in the face of civilization, must have felt something of the voluptuousness which Clubin now experienced. Something like grandeur is felt by one who is made the subject of immense execration.

To be unmasked is a defeat, but to unmask one's self is a victory. It is like intoxication, it is like insolent and satisfied impudence, it is a flaunting nakedness which insults everything before it. Supreme happiness.

These ideas seem a contradiction in a hypocrite, and are not. All infamy is consistent. Honey is gall. Escobar borders on the Marquis de Sade. Proof: Léotade. The hypocrite, being wickedness complete, has within him the two poles of perversity. He is priest on one side and courtesan on the other. His demoniacal sex is double. The hypocrite is the frightful hermaphrodite of evil. He fructifies himself. He engenders and transforms himself. If you desire him charming, look at him; if you desire him horrible, turn him round.

Clubin had within him that complete gloom of confused ideas. He did not perceive them clearly, but he enjoyed them greatly.

A passage of sparks from hell which one might behold at night,—such was the succession of thoughts in this soul.

Clubin remained in this thoughtful state for some

time; he was gazing upon his cast-off honesty with the look which the serpent bestows upon his old skin.

All the world had believed in that honesty, even he himself, to a small extent.

He burst into a second fit of laughter.

They were going to believe that he was dead, and he was rich. They were going to believe that he was lost, and he was saved. What a fine trick played on universal stupidity!

And in that universal stupidity, Rantaine was included. Clubin thought of Rantaine with boundless disdain. The disdain of the weasel for the tiger. That trick in which Rantaine had failed, had succeeded with him. Rantaine had gone off and Clubin was disappearing triumphant. He had substituted himself for Rantaine in the bed of his evil deed, and it was he, Clubin, who had won the prize.

As for the future, he had no well-settled plan of action. He had his three bank notes in the iron box enclosed in his girdle, that certainly was sufficient for him. He would change his name. There are countries where sixty thousand francs are worth six hundred thousand. It would not be a bad plan to go and live honestly in one of those nooks, on the money recaptured from that thief of a Rantaine. To speculate, to enter into business on a grand scale, to increase his capital, to become in serious earnest a millionaire,—that would not be a bad thing either.

At Costa Rica, for example, there were tons of money to be made, as the great trade in coffee was now beginning to be developed. He would see about it.

It mattered little, however. There was time to think on the subject. For the moment, the difficult part was accomplished. To despoil Rantaine, to disappear with the Durande, that was the great matter. It was accomplished. The rest was simple. No obstacle was henceforth possible. Nothing to fear, nothing could arise. He was about to swim ashore, at night he would reach Plainmont, he would climb the cliff, he would go straight to the haunted house, he would enter it without difficulty by means of his knotted rope, concealed beforehand in a hole in the rock; he would find in the empty house his valise containing dry clothing and food, and there he could wait, he was resigned to that. A week would not elapse without the Spanish smugglers, Blasquito, probably, touching at Plainmont; for a few guineas he would get himself transported, not to Torbay as he said to Blasco, to throw conjecture off the track and put it on the wrong scent, but to Pasages, or Bilbao. Thence he would reach Vera Cruz or New Orleans. However, the time had come to throw himself into the sea, the launch was far away, an hour's swim was nothing to Clubin, only a mile separated him from the land, since he was on the Hanways.

At this point in Clubin's reverie, there came an opening in the fog. The formidable Douvres rocks made their appearance.

VII

The Unexpected Intervenes

CLUBIN, haggard, gazed at them.

It certainly was the terrible isolated reef.

Impossible to mistake that misshapen outline. The two twin Douvres reared themselves aloft, hideously, allowing a view of their defile, like a trap, between them. One would have pronounced it the cut-throat of the ocean.

They were quite close at hand. The fog had concealed them, like an accomplice.

Clubin had lost his way in the fog. In spite of all his attention, that had happened to him which happened to two other great navigators: to Gonzalez, who discovered Cape Blanco, and to Fernandez, who discovered Cape Verde. The fog had led him astray. It had appeared to him excellent for the execution of his project, but it had its perils. Clubin had veered to the west, and had erred. The Guernsey passenger, by thinking that he recognized the Hanways, had decided the final turn of the helm. Clubin had believed that he was casting himself on the Hanways.

The Durande, broken open by one of the rocks of the reef, was separated from the two Douvres only by a few cable lengths.

Two hundred fathoms further on was a massive cube of granite. On the steep faces of this rock, several furrows and projections for climbing were visible. The rectilinear corners of these rough walls, with their right angles, suggested the presence of a plateau at the top.

It was "the Man."

The rock of "the Man" rose still higher than the Douvres rocks. Its platform dominated their double and inaccessible point. This platform, while crumbling on the edges, had an entablature, and an indescribable, sculptural regularity. Nothing more desolate and deadly could be imagined. The waves from the open sea lapped tranquilly against the square faces of this enormous black mass, a sort of pedestal for the immense spectres of the sea and of the night.

This aggregate of things was quiet. Hardly a breath in the air, hardly a ripple on the waves. One divined beneath that mute surface of water the vast hidden life of the depths.

Clubin had often seen the Douvres reef from a distance.

He satisfied himself that, in very truth, he was there.

He could not doubt it.

An abrupt and hideous change. The Douvres instead of the Hanways. Instead of one mile, five leagues of sea. Five leagues of sea! the impossible!

The Douvres rock, for the solitary, shipwrecked man, is the presence, visible and palpable, of the last moment. A prohibition of all hope of reaching land.

Clubin shuddered. He had placed himself in the jaws of the shadow. No other refuge than "the Man" rock. It was probable that the tempest would come up during the night, and that the long-boat of the Durande would founder, as it was overloaded. No news of the shipwrecked man would reach the land. No one would even know that Clubin had been left on the Douvres reef. No other prospect than death from cold and hunger. His seventy-five thousand francs would not procure him a mouthful of bread. All that he had built up had ended in this trap. He was the laborious architect of his own catastrophe. No resource, no safety possible. Triumph had turned into a precipice. Instead of deliverance, a prison. Instead of a long and prosperous future, the death agony. In the twinkling of an eye, quick as a flash of lightning, his whole structure had crumbled. The paradise dreamed of by this demon had resumed its true form, the sepulchre.

In the meantime, the wind had risen. The fog, shaken, riddled with holes, rent, was disappearing towards the horizon in huge, shapeless masses. The whole sea reappeared.

The cattle, more and more invaded by the water, continued to bellow in the hold.

Night was approaching; probably, the tempest.

The Durande, gradually set afloat again by the rising tide, swung from right to left, then from left to right, and began to turn upon the reef as upon a pivot.

The moment could be foreseen when a billow would tear her off, and roll her to rack and ruin.

There was less obscurity than at the moment of the shipwreck. Although the day was more advanced, one could see more clearly. The fog, in departing, had carried away a portion of the darkness. The west was clear of all clouds. Twilight has a great, white sky. This vast reflection lighted the sea.

The Durande had run aground on an inclined plane from the stern to the bow. Clubin mounted on the rear of the vessel, which was almost out of water. He fixed his eye intently on the horizon.

The peculiarity of hypocrisy is to be strong in hope. The hypocrite is the man who waits. Hypocrisy is nothing else than a horrible hopefulness, and the foundation of that lie is made of that virtue transformed into a vice.

Strange to say, there is confidence in hypocrisy. The hypocrite trusts himself to some indefinable power in the unknown which permits evil.

Clubin gazed at the expanse.

The situation was desperate; this sinister soul did not despair.

He said to himself that, after this long fog, the vessels which had remained heaved to or at anchor would resume their course, and that perhaps one would pass on the horizon.

And, in fact, a sail did make its appearance.

It was coming from the east and going to the west.

As it approached, the details of the vessel became outlined. It had but one mast and was sloop-rigged. The bowsprit was almost horizontal. It was a coaster.

In less than half an hour it would pass quite close to the Douvres rock. Clubin said to himself: "I am saved."

At a moment like the one in which he found himself, one thinks first of life alone.

This coaster was, perhaps, a stranger. Who knows whether it was not one of the smuggling vessels on its way to Plainmont? Who knows whether it was not Blasquito himself? In that case, not only was life safe, but fortune also; and the encounter of the Douvres reef, by hastening the conclusion, by suppressing the waiting in the haunted house, by winding up the adventure on the open sea, would have been a happy incident.

All the certainty of success frantically re-entered this sombre mind. It is strange with what facility scoundrels believe that success is due them.

There was but one thing to be done. The Durande, entangled in the rocks, mingled her outline with theirs, was confounded with their indentations, among which she formed only one more feature, and would not suffice, in the little daylight remaining, to attract the attention of the vessel now about to pass.

But a human figure, standing out blackly against the whiteness of twilight, erect on "the Man" rock, and making signals of distress, would be perceived without a doubt. They would send a boat to rescue the shipwrecked man.

"The Man" rock was only two hundred fathoms away. It was a simple matter to swim to it, to climb it was easy.

There was not a minute to be lost.

As the bow of the Durande rested on the rock, it was

from the top of the stern, and from the very point where Clubin stood, that it was necessary to plunge for the swim.

He began by making a sounding, and he found that under the stern there was a great depth of water. The microscopic shells of foraminiferæ and polycystines which the tallow on the sounding lead brought up were unbroken, which indicated that there existed very hollow rock caverns where the water was always tranquil, however great the surface agitation.

He undressed, leaving his garments on the bridge. He would find clothes on the coaster.

He retained only the leather girdle.

When he was naked, he raised his hand to his belt, rebuckled it, felt of the iron box within it, rapidly studied with his glance the direction which he must follow among the breakers and the waves, in order to reach "the Man" rock, then, throwing himself head foremost, he made his plunge.

As he dived from a height, he plunged deep. He sank very far into the water, touched the bottom, skirted the submarine rocks for a moment, then struck out for the surface again.

At that moment, he felt himself seized by the foot.

BOOK SEVENTH
THE IMPRUDENCE OF ASKING QUESTIONS OF A BOOK

I
The Pearl at the Bottom of the Precipice

A FEW MINUTES after his brief colloquy with Sieur Landoys, Gilliatt was at Saint-Sampson.

Gilliatt was uneasy and anxious. What had happened?

There was a noise like a frightened beehive in Saint-Sampson. Everybody was at his door. The women were indulging in exclamations. There were people who seemed to be relating something, and gesticulating; a group had formed around them. The words: "What a misfortune!" could be heard. Many faces were smiling.

Gilliatt interrogated no one. It was not his nature to put questions. Moreover, he was too much agitated to talk to indifferent persons. He distrusted rumors, he preferred to learn all the facts at once; he went straight to les Bravées.

His uneasiness was such that he was not afraid even to enter that house. Besides, the door of the ground-floor room stood wide open on the quay. There was a swarm of men and women on the threshold. Everybody was going in, he went in also.

On entering he found Sieur Landoys leaning against the jamb of the door, and the latter said to him in a low voice,—

"You doubtless know what has happened?"

"No."

"I did not wish to shout it to you in the road. It makes one seem like a bird of ill-omen."

"What is it?"

"The Durande is lost."

There was a throng in the room.

The groups were conversing in low tones, as though in a sick chamber.

Those present, the neighbors, curious passers-by, the first comers, kept in a cluster near the door, in a sort of fear, and left unoccupied the end of the room where Mess Lethierry was to be seen standing beside Déruchette, who was sitting and in tears.

He was leaning his back against the wall at the end of the room. His sailor's cap fell over his brows. A lock of gray hair hung down upon his cheek. He said nothing. His arms were motionless; he seemed hardly to breathe. He had the look of a lifeless thing placed against the wall.

One felt, on looking at him, that he was a man within whom life had just fallen into ruins. The Durande being gone, there was no further reason for his existence. He had a soul on the sea, that soul had just gone down. What was he to do now? To rise every morning and go to bed every evening. Never more to await the Durande, never more to see her depart, never more to see her return. What is the remnant of an existence without an object? To eat and drink, and what then?

This man had crowned all his works with a masterpiece, and all his self-devotion by a progress. The progress was abolished, the masterpiece was dead. What was the use of living through a few more empty years? There was nothing to do henceforth. At that age one does not begin again; besides, he was ruined. Poor old man!

Déruchette, seated weeping on a chair beside him, held in both her hands one of Mess Lethierry's fists. Her hands were clasped, his fists clenched. Therein lay the shade of difference between the two states of despondency. In clasped hands, there is something which still hopes; in the clenched fist, nothing.

Mess Lethierry abandoned his arm to her and let her do what she would. He was passive. Henceforth he had only that measure of life which one can have after the stroke of a thunderbolt.

There are certain plunges to the bottom of the abyss which withdraw you from among the living. The people who go and come in your chamber are confused and indistinct; they touch you without reaching you. You are unapproachable to them and they are inaccessible to you. Happiness and despair are not the same respirable elements; when one is in despair, one looks on at the life of others from a distance, one almost ignores their presence; one loses the consciousness of one's own existence; it is in vain that one is flesh and blood; one no longer feels real; one becomes no longer anything but a dream to one's self.

Mess Lethierry's look indicated that condition.

The groups whispered together. They exchanged what they knew. This was the news:—

The Durande had been lost the day before on the Douvres, in the fog, about one hour before sunset. With the exception of the captain, who had not consented to leave the vessel, all the people had escaped in the long-boat. A squall from the southwest, which had followed the fog, had come near wrecking them a second time, and had driven them out to sea beyond Guernsey. During the night they had had the good fortune to encounter the *Cashmere*, which had picked them up and brought them to Guernsey. It was all the fault of the helmsman, Tangrouille, who was in prison. Clubin had behaved nobly.

The pilots, who were numerous in the group, uttered the words: "the Douvres reef," in a peculiar manner. "A poor tavern!" said one of them.

On the table were seen a compass and a bundle of registers and note books; they were, no doubt, the compass of the Durande, and the vessel's papers intrusted by Clubin to Imbrancam and Tangrouille at the moment of the long-boat's departure; a magnificent abnegation on the part of that man, to save even the records at the moment when he was allowing himself to be lost; a small detail full of grandeur, sublime self-forgetfulness.

Admiration for Clubin was unanimous, and unanimous also was the belief that he had been saved after all. The coaster *Shealtiel* had arrived a few hours after the *Cashmere;* it was this coaster which brought the latest information, she had just passed twenty-four hours in the same waters as the Durande. She had lain to during the fog and had tacked during the squall. The skipper of the *Shealtiel* was among those present.

At the moment when Gilliatt entered, this skipper had just finished his report to Mess Lethierry. This report was a correct one. Towards morning, the storm having abated, and the wind become mild, the skipper of the *Shealtiel* had heard bellowing on the open sea. This sound of the meadows, in the midst of the waves, had surprised him; he had directed his course towards it. He had perceived the Durande on the Douvres rocks. The calm had allowed him to approach. He had hailed the wreck. The bellowing of the cattle who were drowning in the hold had been the sole response. The skipper was certain that there was no one on board the Durande. The wreck still held together; and, violent as had been the squall, Clubin could have passed the night there. He was not a man to let go his hold easily. He was not there, hence he had been saved. Many sloops and luggers from Granville and Saint-Malo, when coming out from the fog on the preceding evening, must have passed quite close to the Douvres reef. One of them had evidently picked up Captain Clubin. It must be remembered that the long-boat of the Durande had been full when it quitted the shipwrecked vessel, that it was about to run many risks, that one man more would have overloaded her and might have caused her to founder, and it was this chiefly which had decided Clubin to remain on the wreck; but his duty once fulfilled and a rescuing vessel having presented itself, Clubin had undoubtedly made no scruples about profiting by it. One may be a hero, but one is not a fool. A suicide would have been all the more absurd since Clubin was not to blame. The culprit was Tangrouille, and not Clubin. All this was conclusive; the skipper of the *Shealtiel* was evidently right, and every one expected to see Clubin make his appearance again at any moment. They planned to carry him about in triumph.

Two certainties followed from this recital of the skipper, that Clubin had been saved, and the Durande lost.

As far as the Durande was concerned, one must make up one's mind to it, the catastrophe was irremediable. The skipper of the *Shealtiel* had been present at the last scene in the shipwreck. The extremely pointed rock on which the Durande was, in a manner, nailed had held good all night, and had resisted the shock of the tempest as though it wished to keep the wreck for itself; but in the morning, at the moment when the *Shealtiel,* having ascertained that there was no one on board to save, was on the point of leaving the Durande, there had come one of those massive waves which are like the final bursts of a tempest's wrath. This billow had lifted the Durande furiously, had torn her from the reef, and had hurled her between the two Douvres rocks with the swiftness and directness of an arrow. A "diabolical" crash was heard, the skipper said. The Durande, borne to a certain height by the surges, had been plunged in between the rocks up to her midship frame. She had been fastened afresh, but more solidly than on the submarine reef. There she was destined to remain, deplorably suspended, surrendered to all the fury of the wind and of the sea.

The Durande, according to the statements of the crew of the *Shealtiel,* was already three quarters broken up. She would evidently have sunk during the night, had not the reef sustained her and held her back. The skipper of the *Shealtiel* had studied the wreck with his glass. He gave the details of the disaster with the precision of a mariner; the starboard quarter was stove in, the masts were snapped off, the canvas blown out of the bolt ropes, the shrouds almost cut through, the skylights of the cabin crushed by the fall of a yard, the uprights broken off level with the gunwale, from abreast of the main mast to the taffrails, the dome of the steward's room stove in, the chocks of the long-boat carried away, the round house dismounted, the rudder hinges broken, the tiller-ropes detached, the sheathing torn off, the bitts carried away, the cross beams destroyed, the rail gone, the stern post smashed. All this was the frenzied devastation of the tempest. Of the hoisting crane bolted to the foremast there was nothing left, a complete cleaning-out, gone all to pieces, with its hoisting tackle, its blocks and falls, its snatch block, and its chains. The Durande was dismembered; the sea was now about to tear her to pieces. In a few days, nothing would be left of her.

Nevertheless, the engine, a remarkable fact, and one which proved its excellence, had hardly been affected amid these ravages. The skipper of the *Shealtiel* thought he could affirm that the "crank" had suffered no serious injury. The masts of the vessel had yielded, but the smoke stack of the engine had resisted. The iron guards of the captain's bridge were merely twisted. The paddle-boxes had suffered, the framework had been crushed, but the wheels did not seem to lack a single float. The engine was uninjured. This was the conviction of the skipper of the *Shealtiel*. The engineer, Imbrancam, who had joined the groups, shared this conviction. This Negro, more intelligent than many a white man, was proud of the engine. He raised his arms, with the ten fingers of his black hands outspread, and said to the silent Lethierry: "Master, the machinery still lives."

As Clubin's safety seemed to be assured, and the hull of the Durande having been sacrificed, the engine became the topic of conversation among the groups. They took an interest in it as in a person. They marvelled at its good behavior.

"That's a solid creature!" said a French sailor.

"It's a good thing!" exclaimed a Guernsey fisherman.

"It must have been clever," interposed the captain of the *Shealtiel*, "to get out of that scrape with only two or three scratches."

Little by little this engine became their sole preoccupation. Opinions became warm for and against it. It had friends and enemies. More than one, who had a good old sailing coaster, and who hoped to get back the Durande's customers, was not sorry to see the Douvres reef execute justice on the new invention. The whispering became louder. They discussed almost noisily, still, it was somewhat restrained, and at intervals there came a sudden lowering of voices, under the oppression of Lethierry's sepulchral silence.

The result of the colloquies proceeding in all quarters was as follows:—

The engine was the essential point. It was possible to rebuild the vessel, but not the machinery. To construct another like it, money would be lacking; still more serious, the builders would be lacking. It was called to mind that the builder of the engine was dead. It had cost forty thousand francs. No one in the future would risk such a sum against such a catastrophe; the more so as it had now been proved that steamers could be lost as well as sailing vessels; the present accident to the Durande had destroyed the prestige of all her past success. Nevertheless, it was deplorable to reflect that at that very hour this machinery was still entire and in good condition, and that, in five or six days, it would be dashed in pieces like the vessel. As long as it existed there was, so to speak, no shipwreck. The loss of the engine was alone irremediable. To save the engine would be to repair the disaster.

It was easy to say, save the engine. But who would undertake it? Was it possible?

To plan and to execute are two different things, and the proof is, that it is easy to dream but difficult to perform. Now, if there ever had been a mad and impracticable dream, it was this; to save the engine wrecked on the Douvres. To send a vessel and crew to work on those rocks would be absurd; it was not to be thought of. It was the season of heavy seas; at the first gale, the anchor chains would be sawn asunder by the submarine crests of the rocks, and the vessel would be dashed upon the reef. It would be sending a second shipwreck to the relief of the first. In the hollow of the upper plateau, where the legendary shipwrecked man who had perished of hunger had taken refuge, there was barely room for one man. In order, therefore, to save this engine, it would be necessary for one man to go to the Douvres rock and to go there alone, alone in that sea, alone in that desert, alone five leagues from the shore, alone in that horror, alone for whole weeks together, alone in the presence of the foreseen and the unforeseen; without fresh supplies in the anguish of destitution, without succor in the hour of distress, with no other trace of humanity than that of the ancient shipwrecked wight who had perished there of misery, with no other companionship than that of death. And, besides, how would he set about saving the engine? He must not only be a sailor but a machinist. And amid what difficulties! The man who should attempt that would be more than a hero. He would be a madman. For, in certain vast enterprises when the superhuman seems necessary, bravery is little less than madness. And in fact, after all, would it not be unreasonable to sacrifice one's self for old iron? No. No one would go to the Douvres rocks. The machinery must be given up as well as the rest. The desired deliverer would not present himself. Where was such a man to be found?

This, a little differently expressed, constituted the foundation of all the remarks murmured in that crowd.

The skipper of the *Shealtiel,* who was an old pilot, summed up the thought of all in this exclamation, uttered in a loud voice,—

"No! It is all over. The man who would go there and bring back that machinery does not exist."

"If I do not go," said Imbrancam, "it is because it cannot be done."

The skipper of the *Shealtiel* shook his left hand with that abruptness which expresses the conviction that a thing is impossible, and resumed,—

"If he existed—"

Déruchette turned her head.

"I would marry him," said she.

A silence ensued.

A very pale man stepped out from the midst of the groups, and said,—

"You would marry him, Miss Déruchette?"

It was Gilliatt.

Meanwhile, all eyes had been raised. Mess Lethierry had just straightened himself up erect. A strange light gleamed beneath his brows.

With his fist he grasped his sailor's cap and flung it to the floor, then he gazed solemnly before him, without seeing any of the persons present, and said,—

"Déruchette shall marry him. I give my word of honor on it, before the good God."

II
Much Astonishment on the Western Coast

THE following night the moon rose at ten o'clock. Nevertheless, however good the appearance of the night, the wind, and the sea, no fisherman dreamed of setting out either from Hogue la Pierre, or Bourdeaux, or from Houmet Benet, or from le Platon, or from Port-Grat, or from Vason Bay, or from Perrelle Bay, or from Pezeris, or from le Tielles, or from the Bay of les Saints, or from Petit Bô, or from any port or small harbor of Guernsey. And this was quite simple. The cocks had crowed at midday.

When the cock crows at an unusual hour, the catch of fish fails.

Nevertheless, that evening at nightfall, a fisherman who was returning to Omptolle had a surprise. Off Houmet-Paradis, beyond the two Brayes and the two Grunes, with the beacon of the Plattes-Fougères, in the form of a reversed funnel, on the right, and the beacon of Saint-Sampson, which represents the figure of a man, on the left, he thought that he perceived a third beacon. What beacon was this? When had it been placed on that point? What shoals did it indicate? The beacon immediately answered these questions, it moved; it was a mast. The fisherman's astonishment did not diminish. A beacon suggested a question; a mast was much more suggestive. No fishing was possible. Some one was going out when everybody else was coming in. Who? Why?

Ten minutes later the mast, advancing slowly, came

within a short distance from the fisherman of Omptolle. He could not recognize the vessel. He heard the sound of rowing. There was the noise of two oars. Hence, it was probably a man alone. The wind was from the north; this man was evidently rowing to catch the wind beyond Point Fontenelle. There, he would, probably, hoist his sail. Hence he intended to double Ancresse and Mont Crevel. What was the meaning of this?

The mast passed by, the fisherman ran into harbor.

That same night, chance observers on the west coast of Guernsey, scattered and isolated, made remarks at different hours and at various points.

Just as the Omptolle fisherman had finished mooring his boat, a carter of seaweed half a mile farther on, as he whipped up his horses in the deserted road of Clôtures, near the Cromlech, in the vicinity of Martello Towers six and seven, saw a sail being hoisted on the water, far away on the horizon, in a spot which was little frequented because it was necessary to know it well, towards la Roque-Norde and la Sablonneuse. He paid but little attention to it, however, being intent on his cart and not on boats.

Half an hour, perhaps, had elapsed after the carter perceived this sail, when a plasterer, returning from his work in the town and passing round the Pelée pool, suddenly found himself almost opposite a boat very audaciously making its way among the rocks of the Quenon, the Rousse de Mer, and the Gripe de Rousse. The night was black, but the sea was light, an effect which is frequently produced, and one can then distinguish vessels going and coming on the water. There was no other boat on the sea, except this one.

A little lower down and a little later, a lobster-man, arranging his pots on the sand which separates Port-Soif (Port Thirst) from Port-Enfer (Port Hell), could not understand the manœuvres of a boat gliding between the Boue-Corneille and the Moulrette. A man must be a good pilot, and in great haste to reach his destination, to risk himself there.

As eight o'clock was sounding at the Catel, the innkeeper of Cobo Bay observed, with some bewilderment, a sail beyond the Boue du Jardin and the Grunettes, very near la Suzanne and the Grunes de l'Ouest.

Not far from Cobo Bay, on the solitary point of Houmet on the Vason Bay, two lovers were parting and holding each other back; at the moment when the girl was saying to the youth: "If I go away, 'tis not because I do not like to be with you, but because I have my chores to attend to," their attention was diverted from their parting kiss by a rather large boat which passed by very near them, and directed its course towards the Messellettes.

Monsieur le Peyre des Norgiots, who lived at Cotillon-Pipet, was busy about nine o'clock in the evening examining a hole made by marauders in the hedge of his garden, la Jennerotte; as he observed the damage, he could not help noticing a boat rashly doubling Crocq-Point at that hour of the night.

This was a very hazardous course on the day after a tempest, and with the agitation still remaining in the sea. One was imprudent to select it, unless one knew the channels by heart.

At half past nine, at l'Équerrier, a trawler bringing in his net halted for some time to watch something which must be a boat, between Colombelle and la Souffleresse. This boat was exposing itself greatly. There are sudden and very dangerous gusts of wind there. The "Souffleresse" or Blower rock is so named because it blows unexpectedly on vessels.

At the moment when the moon rose, the tide was full and the sea being spread out in the little strait of Lihou, the solitary keeper of the island of Lihou was greatly startled; he saw a long, black object pass between him and the moon. That lofty, black, narrow form resembled a winding-sheet, erect and walking.; It glided slowly along the top of the sort of wall formed by the piles of rocks. The guardian of Lihou thought he recognized the Black Lady.

The White Lady inhabits the Tau de Pez d'Amont, the Gray Lady inhabits the Tau de Pez d'Aval, the Red Lady inhabits the Silleuse to the north of the Banc-Marquis, and the Black Lady inhabits the Grand-Étacré to the west of Li-Houmet. At night, by moonlight, these ladies come out, and sometimes meet.

This black form might, possibly, be a sail. The long bars of rocks over which it seemed to be walking might, in reality, conceal the hull of a boat sailing behind them, and allow the sail only to be seen. But the guardian asked himself what boat would dare to risk itself at that hour between Lihou and la Pécheresse, and the Angullières and Lérée Point. And with what object? It appeared more probable to him that it was the Black Lady.

Just as the moon had passed the bell tower of Saint-Pierre du Bois, the guard of the Château Rocquaine, as he raised the half of the drawbridge, distinguished at the mouth of the bay, further on than la Haute-Carrée, nearer than la Sambule, a sailing vessel which seemed to be going from north to south.

On this southern coast of Guernsey, there exists, behind Plainmont, at the bottom of a bay, all composed of precipices and rocks, rising perpendicularly from the waves, a singular port which a Frenchman who had sojourned in the island ever since 1855, the same, possibly, as he who writes these lines, had baptized as the "Port on the Fourth Story," a name generally adopted at the present day. This port, which was then called la Moie, is a rock plateau, half natural, half hewn out, elevated about forty feet above the level of the water, and communicating with the waves by two great, parallel beams on an inclined plane. Boats, hoisted by sheer strength of arm by chains and pulleys, mount from the sea and descend again along these beams which are like two rails. There is a staircase for men. This port was greatly frequented at that time by smugglers. Not being very practicable, it was convenient for them.

Towards eleven o'clock, some smugglers, perhaps the very ones on whom Clubin had reckoned, were standing with their bales upon the summit of this platform of la Moie. He who smuggles is on the lookout; they were on the alert. They were astonished by a sail which suddenly appeared beyond the black silhouette of Cape Plainmont. The moon was shining. These smugglers watched that sail, fearing that it was some coastguard boat on its way to station itself in ambush behind the great Hanway.

But the sail passed the Hanways, left the Boue-Blondel behind it on the northwest, and then disappeared in the open sea, amid the pale shadows of the mists on the horizon.

"Where the devil can that boat be going?" said the smugglers to each other.

That same evening, a little after sunset, some one was heard to knock at the door of the Bû de la Rue. It was a young man dressed in brown with yellow stockings, which indicated a junior clerk of the parish. The Bû de la Rue was closed, door and shutters. An old woman, a fisher of the fruits of the sea, who was prowling about the bank with a lantern, hailed the youth, and these words were exchanged by the fishwife and the junior clerk, in front of the Bû de la Rue.

"What do you want, young man?"

"The man who lives here."

"He's not here."

"Where is he?"

"I don't know."

"Will he be here to-morrow?"

"I don't know."

"Has he gone away?"

"I don't know."

"You see, my good woman, the new rector of the parish, the Reverend Ebenezer Caudray, would like to call on him."

"I don't know."

"The reverend gentleman has sent me to inquire whether the man of the Bû de la Rue will be at home to-morrow?"

"I don't know."

III
Tempt Not the Bible

DURING the next twenty-four hours, Mess Lethierry did not sleep, did not eat, did not drink, kissed Déruchette's brow, inquired after Clubin, of whom no news had yet been received, signed a declaration to the effect that he did not intend to present any complaint, and caused Tangrouille to be set at liberty.

He remained the whole of the following day half leaning on the table of the office of the Durande, neither standing nor seated, replying gently when any one spoke to him. Moreover, curiosity having been gratified, solitude reigned at les Bravées. There is much inquisitiveness mingled with eagerness to express sympathy. The door was closed again; Lethierry was left alone with Déruchette. The flash which had gleamed in Lethierry's eyes had died out; the melancholy gaze which he had worn at the beginning of the catastrophe, had returned to him.

Déruchette, who was troubled, had, on the advice of Grâce and Douce, and without saying anything, placed on the table beside him a pair of stockings which he had been engaged in knitting when the news arrived.

He smiled bitterly and said,—

"So they think me a fool."

After a quarter of an hour of silence, he added,—

"These hobbies are good when one is happy."

Déruchette had put away the stockings and taken advantage of the occasion also to remove the compass and the ship's papers, which occupied too much of Mess Lethierry's attention.

In the afternoon, a little before tea time, the door opened and two men entered, clad in black, one old, the other young.

Both these men had a grave air, but their gravity was different; the old man had what may be called state gravity, the young man had natural gravity. Habit gives one; thought, the other.

They were, as their garments indicated, two ecclesiastics, both belonging to the established church.

What would have struck the observer at first sight about the young man was the gravity, which was profound, in his glance, and which evidently resulted from his mind and not from his person. Gravity admits of passion and exalts it by purifying it, but this young man was, first of all, handsome. Although a priest, he was less than twenty-five years old; he seemed to be eighteen. He presented this harmony and also this contrast; a soul which seemed made for exalted passion and a body for love. He was fair, rosy, fresh, very dainty and very graceful in his severe costume, with cheeks like those of a young girl, and delicate hands; he had a lively and natural though subdued air. Everything about him was charm, elegance, and almost voluptuousness. The beauty of his glance corrected this excess of grace. His sincere smile, which displayed the delicate teeth of a child, was pensive and devotional. He had the gracefulness of a page, and the dignity of a bishop.

Beneath his thick blond hair, so golden that it appeared coquettish, his brow was lofty, honest, and well formed. A slight wrinkle with a double curve between his eyebrows, awoke in a confused way the idea of the bird of thought soaring with outspread wings in the centre of this forehead.

One felt, on seeing him, that he was one of those kindly, pure, and innocent beings, whose progress is in inverse sense with that of vulgar humanity, whom illusion renders wise, and of whom experience makes enthusiasts.

His transparent youth allowed his inward maturity to be seen. Compared with the gray-haired ecclesiastic who accompanied him, at the first glance he seemed to be the son, at the second glance he seemed to be the father.

This latter was no other than Doctor Jaquemin Hérode.

Doctor Jacquemin Hérode belonged to the High Church, which is very nearly the same as a papacy without a pope. Anglicanism was distracted at about that epoch by tendencies which have since been affirmed and condensed in Puseyism. Doctor Jaquemin Hérode was of that shade of Anglicanism which is almost a variety of Romanism. He was tall, correct, narrow, and superior. His inner sight hardly pierced to the outside. In place of the spirit, he had the letter. Moreover, he was haughty. His presence was imposing. He seemed less like a "Reverend" than a monsignor. His coat was cut a little like a cassock. His true place would have been Rome. He was a born prelate of the ante-chamber. He seemed to have been created expressly to ornament a pope, and to walk behind the gestatory chair with all the pontifical court, *in abito paonazzo*. . . . The accident of having been born an Englishman, and a theological education turned more towards the Old Testament than the New, had caused him to miss that great destiny. All his splendors were summed up in this: to be Rector of Saint-Pierre-Port, Dean of the Island of Guernsey and Surrogate of the Bishop of Winchester. This was not without glory.

This glory did not prevent Jaquemin Hérode from being a very good sort of man, take him all in all.

As a theologian, he held a good place in the esteem of good judges, and he almost constituted an authority in the Court of Arches, that Sorbonne of England.

He had an air of learning, a knowing and peculiar way of winking his eyes, hairy nostrils, prominent teeth, a thin upper and a thick lower lip, many diplomas, a great stipend, baronets for friends, the confidence of his bishop, and a Bible always in his pocket.

Mess Lethierry was so completely absorbed, that all the effect produced by the entrance of the two priests was an imperceptible frown.

Mr. Jaquemin Hérode advanced, bowed, referred to his recent promotion in a few soberly lofty words, and said that he was come, in accordance with custom, "to introduce" to the notable men, and to Mess Lethierry in particular, his successor in the parish, the new rector of Saint-Sampson, the Reverend Joë Ebenezer Caudray, henceforth Mess Lethierry's pastor.

Déruchette rose.

The young priest, who was the Reverend Ebenezer, bowed.

Mess Lethierry stared at M. Ebenezer Caudray and muttered between his teeth: "a bad sailor."

Grâce brought forward chairs. The two reverend gentlemen seated themselves near the table.

Doctor Hérode began a speech. He had heard that an event had occurred. The Durande had been shipwrecked. As a pastor, he was come to offer his consolation and advice. This shipwreck was unfortunate, but also fortunate. Let us examine ourselves; were we not puffed up with prosperity? The waters of felicity are dangerous, we must not take misfortunes in bad part. The ways of the Lord are unknown to us. Mess Lethierry was ruined. Well? to be rich is a danger. One has false friends. Poverty removes them. One remains alone. *Solus eris.* The Durande brought in, it was said, a thousand pounds sterling a year. That is too much for the wise man. Let us fly temptation, let us disdain gold. Let us accept neglect and ruin with gratitude. Isolation is full of fruits. One obtains grace from the Lord. It was in this solitude that Ajah found the hot springs while leading the asses of his father Zibeon. Let us not rebel against the inscrutable decrees of Providence. Job, that holy man, after his misery had increased in riches. Who knows whether the loss of the Durande would not have its compensations, even temporal? For instance, he, Jaquemin Hérode, had invested capital in a very fine project now in course of execution in Sheffield; if Mess Lethierry wished to embark in this affair the funds which remained to him, he would repair his fortune; it was a great contract of arms for the tzar, who was preparing to subdue Poland. One could make three hundred per cent.

The word tzar appeared to arouse Lethierry. He interrupted Doctor Hérode.

"I'll have nothing to do with the tzar."

The Reverend Hérode replied,—"Mess Lethierry, princes are permitted of God. It is written: 'Render unto Cæsar the things that are Cæsar's.' The tzar is Cæsar."

Lethierry, who had half fallen back into his dream, muttered,—"Who is Cæsar? I don't know him."

The Reverend Jaquemin Hérode resumed his exhortation. He did not insist upon Sheffield. To wish to have nothing to do with Cæsar is to be a republican. The reverend gentleman comprehended that one might be a republican. In that case, let Mess Lethierry turn his attention towards a republic. Mess Lethierry could retrieve his fortune in the United States still better than in England. If he wished to increase what remained to him tenfold, he had only to take shares in a great company for developing plantations in Texas, which employed more than twenty thousand Negroes.

"I'll have nothing to do with slavery," said Lethierry.

"Slavery," replied the Reverend Hérode, "is a sacred institution. It is written: 'If the master smite his slave, he shall not be punished, for he is his money.' "

Grâce and Douce who were in the doorway, were drinking in the words of the reverend rector with a sort of ecstasy.

The reverend gentleman continued: he was, take him all in all, as we have already said, a good man; and whatever might have been his disagreements as to caste, or persons, with Mess Lethierry, he had come very sincerely, to bring him all the spiritual, and even temporal aid, which he, Doctor Jaquemin Hérode, had at his command.

If Mess Lethierry was ruined to such an extent that he could not co-operate advantageously with any Russian or American speculation, why did not he enter the government service, where there were salaried positions? There are fine places, and the reverend gentleman was ready to recommend Mess Lethierry to them. The office of deputy-judge was at that moment vacant in Jersey. Mess Lethierry was esteemed and beloved, and the Reverend Hérode, Dean of Guernsey and surrogate of the Bishop, would do his utmost to obtain for Mess Lethierry the place of député-vicomte of Jersey. The député-vicomte is an officer of importance; he assists as representative of Her Majesty, at the courts of assize, at the debates of the sessions-house, and at the execution of the decrees of justice.

Lethierry fixed his eyes on Doctor Hérode.

"I don't like hanging," said he.

Doctor Hérode, who, up to that point had pronounced all his words with the same intonation, was now seized with a fit of severity, and used a new inflection.

"Mess Lethierry, the death penalty is divinely ordained. God has given the sword in charge to man. It is written: 'An eye for an eye, a tooth for a tooth.' "

The Reverend Ebenezer drew his chair imperceptibly nearer to the chair of the Reverend Jaquemin, and said to him in a manner to be heard by him alone,—

"What this man says is dictated to him."

"By whom? By what?" demanded the Reverend Jaquemin Hérode.

Ebenezer replied in a very low tone,—

"By his conscience."

The Reverend Hérode fumbled in his pocket, pulled out a thick 18mo bound with clasps, laid it on the table and said aloud,—

"Conscience is here."

The book was a Bible.

Then Doctor Hérode became milder. His desire was to be useful to Mess Lethierry, whom he held in high esteem. It was his right and duty as pastor to give counsel, but Mess Lethierry was free.

Mess Lethierry, again taken possession of by his absorption and his grief, no longer listened. Déruchette seated near him and also pensive, did not raise her eyes, and mingled with that conversation the quantity of embarrassment which is afforded by a silent presence. A witness who says nothing is a sort of indefinable weight. However, Doctor Hérode did not seem conscious of it.

As Lethierry made no further replies, Doctor Hérode allowed himself full swing. Counsel comes from man, and inspiration from God. In counsel, said the priest, there is inspiration. It is good to accept counsels, and bad to reject them. Sochoh was seized by eleven devils for having disdained the admonitions of Nathaniel. Tiburianus was struck with leprosy because he thrust the apostle Andrew from his house. Barjesus, magician as he was, became blind for laughing at the words of St. Paul: Elxaï and his sisters, Martha and Marthena, are in hell at the present hour for having despised the warnings of Valencianus, who proved to them as clearly as the day, that their Jesus Christ, thirty-eight leagues in height, was a demon. Oolibama, who is also called Judith, obeyed counsel. Reuben and Peniel hearkened to counsel from on high; their names alone suffice to indicate this. Reuben signifies "son of the vision," and Peniel signifies "the face of God."

Mess Lethierry struck his fist upon the table.

"Parbleu!" he cried, "it was my own fault."

"What do you mean?" asked the Reverend Jaquemin Hérode.

"I say that it was my fault."

"What was your fault?"

"Because I allowed the Durande to return on Friday."

M. Jaquemin Hérode murmured in the ear of M. Ebenezer Caudray: "This man is superstitious."

He continued, raising his voice, and in the tone of instruction,—"Mess Lethierry, it is puerile to believe in Friday. One must not lend faith to fables. Friday is a day like any other. It is frequently a most auspicious date. Melendez founded the city of Saint Augustine on a Friday; it was on a Friday that Henry VII gave his commission to John Cabot; the pilgrims of the *Mayflower* arrived at Provincetown on Friday; Washington was born on Friday, the twenty-second of February, 1732; Christopher Columbus discovered America on Friday, October 12, 1492."

Having said this, he rose.

Ebenezer, whom he had brought with him, also rose.

Grâce and Douce, divining that the reverend gentlemen were about to take their leave, opened both leaves of the door.

Mess Lethierry saw nothing, and heard nothing.

M. Jaquemin Hérode said in an aside to M. Ebenezer Caudray: "He does not even salute us. It is not grief, it is stolidity. We must believe that he has lost his mind."

But he took his little Bible from the table, and held it between his two outstretched hands, as one would hold a bird fearing lest it should fly away. This attitude awakened a certain expectation among the persons present. Grâce and Douce thrust in their heads.

His voice did its utmost to be majestic.

"Mess Lethierry, let us not part without reading a page of the holy book. The situations of life are illuminated by books; the profane use the *Sortes Virgilianæ,* believers take scriptural warnings. The first book at hand, opened at random, gives counsel; the Bible, opened at random, makes a revelation. It is above all, good for the afflicted. That which infallibly springs forth from the Holy Scriptures softens their affliction. In the presence of the afflicted, the holy book must be consulted without choosing the place, and the passage upon which onc alights must be read with candor. What man does not choose, God chooses. God knows what we need. His invisible finger is on the unexpected passage which we read. Whatever be the page, light infallibly proceeds from it. Let us seek no other, let us cling fast to that. It is the word from on high. And destiny is mysteriously revealed to us in the text invoked with confidence and respect. Let us listen and obey. Mess Lethierry, you are in sorrow, this is the book of consolation; you are ailing, this is the book of health."

The Reverend Jaquemin Hérode pressed the spring of the clasp, slipped his nail at a venture between two pages, laid his hand for a moment on the open book, and collected himself, then, dropping his eyes authoritatively, he began to read in a loud voice.

What he read was as follows,—

"Issac walked in the road which leadeth to the well called the well of him that liveth and seeth.

"Rebecca having beheld Isaac, said: 'Who is this man that is come to meet me?'

"Then Isaac brought her into his tent and took Rebecca for his wife, and he greatly loved her."

Ebenezer and Déruchette exchanged glances.

PART II

GILLIATT THE CUNNING

BOOK FIRST
THE REEF

I
THE PLACE WHICH IS HARD TO REACH AND DIFFICULT TO LEAVE

THE BOAT seen from many points on the coast of Guernsey and at various hours during the preceding evening was, as the reader has already divined, the paunch boat. Gilliatt had selected the channel along the coast among the rocks; it was a perilous route, but the most direct. His only thought had been to take the shortest course. Shipwrecks will not wait, the sea is exacting, an hour's delay might be irreparable. He wished to go quickly to the rescue of the imperilled engine.

Gilliatt's chief solicitude on quitting Guernsey appeared to be not to arouse attention. He departed as if trying to escape. He seemed to be seeking concealment. He avoided the eastern coast like a person who found it inexpedient to pass in sight of Saint-Sampson and Saint-Pierre-Port; he slipped—one might almost say that he glided—silently along the opposite coast, which is comparatively uninhabited. Among the shoals, he was obliged to row; but Gilliatt managed his oar according to hydraulic principles; to take the water quietly and to drop it without haste, and in this manner he could proceed through the darkness as rapidly and with as little noise as possible. One might have thought that he was bent on some evil deed.

The truth is that, though he was dashing headlong into

an enterprise which strongly resembled the impossible, and though risking his life with nearly all the chances against him, he feared rivalry.

As the day began to break, those unknown eyes which perchance look down from the open space, could have beheld, on one of the most solitary and dangerous places in the sea, two objects, between which the interval was decreasing because the one was approaching the other. One, almost imperceptible amid the broad swell of the billows, was a sail boat; in that boat there was a man; it was "the paunch," bearing Gilliatt. The other, motionless, colossal, black, reared a singular figure above the waters. Two lofty pillars sustained above the waves in space a sort of horizontal cross-beam, which was like a bridge between their summits. This bridge, so shapeless from a distance that it was impossible to make out what it was, formed one body with the two supports. It resembled a doorway. Of what use was a doorway in that universal opening, the sea? One would have pronounced it a titanic dolmen planted there, in mid-ocean, by a gigantic freak, and built up by hands which have the habit of proportioning their constructions to the abyss. That wild silhouette rose against the clear background of the sky.

The gleams of morning were increasing in the east; the whiteness of the horizon increased the blackness of the sea. Opposite, in the other direction, the moon was setting.

These two columns were the Douvres. The sort of mass encased between them, like an architrave between two jambs, was the Durande.

This reef, holding fast its prey and displaying it to view, was terrible; things sometimes have a sombre and hostile ostentation in the face of man.

There was defiance in the attitude of these rocks. They seemed to be waiting their opportunity.

Nothing could be more haughty and arrogant than their whole appearance: the conquered vessel, the triumphant abyss, the two rocks, all dripping still with the tempest of the day before, seemed perspiring combatants. The wind had moderated, the sea rippled peacefully, some rocks could be made out on a level with the surface, where plumes of foam curled gracefully; a murmur like the humming of bees came from the open sea. All was level, except the two Douvres, erect and upright as two black columns. They were all bearded with seaweed up to a certain height. Their perpendicular flanks glittered like armor. They seemed ready to begin the strife again. One felt that they were rooted in mountains beneath the water. They breathed forth a sort of tragic omnipotence.

Ordinarily, the sea conceals its blows. It prefers to remain obscure. This unfathomable gloom keeps everything to itself. It is very rare that this mystery yields up its secrets. Assuredly, there is something of the monster in disaster, but in unknown quantities. The sea is both open and secret; it hides itself, and does not care to divulge its actions. It accomplishes shipwreck and covers it up; its modesty is manifested by engulfment. The wave is a hypocrite; it slays, conceals its stolen goods, ignores, and smiles. It roars, then foams.

There was nothing of the sort here. The Douvres had an air of triumph, as they raised aloft above the waves the dead Durande. One would have pronounced them two monstrous arms emerging from the gulf, and showing to the tempests this lifeless corpse of a ship. It was something in the nature of an assassin boasting of his deeds.

The sacred horror of the hour contributed to the scene. Daybreak has a mysterious grandeur which is composed of a remnant of dreams and a beginning of thought. At that troubled moment, a little of the spectral is still floating. The sort of immense capital letter H, formed by the two Douvres with the Durande forming the connecting cross line, appeared against the horizon in indescribable, twilight majesty.

Gilliatt was dressed in his sea clothes, a woollen shirt, woollen stockings, shoes with nail-studded soles, a knitted jacket, trousers of coarse, thick stuff, with pockets, and on his head one of those red woollen caps then in use among sailors, which were called in the last century, *galériennes*—"galley slave caps."

He recognized the reef, and went towards it.

The Durande was exactly the reverse of a sunken vessel; she was a vessel hung high in the air.

No task of salvage could be more difficult to undertake.

It was broad daylight when Gilliatt arrived in the waters about the reef.

As we have just said, there was but little swell. The water had only the amount of agitation which is communicated to it by being contracted between the rocks. Every channel, small or large, has this choppy sea. The interior of a strait is always more or less foaming.

Gilliatt did not approach the Douvres without precaution.

He cast the lead a number of times.

Gilliatt had a few things to land.

Accustomed to being absent from home, he kept a stock of provisions for a sudden departure always ready. It consisted of a sack of biscuits, a sack of rye flour, a basket of salt fish and smoked beef, a large can of fresh water, a Norwegian chest, painted with flowers, containing some coarse woollen shirts, his tarpaulin coat, and his leggings, and a sheepskin which he threw over his jacket at night. On quitting the Bû de la Rue he had thrown all these things, with the addition of a loaf of fresh bread, hastily into the paunch. Anxious to be off, he had taken with him no other implements than his blacksmith's hammer, his axe, and hatchet, a saw, and a knotted rope armed with a grappling iron. With a ladder of this description and the knowledge of how to use it, refractory cliffs become accessible, and a good sailor finds available points in the most unpromising precipices. The use which the fishermen of Gosselin have made of a knotted rope can be seen in the island of Sark.

His nets and lines and all his fishing tackle were in his boat. He had placed them there from force of habit, and mechanically, for he was about to sojourn for some time, if he carried out his undertaking, in an archipelago of shoals, where fishing implements are of little use.

At the moment when Gilliatt came alongside the reef, the tide was falling, a favorable circumstance. The receding waves left uncovered at the foot of the little Douvre, several flat or slightly inclined layers of rock which represented, tolerably well, platforms to support a flooring. These surfaces, some narrow, some wide, ranged with irregular spacing along the vertical monolith, were prolonged in a thin cornice up to the Durande, which swelled out between the two rocks. It was gripped there as in a vice.

These platforms were convenient for landing and looking about. The stock of provisions which had been brought in the paunch could be landed there for the time being. But he must make haste. They were only out of water for a few hours. When the tide rose they would sink beneath the foam once more.

It was in front of these rocks, some flat, some sloping, that Gilliatt pushed his boat and lay to.

A wet and slippery coating of seaweed covered them, and their sloping surfaces increased the slipperiness here and there.

Gilliatt took off his shoes and stockings, leaped barefoot upon the seaweed, and moored his boat to a point of rock.

Then he advanced as far as he could on the narrow cornice of granite, arrived beneath the Durande, raised his eyes and surveyed it.

The Durande was caught, suspended, and balanced, as it were, between the two rocks, about twenty feet above the sea. A violent fury of the waves must have been required to hurl it there.

There is nothing astonishing to seafaring men in these frantic blows. To cite only one instance, on the twenty-fifth of January, 1840, in the gulf of Stora, as a tempest was nearly over, with its final surge it struck a brig and hurled it bodily over the shipwrecked hull of the corvette *La Marne,* and fixed it fast, bowsprit first, between two cliffs.

Moreover, only one half of the Durande was in the Douvres.

The vessel, snatched from the waves, had been, in some way, uprooted from the water by the hurricane. The whirlwind had twisted it, the whirlpool of the sea had held it back, and the vessel, thus grasped in contrary directions by the two hands of the tempest, had been broken like a lath. The stern with the engine and the wheels, lifted out of the foam and driven with all the fury of the cyclone into the defile of the Douvres, had entered up to the midship beam, and there she had remained.

The blow of the wind had been well directed to drive that wedge between those two rocks; the hurricane had turned into a club. The bow, carried away and rolled about by the storm, had been broken to pieces on the rocks.

The shattered hold had emptied the drowned cattle into the sea.

A large section of the sheathing of the bow still clung to the wreck, and hung from the riders of the left paddle-box, by a few dilapidated ties, easy to break with the blow of an axe.

Here and there in distant cavities of the reef, planks, strips of canvas, pieces of chain, all sorts of fragments were to be seen lying tranquilly on the rocks.

Gilliatt gazed attentively at the Durande. The keel formed a ceiling above his head.

The horizon, where the limitless expanse of water was barely moving, was serene. The sun was rising superbly from that vast, blue circle. From time to time, a drop of water was detached from the wreck and fell into the sea.

II

The Thoroughness of the Disaster

THE Douvres differed in shape as well as in height. On the little Douvre, curved and pointed, long veins of comparatively soft brick-colored rock could be seen, branching out from base to summit, enclosing the inner part of the granite in its layers. Along the lines where these reddish layers cropped out, there were breaks favorable for climbing. One of these breaks, situated a little above the wreck, had been so enlarged, and worked upon by the dashing of the waves, that it had become a sort of niche where a statue might have been lodged. The granite of the little Douvre was rounded on the surface and soft like touchstone,—a softness which detracts nothing from its durability. The little Douvre terminated in a point like a horn.

The great Douvre, polished, unbroken, smooth, perpendicular, and as though cut after a pattern, was in one piece, and seemed made of black ivory. Not a hole, not a break. The cliff was inhospitable, a convict could not have made use of it for flight, nor a bird for her nest. At the summit, there was, as on the Man rock, a platform; only this platform was inaccessible.

One might climb the little Douvre, but not maintain one's post there; one might sojourn on the great Douvre, but not climb it.

Gilliatt, after his first glance, returned to the boat, unloaded it on the largest of the projections on a level with the water, made of the whole cargo a sort of compact bale, which he tied up in a tarpaulin, fastened to it a sling with its hoisting ring, thrust this bale into a niche in the rock where the water could not reach it, then, from projection to projection, clutching the little Douvre firmly, using both feet and hands, clinging to the smallest niche, he climbed up to the Durande, shipwrecked in the air.

On arriving on a level with the paddle-boxes, he sprang upon the deck.

The Durande presented all the traces of a frightful deed of violence. It was the terrible rape of the storm. The tempest behaves like a band of pirates. Nothing so resembles a deed of crime as a shipwreck. The cloud, the thunder, the rain, the gales, the waves, the rocks,—this group of accomplices is horrible.

Standing on the abandoned deck, one was reminded of something like the furious revelry of the spirits of the sea. Everywhere there were marks of their rage. The strange contortions of certain portions of the ironwork pointed to the mad force of the wind. The lower deck was like the dungeon of a madman, where all was broken.

There is no beast like the sea for dismembering its prey. The waves are full of claws. The wind bites, the tide devours, the billows are jaws. It is a tearing apart and a crushing at one and the same time. The paw of the ocean strikes a blow like that of a lion.

The ruin of the Durande presented this peculiar feature, that it was detailed and minute. It was a sort of terrible plucking asunder, many things seemed done intentionally. One could say: "What malice!"

The fractures of the planking were artistically made. Ravages of this sort are peculiar to the cyclone. To tear in morsels and work like a joiner, such is the caprice of this enormous devastator. The cyclone has some of the studied elegances of the hangman. The disasters which it causes have the look of executions. One would say that it cherishes rancor, that it exercises the refined cruelty of a savage. It dissects while it exterminates. It tortures the victim, it avenges and amuses itself; it descends to acts of pettiness.

Cyclones are rare in our climate, and all the more to be dreaded because they are unexpected. To come in contact with a rock may cause a storm to turn as on a pivot. It is probable that the hurricane had made a spiral on the Douvres and had been abruptly converted into a waterspout on striking the reef, which explained the fact that the vessel had been cast to such a height in these rocks.

When the cyclone is blowing, a vessel weighs no more in the wind than a stone in a sling.

The Durande had received a wound like that of a man who had been cut in two; she was an open trunk, permitting the escape of a mass of fragments similar to entrails. Cordage hung floating and trembling; chains shivered as they swung to and fro, the nerves and fibres of the vessel were bare and exposed. What was not broken was disjointed; fragments of the sheathing of the lining were like curry combs, bristling with nails; all wore the shape of ruin; a handspike was no longer anything but a bit of iron; a sounding lead only a lump of lead; a deadeye was only a bit of wood; a halyard was no longer anything but a scrap of hemp; a coil of rope was no longer anything but a tangled skein; a bolt rope was a mere thread in a hem of a sail; everywhere was the lamentable work of useless demolition, nothing but what was unhooked, unnailed, cracked, wasted, bent, scuttled, annihilated; no adhesion in this hideous heap, everywhere torn, dislocated, ruptured, and,—a peculiarly inconstant and liquid quality which characterizes all confusion, from the confusion of men, which is called battle, to the confusion of the elements, which is called chaos,—all was crumbling, all was flowing, and a stream of planks, hatches, ironwork, cables, and beams had stopped at the edge of the great fracture in the hull, whence the least shock would precipitate the whole into the sea.

What remained of this powerful frame, formerly so triumphant, the whole of that stern suspended between the two Douvres, and on the point, perhaps, of falling, was cracked here and there, and allowed the dark interior of the vessel to be seen through large apertures.

The foam from below spat upon this miserable object.

III
Sound, But Not Safe

GILLIATT had not expected to find only one half of the vessel. Nothing in the details, precise as they were, of the skipper of the *Shealtiel,* had led him to foresee this cutting of the vessel in two. It was probably at the moment when this cut was made, beneath the blinding masses of foam, that that "diabolical crash" heard by the skipper of the *Shealtiel* had taken place. This skipper had, no doubt, tacked ship just before the last gust of wind, and what he had taken for a mass of water was a waterspout. Later on, when approaching to observe the stranded vessel, he had been able to see only the after part of the wreck, the rest, that is to say, the large break which had separated the bow from the stern, being concealed in the narrow pass of the reef.

With that exception, the skipper of the *Shealtiel* had said nothing that was not strictly correct. The hull was lost, the engine intact.

Such chances are frequent in shipwrecks as in conflagrations. The logic of disaster at sea escapes our understanding.

The shattered masts had fallen, the smoke stack was not even bent; the great iron plate which sustained the engine had held it together and kept it in one piece. The plank sheathing of the paddle-boxes was disjointed, very much like the slats of a Venetian blind; but through their interstices the two wheels could be seen in good order. Some of the floats were missing.

The great stern capstan had resisted as well as the engine. It retained its chain, and, thanks to its being stoutly set in a framework of beams, it might still be of service, provided that the strain of the cable did not split the planking. The planking of the deck was giving way at nearly every point. All this diaphragm was shaky.

On the other hand, the fragment of the hull entangled between the two Douvres held firm, as we have said, and seemed solid.

This preservation of the machinery had something derisory about it, and added irony to the catastrophe. The sombre malice of the unknown sometimes bursts forth in this sort of bitter mockery. The machinery was saved, which did not prevent its being lost. The ocean kept it to demolish at its leisure. A cat playing with its prey.

There she was, about to undergo the death agony, and be demolished piece by piece. She was about to serve as a plaything to the savage amusement of the foam. She was to decrease day by day, and as it were, to melt away. What was to be done? It seemed mere folly to imagine. That this heavy block of mechanism and gears, at once massive and delicate, condemned to immobility by its weight, delivered over in that solitude to the forces of demolition, placed by the reef at the discretion of the winds and the waves, could, beneath the pressure of those implacable surroundings, escape slow destruction, it seemed folly just to imagine.

The Durande was the prisoner of the Douvres.

How was she to be delivered?

The escape of a man is difficult; but what a problem was this—the escape of a machine!

IV
A Preliminary Examination

GILLIATT was surrounded only by urgent needs. But the most pressing was to find, in the first place, an anchorage for his boat, then a shelter for himself.

The Durande was settled down more on the port than on the starboard side, the right paddle-box was more elevated than the left one.

Gilliatt climbed upon the right box. From thence he dominated the lower part of the reefs, and, although the gut between the rocks lying in a line with the broken angles behind the Douvres made many turns, Gilliatt was able to study the geometrical plan of the reef.

He began with this reconnaissance.

The Douvres, as we have already pointed out, were like two lofty gables, marking the narrow entrance to a lane of small granite cliffs, with perpendicular faces. It is not rare to find, in primitive submarine formations, these singular corridors, which seem hewn out with a hatchet.

This very tortuous defile was never bare, even at low tide. A very active current always traversed it from end to end. The abruptness of the eddies was good or bad, according to the nature of the reigning wind; sometimes it overcame the swell and made it fall; sometimes it exasperated it. This last effect was most frequently the case; an obstacle sets the sea in a fury, and urges it on to excesses; foam is the exaggeration of the waves.

The wind in a storm undergoes the same compression, in these narrow passages between two rocks, and acquires the same malignity. It is the tempest in a state of strangulation. The immense breath is still immense, and becomes acute. It is a club and a dart. It pierces at the same time that it crushes. Imagine the hurricane contracted, and become a sharp draught through a crevice.

The two chains of rocks, leaving between them this sort of sea street, descended lower than the Douvres in stages of gradually decreasing heights, and plunged together into the waves at a short distance away. There was another narrow channel less elevated than the Douvres passage, but still narrower, which formed the eastern entrance to the defile. It was clear that the double prolongation of the two ridges of rock continued the street under the water as far as "the Man" rock, placed like a square citadel at the other extremity of the reef.

Moreover, at low tide, and this was the moment when Gilliatt was observing them, these two ranges of shoals showed their crests, some dry and all visible, arranged in an uninterrupted file.

"The Man" bounded and buttressed the entire mass of the reef, which was shored up at the west by the two Douvres.

The whole reef, from a bird's-eye view, presented an undulating chaplet, having the Douvres at one end, and "the Man" at the other.

The Douvres reef, taken as a whole, was nothing else than the outcropping of two gigantic layers of granite, almost touching each other, and emerging vertically, like a crest of the ranges which lie at the bottom of the ocean. These immense ridges do exist outside of the abyss. The squall and the swell had torn this crest up into a saw. Only the top was visible; this was the reef. What the water concealed must be enormous. The alley into which the storm had flung the Durande was the space between these colossal layers.

This lane, zigzag like a flash of lightning, was of nearly

the same width at all points. The ocean had made it thus. The eternal tumult develops these eccentric regularities. A sort of geometry emerges from the waves.

From one end to the other of the pass, the two walls of rock presented to each other a parallel face at a distance which was almost exactly measured by the midship-beam of the Durande.

The hollow of the little Douvre, bent and curved over, had furnished a place between the two Douvres for the paddle-boxes; anywhere else, the paddle-boxes would have been crushed.

The double interior façade of the reef was hideous. When, during the exploration of the desert of water called the ocean, one arrives at the unknown things of the sea, all becomes uncouth and shapeless. What Gilliatt could perceive of the defile, from the summit of the wreck, inspired horror. In the granite gorges of the ocean, there often exists a strange permanent representation of shipwreck. The defile of the Douvres had its own, a terrible one. The oxides of the rock had placed, here and there upon the cliffs, red patches resembling pools of clotted blood. It was something like the bloody oozings of a butcher's cellar. There was something of the charnel house in this reef. The rough marine stone, diversely colored, here by the decomposition of metallic amalgams mixed with the rock, there by mould, exhibited in places frightful purples, suspect patches of green, vermillion splashes, awakening the idea of murder and extermination. One would have imagined it to be the bloody wall of a chamber where an assassination had been committed, and that the men crushed there had left traces of their fate; the perpendicular rock bore an indescribable imprint of accumulated agonies. In several places this carnage seemed to be still trickling, the wall was wet, and it seemed impossible to touch it with one's fingers without drawing them back stained with blood. A blight of massacre appeared everywhere. At the base of the double parallel escarpment, scattered on a level with the water, or beneath the waves, or on dry land, in the undermined hollows, monstrous rounded boulders, some scarlet, others black or violet, resembled viscera; one would imagine them to be fresh lungs or rotting livers. One would have said that the bellies of giants had been emptied there. Long red threads, which might have been taken for lugubrious exudations, striped the granite from top to bottom.

Such aspects are frequent in the caverns of the sea.

V

A Word as to the Secret Co-Operation of the Elements

FOR those who, by the chances of voyages, may be condemned to the temporary habitation of a reef in the ocean, the form of the reef is not a matter of indifference. There is the pyramidal reef, a single peak rising from the water; there is the circular reef, something like a ring of huge stones; there is the corridor reef. The corridor reef is the most alarming. It is so not only on account of the agony of the waves between its walls, and the tumult of the closely confined billows, it is so also because of obscure meteorological properties which seem to proceed from the parallel position of two rocks in the open sea. These two straight layers are a genuine electric battery.

A corridor reef has its bearings east and west. This direction is of importance. The first result from it is an action upon the air and the water. The corridor reef acts upon the waves and the wind, mechanically by its form, galvanically by the different magnetic actions possible to its vertical planes, its masses in juxtaposition but counteracted by each other.

This sort of reef attracts to itself all the furious forces scattered in the hurricane, and exercises over the tempest a singular power of concentration.

Hence, in the vicinity of these shoals, there is a certain accentuation of the tempest.

It must be borne in mind that the wind is composite. One thinks of the wind as simple; it is not. This force is not only dynamic, it is chemical; it is not only chemical, it is also magnetic. There is something inexplicable about it. The wind is electrical as much as aerial. Certain winds coincide with the Aurora Borealis. The wind from the Aiguilles bank rolls up waves a hundred feet high, to the amazement of Dumont d'Urville. "The corvette," he says, "did not know whom to obey." Beneath the southern squalls, actual unhealthy tumors swell the ocean, and the sea becomes so horrible that the savages flee to the caves in order to avoid looking at it.

The gales of the northern seas are different; they are all mingled with needles of ice, and these winds, which cannot be breathed, push the sledges of the Esquimaux backwards on the snow. Other winds burn. There is the simoon of Africa, which is the typhoon of China, and the samiel of India. Simoon, typhoon, samiel; one might think them to be demons. They melt the summits of the mountains; a storm vitrified the volcano of Toluca. That hot blast, a whirlwind of inky hue, dashing down upon the red clouds, caused the Vedas to say: "Here comes the black god, to steal the red cows." One feels the presence of the electric mystery in everything.

The wind is full of this mystery. So is the sea. It is also complicated; under the waves of water, which one sees, it has its waves of force, which one does not see. It is composed of everything. Of all confusions, the ocean is the most indivisible and the most profound.

Try to form for yourself a conception of this chaos so enormous that it results in equilibriums. It is the universal recipient; a reservoir for fecundation, a crucible for transformations. It amasses, then disperses; it accumulates, then sows; it devours, then creates. It receives all the sewers of the earth, and converts them into treasure. It is solid in the iceberg, liquid in the wave, impalpable in effluvium. As matter, it is a mass; and, as force, it is an abstraction. It equalizes and marries all phenomena. It is by dint of mingling and disturbance that it arrives at transparency. Soluble diversity is absorbed in its unity.

Its elements are so numerous that it becomes identity, and one of its drops is complete and represents the whole. Because it is full of tempests, it attains equilibrium. Plato saw the dance of the spheres; a strange thing to say, but none the less real: in the colossal, terrestrial journey around the sun, the ocean, with its ebb and flow, is the balance of the globe.

In a phenomenon of the sea, all phenomena are present. The sea is sucked up by the whirlwind as by a siphon; a storm is like a pump; the lightning proceeds from the water as well as from the air; on shipboard, dull shocks are felt, then an odor of sulphur comes from the chain locker. The ocean boils. "The devil has put the sea in his cauldron," said Ruyter. In certain tempests which characterize the equinoxes and the return into equilibrium of genetic forces, vessels beaten by the foam seem to give out a kind of fiery light, and sparks of phosphorus run along the rigging, so mingled with the ropes that the sailors stretch out their hands and try to catch these birds of fire on the wing. After the Lisbon earthquake, a blast as from a furnace pushed towards the city a wave sixty feet high. The oscillation of the ocean is closely connected with the terrestrial quaking.

These immeasurable energies render all cataclysms possible. Towards the close of 1864, a hundred leagues from the coast of Malabar, one of the Maldive Islands sank in the sea. It foundered like a vessel. The fishermen who had set out from it in the morning found nothing in the evening; and they were barely able to vaguely distinguish their villages under the waves; and, on this occasion, vessels were present as spectators at the shipwreck of houses.

In Europe, where it seems as though nature felt herself restrained by respect for civilization, such events are rare and thought impossible. Nevertheless, Jersey and Guernsey once formed part of Gaul; and, at the moment when we write these lines, an equinoctial gale has just demolished the cliff of the First of the Four,[1] on the frontier between England and Scotland.

Nowhere do these panic forces appear more formida-

1. Firth of Forth.

bly conjoined than in that astounding northern strait, Lyse-Fjord. The Lyse-Fjord is the most formidable of all the gut-reefs of the ocean. There the demonstration is complete. It is in the North Sea, in the vicinity of the rough Stavanger Gulf, at the fifty-ninth degree of latitude. The water is heavy and black, with a fever of intermittent storms. In that sea, in the midst of that solitude, there is a great, gloomy street,—a no-man's street. No one passes through it, no vessel risks herself there. A corridor ten leagues long, between two walls three thousand feet high; such is the passage which presents its entrance to the sea. This strait has elbows and angles, like all streets of the sea, which are never straight, being made by the irregular action of the waves. In the Lyse-Fjord, the water is almost always tranquil; the sky is serene; a terrible place. Where is the wind? Not on high. Where is the thunder? Not in the heavens. The wind is beneath the sea, the thunder is in the rock. From time to time, there is a quaking of the water. At certain moments, nearly half way up the vertical cliff, a thousand or fifteen hundred feet above the waves, on the south side rather than on the north, the rock suddenly thunders without there being a cloud in the air, a flash of lightning darts forth from it, then draws back, like those playthings which fly out and spring back into the hands; there are contractions and enlargements, it darts to the opposite cliff, re-enters the rock, then comes forth again, begins anew, multiplies its heads and its tongues, bristles with points, strikes where it can, begins yet again, then is extinguished with singular abruptness. Flocks of birds take their flight. Nothing so mysterious as this artillery proceeding from the invisible. One rock attacks the other. The reefs hurl lightnings at each other. This war does not concern man. The hatred of two walls in an abyss.

In the Lyse-Fjord the wind is converted into effluvium, the rock performs the function of a cloud, and the thunder has its volcanic outbursts. This strange strait is a voltaic pile; the plates of which are represented by its two cliffs.

VI
A Stable for the Horse

GILLIATT was sufficiently well versed in reefs to take the Douvres very seriously. First of all, as we have just said, the question arose of putting the boat in a safe shelter.

The double ridge of reefs which was prolonged in a sinuous lane behind the Douvres, itself formed a group, here and there, with other rocks, and one perceived their ridges and caves opening out into the alley and joined to the principal defile like branches to a tree.

The lower portion of the reefs was carpeted with seaweed, and the upper part with lichens. The uniform level of the seaweed on all the rocks marked the water line of high tide and of slack water. The points not reached by the water had those silver and golden gleams which are imparted to marine granite by the white and yellow lichen. An eruption of conoid shells covered the rock at certain points, the dry rot of granite.

At other points, in the retreating angles where fine sand had accumulated, ridged on the surface by the wind rather than by the water, there were tufts of blue thistle.

In the notches, but little beaten by the foam, one could recognize small holes made by sea-urchins. This shell hedgehog, a living ball, which walks by rolling along on its points, and whose cuirass is composed of more than ten thousand pieces artistically adjusted and welded together, the sea-urchin, whose mouth is called, no one knows why, "Aristotle's lantern," hollows out the granite with his five teeth which gnaw the rocks, and lodges himself in the hole. It is in these little cells that samphire gatherers find him. They cut him in quarters and devour him raw, like an oyster. Some dip their bread in his soft flesh. Hence the name, "sea-egg."

The distant summits of the reefs, left above the water by the receding tide, terminated, directly below the cliff of "the Man," in a sort of creek walled on nearly all sides by the precipice.

Evidently, here was a possible anchorage. Gilliatt observed this creek.

It had the form of a horseshoe and opened in one direction only, to the east wind, which is the least violent on these shores. The water was hemmed in there, and nearly tranquil.

This bay was comparatively safe. Moreover, Gilliatt had not much choice.

If Gilliatt wished to profit by the low tide, he must make haste.

The weather, moreover, remained fine and mild. The insolent sea was now in good humor.

Gilliatt descended, put on his shoes and stockings, cast off his moorings, re-entered his boat, and pushed out into deep water.

Using his oars he coasted along, outside the reef.

On arriving near "the Man," he examined the entrance to the creek.

A fixed ripple in the motionless waves, a furrow imperceptible to any one but a seaman, marked the channel.

Gilliatt studied for a moment this curve, which was almost indistinct in the water; then he sheered off a little, in order to be able to veer at ease, and make the channel well, and quickly, with one turn of the oar, he entered the little inlet.

He sounded.

The anchorage was really excellent.

There the boat would be protected against nearly all the contingencies of the season.

The most dreaded reefs have these quiet nooks. The harbors which one finds in a reef resemble the hospitality of the Bedouin, they are honest and sure.

Gilliatt brought the boat as close alongside of "the Man" as he could, but still far enough away to avoid striking the rocks, and dropped his two anchors. That done, he folded his arms and took counsel with himself.

The boat was sheltered; that was one problem solved; but a second presented itself.

Where was he now to find shelter for himself?

Two retreats presented themselves; the paunch itself, with its little cabin, almost habitable, and the plateau of "the Man,"

From either of these shelters, at low tide, and by leaping from rock to rock, one could reach almost dry-shod the pass of the Douvres where the Durande was.

But low tide only lasts for a moment, and all the rest of the time he would be separated, either from his shelter or from the wreck, by more than two hundred fathoms.

To swim in the water of a reef is difficult; if there is the least sea on, it is impossible.

He must give up the idea of shelter in the boat or on "the Man."

No possible resting-place on the neighboring rocks.

The summits of the lower peaks were covered twice a day by the tide.

The upper peaks were constantly reached by flakes of foam.

An inhospitable drenching.

There remained the wreck itself.

Could one lodge there?

Gilliatt hoped so.

VII
A Chamber for the Traveller

HALF an hour later, Gilliatt, having returned to the wreck, was mounting and descending, from the deck to the lower deck, and from the lower deck to the hold, completing the summary examination of his first visit.

With the assistance of the capstan, he had hoisted upon the deck of the Durande the bale which he had made of the cargo of the boat. The capstan worked well. Bars were not lacking to turn it. Gilliatt had but to make his choice amid that mass of fragments.

Among the refuse he found a cold chisel, which had fallen, no doubt, from the carpenter's box, and which he added to his little stock of tools.

Besides this,—for in destitution everything counts,—he had his knife in his pocket.

Gilliatt worked all day at the wreck, clearing away, consolidating, simplifying.

When evening came, he recognized this fact,—

The whole wreck was quivering in the wind. This carcass trembled at every step which Gilliatt took. There was nothing firm and stable but that portion of the hull containing the engine and which was embedded between the rocks. There the timbers were powerfully buttressed by the granite walls.

It was imprudent to locate himself on the Durande. It was an extra load, and instead of adding weight to the vessel, the important point was to lighten it.

To remain upon the wreck was exactly the contrary of what it was necessary to do.

This ruin required the most careful treatment. It was

like a sick man at the point of dissolution. There would be wind enough to work injury to it.

It was even distressing to be obliged to work upon it. The amount of work which the wreck would be obliged to bear would certainly fatigue it, and perhaps beyond its strength.

Moreover, if any accident were to supervene during the night while Gilliatt was asleep, to be in the wreck was to perish with it. No aid was possible; all was lost. In order to rescue the wreck, he must remain outside of it.

To be outside of it, yet near it; that was the problem.

The difficulty was becoming complicated.

Where was he to find a shelter under such conditions?

Gilliatt reflected.

Only the two Douvres remained. They seemed hardly habitable.

A sort of excrescence on the upper plateau of the great Douvre could be distinguished from below.

Upright rocks with flat summits, like the great Douvre and "the Man," are decapitated peaks. They abound in the mountains and in the ocean. Certain rocks, above all, those which one meets with in the open sea, have notches like trees which have been hacked. They have the appearance of having received a blow from an axe. They are, in fact, subjected to the vast movements to and fro of the hurricane, that wood-chopper of the sea.

There exist other causes for cataclysm, but still more profound. Hence so many wounds on all ancient granite. Some of these giants have had their heads cut off.

Sometimes, from some unknown cause, these heads do not fall, but remain, mutilated, on the truncated summit. This peculiarity is not uncommon. The Roque-au-Diable (Devil's Rock) at Guernsey, and the Table in the valley of Anweiler, present this singular geological enigma under the most surprising conditions.

Something similar had probably happened to the great Douvre.

If the swelling which one perceived on the plateau was not a natural irregularity of the stone, it was necessarily some fragment remaining from the ruined summit.

Perhaps there was a hollow in this rock.

A hole in which to hide one's self; Gilliatt asked no more.

But how was he to reach the plateau? how was he to ascend that vertical wall, as dense and polished as a pebble, half covered with a sheet of viscous hairweed, and having the slippery aspect of a surface that has been soaped.

It was at least thirty feet from the deck of the Durande to the ridge of the plateau.

Gilliatt drew from his box of tools the knotted rope, hitched it to his belt by the grappling-hook and began to climb the little Douvre. The higher he mounted, the rougher became the ascent. He had neglected to take off his shoes, which increased the difficulty of ascent. It was not without exertion that he reached the summit. On arriving at that point, he stood erect. There was only room for his two feet. It would be hard to make it his lodging-place. A Stylite would have been contented with it. Gilliatt, who was more exacting, wanted something better.

The little Douvre curved towards the great one, which made it appear, when seen from a distance, to be saluting it, and the two Douvres, which below were twenty feet apart, were only eight or ten feet apart at the top.

From the point which he had attained, Gilliatt had a more distinct view of the rocky swelling which partly covered the platform of the great Douvre.

This platform rose at least three fathoms above his head.

A precipice separated him from it.

The cliff of the little Douvre as it leaned forward, sloped away beneath him.

Gilliatt detached the knotted rope from his belt, rapidly took in the distances at a glance, and hurled the grapnel upon the platform.

The grapnel scratched the rock, then slipped off. The knotted cord with the grapnel at its extremity, fell back beneath Gilliatt's feet along the little Douvre.

Gilliatt tried again, throwing the rope farther forward, and taking aim at the granite protuberance, where he perceived crevices and scratches.

The cast was so adroit and so neat that the hooks held fast.

Gilliat drew upon it.

The rock broke and the knotted cord returned to strike against the cliff beneath Gilliatt.

Gilliat cast the grapnel a third time.

The grapnel did not fall.

Gilliatt made a trial of the rope. It resisted. The grapnel was anchored.

It had caught in some crevice of the plateau which Gilliatt could not see.

The question now was as to trusting his life to this unknown support.

Gilliatt did not hesitate.

There was the greatest haste. He must take the shortest way.

Moreover, it was almost impossible to descend upon the deck of the Durande for the purpose of devising some other measure. A slip was probable, and a fall was almost certain. One may climb more easily than one can descend.

Gilliatt's movements were precisely like those of all good sailors. He never wasted strength, he only made efforts proportionate to their object; hence the prodigies of rigor which he executed with ordinary muscles; his biceps were no stronger than those of other men, but he had a bolder heart. He added to strength, which is physical, energy, which is moral force.

The thing to be accomplished was formidable.

To cross the interval between the two Douvres, suspended from that thread; such was the problem.

One often encounters in deeds of devotion or duty, interrogation points which seem placed there by death.

"Wilt thou do this?" says the shadow.

Gilliatt gave another pull to test the hook; the hook held good.

Gilliatt wrapped his left hand in his handkerchief, clutched the knotted rope with his right hand, and protected it with his left hand, then, holding one foot in advance and giving a vigorous thrust from the rock with the other, in order that the impetus might prevent his rope from twisting, he precipitated himself from the summit of the little Douvre upon the cliff of the great Douvre.

It was a hard shock.

In spite of the precaution taken by Gilliatt, the rope twisted, and his shoulder struck the rock.

There was a rebound.

His knuckles struck the rock in their turn. The handkerchief was disarranged. They were scratched; barely escaped being broken.

Gilliatt remained hanging for a moment, dizzy.

He was sufficiently master of himself not to let go of the rope.

A few moments passed in jerks and oscillations before he was able to grasp the rope with his feet; but he finally succeeded.

On recovering himself, he glanced below, clinging to the rope with his feet as well as his hands. He was not disturbed about the length of his rope, which had more than once served him for still greater heights. The rope, in fact, trailed on the deck of the Durande.

Gilliatt, sure of being able to descend again, began to climb.

In a few minutes he had reached the platform.

Nothing but what had wings had ever before set foot there. This plateau was covered with guano. Its form was that of an irregular trapezium, a fracture of that colossal granite prism called the great Douvre. This trapezium was hollow in the centre, like a basin. The work of the rain.

Gilliatt's conjecture had, moreover, been correct. At the southern angle of the trapezium, a mass of superimposed rocks was visible, the probable fragments of the crumbling summit. These rocks, like heaps of gigantic paving-stones, left room for any wild beast which might have strayed upon that crest to slip between them. They supported each other confusedly; leaving interstices like a heap of ruins. There existed there neither grotto nor cave, but holes, as in a sponge. One of these holes might admit Gilliatt.

This den had a floor of grass and moss. Gilliatt would be as though in a sheath there.

The alcove was two feet high at the entrance. It grew

smaller as it approached the extremity. There are stone coffins which have this form. The pile of rocks being backed up to the southwest, the lair was assured against the waves, but was open to the north wind.

Gilliatt thought this a good place.

The two problems were solved; the boat had a harbor, and he had a habitation.

The excellence of this habitation consisted in its being within reach of the wreck.

The grapnel attached to the knotted rope, having fallen between two masses of rock, was solidly fastened there. Gilliatt rendered it immovable by placing a large stone upon it.

Then he immediately entered into free communication with the Durande.

Henceforth, he was at home.

The great Douvre was his house, the Durande was his shipyard.

Nothing was more simple than to ascend and descend, to go and come.

He slid rapidly down the knotted rope to the deck.

The day was favorable, he had made a good beginning, he was content, he perceived that he was hungry.

He untied his basket of provisions, opened his knife, cut a slice of smoked beef, bit into his loaf of brown bread, drank a draught from his can of fresh water, and made an admirable supper.

Working well and eating well are two joys. A full stomach resembles a satisfied conscience.

After his supper was finished, a little daylight still remained. He profited by it to begin the lightening of the wreck, which was very urgent.

He had passed a part of the day in sorting the fragments. He laid aside, in the solid compartment where the machine was, all that could be of service,—wood, iron, cordage, canvas. He flung what was useless into the sea.

The cargo of the paunch, hoisted upon the deck by the capstan, was an encumbrance, scanty as it was. Gilliatt perceived a sort of niche, hollowed out at a height which he could reach with his hand, in the wall of the little Douvre. These natural cupboards—not closed in, it is true,—are frequently to be seen in rocks. He thought that it would be possible to entrust his stores to his niche. At the bottom he put his two cases, that containing his tools and that containing his clothes, his two sacks of rye and biscuits, and on the front, a little too near the edge, perhaps, but he had no other place, his basket of provisions.

He took care to withdraw from the box containing his clothes his sheepskin, his hooded tarpaulin, and his tarred leggings.

In order to remove the knotted rope from the power of the wind, he made its lower extremity fast to a rider of the Durande.

As the Durande curved back sharply, the rider itself was considerably curved, and held the end of the rope as well as a closed hand would have done.

The top of the rope remained. To fasten the base was very well, but at the summit of the cliff, as the knotted rope encountered the edge of the platform, it was to be feared that it would be gradually sawed through by the sharp angle of the rock.

Gilliatt rummaged among his stock of reserved fragments, and drew out several strips of canvas, and from a bit of old cable several long pieces of twine, which he stuffed into his pockets.

A mariner would have divined that he was about to pad the section of the knotted rope in contact with the rock, with these bits of canvas and these ends of thread, so as to preserve it from all injury; an operation which is called "serving."

Having supplied himself with rags, he put on his leggings, drew on the tarpaulin over his peajacket, pulled the hood over his red cap, knotted the sheepskin about his neck by its two legs, and thus clothed in this complete panoply, he grasped the rope, henceforth firmly fixed in the flank of the great Douvre, and mounted to the assault of that gloomy tower of the sea.

In spite of his scratched hands, Gilliatt quickly reached the plateau.

The last pale gleams of the setting sun were fading away. It was night on the sea.

The summit of the Douvre retained a little light.

Gilliatt took advantage of this remnant of day, to serve the rope. He applied to it, at the elbow which it made over the rock, a bandage consisting of many thicknesses of canvas, strongly bound at each layer. This was something like the padding which actresses put on their knees for the agonies and supplications of the fifth act.

The serving of the rope finished, Gilliatt, who had been crouching down, straightened himself up.

For the last few moments, while adjusting the strips upon the knotted rope, he had had a confused perception of a singular quivering in the air.

In the evening silence, it resembled the sound which the waving of the wings of an immense bat would produce.

Gilliatt raised his eyes.

A great, black circle was wheeling above his head in the deep, white sky of twilight.

In old pictures these circles can be seen on the heads of saints, only they are of gold on a dark background; this was dark on a light background. Nothing could be stranger. One would have pronounced it to be the aureole of night on the great Douvre.

This circle approached Gilliatt and then retreated; contracting, then widening again.

It consisted of mews, gulls, frigate birds, cormorants, sea mews, a cloud of astonished sea birds.

It was probable that the great Douvre was their home, and that they were come to sleep. Gilliatt had taken a chamber there. This unexpected lodger disturbed them.

A man was something that they had never seen there.

This frightened flight lasted for some time.

They seemed to be waiting for Gilliatt to go away.

Gilliatt, vaguely thoughtful, followed them with his glance.

This winged whirlwind finally took its departure, the circle suddenly resolved itself into a spiral, and the cloud of cormorants alighted upon "the Man" at the other end of the reef.

There they appeared to be consulting and deliberating. Gilliatt, as he betook himself to his granite sheath, and placed a stone under his cheek for a pillow, heard the birds talking for a long time, one after the other, or croaking, each in his turn.

Then they became silent, and all went to sleep; the birds on their rock, Gilliatt on his.

VIII
Importunaeque Volucres

GILLIATT slept well. But he was cold, which caused him to wake from time to time. He had, naturally, placed his feet at the end, and his head on the threshold. He had taken no care to remove from his bed a multitude of rather sharp pebbles, which did not improve his slumber.

He opened his eyes at intervals.

At certain moments he heard deep detonations. They were made by the rising tide entering the caverns of the reef with the noise of a discharge of cannon.

His whole surroundings presented the extraordinary character of a vision; Gilliatt had hallucination around him. The half astonishment of night being added, he beheld himself plunged in the region of unreality. He said to himself, "I am dreaming."

Then he fell asleep again, and in his dreams found himself once more at the Bû de la Rue, at les Bravées, at Saint-Sampson; he heard Déruchette singing; he was among realities. As long as he slept, he thought that he was awake and living; when he woke up, he thought that he was asleep.

In fact, henceforth, he lived in a dream.

Towards the middle of the night, a vast murmur arose in the sky. Gilliatt had a confused perception of it through his slumbers. It is probable that the wind was rising.

Once, when aroused by a shiver of cold, he opened his eyelids a little wider than he had previously done. There were large clouds in the zenith; the moon was flying through the sky, and a large star was pursuing her.

Gilliatt's mind was filled with the diffusion of dreams, and this exaggeration of the state of dreaminess mingled with the wild landscape of the night.

At daybreak he was stiff with cold and sleeping profoundly.

The abruptness of the dawn roused him from this slumber, which might have been dangerous. His alcove faced the rising sun.

Gilliatt yawned, stretched himself and sprang out of his hole.

He had slept so soundly that he did not understand at first.

Little by little, the reality returned to him, and to such a degree that he exclaimed, "Let us breakfast!"

The weather was calm, the sky cold and serene; there were no longer any clouds, the sweeping of the night winds had cleared the horizon, the sun was rising brightly. It was the beginning of a second fine day. Gilliatt felt joyous.

He threw off his peajacket and leggings, rolled them up in the sheepskin, with the wool inside, tied the roll up with a bit of rope, and thrust it to the bottom of his lair, out of reach of possible rain.

Then he made his bed, that is to say, he removed the pebbles.

This done, he let himself slide down the rope to the bridge of the Durande, and ran to the niche where he had deposited his basket of provisions.

The basket was no longer there. As it had been placed very near the edge, the wind had blown it off during the night, had carried it away, and thrown it into the sea.

The wind thus announced its hostile intentions.

It must have had a certain will and some malice, to go in search of that basket there.

It was the beginning of warfare; Gilliatt understood it.

It is very difficult, when one lives in surly familiarity with the sea, not to regard the wind as some one, and the rocks as personages.

The only resource remaining to Gilliatt besides his biscuit and his rye meal was the shell fish with which the shipwrecked man who had died of hunger on "the Man" rock had sustained himself.

Fishing was not to be thought of. Fish do not like the rocks and avoid the breakers. Fishers with pots and drag-nets would waste their labor on these reefs, the points of which are fit only to tear the nets.

Gilliatt breakfasted on a few limpets, which he detached from the stones with difficulty. He came near breaking the knife in the operation.

While engaged on this meagre luncheon, he heard a peculiar tumult on the sea. He looked.

It was the swarm of gulls and sea-mews which had just alighted on one of the low rocks, flapping their wings, knocking against each other and screaming. All were flocking noisily to the same point. This horde were plundering something, with beaks and claws.

That something was Gilliatt's basket.

The basket, tossed upon a point of rock by the wind, had burst open there. The birds had flocked thither. They were carrying away in their beaks all sorts of ragged fragments. Gilliatt recognized his smoked beef and his salt fish from afar.

The birds had entered into rivalry in their turn. They, also, were making reprisals. Gilliatt had deprived them of their habitation; they were depriving him of his supper.

IX

The Reef and the Manner of Using It

A WEEK passed.

Although it was the rainy season it did not rain, which greatly rejoiced Gilliatt.

What he had undertaken, however, was beyond human strength, in appearance, at least. Success was so improbable that the attempt seemed like madness.

Undertakings demonstrate their obstacles and perils when grappled with close at hand. There is nothing like commencing a thing, for seeing how hard it will be to finish. All beginnings offer resistance. The first step which one takes is an inexorable revealer. The difficulty which one touches pricks like a thorn.

Gilliatt was obliged to contend with obstacles immediately.

In order to remove the engine of the Durande from the wreck in which it was three-quarters buried, in order to attempt such a salvage, in such a place, at such a season, with any chance of success, it seemed as though a troop of men were necessary, and Gilliatt was alone; a whole outfit of carpenter's tools and machinery was necessary. Gilliatt had a saw, an axe, a chisel, and a hammer; a good workshop and a group of sheds were required, Gilliatt had not even a roof; provisions and stores were needed, Gilliatt had not even bread.

If any one could have seen Gilliatt at work on the reef during the whole of that week, he would not have been able to make out what the latter was aiming at. He seemed to be no longer thinking of the Durande or of the two Douvres. He was occupied only with what there was among the breakers; he appeared absorbed in saving the petty wreckage. He took advantage of the low tides to strip the reefs of all that the shipwreck had bestowed upon them. He went from rock to rock, picking up what the sea had cast there, fragments of canvas, ends of ropes, scraps of iron, bits of panels, crushed planking, broken yards, here a beam, there a chain, further on a pulley.

At the same time he studied all the crevices of the reef. Not one of them was habitable, to the great disappointment of Gilliatt, who was cold at night in the crevices of the slabs of stones where he lodged on the summit of the great Douvre, and he would be glad to find a better attic.

Two of these cavities were sufficiently spacious; although the natural pavement of the rock was almost everywhere slanting and uneven, one could stand upright and walk in them. The wind and the rain came in at will there, but the highest tides did not reach them. They were close to the little Douvre, and accessible at all hours. Gilliatt decided that one should serve as a storehouse, the other as a forge.

With all the earings and head lines which he could collect, he made bales of the small bits of wreckage, binding the fragments into bundles and the canvas into packets. He lashed them all carefully together. As the rising tide floated these bales, he dragged them across the shoals to his storehouse.

In the hollow of a rock he had found a top rope which enabled him to haul even the larger pieces of timberwork. In the same manner, he drew from the sea the numerous fragments of chains scattered among the breakers.

Gilliatt was astonishingly tenacious and active in this labor. He accomplished everything that he wished. Nothing resists an ant-like perseverance.

At the end of the week, Gilliatt had all the shapeless bric-a-brac of the tempest arranged in order in that granite shed. There was a corner for tacks, and a corner for sheets; the bowlines were not mixed with the halyards; the ribs were arranged according to the number of their holes; the puddenings, carefully detached from the rings of the broken anchors, were rolled in balls; the hearts, which have no sheaves, were separated from the tackle-blocks; the belaying-pins, the bulls' eyes, the out-venter shrouds, the hollow cleats, the pendents, the flukes, the parrels, the stoppers, the booms, occupied different compartments, provided that they were not completely damaged by the tempest; all the timber-work, the cross-trees, post, stanchions, caps, port-lids, fishes, and binding-strakes were piled up separately; wherever it had been possible, the dovetailed planks of the fragments of the ship's bottom had been fitted together again; there was no confusion of the reeflines with the cable-nippers, nor of the crowfeet with the towlines, nor of the pulleys of the shrouds with the pulleys of the white hawsers, nor of the pieces of strake with the pieces of waist; a corner had been reserved for a part of the cat-harpings of the Durande, which held taut the shrouds of the topmast and the futtock shrouds. Each sort of fragment had its place. The whole shipwreck was there, classed and labelled. It was a sort of storehouse of chaos.

A stay-sail, fastened by large stones, though very much riddled with holes, it is true, covered what the rain might damage.

Splintered as had been the Durande's bow, Gilliatt had succeeded in saving both the catheads with their three pulleys.

He found the bowsprit, and had much difficulty in unrolling the gammonings; they adhered very tightly, having been made, as always, at the capstan, and in dry weather. Nevertheless, Gilliatt detached them, since this large rope might be useful to him.

He had also picked up the small anchor, which had remained caught in a hollow of the bottom, where it was uncovered at low tide.

In what had been Tangrouille's cabin, he found a bit of chalk, and he laid it carefully aside. He might have to make marks.

A leather fire bucket and several pails in a tolerably good condition completed this working outfit.

All that remained of the Durande's stock of coal was carried to the storeroom.

In a week this salvage of fragments was finished; the

reef was cleared, and the Durande lightened. Nothing now remained on the wreck but the engine.

The bit of the forward planking which adhered to the after part did not disturb the wreck. It hung without any tension, being sustained by a projection of the rock. Moreover, it was large and wide, and heavy to drag, and it would have encumbered the storehouse. This strip of planking had the appearance of a raft. Gilliatt left it where it was.

Gilliatt, profoundly thoughtful during this labor, sought in vain for the figurehead or "doll" of the Durande. It was one of the things which the waves had carried away forever. Gilliatt would have given his two hands to find it, had he not stood in such need of them.

At the entrance of the storehouse, and outside of it, two heaps of refuse were visible; one of iron, fit for reforging, the other of wood, fit for burning.

Gilliatt was at work by daybreak. He took not a moment's rest, except the hours of sleep.

The cormorants flying hither and thither watched him at his work.

X

The Forge

THE storehouse completed, Gilliatt made his forge.

The second cavity selected by Gilliatt offered a den, a sort of narrow but deep gut. He had had an idea of lodging there, but the north wind blew so incessantly and so obstinately in this passage, that he had been obliged to give it up. The draught had suggested to him the idea of a forge. Since this cavern could not be his chamber, it should be his workshop.

To force the obstacle into service is a great stride towards triumph. The wind was Gilliatt's enemy. Gilliatt undertook to make it his servant.

What is said of certain men called "Jack of all trades and master of none," may be said of cavities in rock; what they offer, they do not give. One rock cavity is a bathing-room, but it allows the water to flow off through a fissure; another is a chamber, but without a ceiling; another is a bed of moss, but wet; another is an arm-chair, but of stone.

The forge which Gilliatt wished to establish was sketched out by nature; but nothing was more difficult to accomplish than to conquer this rough outline and render it manageable, and to transform this cavern into a workshop. With three or four large stones hollowed out in funnel shape and terminating in a narrow fissure, chance had created a vast, shapeless bellows, much more powerful than those huge old forge bellows fourteen feet long, which gave, at the base, with every puff, ninety-eight thousand square inches of air. Here it was quite a different matter. The proportions of the hurricane are not to be calculated.

The excess of power was an embarrassment; it was difficult to regulate this blast.

The cavern had two inconveniences: the wind traversed it from end to end, also the water.

It was not the waves of the sea, but a small, perpetual trickle, resembling a dripping more than a torrent.

The foam, dashed incessantly upon the reef by the surf, sometimes more than a hundred feet into the air, had finally filled with sea water a natural cask situated in the lofty rocks which overlooked the excavation. A little in the rear, the overflow of this reservoir formed in the cliff a slender waterfall, an inch in width, which descended perhaps four or five fathoms. A contingent of rain was added. From time to time a passing cloud emptied a shower into this inexhaustible reservoir which was always overfull. This water was brackish and not drinkable, but limpid, though salt. The fall trickled gracefully from the extremities of the hairweed, as from the tips of locks of hair.

It occurred to Gilliatt to make use of this water to

regulate the draught. By means of a funnel made of two or three pieces of planks, nailed together and adjusted in haste, one of which had a shut-off, and of a very large bucket placed beneath as a lower reservoir, without check or counterbalance, only completing the arrangement by a nozzle below and suction holes above, Gilliatt, who was, as we have already said, something of a blacksmith and mechanic, succeeded in devising—to serve in place of the forge bellows, which he did not possess—an apparatus less perfect than what is now called a *cagniardelle,* but less rudimentary than what used to be called in the Pyrenees a *trompe.*

He had some rye flour, he made paste of it; he had some untarred manilla rope, he turned it into oakum. With this oakum and paste and a few bits of wood, he stopped up all the fissures in the rocks, leaving only a small air passage, made from a small piece of the tube, to a powder flask which he had found on the Durande, and which had served for loading the signal gun. This air nozzle was directed horizontally upon a large flagstone where Gilliatt located the forge hearth; a stopper made from a bit of sail cord closed it when needful.

After this, Gilliatt piled up wood and coal on this hearth, struck his steel on the rock itself, dropped the spark on a handful of tow, and with it ignited the wood and the coal.

He tried the draught. It worked admirably.

Gilliatt felt the pride of a Cyclops, master of air, water, and fire.

Master of the air, he had given the wind a sort of lungs, created in the granite a respiratory apparatus, and changed the draught into a pair of bellows. Master of water, of the little cascade he had made a *trompe.* Master of fire, from this inundated rock he had caused flames to flash.

The excavation being nearly everywhere open to the sky, the smoke dispersed freely, blackening the overhanging cliff. These rocks, which seemed forever made for foam, grew black with soot.

Gilliatt took for his anvil a large boulder, of very close grain, which presented nearly the desired form and dimensions. It was a very dangerous base, as it was liable to being split by blows. One of the extremities of this block, which was rounded and terminated in a point, could, in case of need, take the place of the conoid double-horn, but the other, the pyramidal double-horn, was lacking. It was the ancient stone anvil of the Troglodytes. The surface, polished by the waves, had almost the firmness of steel.

Gilliatt regretted that he had not brought his anvil. As he had not been aware that the Durande had been cut in twain by the tempest, he had hoped to find the carpenter's chest and all his ordinary tools in the forecastle. But it was precisely the forepart which had been carried away.

The two excavations found on the reef by Gilliatt were close together. The storeroom and the forge communicated with each other.

Every evening, when his day's work was finished, he supped on a little biscuit softened in water, a sea-urchin, a hermit crab, or some sea-chestnuts, the only game possible among these rocks, and, shivering like the knotted rope, he ascended to sleep in his hole on the great Douvre.

The sort of abstraction in which Gilliatt lived was increased by the very material nature of his occupations. Reality in strong doses frightens. Physical labor with its innumerable details detracted nothing from his amazement at finding himself there and being engaged in his present work; but the very singularity of the task undertaken by Gilliatt maintained him in a sort of ideal twilight region.

It seemed to him at moments that he was dealing blows with his hammer in the clouds. At other moments it seemed to him that all his tools were weapons. He had the singular feeling of a latent attack which he was restraining or preventing. Untwisting ropes, unravelling threads from a sail, propping two planks against each other, seemed like fashioning weapons of war. The thousand minute cares of this case of salvage came at last to resemble precautions against intelligent aggressions, very thinly disguised and very transparent. Gilliatt did not know the words which render the ideas, but he perceived the ideas. He felt himself less and less a workman, and more and more a man of war.

He was there in the character of subduer. He almost understood it. A strange enlargement for his mind.

Moreover, there was about him, as far as the eye could reach, the immense vision of wasted labor. Nothing is more disquieting than to behold the diffusion of forces working in the unfathomable and in the limitless. One seeks the object of these forces. Space always in movement, the indefatigable water, clouds which ever seem in haste, the vast, obscure effort, all this convulsion is a problem.

What is accomplished by this perpetual trembling? What do these gales construct? What do these shocks build? These shocks, these sobs, these howls, what do they create? With what is this tumult occupied? The ebb and flow of these questions is as eternal as the sea.

Gilliatt knew what he was doing, but the agitation of the vast plain confusedly perplexed him with its enigma. Unconsciously to himself, mechanically, imperiously, by pressure and penetration, without any other result than being unconsciously and almost fiercely dazzled, Gilliatt, being a dreamer, blended with his own work the prodigious, useless labor of the sea. How, in fact, can one be there and escape the mystery of the frightful, toilsome waves? How help meditating, so far as meditation is possible, on the vacillation of the waves, the wrath of the foam, the imperceptible wear and tear of the rock, the senseless breathing of the four winds? What terror for the thought is that perpetual recommencement, the ocean well, the Danaïdean pouring, all that pain for nothing!

For nothing? no! But, O! Unknown, thou alone knowest why!

XI
A Discovery

A REEF in the vicinity of the coast is sometimes visited by men; a reef in the open sea, never. Why should any one go there? It is not an island. No fresh supply of provisions is to be hoped for, no fruit trees, no pasturages, no cattle, no springs of water fit to drink. It is bareness in a solitude. It is a rock with cliffs above the water and sharp points below the water. Nothing is to be found there but shipwreck.

Reefs of this species, which the ancient dialect of the sea calls "les Isolés," are, as we have said, strange places. The sea is alone there, it does what it wills. No terrestrial apparition disturbs it. Man frightens the sea; it distrusts him; it hides from him what it is and what it does. In the reef it regains assurance; man will not come there. The monologue of the waves will not be troubled. It works at the reef, repairs its injuries, sharpens its points, renders it bristling, makes it over, maintains it in condition. It undertakes the piercing of the rock, disintegrates the soft stone, denudes the hard stone, removes the flesh, leaves the skeleton, searches, dissects, bores, pierces, channels, puts the cæca in communication, fills the reef with cells, imitates the sponge on a grand scale, hollows out the inside, carves the outside. In this secret mountain which belongs to it, it makes caverns, sanctuaries, palaces; it possesses all manner of hideous and splendid vegetation, composed of floating grasses which bite, and of monsters which take root. Beneath the shadow of the water it conceals this frightful magnificence. In the isolated reef, nothing watches it, spies upon it, or disturbs it; there it develops, at its ease, its mysterious side which is inaccessible to man. There it deposits its living and horrible secret things. All the unknown wonders of the sea are there.

The promontories, capes, headlands, shoals, and reefs are, we insist upon it, true structures. The geological formation is but little in comparison with the oceanic formation. The reefs, those homes of the billows, those pyramids and syringes of foam, belong to a mysterious art which the author of this book has somewhere named Art in Nature, and have an excessive sort of style. The effect of chance there seems to be by design. These structures are multiform. They possess the confusion of the coral formation, the sublimity of the cathedral, the extravagance of the pagoda, the amplitude of the mountain, the delicacy of the jewel, the horror of the sepulchre. They have cells like a wasp's nest, lairs like a menagerie, tunnels like a mole burrow, dungeons like a prison, ambuscades like a camp. They have doors, but they are barricaded; columns, but they are truncated; towers, but they are leaning; bridges, but they are broken; their compartments are adapted to one use and only one; this is only for birds, that is only for fish. There is no passing. Their architectural figure is transformed, confused; it is in accordance with the law of statics and contradictory to it; it breaks off, stops short, begins as an archivolt, ends in an architrave; block on block; Enceladus is the mason.

An extraordinary system of dynamics here exhibits its problems, solved. Alarming pendentives threaten but do not fall. One knows not how these dizzy structures are held together. Everywhere they overhang and deviate from the perpendicular; there are gaps, senseless suspensions; the law of this Babel hides itself; the great unknown architect makes no plans, yet accomplishes everything; the rocks piled up in confusion compose a huge monument; no logic, a vast equilibrium. It is more than solidity, it is eternity.

At the same time it is disorder. The tumult of the waves seems to have passed into the granite. A reef is the tempest petrified. Nothing moves the mind more than that wild architecture, always crumbling, yet always erect. All things there lend assistance to each other, and are opposed to each other. It is a combat of lines whence results an edifice. One recognizes the collaboration of those two enemies, the ocean and the hurricane.

This architecture has its terrible masterpieces. The Douvres reef was one of them.

The sea had fashioned and perfected this one with formidable love. The surly waters licked it. It was hideous, treacherous, obscure; full of caverns.

It had a whole venous system of submarine holes, branching out in the fathomless depths. Many orifices of this inextricable boring were dry at low water. One could enter at one's own risk and peril.

Gilliatt was obliged to explore all these grottoes in order to save his wreckage. There was not one which was not frightful. Everywhere in these caverns was reproduced, with the exaggerated dimensions of the ocean, that aspect of the slaughter-house and the butcher's shambles strangely imprinted on the passage of the Douvres. He who has not seen, in excavations of this kind, these frightful frescoes of nature on the wall of eternal granite, can form no idea of them.

These ferocious grottoes were treacherous; one must not tarry too long in them. High tide filled them to the very ceiling.

Rock limpets and sea mosses abounded there.

They were encumbered with boulders, piled in a heap at the extremities of the vaults. Many of these boulders weighed more than a ton. They were of all sizes and all colors; the majority appeared to be bleeding; some, covered with hairy and glutinous seaweed, seemed great green moles burrowing among the rocks.

Many of these caves terminated abruptly in a low, spherical vault. Others, arteries of a mysterious circulatory system, were prolonged in the rock in dark and tortuous fissures. They were the streets of the abyss. A man could not pass through these fissures, for they gradually contracted. A lighted torch revealed dripping obscurity.

Once, Gilliatt in his search ventured into one of these fissures. The state of the tide was favorable. It was a fine, calm, sunny day; no accident of the sea which could increase the risk was to be feared.

Two necessities urged Gilliatt to these explorations, as we have already pointed out:—the necessity of seeking useful fragments to save, and that of finding crabs and crawfish for his sustenance. Shell fish began to fail him in the Douvres.

The fissure was contracted and passage almost impossible. Gilliatt saw light beyond. He made an effort, drew himself together, writhed to the utmost of his ability, and advanced as far as possible.

He found himself, without suspecting it, precisely in the interior of the rock on the point of which Clubin had run the Durande. Gilliatt was beneath this point. The rock, abrupt on the exterior, and inaccessible, was hollow within. There were galleries, wells, and chambers, as in the tomb of an Egyptian king. This undermining was one of the most complicated among those labyrinths, the work of the water, the indefatigable sapper of the sea. The branches of this cavern beneath the sea probably communicated with the immense watery expanse outside by more than one issue, some yawning on a level with the waves, others deep, invisible funnels. It was quite close to this place that Clubin had cast himself into the sea, but Gilliatt did not know it.

Gilliatt in that crocodile's crevice where, it is true, crocodiles were not to be feared, writhed, and climbed, bumped his head, bent, straightened up again, lost his footing, and regained it again, advanced painfully. Little by little the passage widened, a glimmer of half daylight appeared, and Gilliatt suddenly entered an extraordinary cavern.

XII
THE INTERIOR OF A SUBMARINE EDIFICE

THIS glimmer of daylight came opportunely.

One step more and Gilliatt would have fallen into water that was, perhaps, unfathomable. The waters of such caves are so cold, and paralyze so instantaneously that often the stoutest swimmers remain in them forever.

Moreover, there is no way of mounting and clinging to the cliffs between which one is immured.

Gilliatt stopped short. The crevice from which he had emerged terminated in a narrow and slippery exit, a sort of corbelling in the perpendicular wall. Gilliatt placed his back to the wall and gazed about.

He was in a great cave. Above him there was something like the lower part of a huge skull. This skull had the appearance of being recently dissected. The dripping nerves of the striated rocks imitated on the vault the branchings of the fibres and the jagged sutures of a cranium. For ceiling, the stone; for floor, the water; the sea waves confined between the four walls of the grotto seemed like large, trembling paving-slabs. The grotto was closed on every side. Not a window, not an airhole; not a breach in the wall, not a crack in the vault. All this was lighted from below, by the water. The resplendence was indescribable.

Gilliatt, the pupils of whose eyes had been dilated during his dark passage through the corridor, distinguished every object in this twilight.

He was acquainted, through repeated visits, with the caves of Plémont in Jersey, the Creux-Maillé in Guernsey, the "Shops" in Sark, so named because of the smugglers who deposited their merchandise there; none of these marvellous caves was to be compared with the subterranean and submarine chamber into which he had now penetrated.

Gilliatt beheld in front of him, beneath the waves, a sort of flooded arch. This arch, a natural ogive fashioned by the water, stood out dazzlingly between its two deep, black supports. It was through this submerged porch that the light from the open sea entered the cavern. A strange daylight, the effect of engulfment.

This light spread out under the water like a large fan and was reflected from the rock. Its rectilinear rays, cut into long, straight bands on the opacity of the bottom, growing lighter or darker from one crevice to another, seemed as if refracted through layers of glass. There was daylight in this cavern, but an unknown daylight. There was nothing of the earthly in this brilliance. One could fancy one's self in another planet. The light was an enigma; one would have thought it the glaucous light from the eye of a sphinx.

This cave represented the interior of an enormous and splendid skull; the vault was the cranium; the arch was the mouth; the eye sockets were lacking. That mouth, swallowing and giving forth the ebb and flow of the tide, yawning in the full external midday, drank in light and belched forth bitterness. Certain creatures, intelligent and wicked, are like that. The ray of sunlight, as it traversed this porch, obstructed by a vitreous medium of sea water, became as green as a ray from Aldebaran. The water, all filled with that liquid light, appeared like a melted emerald. A shade of aquamarine of unbelievable delicacy, gently tinged the whole cavern. The vault, with its almost cerebral lobes, and its crawling ramifications, similar to outspreading nerves, had the tender reflection of chrysoprase. The sheeny pools of the waves, reflected from the ceiling, were decomposed and recomposed in endless succession, stretching and contracting their golden scales with the movements of a mysterious dance. It produced a spectral impression; the mind wondered what prey or what expectation rendered this magnificent network of living fire so joyous.

From the reliefs of the vault and the rough points of

the rock hung long, delicate vegetation, probably bathing their roots through the granite, in some sheet of water above, and telling off, one after the other, at their extremities, a drop of water, a pearl. These pearls fell into the gulf with a slight, gentle splash. The startling effect of this whole was indescribable. Nothing more charming could be imagined, nothing more mournful could be found.

It was a wondrous palace where Death sat contented.

XIII
What One Sees There, and What One Gets a Glimpse of

DAZZLING gloom: such was this surprising place.

The palpitation of the sea made itself felt in this cavern. The external oscillation swelled, then depressed, the internal sheet of water with the regularity of respiration. One seemed to be conscious of a mysterious soul in that great green diaphragm, thus rising and falling in silence.

The water was magnificently limpid, and Gilliatt distinguished in it, at various depths, submerged stations, projecting surfaces of rock, of a darker and still darker green. Certain obscure depths were probably unfathomable.

On each side of the submarine porch, rough outlines of flattened arches, full of shadows, indicated little lateral caves, side aisles of the central cavern, accessible, possibly, at the period of very low tides.

These crevices had sloping ceilings, with more or less spreading angles. Tiny beaches a few feet wide, laid bare by the excavations of the sea, stretched under these obliquities and were lost there.

Here and there seaweeds more than a fathom in length undulated beneath the water like hair waving in the wind. One caught glimpses of forests of sea-plants.

The whole wall of the cave, under the water and out of the water, from summit to base, from its vault to the point where it merged into the invisible, was hung with these prodigious blooms of the ocean, so rarely perceived by the human eye, which old Spanish navigators called *praderías del mar,*—"meadows of the sea."

A luxuriant moss, which possessed all the shades of olive, concealed and enlarged the swellings of the granite. From all the projecting surfaces sprang slender crimped ribbons of the wrack from which fishermen make barometers. The light breath of the cavern waved these shining bands to and fro.

Beneath this vegetation the rarest jewels in the casket of the ocean were both hidden and displayed, ivory shells, conch shells, mitre shells, helmet shells, purple shells, whelks, and turreted murexes. Bell-shaped limpets, resembling microscopic huts, adhered to the rocks in every direction, and were grouped together in villages, in whose streets roamed the beetles of the sea. As pebbles could enter this cavern only with difficulty, shell fish took refuge there. Shell fish are the great lords, who, all bedecked with embroidery and gold lace, avoid the rude and uncivil contact of the populace of pebbles. The shining heap of shells formed beneath the waves, in some spots, ineffable radiations, across which one caught a glimpse of a throng of azures and pearly tints and golds,—of all the shades of the water.

On the wall of the cavern, a little above the line of high tide, a magnificent and singular plant was attached like a border to the hangings of wrack, continuing and completing it. This plant, fibrous, thick, inextricably bent and almost black, presented to the eyes wide expanses, tangled and obscure, dotted everywhere with innumerable little flowers the hue of lapis-lazuli. In the water these flowers seemed to take fire, and one fancied them blue living flame. Outside of the water they were flowers, under the water they were sapphires, so that the waves, as they rose and inundated the base of the grottoes clothed with these plants, covered the rock with carbuncles.

At each surge of the billows, swelling like lungs, these flowers were bathed and shone resplendent; at each fall they were extinguished; a melancholy resemblance to destiny. It was inspiration, which is life; then expiration, which is death.

One of the marvels of this cavern was the rock. This rock, now a wall, now an arch, now a binding beam or a pilaster, was in places rough and bare, then, close beside these, the most delicate natural carvings. An indescribable something, which had much intelligence, was mingled with the massive stupidity of the granite. What an artist is the abyss! Such and such a section of wall hewn squarely and covered with round bosses in various positions, presented a vague bas-relief; before this sculpture, which contained something of the cloudlike, one could dream of Prometheus making rough sketches for Michael-Angelo. It seemed as though that genius might, with a few blows of the hammer, finish what the giant had begun. In other spots the rock was damascened like a Saracen buckler, or inlaid with niello like a Florentine fountain basin. It had panels which seemed made of Corinthian bronze; then arabesques, like the gate of a mosque; then, like a runic stone, obscure and mystic imprints of nails. Plants with small, twisted branches and tendrils, interlacing above the gold of the lichens, covered it with filigree. This cavern was in some respects like an Alhambra. It was the union of savagery and goldsmith's work in the august and shapeless architecture of chance.

The magnificent moulderings of the sea covered the angles of the granite as with velvet. The cliffs were festooned with magnificent liana grandiflora, hanging gracefully, which ornamented the walls as if by intelligent designs. Wall pellitory with odd clusters displayed its tufts tastefully and appropriately. All the coquetry possible to a cavern was there. The surprising Eden-like light which proceeded from beneath the water, at one and the same time a marine penumbra and an Elysian radiance, softened down all lineaments into a sort of visionary diffusion. Each wave was a prism. The contours of things beneath these rainbow-hued undulations had the chromatic shades of optical lenses made too convex; solar spectres floated beneath the water. One thought that one beheld fragments of submarine rainbows floating in this auroral pellucidness. Elsewhere, in other corners, there was a kind of moonlight in the water. All splendors seemed amalgamated there to accomplish some unknown and hidden deed of darkness. Nothing could be more disquieting and more enigmatic than such sumptuousness in that cave.

Enchantment was the dominating note.

The fantastic vegetation and the shapeless stratification agreed and were harmonious. This union of wild things was a happy one. The ramifications clung fast while having the appearance of touching lightly. The caress of the savage rock and of the untamed flower was profound. Massive pillars had for capitals and ligatures frail garlands constantly a-quiver, one thought of the fingers of fairies tickling the feet of behemoths, and the rock sustained the plant, and the plant strained the rock in its embrace, with a monstrous grace.

The result of these mysteriously adjusted deformities was an indescribably sovereign beauty. The works of nature, no less supreme than the works of genius, contain something of the absolute, and are imposing. Their unexpectedness makes them imperiously obeyed by the mind; one is conscious of a premeditation which is outside of man, and they are never more striking than when they make the exquisiteness of the terrible stand out in sudden relief.

This unknown grotto was, so to speak, and if such an expression be admissible, elevated to the stars. One there experienced all the unexpected effects of stupor. What filled this crypt was the light of the Apocalypse. One was not quite sure that the thing existed. One had before one's eyes a reality stamped with impossibility. One gazed at it, one touched it, one was there; only, it was difficult to believe in it.

Was it daylight which came through that window beneath the sea? Was it water which trembled in that gloomy basin? Were not those arches and porches the celestial clouds imitating a cavern? What stone was this under foot? Was not this support on the point of becoming disintegrated and turning into vapor? What jewelry of shells was that of which one caught a glimpse? At what distance was one from life, from earth, from men? What was this rapture, mingled with these shadows? Unprecedented, almost sacred emotion, to which was added the gentle uneasiness of grass beneath the water.

At the extremity of the cave, which was oblong, under a cyclopean archivolt of singularly correct design, in an almost indistinct hollow, a sort of cavern within the cave, and of tabernacle within the sanctuary, behind a sheet of green light interposed like a temple veil, a stone with square sides could be seen bearing a resemblance to an altar. The water surrounded this stone on all sides. It seemed as though a goddess had just descended from it. One could not refrain from imagining beneath that crypt, on that altar, some celestial nude figure, eternally pensive, whom the entrance of a man had caused to hide. It was difficult to conceive of that august cell without a vision within it, the apparition evoked by reverie reconstituted itself; a flood of chaste light on shoulders hardly seen, a brow bathed with dawn, an Olympian oval of countenance, mysterious roundness of breasts, modest arms, tresses falling loose in the aurora, ineffable hips modelled in whiteness against a sacred mist, the form of a nymph, the glance of a virgin, a Venus rising from the sea, an Eve springing from chaos. Such was the dream in which it was impossible not to indulge. It was improbable that there should not be a phantom there. A wholly nude woman, bearing a star within her, had probably just been on that altar. On that pedestal, whence emanated an unspeakable ecstasy, one imagined a whiteness, living and erect. The mind pictured to itself, amid the mute adoration of that cavern, an Amphitrite, a Tethys, some Diana who could love, a statue of the ideal formed of radiance and gazing sweetly on the gloom. It was she who, at her departure, had left behind her in the cavern that brightness, a sort of light perfume, which had emanated from the body of that star. The dazzling radiance of the phantom was no longer there, one did not behold that figure made to be seen only by the invisible, but one felt it; one was seized with that trembling which is voluptuous delight. The goddess was absent, but the divinity was present.

The beauty of the cave seemed made for that presence. It was because of that deity, of that fairy, of that pearly iridescence, of that queen of the zephyrs, of that Grace born amid the waves, it was because of her, so at least one fancied, that the subterranean cave was thus sacredly walled up, so that around this divine phantom nothing could ever disturb the obscurity, which is a form of respect, and the silence, which is a majesty.

Gilliatt, who was a sort of seer of nature, dreamed in confused emotion.

All at once, a few feet below him, in the charming transparencies of that water which was like liquid precious stones, he perceived something indescribable. A sort of long rag was moving in the oscillation of the waves. This strip of rag was not floating, it was swimming; it had a purpose, it was going somewhere, it was swift. This rag had the form of a jester's bauble with points; these points, which were flabby, were waving. They seemed to be covered with a dust impossible to moisten. It was more than horrible, it was foul. There was something of the chimera about the thing; it was a creature, unless it was an illusion. It seemed to direct itself towards the dark side of the cave, and to sink into the depths. The dense waters grew darker above it, as this sinister form glided by and disappeared.

BOOK SECOND
LABOR

I
The Resources of One Who Lacks Everything

THIS CAVE did not release men easily. Entrance to it was not easy, the exit was still more difficult. Nevertheless, Gilliatt extricated himself from it, but he never returned to it. He had found nothing there of which he was in search, and he had no time to be curious.

He put his forge into immediate activity. He lacked tools, he made them.

For fuel, he had the wreck; for a motor, the water; the wind for bellows, a stone for an anvil; for art, his instinct; for power, his will.

Gilliatt entered ardently upon this gloomy labor.

The weather appeared to be complaisant. It continued dry and as little equinoctial as possible. The month of March had arrived, but tranquilly. The days were growing long. The blue of the sky, the vast gentleness of the movements of the expanse, the serenity of midday, seemed to exclude all evil intent. The sea was gay in the sunlight. A preliminary caress spices treachery. The sea is not avaricious of such caresses. When one has to do with a woman,[1] one must distrust her smile.

There was but little wind; the hydraulic bellows worked all the better for it. An excess of wind would have hindered rather than helped.

1. The sea is feminine in French.

Gilliatt had a saw; he made himself a file; with the saw he attacked the wood, with the file he attacked the metal; then he availed himself of the blacksmith's two iron hands, a pair of tongs and pincers; the tongs grip, the pincers manipulate; the one acts like the wrist, the other, like the finger. A set of tools is an organism. Little by little, Gilliatt provided himself with auxiliaries, and constructed his armory. With a piece of sheet iron he made a hood for the hearth of his forge.

One of his principal cares was sorting and repairing pulleys. He put into working condition the blocks and sheaves of the falls. He cut off all the splintered parts of all the broken beams, and shaped the ends afresh; he had, as we have said, for the needs of his carpentering work, a quantity of timbers stored up and matched according to their forms, dimensions, and kind, oak on one side, pine on the other; curved pieces, like the riders, separate from the straight pieces like the binding-strakes. They constituted his reserve of fulcrums and levers, of which he might stand in great need at any given moment.

Any one who is meditating a hoisting apparatus must provide himself with beams and tackle; but this was not sufficient; rope was needed. Gilliatt repaired the cables and warps. He ravelled the tattered sails and succeeded in extracting from them excellent twine, of which he made cord; with this cord he joined the ropes. Only, these joints were liable to rot; these cords and cables must be speedily used, and Gilliatt had been able to make only white rope, as he lacked tar.

The ropes being repaired, he repaired the chains.

Thanks to the lateral point of the stone anvil, which took the place of the conical double-horn, he was able to forge coarse but solid rings. With these rings he attached the ends of the broken chains to each other, and made long pieces.

To forge alone, and without assistance, is more than hard; nevertheless, he managed it. It is true that he had to forge only pieces small in size; he could work them with one hand with the pincers, while he hammered them with the other.

He cut into fragments the round iron railings of the captain's bridge; at one end of each fragment he forged a point, at the other, a large flat head, and these made huge spikes about a foot long. These spikes, much used in making pontoon bridges, are useful for fixing in the rocks.

Why did Gilliatt take all this trouble? The reader will see.

He was obliged to renew the edge of his axe and the teeth of his saw many times. For the saw he had made a hand file.

Occasionally, he made use of the capstan of the Durande. The hook of the chain broke. Gilliatt forged another.

With the aid of his pincers and tongs, and making use of his chisel as a screwdriver, he undertook to take apart the two paddle-wheels of the vessel, and he succeeded. It will not be forgotten that this was possible, it was a peculiarity of their construction. The paddle-boxes which had covered them, served to pack them in, for with the plank of the two boxes, Gilliatt hammered and joined together two cases, in which he deposited, piece by piece, the two wheels, carefully numbered.

His bit of chalk proved precious to him for this numbering.

He placed these two cases on the most solid part of the Durande's deck.

These preliminaries concluded, Gilliatt found himself face to face with the supreme difficulty. The question of the machinery presented itself.

It had been possible to take the wheels apart; to take the machinery apart was impossible.

In the first place, Gilliatt was but little acquainted with this mechanism. By working at haphazard, he might do it some irreparable injury. Next, in order even to attempt to take it apart, bit by bit, if he had been so imprudent as to do so, other tools were necessary than those which can be fabricated with a cavern for a forge, an air draught for bellows, and a stone for an anvil. In attempting to take the machinery apart, he ran the risk of breaking it in pieces.

Here one might believe one's self absolutely face to face with the impossible.

It seemed as though Gilliatt were driven to the foot of that wall,—the impossible.

What was he to do?

II

How Shakespeare and Æschylus Can Meet

GILLIATT had his own idea.

Since the time of that mason-carpenter of Salbris, who, in the sixteenth century, in the infancy of science,—long before Amontons had discovered the first law of friction, Lahire the second, and Coulomb the third—without counsel, without guidance, with no other aid than that of a child, his son, with an ill-shaped set of tools, resolved at one stroke, during the lowering of the great clock of the Church of Charité-sur-Loire, five or six problems of statics and dynamics intermingled like the wheels in an entanglement of carts, and presenting an obstacle simultaneously, since that superb and marvellous feat which found means without breaking even a brass wire, and without unsettling a gearing, to lower in one piece, by a wonderful simplification, from the second story of the bell tower to the first, that massive case of the hours, all of iron and copper, "as large as the chamber of the night watchman," with its movement, its cylinders, its barrels, its drums, its hooks and balances, its spindle for the hour hand and its spindle for the minute hand, its horizontal pendulum, its escapements, its masses of big chains and little chains, its stone weights, one of which weighed five hundred pounds, its striking weight and chimes, its jacks that strike the hours,—since the day of that man who had performed that miracle, and whose name is no longer known, nothing parallel to what Gilliatt meditated doing had ever been undertaken.

The operation which Gilliatt had undertaken was worse, perhaps; that is to say, still more beautiful.

The weight, the delicacy, the intricacy of difficulties were no less in the case of the Durande's machinery, than in that of the clock of Charité-sur-Loire.

The Gothic carpenter had an assistant, his son; Gilliatt was alone.

A crowd of spectators was there, who had come from Meung-sur-Loire, Nevers, and even from Orleans, who could, in case of need, render assistance to the mason of Salbris, and who encouraged him by their friendly uproar. Gilliatt had around him no other noise than that of the wind, and no other throng than the waves.

Nothing equals the timidity of ignorance, except its temerity. When ignorance sets out but to dare, it is because it has a compass within it. This compass is the intuition of the true, often more clear in a simple than in an enlightened mind.

Ignorance invites to an attempt. Ignorance is reverie, and reverie is a curious force. Knowledge sometimes disconcerts, and often dissuades. Gama, had he known, would have recoiled before the cape of storms. If Christopher Columbus had been a good cosmographer, he would not have discovered America.

The second person to ascend Mont Blanc was a learned man, Saussure; the first was a shepherd, Balmat.

These cases, let us remark in passing, are the exception, and all this detracts nothing from science, which remains the rule. The ignorant man may discover, the learned man alone invents.

The boat was still anchored in the cove of "the Man," where the sea left it tranquil. Gilliatt, it will be remembered, had arranged something so as to maintain free communication with his vessel. He proceeded thither, and carefully measured her beam at various points, particularly her midship-frame. Then he returned to the Durande, and measured the greatest diameter of the bottom of the machinery. This diameter, minus the wheels, of course, was two feet less than the greatest beam of the boat. Hence, the engine could go in the boat.

But how was he to get it into the boat?

III

Gilliatt's Masterpiece Comes to the Succor of Lethierry's Masterpiece

SOME time later, any fisherman who should have been foolish enough to loiter about that coast at that season, would have been repaid for his hardihood by the sight of something singular between the Douvres.

This is what he would have perceived; four stout beams, equally spaced, running from one Douvre to the other, and forced, as it were, between the rocks, which is the best sort of solidity. On the side of the little Douvre, their ends rested and were buttressed against projections of the rock; on the side of the great Douvre, these extremities must have been violently driven into the cliffs by blows from the hammer of some powerful workman standing upon the very beam which he was forcing in. These beams were a little longer than the width of the passage; hence the firmness of their insertion; hence, also, their adjustment on an inclined plane. They touched the great Douvre at an acute, and the little Douvre at an obtuse, angle. They sloped slightly, but unequally, which was a defect. But for this defect, one might have said that they were arrayed for the reception of the platform of a bridge. To these four beams were attached four sets of tackle, each furnished with its tye and fall and having this bold peculiarity, that the block and fall with two sheaves was at one end of the beam, while the simple pulley was at the opposite end. This separation, too great not to be dangerous, was probably necessitated by the operations to be accomplished. The blocks were strong and the pulleys solid. To these sets of tackle, cables were attached, which at a distance appeared like threads, and below this aërial apparatus of falls and timber-work, the massive wreck, the Durande, seemed suspended by these threads.

It was not yet suspended. Perpendicularly, beneath the timbers, eight openings had been made in the deck, four on the starboard and four on the port side of the engine, and eight others beneath these, in the bottom. Cables descending vertically from the four tackles entered the deck, then emerged from the bottom, through the openings on the starboard side, passed under the keel and under the engine, and re-entered the ship again through the port openings and, reascending, traversing the bridge afresh, returned and were coiled round the four pulleys of the beam, where a sort of burton tackle seized them and made of them a bundle bound to a single cable, and capable of being guided by a single arm.

A hook and a deadeye, through the hole of which the single cable was passed and wound, completed and, when necessary, checked the apparatus. This combination forced the four tackles to work together and, a complete check on the suspending forces, a dynamic rudder, in the hand of the pilot of the operation, maintained the rigging in equilibrium.

The very ingenious adjustment of this burton possessed some of the simplifying qualities of the Weston-pulley of to-day, and of the antique polyspast of Vitruvius. Gilliatt had invented this, although he knew neither Vitruvius, who no longer existed, nor Weston, who did not as yet exist. The length of the cables varied according to the unequal slope of the beams, and corrected this defect to some extent. The ropes were dangerous, the untarred cables might break, chains would have been better; but chains would have run badly through the blocks.

All this apparatus was full of defects but, as made by one man, was amazing.

However, we abridge the explanation. The reader will understand that we omit many details which would render the matter clear to members of the craft and obscure to all others.

The top of the engine's smoke stack passed between the two middle beams.

Gilliatt, without suspecting it, an unconscious plagiarist of the unknown, had reproduced, after a lapse of three centuries, the mechanism of the carpenter of Salbris, a rudimentary and incorrect mechanism, hazardous to him who should dare to make use of it.

Let us remark here that even the grossest faults do not prevent a mechanism from working after a fashion. It limps, but it walks. The obelisk on the square of St. Peter's at Rome was erected contrary to all laws of statics. Tzar Peter's coach was so constructed that it seemed as though it must upset at every step; but it moved onward all the same. What deformities were in the machinery of Marly! Everything there was out of perpendicular. But, none the less, it furnished Louis XIV with water.

At all events, Gilliatt had confidence. He had even counted upon success so far as to fasten in the rail of the paunch, one day when he went there, two pairs of iron rings opposite each other, on the two sides of the boat, spaced in the same way as the four rings of the Durande, to which were attached the four chains of the smoke stack.

Gilliatt evidently had a very complete and well-defined plan. Having all the chances against him, he wished to place all precautions on his side.

He did things which appeared useless, a sign of attentive forethought.

His manner of procedure would have puzzled, as we have already remarked, an observer or even a connoisseur.

A witness of his labors who should have beheld him, for instance, with unprecedented efforts and at the risk of breaking his neck, drive, with his hammer, eight or ten great spikes which he had forged, into the base of the two Douvres, at the entrance to the defile of the reef, would have found some difficulty in comprehending the reason for these spikes, and would probably have inquired to what purpose all this useless trouble.

Then, if he had beheld Gilliatt measuring the fragment of the bulwark of the bow which, as the reader will remember, remained clinging to the wreck, then attaching a strong warp to the upper edge of this fragment, cutting away with his axe the dislocated timberwork which held it, drag it out of the passage with the receding tide assisting by pushing the bottom while Gilliatt tugged at the top, and then, with great difficulty, attaching, with the small cable, this heavy mass of planks and beams, larger than the very entrance of the defile, to the spikes sunk in the base of the little Douvre,—the observer would have understood still less, perhaps, and would have said to himself that if Gilliatt wished, for the convenience of his operations, to clear the strait of the Douvres of this encumbrance, he had only to let it fall into the tide, which would have carried it out with the current.

Gilliatt probably had his reasons.

In order to fix his spikes in the base of the Douvres, Gilliatt took advantage of all the fissures in the granite, enlarged them where needful, and first drove in wedges of wood, in which he afterwards planted the iron spikes. He made a beginning of the same preparations in the two rocks which reared themselves at the other extremity of the reef strait, on the east; he stuffed all their crannies with wooden plugs, as though he wished to hold these crannies also in readiness to receive clamps; but this appeared to be a simple precaution, for he drove in no spikes. It will be understood that, out of prudence, in his penury, he could only expend his materials in proportion to his needs, and at the moment when the necessity presented itself. It was another complication added to so many other difficulties.

A first labor achieved, a second arose. Gilliatt passed from one to the other without hesitation, and took this giant's stride with resolution.

IV
Sub Re

THE aspect of the man who wrought these things had become terrifying.

Gilliatt, in this multiple toil, expended all his forces simultaneously; it was with difficulty that he renewed them.

Through privations on the one hand and weariness on the other, he had grown thin. His hair and beard had grown long. He had but one shirt left which was not in rags. He was barefooted, the wind having carried away one of his shoes, and the sea, the other. Splinters from the rudimentary and very dangerous anvil which he used had made little wounds on his hands and arms, the spatterings of toil. These wounds—scratches rather than wounds,—were superficial, but irritated by the sharp air and the salt water.

He was hungry, thirsty, and cold.

His can of fresh water was empty. His rye flour had been used or eaten. All that was left for him was a little biscuit.

He broke it with his teeth, as he now lacked water wherewith to soak it.

Little by little, day by day, his strength decreased.

This redoubtable rock was sapping his life.

Drinking was a problem; eating was a problem; sleeping was a problem.

He ate when he succeeded in catching a sea-louse, or a crab; he drank when he saw a sea-bird alight on a point of rock. He climbed thither, and found a hollow with a little fresh water. He drank after the bird, sometimes with the bird; for the mews and the gulls had become accustomed to him, and did not fly away at his approach. Gilliatt, even at his hours of greatest hunger, did them no harm. It will be remembered that he had a superstition with regard to birds. The birds, on their side, were not afraid of him, now that his hair was shaggy and wild, and his beard long; this change of visage reassured them; they no longer thought him a man, but believed him to be a beast.

The birds and Gilliatt were now good friends. These poor creatures aided each other. As long as Gilliatt had had flour, he had crumbled up for them the cakes which he made: now, in their turn, they pointed out to him the spots where there was water.

He ate his shell fish raw: shell fish quench thirst to a certain extent. He cooked the crabs; having no pot, he roasted them between two stones heated in the fire, after the manner of the savage inhabitants of the Faroë Islands.

In the meantime, the equinoctial weather had appeared to some extent; rain had come; but a hostile rain. No sheets, no downpours, but long, fine, sharp, icy, penetrating needles, which pierced through Gilliatt's garments to the very skin, and his skin to the very bone. This rain furnished but little water to drink, and wet him none the less.

Chary of assistance, lavish of misery, such was this rain, unworthy of heaven. Gilliatt had it upon him for more than a week, day and night. This rain was an evil action from on high.

At night, in his hole in the rock, he slept only from the utter exhaustion of labor. The huge sea gnats came and stung him, and he awoke covered with pustules.

He had fever, which sustained him; fever is a help which destroys. He instinctively chewed lichens or sucked the leaves of wild cochlearia, the meagre shoots of the dry crevices of the reef. However, he paid but little heed to his sufferings. He had not the time to turn his attention from his work because of them; the engine of the Durande was in good condition. That sufficed for him.

Every moment, as the necessities of his work required,

he threw himself into the water, then came out again. He entered the water and emerged from it as a man passes from one chamber in his dwelling to another.

His garments were never dry. They were soaked with the incessant rain, and with sea water, which never dries. Gilliatt lived in a constant state of moisture.

To live in wet clothing is a habit which can be acquired. Poor groups of Irish, old men, mothers, young girls almost naked, children, who pass the winter in the open air, beneath the pouring rain and the snow, huddled close together in the corners of houses in the streets of London, live and die in this condition.

To be soaked without, and to be thirsty; Gilliatt endured that strange torture. At times he sucked the sleeve of his peajacket.

The fire which he made scarcely warmed him. Fire in the open air is only half a comfort; it burns on one side and freezes on the other.

Gilliatt was in a perspiration, and yet shivering.

Everything around Gilliatt offered resistance in a sort of horrible silence. He was conscious of this enmity.

Things have a gloomy *non possumus*.

Their inertia is a lugubrious warning.

An immense ill will surrounded Gilliatt. There were burns and shiverings. The fire bit him, the water chilled him, thirst gave him fever, the wind rent his clothes, hunger ruined his stomach. He suffered the weight of an exhausting combination of circumstances. The obstacle, silent, vast, with the apparent irresponsibility of fate, but full of indescribable and savage unanimity, converged from all points upon Gilliatt. Gilliatt felt it bearing down inexorably upon him. There was no means of escape. It was almost like a living person. Gilliatt was conscious of a sombre rejection, and of a hatred exerting an effort to subdue him.

It depended only upon himself to flee, but, since he remained, he had to deal with this impenetrable hostility. Not being able to put him outside, it put him under. It? The unknown. It clasped him close, it compressed him, it took his place from him, it deprived him of breath. He was bruised by the invisible. Every day the mysterious vise was tightened one turn.

Gilliatt's situation amid these disturbing surroundings resembled an ambiguous duel in which one party is the victim of treachery.

The coalition of obscure forces environed him. He was conscious of the existence of a resolution to get rid of him. It is thus that the glacier expels the wandering block of stone.

Almost without having the appearance of touching him, this secret coalition had reduced him to rags, to bleeding, driven him at bay, and, so to speak, crippled him before the battle. He worked on, none the less, untiringly, but in proportion as the work was done, the workman was undone. One would have said that brute nature, fearing the soul, had adopted the expedient of wearing out the man. Gilliatt persisted, and waited. The abyss had begun by exhausting him. What would the abyss do next?

The double Douvre, that dragon made of granite, and lying in ambush in the open sea, had admitted Gilliatt. It had allowed him to enter, and to do what he wished. This reception resembled the hospitality of yawning jaws.

The desert, extent, space, where there are so many refusals for man, the mute inclemency of phenomena pursuing their courses, the great general implacable and passive law, the ebb and flow, the reef, the black Pleiades, each point of which is a star with whirlwinds, the centre of an irradiation of currents, an unknown plot of the indifference of things against the temerity of a being, winter, the clouds, the besieging sea, enveloped Gilliatt, beset him, closed in upon him, in a measure, and separated him from the living like a dungeon cell rising round a man.

Everything against him, nothing for him, he was isolated, abandoned, weakened, undermined, forgotten. Gilliatt had his empty storeroom, his broken or weakened tools, hunger and thirst by day, cold by night, wounds and tatters, rags on the suppurating spots, holes in his clothes and in his flesh, torn hands, bleeding feet, emaciated limbs, a livid countenance, and a flame in his eyes.

A superb flame is the visible will. The eye of man is

so made that one perceives his virtue in it. Our eyes reveal the quantity of man there is in us. We assert ourselves by the light which lies under our eyelids. Small consciences blink their eyes, great ones dart lightnings. If nothing glows beneath the lids, it is because nothing in the brain thinks, nothing in the heart loves. He who loves wills, and he who wills lightens and breaks forth in brilliancy. Resolution lends fire to the eye, an admirable fire which is composed of the combustion of timid thoughts.

The obstinate are the sublime. He who is merely brave acts from impulse; he who is merely valiant has but a temperament; he who is only courageous has only a virtue; the man obstinate in the true sense has greatness. Nearly the whole secret of great hearts lies in this word, *perseverando*. Perseverance is to courage what the wheel is to the lever, it is the perpetual renewing of the fulcrum. Whatever the goal may be, in earth or heaven, the whole secret lies in proceeding to that goal; in the first case, one is Columbus; in the second case, one is Jesus. The cross is madness; hence its glory. Not to allow one's conscience to discuss, nor one's will to be disarmed, it is thus that one obtains suffering and triumph. In the order of moral facts, to fall does not preclude soaring. Ascension springs from the fall. The mediocre allow themselves to be dissuaded by a specious obstacle; the strong do not. To perish is their perhaps; to conquer is their certainty. You may give Stephen all sorts of good reasons for not allowing himself to be stoned. The disdain of objections raised by reason brings forth that sublime victory which is called martyrdom.

All Gilliatt's efforts seemed chained to the impossible, success was feeble or slow, and he had to spend much to obtain a little; that is what made him magnanimous, that is what rendered him pathetic.

The misery of his solitary work lay in the fact that, in order to erect four beams above a stranded vessel, in order to cut out and isolate in that vessel the part that could be saved, in order to adjust to that wreck within a wreck four sets of tackle with their cables, so many preparations, so many labors, so much groping, so many nights on the hard rock, so many days in pain had been necessary. Fatality in the cause, necessity in the effect. This wretchedness Gilliatt had more than accepted; he had chosen it. Fearing a competitor, because a competitor might prove a rival, he had sought no assistance. The overwhelming enterprise, risk, danger, multiplied by itself, the possible engulfment of the rescuer by what he was rescuing, famine, fever, destitution, distress,—he had taken all these upon himself alone. He had been thus egotistic.

He was beneath a sort of frightful pneumatic chamber. His vitality was leaving him, little by little. He hardly perceived it.

Exhaustion of strength does not exhaust the will. Faith is only a secondary power, to will is the first. The proverbial mountains which faith moves are nothing beside that which the will accomplishes. All the ground which Gilliatt lost in vigor he made up in tenacity. The reducing of the physical man under the repressing action of this savage nature ended in the growth of the moral man.

Gilliatt was not conscious of fatigue, or, to speak more correctly, he would not yield to it. The refusal of the soul to succumb to the weaknesses of the body is an immense force.

Gilliatt saw the steps by which his work progressed, and saw nothing else. He was wretched without knowing it. His goal, which he had almost attained, affected him with hallucinations. He endured all these sufferings without any other thought occurring to him than this: Forward! His work had mounted to his brain. Will intoxicates. One can become intoxicated with one's own soul. This intoxication is called heroism.

Gilliatt was a sort of Job of the ocean.

But a Job struggling, a Job combating, and facing his scourges, a conquering Job, and, if such words are not too grand for a poor sailor fisherman of crabs and lobsters,—a Promethean Job.

V
Sub Umbra

SOMETIMES, at night, Gilliatt opened his eyes and looked at the darkness.

He felt himself strangely moved.

His eyes opened upon blackness. A lugubrious situation, full of anxiety.

There is such a thing as the pressure of the gloom.

An indescribable roof of shadows: a deep obscurity inaccessible to the diver; light mingled with that obscurity, an indescribably subdued and sombre light; brightness shattered to bits; is it seed? is it ashes? Millions of torches, no illumination; a vast combustion, which does not reveal its secret; a diffusion of fire in dust, which seems a flight of sparks stopped in their career; the disorder of the whirlwind, and the immobility of the sepulchre, the problem presenting the opening of a precipice, the enigma showing, yet concealing its face, the infinite masked with blackness,—such is night. This superposition weighs heavily on man.

This amalgamation of all mysteries at once, of the cosmic mystery as well as of the mystery of fate, overwhelms the human head.

The pressure of the gloom acts in inverse sense on different sorts of souls. Man, in the presence of night, recognizes himself as incomplete. He beholds the obscurity, and is conscious of his weakness. In the presence of night, man is blind. Man, face to face with night, struggles, kneels, prostrates himself, lies prone, crawls towards a hole, or seeks wings for himself. Almost always he desires to flee from that shapeless presence of the Unknown. He asks himself what it is; he trembles; he bends; he ignores; sometimes, also, he desires to go towards it.

To go whither?

Yonder.

Yonder? What is that? And what is there?

This curiosity is evidently that of things forbidden, for in that direction all the bridges around man are broken. The arch of the infinite is lacking. But the forbidden, being a gulf, attracts. Where the foot cannot tread, the eye can reach; where the eye cannot penetrate, the mind can soar. There is no man, however feeble and insufficient he may be, who does not make the attempt. Man, according to his nature, is searching or at a stand-still in the presence of night. For one sort it is a repression; for the other, an expansion. The spectacle is gloomy. The indefinable is mingled with it.

Is the night serene? There is a background of gloom. Is it stormy? There is a background of vapor. The illimitable refuses itself and offers itself at one and the same time, closed to experiment, open to conjecture. Innumerable punctures of light render the bottomless obscurity more black. Carbuncles, scintillations, stars, presences in the unknown revealed, frightful challenges to approach and touch that brightness. They are the landmarks of creation in the absolute; they are milestones where there are no longer distances; they are some impossible yet real system of numbering the fathoms of the infinite depths. A microscopic point which shines out; then another, then another, then another; it is the imperceptible, it is the enormous. This light is a hearth, this hearth is a star, this star is a sun, this sun is a universe, this universe is nothing. Every number is zero in the presence of the infinite.

These universes, which yet are nothing, exist. On realizing their existence, one feels the difference between being nothing and not being at all.

The inaccessible added to the inexplicable, such is the sky.

From this contemplation a sublime phenomenon is given forth; the enlargement of the soul through awe.

The sacred terror is peculiar to man, the beast knows

not this fear. Intelligence finds both its eclipse and its proof in this august terror.

The shadow is a unity; hence the horror. At the same time it is complex; hence terror. Its unity masses itself in our spirit and takes away the desire of resistance. Its complexity causes one to gaze on all sides; it seems as though one had to fear sudden attacks. One surrenders, and yet is on one's guard. One is in the presence of All, hence submission; and of Many, hence defiance. The unity of the darkness contains a multiple. A mysterious multiple, visible in matter, apparent to the thought. And it is silent,—another reason for being on the watch.

Night—he who writes this has said so elsewhere—is the peculiar and normal state of the special creation of which we form a part. Daylight, brief in duration as in space, is but the proximity of a star.

The universal miracle of night is not accomplished without friction, and all frictions of such a machine are contusions to life. The friction of the machine is what we call evil. We feel, in this obscurity, evil, a latent contradiction to the divine order, a virtual blasphemy of the fact rebellious to the ideal. Evil complicates the vast cosmic whole with some thousand-headed monstrosity. Evil is everywhere present for the purpose of protesting. It is hurricane, and it torments the progress of a ship; it is chaos, and it hinders the blossoming forth of a world. Good has unity; evil has ubiquity. Evil confuses life, which is logic. It causes the fly to be devoured by the bird, and the planet by the comet. Evil is an erasure on creation.

The nocturnal obscurity is full of vertigo. Any one who sounds it sinks into it and struggles there. There is no fatigue to be compared to this examination of the shadows. It is the study of an obliteration.

There is no definite point where the mind can rest. There are points of departure, no points of arrival. The interlacing of contradictory solutions, all the branchings of doubt presented at the same moment, the ramifications of phenomena exfoliating without limit beneath an indefinite impulse, all laws pouring into each other, a fathomless promiscuousness which causes mineralization to vegetate, vegetation to live, thought to weigh, love to radiate, and gravitation to love; the immense attacking front of all questions developing itself in the limitless obscurity; the half-perceived making a rough sketch of the unknown; cosmic simultaneousness in full view, not to the gaze but to the intelligence in vast, indistinct space; the invisible become a vision. This is the shadow. Man is beneath it.

He knows not the details, but he bears, in a quantity proportioned to his mind, the monstrous weight of the whole. This obsession drove the Chaldæan shepherds to astronomy. Involuntary revelations proceed from the pores of creation; an exudation of science takes place, in a manner, of its own accord, and runs over the ignorant man. Every solitary man, beneath this mysterious impregnation, becomes, often without himself being aware of it, a natural philosopher.

Obscurity is indivisible. It is inhabited. Inhabited without displacement by the absolute, inhabited also with displacement. One moves in it, a disturbing thing. A sacred formation accomplishes its phases there. Premeditations, powers, voluntary destinies, these elaborate in common a vast work. A terrible and horrible life lies within it. There are vast evolutions of stars, the stellar family, the planetary family, the zodiacal pollen, the *Quid divinum* of currents, of the effluvia of polarizations and attractions; there is union and antagonism, a magnificent ebb and flow of universal antitheses; the imponderable set at liberty in the midst of centres; there is sap in the globes, light outside of the globes, the wandering atom, the scattered germ, curves of fecundation, encounters of coupling and of combat, unprecedented profusions, distances which resemble dreams, dizzy motions, worlds driven into the incalculable, prodigies pursuing each other in the gloom, a mechanism once for all, breezes of spheres in flight, wheels which one feels turning; the learned man conjectures, the ignorant man consents and trembles; this *is* and hides itself; it is impregnable, it is out of reach, it is beyond approach. One is convinced even to oppression. Man is confronted by some strange dark evidence. One cannot grasp anything. One is crushed by the impalpable.

Everywhere, the incomprehensible; nowhere, the unintelligible.

And add to this the formidable question: Is this Immanence a Being?

One is beneath the shadow. One gazes. One listens.

Meanwhile, the sombre earth advances and rolls on; the flowers are conscious of this enormous movement, the catch-fly opens at eleven o'clock at night, and the day-lily at five in the morning. Striking regularity.

In the other depths, the drop of water becomes a world, the infusoria swarm, giant fecundity springs from the animalcules, the imperceptible displays its grandeur, the inverse sense of immensity manifests itself; a single diatom in the space of one hour produces thirteen hundred million diatoms.

What a propounding of all riddles simultaneously!

The irreducible is there.

One is constrained to faith. Belief by force, such is the result. But it is not enough to have faith, in order to be tranquil. Faith feels a singular and indescribable need of form. Hence religions. Nothing is so oppressive as a belief without outline.

Whatever one may think, whatever one may wish, whatever resistance one may have within one's self, to look at the darkness is not to look but to contemplate.

What is to be done with these phenomena? How is one to move under their convergence? To resolve this pressure into its simple components is impossible. What reverie is one to adjust to all these mysterious circumstances? What abstruse, simultaneous, stammering revelations, rendered obscure by their very mass, a sort of lisping of the word! The darkness is a silence, but this silence says everything. One resultant detaches itself from it majestically, God. God, that is the incompressible idea in man. Syllogisms, differences, negations, systems, religions, pass over it without diminishing it. This idea, darkness affirms in its entirety. Formidable Immanence. The formidable agreement of forces is manifested by the maintenance of all this obscurity in equilibrium. The universe hangs suspended; nothing falls. Incessant and tremendous displacement goes on without accident and without fracture. Man participates in this movement of translation, and the amount of oscillation which he undergoes he calls destiny. Where does destiny begin? Where does nature end? What difference is there between an event and a season, between a grief and a shower, between a virtue and a star? Is not an hour a wave? The wheel-work continues, without replying to man, its impassive revolutions. The starry heaven is a vision of wheels, balances, and counterpoises. It is supreme contemplation, reinforced by supreme meditation. It is the whole of reality, plus the whole of abstraction. There is nothing beyond it. One feels one's self caught, and is at the mercy of that shadow. No escape is possible. One sees that one is in the gearing and is an integral part of an unknown whole, one feels the unknown within fraternizing mysteriously with an unknown outside of one.

This is the sublime announcement of death. What anguish and, at the same time, what rapture! To adhere to the infinite, to be led by that adherence to attribute to one's self a necessary immortality, who knows? a possible eternity, to feel in that prodigious surge of the deluge of universal life, the insubmergible persistency of the ego! to gaze at the stars and to say, "I am a soul like you!" to gaze at the darkness and say, "I am an abyss like thee!"

These enormities constitute Night.

All this, intensified by solitude, weighed upon Gilliatt.

Did he understand it? No.

Did he feel it? Yes.

Gilliatt was a great disturbed intellect and a great untutored heart.

VI
GILLIATT BRINGS THE PAUNCH INTO POSITION

THIS rescue of the engine planned by Gilliatt was, as we have already said, a veritable escape from prison, and every one knows the patience and industry required for an escape. Industry is carried to the miraculous; patience even to agony. A prisoner, Thomas, for example, at Mont-Saint-Michel, finds the means of secreting half a wall inside his straw pallet. Another, at Tulle, in 1820, cuts the lead from the promenade platform of the prison,—with what knife? impossible to divine; melts this lead,—with what fire? no one knows; runs this lead into a mould made of bread crumbs, and with this mould makes a key, and with this key opens a lock, only the keyhole of which he had seen. With these incredible displays of skill, Gilliatt was endowed. He could have ascended and descended the cliff of Boisrosé. He was the Trenck of a wreck, and the Latude of an engine.

The sea, which was the jailer, kept watch over him.

However, as we have said, wretched and unpleasant as the rain was, he had put it to use. He had, to some extent, replenished his stock of fresh water; but his thirst was unquenchable, and he emptied his can almost as rapidly as he filled it.

One day,—the last day of April, I think, or the first of May,—all was at length in readiness.

The flooring of the engine was framed, as it were, between the eight cables of the tackle, four on each side. The sixteen openings through which these cables passed, were connected on the deck and beneath the hull by saw-cuts. The planking had been cut through with the saw, the timbers with the axe, the iron with the file, the sheathing with the chisel. The part of the keep above which the engine rested was cut squarely and was ready to lower with the machine while supporting it. All this frightful swinging hammock was now held by a single chain, which in its turn depended only upon a single stroke of the file. At this point of achievement, so near the end, haste is prudence.

The tide was low, the moment favorable.

Gilliatt had succeeded in dismounting the shaft of the paddle-wheels, the end of which might present an obstacle, and retard the descent. He had succeeded in fastening this heavy piece vertically in the very framework of the engine.

It was time to make an end of it. Gilliatt was not fatigued, because he would not yield to it, as we have said, but his tools were. The forge was gradually becoming impracticable. The stone anvil had split. The draught had begun to work badly. As the little hydraulic fall was of sea water, saline deposits had formed in the joints of the apparatus and interfered with its working. Gilliatt went to the inlet of "the Man," surveyed the paunch, assured himself that all there was in good condition, particularly the four rings fixed to starboard and port, then raised the anchor and rowed the boat back to the two Douvres. The passage between the Douvres was wide enough to admit the boat. There was also sufficient depth. Gilliatt, from the very first day, had recognized the fact that the boat could be brought directly under the Durande.

The labor, however, was excessive, it required the precision of a jeweller, and this insertion of the bark into the reef was all the more delicate because, for Gilliatt's purpose, it was necessary to enter stern foremost, with the rudder ahead. It was important that the mast and the rigging of the paunch should remain free from the wreck, on the side towards the entrance.

These embarrassments in the manœuvre rendered the operation difficult even for Gilliatt himself. It was no longer, as in the inlet of "the Man," a question of a turn of the helm; he must push, drag, row, and sound, all at the same time. Gilliatt spent no less than a quarter of an hour over it. But he succeeded.

In fifteen or twenty minutes the boat was adjusted beneath the Durande. It lay almost wedged in. By means of his two anchors, Gilliatt moored the paunch head and stern. The largest of them was so placed as to resist the strongest wind that was to be feared, which is the west wind. Then, by the aid of a lever and a capstan, Gilliatt lowered into the boat the two cases containing the dismounted wheels, whose slings were all ready. These two cases furnished the ballast.

Having got rid of his two cases, Gilliatt attached to the hook of the capstan chain the sling of the regulating tackle, intended to check the pulley.

For Gilliatt's purpose, the defects of the paunch became useful qualities; she was not decked over, the cargo would have more depth, and could rest in the hold. Her mast was well forward, too far forward, perhaps; the cargo would have more room and, the mast being thus beyond the wreck, nothing would hinder the exit; it was nothing but a wooden shoe, and nothing is so stable and solid on the sea as a wooden shoe.

All at once, Gilliatt observed that the sea was rising. He looked to see whence the wind was coming.

VII
Sudden Danger

THERE was not much breeze, but what there was was blowing from the west. It is a bad habit which the wind is fond of during the equinoxes.

The rising tide behaves differently in the Douvres reef, according to the wind that is blowing. According to the gust that impels it, the tide enters this corridor from the east or from the west. If the sea enters from the east, it is favorable and gentle; if it enters from the west, it is furious. This arises from the fact that the east wind, blowing from the land, has but little breath; while the west wind, which traverses the Atlantic, brings with it all the force of that immensity. Even very little apparent breeze, if it comes from the west, is disquieting. It rolls large billows from the limitless expanse, and forces too much water at once into the strangled passage.

Water rushing into any narrow place is always frightful. It is with water as with a crowd; a multitude is a liquid; when the quantity which can enter is less than the quantity which desires to enter, a crush ensues in the case of the crowd and convulsion in the case of the water. As long as the west wind reigns, were it but the feeblest breeze, the Douvres undergo this assault twice a day. The sea rises, the tide presses, the rock resists, the mouth opens but slightly, the waters forcibly thrust in, leap and roar, and a frantic swell beats the two inner faces of the gorge. So that the Douvres, in the slightest west wind, present this singular spectacle: outside, on the sea, calm; within the reef, a storm. This local and restricted tumult has none of the characteristics of a tempest; it is only a riot of the waves, but it is terrible.

As for the north and south wind, they pass across the reef, and make but little surf in the narrow passage. The entrance on the east, a fact which must be remembered, adjoins "the Man" rock; the formidable western opening is at the opposite extremity, precisely between the two Douvres.

It was at this western opening that Gilliatt found himself with the stranded Durande and the paunch moored beneath it.

A catastrophe seemed inevitable. There was but little wind, yet sufficient to produce this threatened catastrophe.

In a few hours, the swell of the rising tide would rush in full force through the Douvres strait. The first waves were already roaring. This swell, and eddy of the whole Atlantic, would have the entire sea behind it. No squall, no wrath; but one simple, supreme wave, containing within itself a force of impulsion which, setting out from America to end in Europe, has a spring of two thousand leagues. This wave, a gigantic wedge from the ocean, would encounter the opening in the reef and piling up against the two Douvres, the entrance towers, the pillars of the straits—swollen by the flood tide, swollen by the obstacle, repulsed by the rock, overdriven by the breeze, would violently strike the reef, would penetrate into it, with all the contortions of the obstacles encountered, and all the frenzies of the impeded billows, between the two walls, would find the boat and the Durande there, and would crush them.

Against this eventuality a shield was necessary, and Gilliatt had it.

The sea must be prevented from entering at one dash; it must be prohibited from dashing, yet allowed to rise; its passage must be barred, yet entrance not refused; it was necessary to resist it, yet yield to it, to prevent the compression of the water in the gorge, wherein lay the whole danger; to replace irruption by introduction, to deprive the billows of their eagerness and their brutality, to constrain this fury to mildness. For the obstacle which irritates, substitute the obstacle which appeases.

Gilliatt, with that dexterity of his which is stronger than force, executing the manœuvre of a chamois in the mountains or a monkey in the forest, utilizing for his tottering and dizzy strides the slightest projecting stone, leaping into the water and emerging again, swimming in the eddy, climbing the rock, a rope between his teeth, a hammer in his hand, detached the small cable which held the section of the forward part of the Durande suspended, and also fast to the base of the little Douvre, fashioned out of some bits of hawser a sort of hinges attaching this section to the large spikes fixed in the granite, made this bulwark of planks swing on these hinges like the gate to a dry dock, presented it, as one turns a rudder sidewise, to the waves which pushed one end of it against the great Douvre, while the rope hinges retained the other end against the little Douvre. He fixed upon the great Douvre, by means of the spikes awaiting him, which he had placed there in advance, the same kind of fastenings as on the little one, and moored this vast mass of wood solidly to the two pillars of the gorge, crossed this barricade with a chain, like a baldrick on a cuirass, and, in less than an hour, this barrier rose against the tide, and the sea lane of the reef was closed as by a door.

This powerful construction, a heavy mass of beams and planks, which, lying flat, would have been a raft, and erect was a wall, had, with the aid of the water, been handled by Gilliatt with the dexterity of a juggler. One might almost say that the trick was performed before the rising tide had had time to perceive it.

It was one of those cases when Jean Bart would have uttered that famous saying which he addressed to the waves every time he escaped shipwreck: "Cheated the Englishman!" When Jean Bart wished to insult the ocean, he would call it "the Englishman."

Having barred the entrance to the strait, Gilliatt thought of his boat; he paid out sufficient cable on both anchors to allow it to rise with the tide. An operation analogous to that which old sailors were wont to call "anchoring with springs." In all this Gilliatt had not been taken unawares, the emergency had been foreseen; a member of the craft would have recognized the fact by two top-rope pulleys lashed as snatch blocks to the stern of the boat, through which passed two cables, the ends of which served as bolt ropes to the rings of the two anchors.

Meanwhile, the flow of the tide had increased, half-tide had arrived; it is at this point that shocks from the waves of the tide, even when peaceful, can be rough. What Gilliatt had calculated was realized. The flood rolled violently towards the barrier, struck it, swelled against it, and passed under it. Outside was the heavy swell; inside, the water rose quietly. Gilliatt had created a sort of Caudine Forks of the sea. The tide was vanquished.

VIII

Change Rather than Conclusion

THE dreaded moment had come.

The question now was to place the machinery in the boat.

Gilliatt was thoughtful for several minutes, holding the elbow of his left arm in his right hand, and his brow in his left hand.

Then he mounted the wreck, one portion of which, containing the engines, was to be detached, while the other portion, the hull, was to remain.

He cut the four slings which fastened the four chains of the smoke stack to the starboard and port sides of the Durande. As the slings were merely of rope, his knife served for this purpose.

The four chains, now free and unfastened, hung down along the smoke stack.

From the wreck, he climbed up to the apparatus which he had constructed, stamped upon the timbers, inspected the tackle, looked at the pulleys, felt of the cables, examined the pieces with which they were eked out, made sure that the untarred rope was not thoroughly saturated, saw that nothing was lacking, and that nothing was giving way, then, leaping from the summit of the binding-strakes upon the deck, he took up his position near the capstan, in the part of the Durande which was to remain hanging to the Douvres. That was to be his post of labor.

Grave, moved solely by useful emotion, he cast a final glance at the blocks and falls, then seized a file, and began to work at the chain which held all in suspense.

The grating of the file could be heard amid the roaring of the sea.

The chain of the capstan, attached to the regulating burton, was within Gilliatt's reach, close to his hand.

All at once, there came a cracking. The chain into which the file was biting, when not more than half cut through, had just broken; the whole apparatus began to waver. Gilliatt had barely time to seize the burton tackle.

The broken chain struck the rock, the eight cables stretched, the whole mass, cut and sawed through, tore itself from the wreck, the belly of the Durande opened, the iron flooring of the engine, weighing on the cables, made its appearance below the keel.

If Gilliatt had not seized the burton in time, a fall would have ensued. But his controlling hand was there, and it was a descent instead.

When the brother of Jean Bart, Pieter Bart, that powerful and sagacious drunkard, that poor fisherman of Dunkirk, who addressed the Grand Admiral of France familiarly "thou," saved the Langeron galley, wrecked in the Bay of Ambleteuse,—when, in order to rescue that heavy floating mass from the breakers of the furious bay, he rolled up the mainsail and tied it with sea rushes, when he wished these rushes to give the sail to the wind by breaking of their own accord,—he trusted to the parting of the rushes as did Gilliatt to the snapping of the chain, and it was the same eccentric hardihood, crowned with the same success.

The burton tackle which Gilliatt seized, held firm and worked admirably. Its function, as the reader will remember, was the controlling of many forces brought together into one and reduced to simultaneous action. This burton was somewhat similar to the bridle of the bowline; only, instead of trimming a sail, it served to balance a mechanism.

Gilliatt, erect, with his hand on the capstan, had, so to speak, his finger on the pulse of the apparatus.

Here Gilliatt's inventive genius shone forth.

A remarkable coincidence of forces was produced.

While the machinery of the Durande, detached in a mass, was descending towards the boat, the boat was rising to meet the machinery. The wreck and the rescuing boat helped each other in inverse sense, by coming to meet each other. They sought each other and spared each other half the toil.

The tide swelling noiselessly between the two Douvres, raised the boat and brought it nearer the Durande. The sea was more than vanquished, it was tamed. The ocean became a part of the mechanism.

The water as it rose lifted the boat without any shock, softly, almost with precaution, and as though it were made of porcelain.

Gilliatt combined and proportioned the two labors, that of the water and that of the apparatus, and motionless beside the capstan, a sort of redoubtable statue, obeyed by all the movements at once, regulated the slowness of descent by the slowness of the rise.

There was no shock in the water, no jerk from the blocks and falls. It was a strange collaboration of all natural forces, conquered. On the one hand, gravitation, bearing the engine; on the other, the water bearing the bark. The attraction of the planets, which is the tide, and the attraction of the earth, which is weight, seemed to have entered into an understanding to serve Gilliatt. Their subordination knew no hesitation or halt, and, beneath the dominance of a mind, these passive forces became active auxiliaries. Moment by moment the work advanced; the interval between the boat and the wreck insensibly diminished. The approach was made in silence and with a sort of terror of the man who was there. The elements had received an order and were executing it.

Almost at the precise moment when the tide ceased to rise, the cables ceased to pay out. Suddenly, but without commotion, the tackle halted. The machinery had reached its resting-place in the boat. There it stood, erect, motionless, solid. The supporting iron floor rested its four corners evenly in the hold.

It was done.

Gilliatt gazed, in bewilderment. The poor creature was not spoiled by his joy; he underwent the weakening effect of an immense happiness, he felt his limbs give way beneath him, and in the hour of his triumph, he, who hitherto had never had a single quiver, now began to tremble.

He gazed at the boat under the wreck, and the machinery in the boat. He did not seem to believe it was true. One would have said that he had not expected to accomplish what he had done. A prodigy had been wrought by his hands, and he looked upon it with amazement.

This bewilderment did not long continue.

Gilliatt started like a man who is just waking up, seized the saw, cut the eight cables, then, separated from the boat by half a score of feet only, thanks to the rising of the tide, he jumped into it, took a coil of rope, made four slings, passed them through the rings prepared in advance, and fastened to the sides of the boat the four chains of the smoke stack which only an hour before had been still attached to the sides of the Durande.

The smoke stack secured, Gilliatt disengaged the upper part of the machinery. A square piece of the platform of the Durande's bridge adhered to it. Gilliatt removed the nails, relieved the boat of this encumbrance of beams and planks, which he flung upon the rock. A useful lightening.

However the sloop, as might have been foreseen, bore herself well under the weight of the machinery. The paunch was loaded only to a good floating line. The engine of the Durande, although heavy, weighed less than the heap of stones and the cannon once brought back from Herm by the paunch.

So everything was finished. Nothing was left but to take his departure.

IX
Success Snatched Away as Soon as Granted

ALL was not finished.

No course was more plainly indicated than to reopen the narrow entrance closed by the piece of the Durande's planking and at once push the boat outside of the reef. At sea, every minute is urgent. There was but little wind, hardly a ripple on the ocean; the evening was very beautiful and promised a fine night. It was slack water, but the ebb tide was beginning to make itself felt; the moment was favorable for setting out. There would be the ebb tide on which to go out of the Douvres, and the flood tide with which to return to Guernsey. Saint-Sampson might be reached by daybreak.

But an unexpected obstacle presented itself. There had been a defect in Gilliatt's foresight.

The engine was free, the smoke stack was not.

The tide, by bringing the boat close to the wreck suspended in the air, had lessened the perils of the descent, and shortened the process of rescue; but this diminution of interval had left the top of the funnel entangled in the yawning frame formed by the hull of the Durande. The smoke stack was caught there as between four walls.

The service rendered by the tide was complicated by this sly trick. It seemed as though the sea, constrained to obedience, had indulged in an afterthought.

It is also true that what the flood tide had done the ebb tide was about to undo.

The smoke stack, a little more than three fathoms in

height, was buried eight feet deep in the Durande; the water level would sink about twelve feet; the smoke stack, descending with the boat on the ebbing tide, would have four feet to spare, and could get free.

But how much time would this release require? Six hours.

In six hours it would be nearly midnight. How attempt to get out at such an hour, what channel was to be followed among all those breakers,—so labyrinthine even in daylight,—and how risk one's self in the dead of a dark night in that ambush of shoals?

There was nothing to be done but wait until the morrow. Those six hours lost would entail the loss of at least twelve.

He must not even think of expediting the work by opening the entrance to the reef. The barrier would be necessary at the next high tide.

Gilliatt was obliged to rest.

Folding his arms was the only thing which he had not yet done during his sojourn on the Douvres reef.

This forced inaction irritated and made him almost vexed with himself, as though it were his fault. He said to himself, "What would Déruchette think of me, if she saw me here doing nothing?"

Nevertheless, this renewal of his strength was not useless, perhaps.

The paunch was now at his disposal; he decided to pass the night on board.

He went in search of his sheepskin on the great Douvre, descended again, supped on a few limpets and two or three sea chestnuts, drank, being very thirsty, the last few mouthfuls of fresh water from his almost empty can, wrapped himself in his sheepskin, the wool of which made him comfortable, lay down beside the engine like a watch dog, pulled his red galley cap over his eyes, and fell asleep.

He slept profoundly. A man has such slumbers after accomplishing labors of this kind.

X

THE WARNINGS OF THE SEA

HE was awakened in the middle of the night abruptly, and as though jerked by a spring.

He opened his eyes.

The Douvres above his head were illuminated as by the reflection of a great white glow. Over the whole dark front of the reef was a light, like the reflection of a fire.

Whence came that fire?

From the water.

The appearance of the sea was extraordinary.

It seemed as though the water were on fire. As far as the eye could reach, inside the reef and beyond, the whole sea was in a blaze. This blaze was not red: it had nothing of the great living flame of craters and furnaces. No sparkle, no heat, no crimson, no noise. Bluish trails on the waves imitated the folds of a winding-sheet. A large pallid light shivered over the water. It was not a conflagration; it was the spectre of one.

It was something like the livid illumination of a sepulchre by an unearthly flame.

Let the reader imagine shadows ignited.

Night, the vast, troubled, and diffuse night, seemed to be the fuel of this chilly fire. It was an indescribable light made of blindness. Gloom entered as an element into that phantom light.

The mariners of the channel are acquainted with all these indescribable phosphorescences, which are full of warnings for the navigator. They are nowhere more surprising than in the Grand V, near Isigny.

In this light, objects lose their reality. A spectral inner

light renders them transparent, as it were. Rocks are no longer anything but lineaments. The anchor cables seem bars of iron raised to a white heat. The nets of the fishermen under water seem of knitted fire. One half of the oar is of ebony; the other half, beneath the wave, is silver. The drops of water stud the sea with stars, as they fall from the oar. Every boat trails a comet behind it. The sailors, wet and luminous, seem like men on fire. One plunges one's hand into the water, and withdraws it gloved in flame; this flame is dead, one does not feel it. Your arm is a blazing brand. You see the forms which are in the sea rolling along beneath the water as in a liquid fire. The foam sparkles. The fish are tongues of fire and fragments of serpentine lightning in the pale depths.

This light had struck across Gilliatt's closed lids. It was this that had wakened him.

His waking was opportune.

The tide had ebbed; a new flood tide was beginning. The smoke stack of the engine, disengaged during Gilliatt's sleep, was on the point of entering once more the yawning wreck above it.

It was slowly rising towards it.

Only a foot was lacking before the smoke stack would enter the Durande once more.

It requires about half an hour for the tide to rise a foot. If Gilliatt desired to take advantage of this deliverance, which had again become doubtful, he had half an hour before him.

He started to his feet.

Urgent as was the situation, he could not help standing for a few moments, gazing at the phosphorescence, and meditating.

Gilliatt knew the sea thoroughly. Although it was angry with him, and although often ill-treated by it, he had long been its companion. That mysterious being called the ocean could have nothing in its thoughts that Gilliatt could not divine. Gilliatt, by dint of observation, reverie, and solitude, had become a weather prophet, what is called "weatherwise."

Gilliatt ran to the ropes and paid out more cable; then, as it was no longer held by the small bower anchor, he seized the boat hook, and bearing against the rocks, he pushed the boat towards the entrance, a few fathoms beyond the Durande, and quite close to the barrier. In less than ten minutes, the paunch was withdrawn from beneath the stranded carcass. No more danger of the smoke stack being caught in the trap again. The tide might rise now.

But Gilliatt had not the air of a man who is on the point of taking his departure.

He looked at the phosphorescence again and raised his anchors; but it was not to start, his intention was to moor the boat afresh, and very firmly, near the exit.

Up to that time, he had used only the two anchors of the boat, and he had not, as yet, made use of the little anchor of the Durande, which he had found among the rocks, as the reader will remember. This anchor he had placed all ready for emergencies, in one corner of the paunch, with a quantity of hawsers and pulleys, and its cable very solidly made fast in advance, with stoppers which prevented its dragging. Gilliatt let go this third anchor, taking care to attach the cable to a small rope, one end of which was fastened to the ring of the anchor, and the other end of which was rigged to the windlass of the boat. In this manner, he effected a sort of triple mooring, much stronger than mooring with two anchors.

This denoted lively anxiety and a redoubling of precautions. A sailor would have recognized in this operation something similar to anchoring in stormy weather, when a current is to be feared that might set the vessel to the leeward.

The phosphorescence which Gilliatt was watching, and on which he kept his eye fixed, was threatening perhaps, but aided him at the same time. Without it he would have been the prisoner of slumber, and the dupe of the night. It had awakened him and it gave him light.

It produced an equivocal daylight on the reef. But the brilliancy, disquieting as it appeared to Gilliatt, had this advantage: it rendered the danger visible to him, and made his manœuvring possible. Hereafter, when Gilliatt should desire to set sail, the boat bearing the machinery was free.

Only Gilliatt seemed to be thinking less and less of

departure. The boat being secured, he went in search of the stoutest chain in his storehouse, and, attaching it to the spikes driven in the two Douvres, with this chain he fortified on the inside the rampart of planks and beams already protected on the outside by the other cross chain. Instead of opening the exit, he barricaded it more completely. The phosphorescence still lighted him, but it was decreasing. The daybreak was beginning to appear.

All at once, Gilliatt bent his ear and listened.

XI

A Word to the Wise Is Sufficient

It seemed to him that he heard a feeble and indistinct sound somewhere in the immense distance.

The depths, at certain hours, give forth a murmuring roar.

He listened a second time. The distant noise began anew. Gilliatt shook his head like some one who knows what he is about.

A few minutes later, he was at the other extremity of the lane of the reef at the eastern entrance, open hitherto, and, with mighty blows of the hammer, he was driving huge spikes into the granite of the two sides of that entrance close to "the Man" rock, as he had done in the case of the entrance to the Douvres.

The crevices of these rocks were all prepared and well furnished with wood, almost all of which was heart of oak. The reef was much shattered on this side, there were a great many cracks, and Gilliatt could fix even more spikes here than at the base of the two Douvres.

At a sudden movement, and as though it had been blown out, the phosphorescence was extinguished; the morning twilight, growing more luminous every instant, replaced it.

After driving in the spikes, Gilliatt dragged beams, then ropes, then chains, and, without taking his eyes from his work, without allowing his attention to be distracted for a moment, he began to construct across "the Man" entrance, with beams fixed horizontally and bound together by cables, one of those openwork barriers which science has now adopted, and which it styles breakwaters.

Those who have seen, for instance, at la Rocquaine in Guernsey, or at Bourg-d'Ault in France, the effect produced by a few piles fixed in the rock, understand the power of these very simple appliances. The breakwater is a combination of what is called in France, *épi,* with what is called in England, dike. Breakwaters are the chevaux-de-frise of fortifications against tempests. One can contend with the sea only by taking advantage of the divisibility of this force.

Meanwhile, the sun had risen, perfectly unobscured. The sky was clear, the sea was calm.

Gilliatt hastened his work. He, also, was calm, but there was anxiety in his haste.

He went, with long strides, from rock to rock, from the barrier to his storehouse, and from his storehouse to the barrier. He returned dragging in frantic haste now a rider, now a binding-strake. The utility of this provision of timber made itself manifest. It was evident that Gilliatt was face-to-face with an emergency which he had foreseen.

A strong iron bar served him as a lever wherewith to move the beams.

The work was executed so rapidly that it was a growth rather than a construction. One who has never seen a military pontooner at work can form no idea of this rapidity.

The eastern entrance was still narrower than the western one. The gap was only five or six feet wide. The smallness of this opening helped Gilliatt. The place to be fortified and closed being very restricted, the barrier would be more solid and might be more simple. Hence, horizontal beams sufficed; upright pieces were useless.

The first crossbeams of the breakwater being laid, Gilliatt mounted on them and listened.

The roaring was becoming significant.

Gilliatt proceeded with his construction. He buttressed it with the two catheads of the Durande fastened to the framework of the beams by halyards passed through their three pulley sheaves. He made fast the whole with chains.

This construction was nothing else than a sort of colossal hurdle, with beams for rods and chains for wattles.

It seemed woven as much as built.

Gilliatt multiplied the fastenings, and added spikes where needed.

Having had a great deal of round iron from the wreck, he had been able to lay in a great stock of spikes.

As he worked he crunched biscuit between his teeth. He was thirsty but he could not drink, having no more fresh water. He had emptied his can at supper on the preceding evening.

He piled up four or five more timbers, then mounted the barrier again, and listened.

The noise on the horizon had ceased. All was still.

The sea was smooth and superb, it deserved all the madrigals which worthy citizens address to it when they are satisfied with it,—"a mirror," "a pond," "like oil," "playful," "a lamb." The deep blue of the sky responded to the deep green of the ocean. The sapphire and the emerald could admire each other. They had no occasion to reproach themselves. Not a cloud on high, not a fleck of foam below. Through all this splendor the April sun was rising magnificently. It was impossible to see finer weather.

On the extreme horizon, a long black file of birds of passage streaked the heavens. They were flying rapidly. They were directing their course towards the land. It seemed as though they were fleeing as well as flying.

Gilliatt betook himself again to raising the height of the breakwater.

He raised it as high as he could, as high as the curve of the rocks permitted.

Towards midday the sun seemed to him hotter than it should be. Noon is the critical hour of the day. Gilliatt, standing erect on the strong hurdle which he had just finished, stopped once more to survey the expanse.

The sea was more than tranquil, it was stagnant. Not a sail was to be seen. The sky was everywhere clear; only, from blue it had become white. This white was singular. In the west, on the horizon, there was a small spot of sickly hue. This spot remained motionless in the same place, but increased in size. Near the reef, the waves rippled very gently.

Gilliatt had done well to build his breakwater.

A tempest was approaching.

The abyss had decided to give battle.

BOOK THIRD
THE BATTLE

I
Extremes Meet

NOTHING is so threatening as a late equinoctial storm. The sea presents a savage phenomenon which might be designated as the arrival of the winds from the open ocean.

At all seasons, especially at the time of the syzygies, at the moment when it is least to be expected, the sea suddenly becomes strangely tranquil. The vast perpetual movement is allayed; something like lulling to sleep; it becomes languid; it seems as though it were going to take a rest; one might fancy that it was fatigued. Every rag of bunting, from the pennon of a fishing smack to the flag of a man-of-war, droops along the mast. The admiral's, the royal, and the imperial standards,—all are asleep.

All at once these streamers begin to wave gently.

This is the moment, if there are clouds, to watch the formation of the cirrhus; if the sun is setting, to examine the red glow of the evening; if it be night and there is a moon, to study halos.

At that moment, the captain or commander of the squadron who is so lucky as to possess one of those storm indicators, whose inventor is unknown, observes this glass carefully and takes his precautions against the south wind, if the mixture bears the aspect of dissolved sugar; and against the north wind if it exfoliates in crystallizations similar to thickets of fern or groves of fir trees.

At that moment, the poor Irish or Breton fisherman, after having consulted some mysterious gnomon engraved by the Romans or by demons, on one of those enigmatical upright stones which are called in Brittany "menhir," and in Ireland "cruach," hauls his boat upon the shore.

Meanwhile, the serenity of sky and sea continues. The morning rises radiant and the dawn smiles. This was what filled the ancient poets and soothsayers with religious awe, horrified that any one could believe in the falsity of the sun. *Solem quis dicere falsum audeat?*

The sombre vision of the latent possible is interdicted to man by the fatal opacity of surrounding things. The most formidable and most perfidious of aspects, it is the mask of the deep.

The saying, "A snake in the grass," should be "A tempest beneath the calm."

Several hours, sometimes several days, pass thus. Pilots point their glasses here and there. The faces of old seamen wear an expression of severity, which partakes of the secret vexation of expectancy.

Suddenly, a great confused murmur is heard. There is a sort of mysterious dialogue in progress in the air.

Nothing is to be seen.

The expanse remains impassive.

Still the noise swells, increases, rises. The dialogue becomes emphatic.

There is some one behind the horizon.

A terrible some one,—the wind.

The wind,—that is to say, that populace of Titans which we call Gales.

The immense rabble of the gloom.

India called them the Marouts; Judea, the Cherubim; Greece, the Aquilones. They are the invincible wild birds of the Infinite. These winds rush onward.

II

The Winds from the Open Ocean

WHENCE come they? From the incommensurable. For the spread of their wings they require the diameter of the ocean gulf. Their huge pinions need the indefinite space of solitudes. The Atlantic, the Pacific, those vast blue openings, are what suits them. They render them sombre. There they fly in flocks.

Commander Page once saw seven waterspouts at one time, on the high seas. There they are ferocious. They premeditate disasters. Their labor is the eternal rise and fall of the waves. What they can do no one knows, what they wish no man can say. They are the sphinxes of the abyss; and Vasco da Gama is their Œdipus. In that obscurity of the expanse ever moving, they appear as cloud faces. He who perceives their livid features in that dispersion which is the horizon of the sea, feels himself in the presence of irreducible force. One would say that human intelligence disquiets them, and that they are resenting it.

Intelligence is invincible, but the elements are impregnable. What is to be done against the undiscernible? The breeze turns into a club, then becomes a breeze again. The winds combat by crushing, and defend themselves by vanishing. He who encounters them is driven to the use of artifices. Their varying assault, full of rebounds, confuses. They have as much power of flight as of attack. They are impalpable, and tenacious. How is one to conquer them? The prow of the ship Argo, carved from an oak from the grove of Dodona, at once both prow and pilot, was wont to speak with them. They treated that goddessprow brutally. Christopher Columbus, seeing them advance toward the *Pinta,* mounted the poop and addressed to them the first verses of the Gospel according to St. John. Surcouf defied them: "Here's the gang," he said. Napier fired cannon at them. They hold the dictatorship of chaos.

They control chaos. What do they do with it? Something implacable. The den of the winds is more monstrous than the den of lions. What corpses beneath those bottomless depths! The winds push on the great obscure and ghastly mass without pity. They are heard at all times but they listen to nothing. They commit deeds which resemble crimes. One knows not upon whom they cast the white fragments of foam which they tear away. What impious ferocity in shipwreck! What an affront to Providence! They appear, at times, to be spitting into the face of God. They are the tyrants of the unknown regions. *Luoghi spaventosi,* murmured the mariners of Venice,—regions of terror.

The shuddering expanses submit to their deeds of violence. What takes place in those great deserted regions is inexpressible. Some equestrian shape seems to be galloping through the shadow. The air makes a noise like that of a forest. One sees nothing, but hears troops of cavalry. It is midday; all at once, it changes into night;—a tornado passes by: it is midnight; suddenly, it becomes day,—the polar effluvium has been lighted. Whirlwinds pass in opposite directions, a sort of hideous dance, a trampling of scourges on the element. A too-heavy cloud breaks in the middle and falls piecemeal into the sea. Other clouds, full of crimson, lighten and thunder, then grow lugubriously dark; the cloud, emptied of its thunder, turns black, it is an extinguished coal. Sacks of rain burst into fog. Yonder, where it rains, there is a fiery furnace; there a wave, from whence darts forth a flame. The white gleam of the sea beneath the downpour lights up surprising distances. One beholds thicknesses, wherein resemblances wander and grow deformed. Monstrous navels form hollows in the clouds. The vapors whirl, the waves spin, intoxicated Naïads roll; as far as the eye can see, the massive and flaccid sea moves without displacement; all is livid; desperate cries proceed from the pallor.

In the depths of the inaccessible obscurity shiver great sheaves of gloom. At times there comes a paroxysm. The rumor becomes a tumult, just as the wave becomes a surge. The horizon, a confused pile of billows, endless oscillation, murmurs in a constant bass; sudden bursts of uproar break out; one thinks that one hears hydras sneezing. Cold blasts come, then hot ones. The trepidation of the sea announces a terror which is all-expectant,—it is quietude, anguish, profound terror of the waters. Suddenly the hurricane, like a beast, comes down to drink from the ocean; unprecedented suction; the water ascends towards the invisible mouth, a cupping-glass is formed, the tumor swells,—it is the waterspout, the Prester of the ancients, a stalactite above, a stalagmite below; a double, inverse, whirling cone; one point balanced upon the other; the kiss of two mountains, a mountain of foam rising, a mountain of cloud descending; a terrible coition of the wave and the shadow. The waterspout, like the pillar of the Bible, is cloudy by day and luminous by night. In the presence of the waterspout, the thunder holds its peace. It seems to be afraid of it.

The vast commotion of solitudes has a gamut; a formidable crescendo: the blow, the gust, the squall, the storm, the wild hurricane, the tempest, the waterspout; the seven chords of the lyre of the winds, the seven notes of the abyss. The sky is a breadth, the sea is a roundness; a breath passes, nothing remains of all this; all is fury and confusion.

Such are these forbidding places.

The winds rush, fly, swoop down, finish, begin again, soar, hiss, roar, laugh; frantic, wanton, unbridled, taking their ease on the irascible wave. These howlings have a harmony. They make the whole sky sonorous. They blow into the cloud as into a trumpet; they put their mouths to space, and they sing in the infinite with all the mingled voices of clarions, conch-shells, bugles, and trumpets, a sort of Promethean flourish. He who hears them is listening to Pan. The frightful thing about it is that they are playing. Theirs is a colossal joy, composed of truce, day and night, at all seasons, at the tropics as at the poles; sounding their distracting trumpet, they follow through the thickets of the clouds and the waves, the great black hunt of shipwrecks. They are the masters of the hounds. They amuse themselves. They make the waves, their dogs, bark at the rocks. They gather and disperse the clouds. They knead the suppleness of the immense water as with millions of hands.

The water is supple because it is incompressible. It glides away from under the effort. Borne down on one side, it escapes on the other. It is thus that the water becomes a wave. The wave is its liberty.

III
The Sea and the Wind

We see the tides of the water; we do not see the tides of the air. The atmosphere, like the ocean, has its own ebb and flow, even more gigantic, and rising, like a vast tumour, toward the moon.

Unity begetting complexity—that, we were just saying, is the law of laws.

The mechanism of the atmosphere is simple.

A libration develops between atmospheric electricity and terrestrial magnetism.

The tropics are boilers, the poles are condensers; the compression is equal to the expansion; there is a discharge from above, along the equator, and a return takes place from beneath, at the poles. This to-and-fro movement is the wind.

All nature is an exchange.

Two circles of wind, one polar, the other equatorial, roll unendingly around the globe.

Beneath this turning double ring the earth revolves.

Colossal vision.

The meeting of the two circles of wind at right angles jars and cracks the atmosphere and causes those fractures we call storms.

Out of these fractures come the whirlwinds. The first obstacles encountered by the whirlwinds give them their gyratory motion. A rock in the middle of the water, like the Peak of Teneriffe or even the Douvres reef, is sufficient. Away they go spiraling across space, trailing the sea in their coils. A cyclone will twist a three-decker the way a washerwoman wrings out a piece of cloth. Think of a gigantic serpent of air, a league tall and three or four hundred leagues long, whirling with frightful speed over the ocean.

The wind deals harshly with the sea. Its assault is great enough to disturb that vast rhythm we call the tide. The tormented waters rebel. Long clouds, electric bladders, puff up, and in their bosoms you can recognize, by a misshapen swelling, the thunder held prisoner like a dead animal in a boa's stomach. The foam streams in a thousand undulations over the flanks of the sandbank like the linen robe over the hips of Venus Anadyomene. The barometer sinks, then rises, then drops; there is the same dark play in the storm. You hear the sob of creation. The sea is the great weeper. She is filled with complaint; the ocean laments for all that suffers. Beneath the water the effluences come and go, at a speed of seventy thousand leagues a second, from the boreal pole with its single volcano, Hekla, to the austral pole with its two, Erebus and Terror. The liquid contends with the gaseous. The defenseless solitudes suffer the jars of this savage tournament. If no one is there, deluges; if man is there, shipwrecks. Such is the tremendous hazard of the darkness.

The winds rise and fall; their rising is life; their falling is calamity.

Under the equator's circle of wind is a continual rumbling of thunder.

The earth's rotation causes the left banks of the rivers of the southern hemisphere to erode.

Let us state this majestic geometry with exactitude.

There is always an electric polarity in the circles of the wind-spirals; one semicircle is positive and the other is negative. This is shown by the electroscope. The line of translation which follows the cyclone's center separates the two forms of electricity. At the center the force diminishes.

At the center of the cyclone, absolute calm. The forces are in equilibrium. The tempest is at peace with itself.

The cyclone's plane of rotation changes as it rises toward the cold regions. In the tropics the cyclone is a tangent, at the poles it is a secant. Picture it as a disk, flat at first, then righting itself.

A cyclone on the move can upset the barometer at a distance of nine hundred miles.

The atmosphere has a network of veins through which the winds glide. Sometimes this network becomes congested. A tempest is the rupture of an aneurism.

Variable in the immovable—such, we insist, is this body of laws. Numberless combinations are added to it, which in the end make a wilderness out of four or five apparently simple laws. Every fact is a logarithm; one added term ramifies it until it is thoroughly transformed. In the general aspect of things the great lines of creation take shape and arrange themselves into groups; beneath lies the unfathomable. Physics has an implied limit, which is chemistry. There is a base under the laws of nature.

Because of nature's unity it has been concluded that she is simple. An error. Everywhere, in what the older science called elements, to-day's science has discovered complexities. Seawater, for example, which to Pythagoras was simple, was described last year as being composed of twenty-five substances; this year (1864) analysis has added two more, boron and aluminum, which makes twenty-seven.

Phenomena intersect; to see but one is to see nothing. There is no end to the profusion of natural disasters. They follow the same law of development as all other riches: circulation. One becomes part of another. From the penetration of phenomenon into phenomenon is born the prodigy.

The prodigy is the masterpiece among phenomena. Sometimes the masterpiece is a catastrophe. But in the workings of creation—prodigious decomposition immediately recomposed—nothing is purposeless.

Copulation is the first stage, giving birth is the second. The universal order is a magnificent wedding. In disorder there can be no fecundation. Chaos is a celibate. We attend unceasingly the marriage of our first parents. Adam and Eve are eternal: Adam is the globe, Eve the sea.

When it wishes to be, the sea is gay. No other joy has the radiance of the sea. The ocean is brightness itself. Nothing can cast a shadow upon it save the cloud, and it chases the shadow away with a puff. If you do not look beneath the surface, the ocean is liberty—and equality also. At this level every gleam radiates contentedly. The all-encompassing merriment of the clear sky sprawls everywhere. The tranquil sea is a holiday. No siren's call is sweeter or more seductive. Not a sailor but would be tempted to set out. There is nothing to equal this serenity; the whole immensity is but a caress. The waters sigh and the reef sings, the algae kiss the rock, the gulls and the pintails fly, and the soft meadows of the sea undulate from billow to billow; under the halcyons' nests the water seems like a nurse, the wave like a cradle, while the sun covers over those formidable hypocrisies of the deep with a blinding layer of light.

Here appearances are so fleeting that for him who observes it long, the sea's aspect becomes purely metaphysical; its brutality degenerates into abstraction. It is a quantity that decomposes and is recomposed. It is an expansible quantity, partaking of infinity. Arithmetic, like the sea, is an undulation without any possible end. The wave is futile like the cipher. The wave, too, requires an inert coefficient. The reef gives it a value as the zero does the figure. The sea, like the number, has a transparency by which the depths beneath them may be perceived. They hide, efface themselves, are reconstructed, cannot exist by themselves, wait to be used, multiply in the darkness as far as the eye can reach, are always there. Nothing else presents the idea of numbers like the aspect of the water.

Over this reverie hovers the hurricane.

We are awakened from abstraction by the tempest.

* * *

Mare portentosum.

The great solitary water, this diffuse mobility, this sheet of storms, so calm underneath, communicates by hidden arteries with those volcanoes of mud which eject the internal humus, revealing to us that, like man, the globe has its skin, the land—and its mucus, the mire. The globe is obviously an animated being. Is it alive? That is the question. Between animation and life there exists a subtle difference: the personality, the enormous I. Who would dare affirm it? who could deny it?

Be that as it may, the waters belong to the winds. The sea submits to the breeze. The result is an inexhaustible variety of apparent facts, contradictory on the surface but basically in agreement, whose numberless transformations have given trouble to Hippocrates, Aristotle, Avicenna, Albertus Magnus, Galileo, Porta, Huygens, Mariotte, Volta, Vallisnieri, Spallanzani, Beccaria, Wheatstone, Lyell, Coulvier-Gravier, Maury, Peltier, Maxadorf, Schoenbein, Humboldt, even the ingenious Matthew de la Drôme and those wise and learned writers, Margollé and Zurcher, the two historians of the wind.

The air's breath, the capricious whim, *flat ubi vult,* seems to laugh to-day at the wires of Snow-Harris, just as once it laughed at the two swords of King Artaxerxes and Queen Parysatis.

Those swords were the embryo of the lightning-conductor.

The atmosphere, forty miles thick, expandable to seventy-five, has been weighed by Galileo, equilibrated with mercury by Torricelli, inventor of the barometer, measured by Pascal from the top of the Tower of St. Jacques, separated into its elements by Lavoisier. And there we stand.

Who knows where science will stop? Who knows whether man will not succeed in forging the key to the wind?

To catch the hurricane, science makes a net whose meshes are being multiplied; the London observatory has Admiral Fitzroy's twenty-six charts, and the Paris observatory compiles the Storm Atlas. Science has reached the point of fathoming the weather, and almost of predicting it, by assembling data and by calculations, and projecting as far across the ocean as possible all the lines of equal barometric pressure. The shapes of these curves mark the variations of the atmosphere.

One part of the enigma has been guessed; the other data are under study.

The despotic winds do obey; something commands that fantastic, scattered troop there are laws to its madness—laws so great that merely to state them is terrifying.

The nineteen-year lunar period observed by Grand-Jean de Fouchy, the forty-one-year solar period of maximum sunspot activity, the crowded transit of shooting stars on the climacteric nights of August 10 and November 12—that whole mysterious body of laws rules the dull compass card. The aurora is a signal that raises the hurricane. A meteor falls into the sun, a storm breaks out on earth: is it extraordinary coincidence or law of nature?

There are prodigious pressures. Other immeasurable circumstances are perceived but dimly. From October 10, 1781, to March 25, 1782, while the fifty-fifth star in Hercules was in process of extinction, the ocean was convulsed with storms. Schwabe vouches for the solar event, Slough for the stellar. Why not? An ant weighs upon the earth; a star can well weigh upon the universe. Who knows to what extent we depend upon the variations of the *Gamma* star of Antinoüs, on *Delta* of Cepheus, and on *Alpha* of the Dragon? Who knows the dimensions of cosmic influence? the length of emanations? Do we not in some measure feel, in the repercussions upon our own planetary system, all those distant yet enormous presences—Sirius, Mira Ceti, Argo at times attaining nearly the intensity of Canopus, and Hevelius' oscillations of Hydra? Humboldt dreamed of them. Can we be sure that the passage of sixteen thousand bolides in a night counts for naught, for example, in a windstorm such as the one which drove the sea back over the land near Elliott Key, so that ships cast anchor in forests? When the seamen of the *Ledbury-Snow* awoke, they perceived their anchor caught in the top branches of a tree beneath the surface of the water.

There is no interruption in creation; no broken arch, no lapse; an action and its consequences embrace all nature; the chain may be longer or shorter, but never breaks. Climb this immense knotted cord, take one fact after another, and you will progress from the vibrio to the constellation. The immanent marvel has its own cohesion. Nothing is wasted; no effort is lost. The useless does not exist. The universe has what is necessary and only what is necessary.

The astral influence combines with the terrestrial. Are not the phenomena inherent in the contraction of the earth's circle of rotation, for example, connected with the furious rush of certain polar winds, and in particular with those violent winds of Norway which once, in a single day, caused a drop in the barometer of twenty-one millimeters at Skudenes and of thirty-one at Christiansand?

The unfathomable has its machinery; Laplace called it *celestial mechanics.* Its wheels are invisible to us, so huge are they. Its lever arms go from what we name reality to what we name abstraction. They exert their power right down to the geometric point. No method of measurement, no dreaming, can give an idea of this propagation of vitality along increasing or lessening proximities—the dizzying growth from the indefinite to the infinite. The infinitely great reaches to the infinitely small, and the infinitely small to the infinitely great. Take a pinch of tripoli, one cubic inch; in that cubic inch of impalpable powder there are forty-one billion skeletons. What difference can you make out between those ashes and that other dust we call the Milky Way? Which is the more marvellous of the two?

Here is the diatom, there the star. Above, just as below, specks; below, as above, vastnesses.

Relativity being the sole measure, the microscopic world has its own colossi. Alongside the crepuscular monad, the hooded colpode is as the whale to the minnow. Between the microscopic universe and the telescopic universe there is identity. The big end of the spyglass is the whole question.

Man himself, this giant of intelligence and will, is microscopic. A billion men, the entire population of the globe, could be contained in a coffin a thousand feet high, a thousand feet wide, and six thousand feet long. Hollowed out, the smallest of the Alps would suffice for the sarcophagus of the human race.

Life is an ever-closer communication, the forging of a chain. What we call death is the changing of a link. No breach of continuity being possible, the perpetuity of the self is the necessary result of the immanent fact. Forgetfulness of having been would be a break in the chain. We mean absolute forgetfulness; for the possibility of momentary forgetfulness, in which the persistence of the personality loses nothing, is proved by sleep. Our life on earth is probably a kind of sleep. The immortality of the soul is nothing other than the universal cohesion of creation ruling the individual as it rules the universe.

What this cohesion is, what this immanence, is impossible to imagine. It is at once the amalgam out of which solidarity is born, and the self which creates directions. It is all explained in the word, Radiation. The interweaving of creatures with their emanations is creation. We are simultaneously points of arrival and points of departure. Every being is the centre of a world.

There is a work of the whole composed of all the works of isolation being swept along toward a common goal, without even the workers' knowledge, by the one great central soul.

The immanence of creation is beyond imagination; no less so are its workings. The possibilities of supreme power are unknown. Man does not know the power of man. And if the works of man are so transformative a force, to speculate about the works of divinity makes the mind reel. A woman weeps; the chemist Smithson is present, he collects a drop of the liquid, and a woman's tear becomes a chemical formula from which a branch of science will develop. Quentin Matsys or Benvenuto Cellini manipulates a bit of iron for a few hours, they leave their mark upon it, and the iron has become more precious than gold. Byron pays his stationer a shilling for a bottle of ink that he will sell to his publisher for a hundred thousand francs. And we are confining ourselves to statements of material results; the moral result is far more surprising still. A man's toil filtered through a mass of metal or stone, a canvas, a sheet of paper, causes it to undergo so great a sublimation that from the gross matter that it was, it becomes idea. Out of toil there emerges a metaphysical dynamics resistant to all formulas but productive of forces and values. Execution is a second creation; the first creation is but the setting into motion. First was the slime, then intelligence. Picture a papyrus becoming the *Iliad.* If such things can be done by the Prometheuses here below, surprising the creator and robbing him of his secret, what will not the providences above accomplish! what will not the Creator Himself perform? *Quid domini facient, audent cum talia fures!*

The data of this universal activity defy all nomenclature. There is no way to define them; they are not to be circumscribed. Contraries wed; distances are points of contact. What appears to be divorce, is marriage. Hatred ends as love. Beneath the combat is the kiss. Everything is a coefficient. You think you are at one pole, you are at the other. Union is never tighter than when separation seems most irremediable. The mountain is as unaware of movement as the infusoria are of sleep. Yet it is the infusoria that make the mountain. All Australia is a coral, constructed by an insect.

Everywhere the unexpected. The similarities are no less strange than the contrasts. It is extraordinary that *this* should be like *that.* One phenomenon closely copies the other. God repeats himself. The All-Powerful is the plagiarist of the Creator, and it is in the presence of the plagiarism that you sense most profoundly the overwhelming force of the sublime. We have indicated elsewhere[1] the identity of form of the sun and the spider. These repetitions are the miracle of invention. We contemplate in bewilderment, we listen distraught. The voices of the infinite echo the awesome depths.

Striking resemblances, recognizable at zodiacal distances—what could be more astounding? What a dem-

1. *Légende des Siècles.*

onstration of unity! The comet soars like the dragonfly. A nebula is, as it were, a universe in the cocoon. The firmament and the drop of water have the same model; both contain worlds. The reptility of the caterpillar resembles our miseries and our vices; there are wings within. Temper and tempest issue from the same mold. Such parallels might be multiplied indefinitely.

One should never tire of insisting on the unity of the laws of nature; it reveals the unity of being.

In these logarithmic wonders of a creative fruitfulness ceaselessly refilling the same urn with fresh water from the same spring, certain infirm philosophies have seen only sterility. It would take little more for them to be accusing God of senility: Thou art mouthing the same old words, Jupiter. The serious thinker is perhaps even more carried away and amazed by these great parallelisms than by the lightning shocks of the unforeseen. Harmony is a line that extends majestically as far as the eye can reach. Its straightness electrifies us. At certain moments we divine, we feel, that the law is about to confirm itself in a new form; we see God coming. It is the supreme understanding! we come close to surprising Him in the process. A little more, it seems, and we ourselves should be creating. So that is how He works! We have the vertiginous feeling of placing our hand upon the divine instrument.

Here he works by antithesis, there by identicalness. Nothing could be more sublime. There is but one pattern. The law of the spirit follows the same rules of gravitation as the law of the stars; the material echoes the moral; equilibrium is the proof of equity; man is the planet of the truth. God makes everything the same way. The universe is his synonymy. The unshakable is analogous to the ephemeral. God varies his edifice, not his geometry; his effects, not his rules. The rotary movement of the volvox serves him for the evolution of the globe; he does not trouble to invent another form: since it serves for the organism, it's good enough for you, O universe; and there is something terrifying about the calmness of omnipotence copying itself. Creation unfolds out of unity. The burgeoning is varied, the root is the same. Amid these mystic symmetries it is natural to succumb to awe. The infinitely great is counterbalanced by the infinitesimally small; harmony is counteracted by confusion; immobility is nothing other than a stationary whirlwind; the Milky Way resembles a cloud; the scud resembles a mountain chain; a river flows in the tree, twists about in its ramifications, the stream is multiplied in minute detail; the sap is blood; light is a wave; movement is combustion; to live is to burn; to consummate is the same as to consume; all activity is alike; all matter is handled the same way; the element dissolves in the atom; unity in layers—that is the universe; there is no difference between a handful of ashes and a handful of worlds: the same conditions of being, almost the same appearance, with slight differences in duration; the same perpetual remoulding; the same anvil above and below; the work, here panting, there passive, bursts forth in the same manner, in the momentary as in the inextinguishable, and the dreamer, mute with conviction and surprise, watches the fire of the forge crumble into sparks, and the fire of the abyss into stars.

Our cosmic dependence—proven now, but which myopic science seeks to circumscribe—will become ever more manifest. The terrestrial phenomenon, to-day still obscure, is a zodiacal derivative.

Sidereal evolutions bring about the displacement of our seasons. It takes the magnetic needle six hundred and twenty years to complete its oscillation to the west and to the east of the meridian. Thus the present oscillation, begun in 1660, will not be finished until 2280. The law of storms is related to this oscillation. In this revolution of six hundred and twenty years, now the Asiatic pole is the colder one, now the American. Oneness and attachment assert themselves under many other forms as well. Franklin proved that the northeasterlies have their source in the southwest. South of the equator, cyclones turn clockwise, and north of the equator counterclockwise. Explosions of firedamp in the ground coincide with equinoctial storms at sea. Formidable arcana that navigators must study.

Phenomena may well be suspected of anything, are capable of anything. Hypothesis proclaims the infinite;

that is what gives hypothesis its greatness. Beneath the surface fact it seeks the real fact. It asks creation for her thoughts, and then for her second-thoughts. The great scientific discoverers are those who hold nature suspect. They suspect her of enlargement, prolongation, obscure unfoldment, of shoots reaching out in every direction, of boundless vegetation; they suspect her of extensions into the invisible. It is toward these extensions that hypothesis directs its sublime groping. He who glimpses these extensions into the invisible realm of creation is the magus; he who glimpses these extensions into the invisible realm of destiny is the prophet.

Nature is suspect in all directions. Her immensity authorizes suspicion. What she does is not what she seems to do; what she wills is not what she seems to will. Over the invisible she places the mask of the visible, so that what we do not see escapes us, and what we see deceives us. Hence the arguments furnished to atheism by nature, that plenitude of God. Nature has no candor. She shows herself to man with her face turned away. She is appearance; happily she is also transparency. How strange: we go much less astray with her when we guess, perhaps, than when we calculate. Aristotle sees further than Ptolemy. When the Stagyrite dreamer affirmed that the successive motion of the winds follows the apparent motion of the sun, he almost put his finger on Galileo's findings. A mathematician is a savant only on condition that he be also a sage. Nature eludes calculation. Number is a grim pullulation. Nature is the thing that cannot be numbered. An idea makes more work than adding a column of figures. Why? because the idea shows the whole, whereas addition cannot make the total. The infinite in its splendor and oneness fecundates the intelligence; numbers, those millipedes, dissect and devour it. The savant who throws himself into a pit of figures is like the Brahman who throws himself into a snake-pit. Calculation does indeed obtain some admirable results, provided it never becomes entangled with hypothesis. Petty calculation disdains conjecture; major calculation takes it into account. Calculation can only multiply; hypothesis sometimes creates. The limit of calculation is the exact, the limit of hypothesis is the absolute—a field deep enough in other respects.

Mathematics collides with the impossible; it meets with the overturned 8: ∞, infinity; hypothesis collides only with mystery. To try to square the circle is absurd; to seek the philosopher's stone is not.

Venerable nature, held sacred yet forever under suspicion: such is the law of ancient Magianism and of modern science, such is the point of departure for the spirit of discovery. Astronomers and chemists are the mask-snatchers. Somebody asked one day in the Portico: Which goddess would you like to see unclothed? Plato answered: Venus. Socrates answered: Isis. Isis is Truth. Isis is Reality. In the absolute the real is identical with the ideal. It is Jehovah, Satan, Isis, Venus; it is Pan. It is Nature.

Nature abounds in false bottoms. She is Daedalian, mixing up all the tracks on all the lines. In our short view her apparent directions run contrary to her actual inclinations. The facts have an interior current different from the surface current. Nature's secret is known to one being alone, the very being that is the secret. Ever since there have been thinking creatures on earth, nature has been spied upon with unquiet looks, sometimes even with black looks. *Transversa tuentibus.* She is suspected: by the ascetic, of orgies; by the savant, of illusion; by the philosopher, of evil toward the good. For one man she is a libertine, for another a liar, for the third a savage. She is none of these. Only, she has what we lack: time and space. Nothing presses her and nothing restricts her. Her line is not straight, and so eludes us. To reach her goal she takes the roundabout road of infinity.

She meanders in a realm of possibility which is not ours. Not having our limitations, she has not our morals. She would be monster were she not marvel. For her, as we have said elsewhere, the end justifies the means. Only the absolute has that right. Probably one who is without gauge can be without scruple. Hence the cataclysms, those violent measures taken by the irresponsible.

Hence also the dire monsters. The ancient Python is no fable. The Hecatoncheires exists in the infinitesimal;

why should it not exist in the infinitely large? Bonnet of Geneva, a naturalist whose studies were all-encompassing, believed in the existence of a myriapod of a size proportionate to the ocean. He had received one hundred and thirty-nine observations on it that he considered definite.

The solitudes of the water are unexplored. They have caeca. At each of the two poles alone there is an unknown surface five million square miles in extent. What lives there?

Magnetic life is centralized at the poles. They are prodigious reservoirs of creatures.

The Kraken, in which Buffon believed, is a polar Python.

These swarms of life fling terrifying specimens our way from time to time. Cuvier rediscovered the dragon.

The ornithorhynchus is a griffin. The Aepyornis is the roc of the Arabian Nights. One of the palace huts of the kings of Madagascar has a roof made of three Aepyornis feathers. These vast plumes have a wingspread appropriate for a colossal eagle, and modern science—willing advocate of the little, and of the diminishing hypothesis—was wrong in declaring the Aepyornis a brevipennate.

Fossils have similarly demonstrated the existence of another gigantic bird, the moa. Its leg exceeds the height of a man (femur: eighteen inches; tibia: three feet, three inches; metatarsus: twenty inches; great toe: ten inches).

Zoology is as limitless as cosmography.

The Hydra is sufficiently proved in water by the shark and on land by the crocodile.

Other animal terrors, even stranger, make up part of creation. Perhaps we shall meet some of them in the course of this book.

There is in creation an Unknown. It has its reasons, which are beyond our comprehension. The Unknown is extravagant in frightfulness as in splendor. Its successes in the ghastly make one shudder. Man's dream is an attempt that is always exceeded by creation; there is something more nocturnal than thought: it is fact. The reality outdistances the nightmare. Our phantoms are abortions.

Nature creates them after we do or before we do—and more complete. In Cayenne, over sleeping men, flies the bat-winged vampire. The Unguessed, the Invisible, the Possible: plumb these three abysses. Let us not quibble about the boundless. Quibbling will not circumscribe; denial will not limit. In spite of our optimism, there are creatures of dread. Terror exists, in things of flesh and blood. It is under us and upon us. Even when we touch it, even when it possesses us, it keeps its unlikelihood, and, being so full of horror, seems not to be. The unexpected lies in wait for us. It makes its appearance, seizes us, devours us, and still scarcely seems real. Creation is full of vertiginous formations that envelop us and of which we are skeptical. Either there is too much magnificence or there is too much deformity. Here an exuberance of harmony, there an excess of chaos. God exaggerates. Down below as up above, He goes too far. The undulations of vitality are as limitless and as indefinite as ripples in the water. They twist and tangle, unravel, and tie themselves into new knots. The zones of universal reality writhe, above and beneath our horizon, in endless spirals. Life is the prodigious serpent of the infinite. Neither head nor tail, neither beginning nor conclusion: coils without number. There are rings of stars, and there are rings of acari. Everything holds together. As we have said elsewhere, the world is two Babels moving in contrary directions, one lunging, the other rising. The surprising thing would be if we understood it. At the very most we arrive at a conjecture. Which of our methods of measuring could we apply to this eddying mass that is the universe? In the presence of these profundities our sole ability is to dream. Our conception, quickly winded, cannot follow creation, that vast breath. Our hypotheses, bewildered as they are, consider with stupefaction the unexpressable ramifications of the possible, and the dilatations of reality in all directions. God attains the inconceivable in the mollusk of the sea as well as in the star of the heavens. His very excess sometimes leads us to deny Him. The unfathomable logarithms of His combinations fascinate us or revolt us, but, whether we are fascinated or revolted, overwhelm us. His infinite presence in the minutest fact disconcerts us. It flashes forth especially in extreme phenomena, in the hideous or splendid marvels that one might call border incidents. These are in fact the beginnings of regions. So much reached, so much established, so much recorded and undergone—we understand nothing more. The imagination declines to plunge and soar; knowledge refuses to grope. Beyond the monster there is only the phantom. We do not want to know any more. It is all right, enough, we are saturated, we have had our fill. The brain, as far as knowledge is concerned, is but a limited container. In a human being, too deep an acquaintance with reality would appear folly to other human beings, complete knowledge would look like madness, and the unfortunate soul who succeeded in meeting the Great Unknown face to face on the summit of all things would descend from Sinai only to enter Bedlam.

Let us not heave our lead too far forward.

Let us confine ourselves, from the cosmic point of view, to accepting what is, complicated by what can be. The real is the asymptote of the possible; their meeting point is at infinity. In the universe, which envelops us and pervades us, nothing, except the absurd, except that which commits suicide, may be denied *a priori*. The incomprehensible takes up too much room for any to be left for the improbable. Since there are comets, there may well be the Python. The edge of darkness can no more be found than the edge of light. The Unknown works in both directions. The miasma has its logic like the ray, and logic is life.

The Why of disasters is beyond our understanding. To what purpose this catastrophe? What was the use of this fire, this flood, this earthquake, this shipwreck, this plague, this eruption? What is the function of calamities?

Outside of man, what reason has One to do what One does? From what angle does the mysterious ordainer see causes and effects? Is there any sense in the elements, those intermediaries between him and us? They often seem to us mad, sometimes insensate. Lavoisier spoke of *the extravagance of the air.* There are forces in the darkness whose way of acting disconcerts us. It would seem that we living beings have to reckon, if not with invisible creatures of spite, at least with some sort of unknown blind agencies charged with a portion of the conduct of things. These obscure forces govern in their fumbling way the human race.

Let this be said, however: between blind and obscure it is necessary to make a distinction. Impenetrability is not blindness. That these forces are dark does not prove that they are unconscious. They are sufficiently active not to be merely passive. We call them Forces; perhaps they are Powers. The *Ubi Vult* indicates intention in a puff of wind.

What does the wind say? To whom does it speak? What is its interlocutor? Into what ear does it murmur? near the ground it is sometimes quiet; in the high latitudes, never. It is the voice. All other sounds stop or break off; this one persists. The wandering of the wind fills the air. It is the great stubborn murmur. Is it a monologue? Is it a reply? Nothing could be more monotonous and more sublime. This drivel of the abyss was taken in bad part by many philosophers of old. The pantheistic gymnosophists, accustomed to calling nature to account, were indignant over it. Why this whistling, ever the same? Why this grating, ever the same? what was the use of this bawling to the heavens to repeat the same things endlessly? *vary your exclamations!* A Cynic philosopher who supported himself on a stick that was sold after his death for a talent, five thousand francs today, Peregrinus Proteus, walked along the seashore in heavy windstorms shrugging his shoulders. He listened to the clamor of the winds as he would to the pleading of lawyers. He seemed to be reproaching the cold blasts for always recommencing their eternal scoldings, and to be criticizing the tempest in the same terms, for boring its audience and for deafening people, before drowning them, with all those cruel banalities. He would gladly have told the storm to first drown its voice.

The wind in itself is not a force: it is only an effect of velocity, but velocity is energy. Such a force, after all, that the sudden arrest of speed results in instantaneous combustion. The burst of energy is resolved into fire and produces a percussion.

By velocity the zephyr becomes a projectile. Speed crushes. The bound that gives the tiger its power also makes the hurricane. In 1836 a blast of wind passing through London at ten o'clock in the morning was in Stettin at ten in the evening. Another, on February 27, 1860, in half an hour rolled twenty-two million tons of air over Paris. Still another, on May 23, 1865, dumped over two million cubic yards of water in thirty minutes, also on Paris. And alongside the winds of Africa and Asia the winds of Europe are as nought.

Some meteorologists affirm that at times a cyclone, like a cannon ball, does fifteen hundred miles an hour. There is some exaggeration there, we think.

The mighty blows struck by these velocities are amazing. One passing blast snatches a carronade from the bridge of the frigate *Sané*; another, near St. Luc in Jersey in 1854, throws a hundred-and-twenty-eight-foot wall down flat in one piece like a sheet of paper; another, in 1863, near St. Martin in Guernsey, dismembers a large mill, breaks its crosspiece in full flight, and fifty paces away buries those two great beams in the earth with their slats, like a couple of feathers; another, on June 7, 1859, razes a street in Granville; another, in the vicinity of St. Pol-de-Léon, hurls twenty-four church bells to the ground. Another, in Corrèze in June 1865, in fifteen minutes tears the commune of Meilhard to shreds, shatters two hundred roofs, and scatters an entire hamlet into the air—Sauviate, of which not more than one house remains. Another dries up a forest; another reaches beneath the sea to break up madrepores and carries gigantic fragments of them into the valleys of the island of Bourbon; another reduces Kingstown from six hundred houses to fourteen ruins. The fleets fare no better. In a single buffet the wind takes two ships in Orelana, three in Duquesne, four in Anson, four in Rodney, everything in Medina Sidonia.

With regard to the wind's prodigies of strength such as those, legend is in agreement with science, and naturally goes a bit further. The people of Iceland complained one day about the harshness of their climate; they said that Hekla was not an adequate fireplace for keeping them warm. "Attach a tow-rope to your island," the pole wind shouted to them, "and I shall pull Iceland wherever you wish."

These forces are in jealous possession of the wide spaces. The wind guards the sea with proprietary acrimony. It defends against human encroachment the hells that it hides and the paradises that it shelters; it defends the volcanoes of the South Pole, Erebus and Terror, against Dumont d'Urville, just as it does Tahiti against Cook. But the European pioneer persists nevertheless; he persists from every kind of motive: Marco Polo, to reach Great Cathay; Rubruquis, to convert the Grand Khan; Diaz, to find Prester John; Pigolano, in order to be named *maestrante* of the knighthood of Seville; Quirino Buscon, in order to discover the convent of Plusimanos, where, under the name of Malabestia, the devil rings the bells. Others have the divine and sure instinct for civilizing, and they brave shipwreck for progress' sake. Discard the false weight of glory, and take a balance: in the scales of civilization all the armies of Cyrus and Sesostris, and the phalanxes of Alexander, and Caesar's legions, weigh less than the hundred and sixty men who followed Vasco da Gama and the hundred and eighteen men who accompanied Cook.

Navigation is education. The sea is a hard school. Cohabitation with these unmanageable phenomena produces a rough race of men who deserve to be cherished, the mariners. There are no other conquerors but them. Ulysses the voyager accomplishes more than Achilles the fighter. The sea drenches man; the soldier is only iron, the mariner is steel. Behold them at the port, these seamen, quiet martyrs, silent in triumph, virile characters in whose glance is the religion that comes out of the deep. Add this: navigation is the opposite of war. Navigation civilizes barbarism, war barbarizes civilization. What the mariners do may be freely admitted. But the strange thing is that man admires carnage more than discovery. He insists on having both sides of the brute: ferocity plus stupidity. Hence all the butchery. Hence armies for the sake of war and war for the sake of armies. The day when Van Diemen is more popular than Caesar, the day when the compass is preferred to the sword, the day when love of mariners replaces love of soldiers, on that day will peace be made.

Humanity will enter into possession of its two estates, the totality of the earth and the totality of life.

In the meantime, civilization will go on brutalizing the sailor in its shameful way. In 1863, to cite only the one year, the English navy received twenty-five thousand five hundred and thirteen whip-lashes.

Given by whom? by the officer to the seaman. Which of the two was degraded?

It is by the sea that the land is conquered. A vast labor, under endless investigation. The entire sea covers a perilous, half-understood region.

Yet the end is being reached. Little by little, step by step, slowly, scientifically. In the past twenty years alone, through studies of the sea, thanks to the fine work of the brilliant hydrographer Maury, ten days have been cut from the equator crossing, fifteen from the China voyage, fifty from the passage to Australia.

Man trespasses; space seems to consent. The ocean appears about to capitulate. The storm draws back, not without violent protest. The fury of the winds is a barrier. The first relay post of the northern gales is at the Pillars of Hercules: Calpe and Abila are breached; then, on the underside of Africa, before the vessel of men there looms, immobile across the ocean, upright—gazing out, as it were, from beneath its double brow of clouds—the menace of Cape Nun. Passage forbidden. Man passes. The winds make concessions, the fluid obstacle offers no resistance to Gilianez, who doubles to Point Bojador; to Cadamosto, who discovers the Canaries; to Fernandez, who discovers Cape Verde, to Alvarez Cabral, who discovers the Azores; to Jacques Lemaire, who doubles Cape Horn, where the Andes terminate in volcanoes; to Sebastian del Cano, who continues the voyage of Magellan; to Clarke, who continues Crook's work; to a hundred more. The winds resist Dumont d'Urville, trying to penetrate "the ancient blue ice packs." They destroy Lapeyrouse and Franklin. They are easier on Anson, that hero who was part pirate; they restore the

Centurion to him in the Ladrones, and by their permission he is able to return to London, to the sound of drums and trumpets, with thirty-two carriages laden with Spanish piasters. The winds had already been complaisant toward England, notably in the time when Cartis-Mandua, queen of the Brigantes, sent her pirogue flotillas against Rouen. There are moments when you think you can catch a glimpse of their disdain. They obey man whether he is for or against civilization. With the same impartiality they convey Attila to Italy and Columbus to America. The wind seems to be the great indifferent force of the sinister. In short, the storms bend, relent, break, turn tail, yield, let man alone; at times it is like a rout, they submit to defeat, Drake finds California, Tasman Australia, the winds retreat as far as they can into the solitudes, take refuge in inaccessible places, exile themselves to unknown regions, one almost forgets about them, where are they? and suddenly here they are, it is as if nothing has been accomplished, with a single beating of wings they retake everything.

We were in their territory, they are in ours.

They seek their revenge. They come to seek out man, they are furious. They declare war on him on a thousand fronts at once, in Asia at the same time as in Europe. In one month, almost in one day, they crush six-story houses in London under factory smoke stacks, the brick towers toppled with a puff; in a few minutes they sink in the Thames, at Bugsby Hole, sixty barges loaded with coal; they lay the Indian quarter of Chandernagore in ruins; at Calcutta they jumble the English, French, and American navies together in the same destruction.

They make sorties. They quit their remote fastnesses. They hurl themselves upon the earth.

Why?

To do evil?

Yes and no.

The wind is on the one hand a scourge and on the other a blessing.

And it is the blessing that is its greater side.

Certain calamities cause us to doubt providence. Terrible Nature seems to say: Ah! thou does not believe in

God. Well, thou art right. A deluge, a plague, an earthquake—these are atheism taken at its word.

Fortunately the evil is only its obverse side; the good is creation's face.

A storm is an act of dictatorship on the part of darkness, reëstablishing equilibrium.

Let us say in passing: When, in the social realm, a man has any pretension to doing that sort of thing, the parody has just one flaw, he lacks the infinite. A human earthquake is a crime. Man imitating God's authority remains petty and becomes horrible. The monkey is the beginning of the demon.

Dictatorship implies infinitude and eternity.

The hurricanes are prodigious locomotives hauling the rains of the high seas toward the earth. To the plants they bring carbonic acid, nitre, ammonia. To the vast universal fermentation they bring ozone, the disinfectant that is measured out by infinity.

Without them the earth would be without rivers, forests, prairies, fruits, or flowers. They make the air breathable, they make the earth habitable, they make man possible. They are charged with sweeping away miasmas. They are charged with the provision of water. The marvelous drainage of the atmosphere! The usefulness of the destructive elements! Take water away and figure out what is left. These ruffians are distillers. Every time you see a cloud, you see their retort and their alembic. The water reservoir is salty, otherwise it would stagnate. From the drop of ocean water, the winds make the raindrop. Without them the terrestrial world would consist of two deserts, one liquid and one solid. All that is out of the water would be dryness. The earth would be stone. The globe would be the bare cranium of an enormous death's-head rolling through the heavens.

IV

Explanation of the Noise to Which Gilliatt Listened

THE great descent of the winds towards the earth takes place at the equinoxes. At these periods the balance of the tropics and the poles sways up and down, and the colossal atmospheric tide pours its flood upon one hemisphere and its ebb upon the other. There are constellations which signify these phenomena,—Libra, the balance, and Aquarius, the water-bearer.

It is the time of tempests.

The sea waits and preserves silence.

Sometimes the sky wears an evil look. It is pallid, a great dim veil obstructs it. Mariners gaze with anxiety at the irritated aspect of the gloom.

But it is its satisfied aspect which they fear the most. A smiling equinoctial sky is the storm showing a velvet paw. When the skies are thus, the Tower of Weepers at Amsterdam is filled with women scanning the horizon.

When the vernal or autumnal tempest is behind time, it is only gathering up strength. It hoards up for ravages. Beware of arrearages. Ango was wont to say: "The sea is a good paymaster."

When the delay has been too long, the sea displays its impatience only by more calm. But the magnetic tension is manifested by what may be called the inflammation of the water. Gleams leap from the waves. Electric air, phosphoric water. Sailors feel languid. This time is particularly perilous for ironclads; their iron hulls may be productive of variations of the compass, and destroy them. The transatlantic steamer *Iowa* perished from this cause.

For those who are familiar with the sea, its aspect at such moments is strange: one would say that it desired and feared the cyclone. Certain unions, though strongly urged by nature, are accepted in this fashion. The lioness in heat flees before the lion. The sea is also in heat. Hence its trembling.

The immense marriage is about to take place.

This marriage, like the bridals of the emperors of old, is celebrated by exterminations. It is a festival seasoned with disasters.

Meanwhile, from the distance, from the open sea, from the impregnable latitudes, from the livid horizon of solitudes, from the depths of boundless liberty the winds arrive.

Pay attention, it is the equinoctial fact.

A tempest is a thing that plots mischief. Ancient mythology caught a glimpse of these indistinct personalities, mingled with vast, diffused nature. Æolus lays his plans with Boreas. The alliance between element and element is necessary. They distribute the task among themselves. Impulsions must be communicated to the wave, to the cloud, to the effluvium; night is an auxiliary; it is important that it should be employed. There are compasses to be falsified, beacons to be extinguished, lighthouses to be masked, stars to be hidden. The sea must coöperate. Every storm is preceded by a murmur. Behind the horizon the preliminary whispering of the hurricanes is in progress. The noise one hears lies far away in the gloom, above the frightened silence of the sea.

Gilliatt had heard that redoubtable whisper. The phosphorescence had been the first warning; this murmur was the second.

If the demon Legion exists, it is assuredly he who is the Wind.

The wind is multiple, but the air is one.

Hence this result: all storms are mixed. The unity of the air exacts this.

The whole abyss is involved in a tempest. The entire ocean is contained in a squall. Its total forces enter into it in line, and take part. A wave is the gulf from below;

a gust is the gulf from above. To have to deal with a squall is to have to do with all the sea and all the sky.

Messier, the naval authority, the thoughtful astronomer of the little lodge at Cluny, said: "The wind is from everywhere, and is everywhere." He did not believe in imprisoned winds, even in inland seas. There were no Mediterranean winds for him. He said that he recognized them on their passage. He affirmed that on such a day, at such an hour, the foehn of Lake Constance, the ancient Favonius of Lucretius, had traversed the horizon of Paris; on another day the bora of the Adriatic; on another day, the gyrating Notus which is said to be shut up in the circle of the Cyclades. He indicated its emanations. He did not think that the south wind which whirls between Malta and Tunis, and the south wind which blows between Corsica and the Balearic Isles, were unable to escape. He did not admit that there were winds confined like bears in cages. He said: "All rain comes from the tropics, and all lightning from the poles." The wind is, in fact, saturated with electricity at the intersection of the colures, which marks the extremities of the axis, and with water at the equator; and it brings us liquid from the equatorial line and air from the poles.

Ubiquity, that is the wind.

This, of course, does not mean that windy zones do not exist. Nothing is more firmly established than these afflations with continual currents, and some day, aerial navigation by means of air-ships, which in our mania for the Greek we call *aëroscaphes,* will utilize the principal currents. The canalization of the air by the wind is incontestable; there are rivers of wind, streams of wind, and brooks of wind; only these branchings in the air are made in a directly opposite way from branchings of the water; here it is the brooks which flow from the streams, and the streams from the rivers, instead of falling into them; hence, instead of concentration, dispersion.

It is this dispersion which constitutes the solidarity of the winds and the unity of the atmosphere. One molecule displaced, displaces another. The whole wind moves together. To these deep-seated causes of amalgamation, add the relief of the glove, piercing the atmosphere by all its mountains, causing knots and torsions in the courses of the wind, and determining counter-currents in all directions. Unlimited irradiation.

The phenomenon of the wind is the oscillation of two oceans, one upon the other; the ocean of air superimposed on the ocean of water, rests upon this flight and wavers on this trembling.

The indivisible is not to be put into compartments. There is no partition between one flood and the other. The Channel Islands feel the influence of the Cape of Good Hope. Universal navigation contends against a single monster. The whole sea is the same hydra. The waves cover the sea as with a coat of scales. The ocean is Ceto.

Upon that unity descends the innumerable.

V

Turba, Turma

FOR the compass there are thirty-two winds, that is to say, thirty-two directions; but these directions may be subdivided indefinitely. The wind, classed by its directions, is the incalculable; classed by its kinds, it is the infinite.

Homer would have shrunk from the enumeration of them.

The polar current comes in contact with the tropical current. Heat and cold suddenly combine, equilibrium begins with the shock; the surge of the winds springs forth from it, swollen, scattered, and torn in all directions into fierce tricklings. The dispersion of the gusts shakes the prodigious tangle of air to the four corners of the horizon.

All the winds blow there: the wind from the Gulf Stream, which pours out so much fog on Newfoundland;

the wind from Peru, a region with a mute heaven where no man has ever heard thunder; the wind of Nova Scotia, where flies the great auk, *Alca impennis,* with striped beak; the typhoons of the China Sea; the wind of Mozambique, which abuses the *pangays* and junks; the electric wind of Japan, announced by the gong; the African wind, which dwells between Table Mountain and the Devil's Peak, and which there gains its liberty; the wind of the equator, which passes above the trade winds and describes a parabola whose apex always points to the west; the Plutonian wind, which issues from craters, and which is the terrible breath of the flame; the strange wind peculiar to the volcano of Awu, which always causes an olive-hued cloud to rise in the north; the monsoon of Java, against which the casemates called "hurricane houses" are built; the north wind with its branches, which the English call "bush winds"; the curved gusts of the Straits of Malacca observed by Horsburgh; the powerful southwest wind, called *Pampero* in Chile and *Rebojo* at Buenos Aires, which bears the condor far out to sea and saves it from the pit where the savage, lying flat on his back and bending his great bow with his feet, is lying in wait for it under an oxhide freshly flayed; the chemical wind, which, according to Lemery, makes thunder stones in the cloud; the Harmattan of the Kaffirs; the Polar snow wind which harnesses itself to the fast ice and drags the eternal icebergs; the wind from the Gulf of Bengal, which goes as far as Nijni-Novgorod to sack the triangle of wooden booths, wherein is held the Asiatic fair; the wind of the cordilleras, agitator of great waves and great forests; the wind of the Australian archipelagoes, where the honey hunters ferret out the wild hives concealed beneath the armpits of the branches of the giant eucalyptus; the sirocco, the mistral, the hurricane, the winds of drought, the winds of inundation, the diluvial, the torrid; those which cast into the streets of Genoa the dust from the plains of Brazil, those which obey the diurnal rotation, those which act in opposition, and which caused Herrera to say: *"Malo viento torna contra el sol"* (it's an evil wind that turns contrary to the sun); those which go in couples, conspiring to overthrow, the one undoing what the other does, and the ancient winds which assailed Christopher Columbus on the coast of Veragua, and those which, for the space of forty days, from the twenty-first of October to the twenty-eighth of November, 1520, delayed and rendered doubtful Magellan's entrance into the Pacific, and those which dismasted the Armada and blew upon Philip II.

There are still others, and how is their end to be reached? The winds which carry toads and grasshoppers, and drive before them clouds of living things across the ocean; those which effect what is called "the veering of the wind," and whose function is to cause shipwrecks; those which, with a single breath, displace the cargo in the vessel and compel her to continue her course leaning over; the winds which construct the circum-cumuli; the winds which mass the circum-strati; the heavy, blind winds swollen with rain; the hail winds; the fever winds; those whose approach sets the salt springs and the sulphur springs of Calabria boiling; those which make the hair of the African panthers sparkle as they roam the thickets of Cape Ferro; those which come shaking from the cloud, like the tongue of a poisonous serpent, the frightful forked lightning; those which bring black snow. Such is the legion.

The Douvres reef, at the moment when Gilliatt was constructing his breakwater, heard its distant gallop.

We have just said that the wind is the combination of all the winds.

This whole horde was arriving.

On the one hand, this legion.

On the other, Gilliatt.

VI
Gilliatt Has His Choice

THE mysterious forces had chosen their time well.

Chance, if such a thing exists, is far-seeing.

As long as the boat had been stabled in "the Man" inlet, as long as the machinery had been boxed into the wreck, Gilliatt was impregnable. The boat was safe, the machinery was under shelter; the Douvres, which held the machinery, condemned it to slow destruction, but protected it against surprise. In any case, one resource remained to Gilliatt: if the machinery were destroyed, Gilliatt was not destroyed. He had the boat to save himself.

But to wait until the boat was withdrawn from the anchorage where it was inaccessible, to let it be entangled in the defile of the Douvres, to wait patiently until it also was caught by the reef, to permit Gilliatt to effect the salvage, the lowering and embarkation of the engine,—not to interfere with this marvellous work, which placed everything in the boat, to consent to this success,—therein lay the trap. There the sombre ruse of the abyss, a sinister sort of feature, allowed itself to be glimpsed.

At that hour, the machinery, the boat, and Gilliatt were all within the gorge of rocks. They formed but one group. The boat dashed on the reef, the machinery sent to the bottom, Gilliatt drowned, was all the matter of a single effort directed upon a single point. All could be finished at once, at the same time, and without dispersion. All could be crushed with one blow.

No situation could be more critical than was that of Gilliatt.

The sphinx suspected by the dreamers in the depths of the gloom seemed to be posing him a dilemma: Stay, or leave.

To leave was madness; to stay was frightful.

VII
THE COMBAT

GILLIATT climbed upon the great Douvre.

From thence he surveyed the whole sea.

The west was startling. A wall was rising from it. A great wall of cloud, barring the expanse from side to side, was mounting slowly from the horizon towards the zenith. This wall, rectilinear, vertical, without a flaw through all its height, without a rent in its ridge, appeared built with the square, and levelled with the plumb line. It was a cloud which resembled granite. The escarpment of this cloud, perfectly perpendicular at its southern extremity, curved a little towards the north, like a bent piece of sheet iron, and presented the vague slope of an inclined plane. This wall of fog enlarged and grew, without its entablature ceasing for a moment to appear parallel to the line of the horizon, almost indistinct in the gathering gloom. This wall of air rose in one piece, in silence. Not an undulation, not a wrinkle, not a projection, to deform or displace it. This immobility in movement was dismal.

The sun, pallid behind some indescribable, unhealthy transparency, illuminated this apocalyptic outline. The cloud had already invaded half of space. One would have pronounced it the frightful slope of the abyss. It was something like the rising of a mountain of shadow between earth and heaven.

It was the ascent of night in broad daylight.

There was the heat in the air, as from a stove. A reek as from a vapor bath was given off by this mysterious accumulation. The sky, which had been blue, turned to white, and from white had become gray. The sea beneath, dull and leaden-hued, was another enormous slate. Not a breath, not a wave, not a sound. As far as the eye could reach, the desert ocean. Not a sail to be seen on either side. The birds had hidden themselves. One felt conscious of treachery in the infinite.

The enlargement of all this shadow increased insensibly.

The moving mountain of vapors which was directing its course towards the Douvres, was one of those clouds which may be called the clouds of combat. Sinister clouds. Through these obscure masses, you know not what monster is squinting at you.

The approach was terrible.

Gilliatt scrutinized the cloud intently, and muttered between his teeth: "I am thirsty, you are going to furnish me with water."

He remained motionless for a few moments, with his eyes fixed on the cloud. One would have said that he was taking the measure of the tempest.

His galley cap was in the pocket of his peajacket, he drew it out and put it on. He took his reserve of clothing from the hole in which he had slept so long; he put on his leggings and donned his tarpaulin coat, like a knight putting on his armor at the moment of battle. The reader knows that he no longer had any shoes, but his bare feet were hardened to the rocks.

His war toilet completed, he scanned his breakwater, grasped his knotted rope, briskly descended from the plateau of the Douvre, set foot on the rocks below, and ran to his storehouse. A few moments later, he was at work. The vast, mute cloud could hear the blows of his hammer. What was Gilliatt doing? With what spikes, ropes, and beams he had left, he was constructing a second breakwater across the eastern entrance, ten or twelve feet behind the first.

The silence was still profound. The blades of grass in the crevices of the rock did not quiver.

Suddenly, the sun disappeared; Gilliatt raised his head.

The rising cloud had just reached the sun. It was like an extinction of the day, replaced by a mixed and pallid reflection.

The wall of cloud had changed its aspect. It no longer preserved its unity. It had wrinkled horizontally on touching the zenith, whence it overhung the rest of the sky. It now had its strata. The formation of the tempest was there sketched out like the section of a trench. One could distinguish the layers of rain and the layers of hail. There was no lightning, but a horrible, diffused light, for the idea of horror may be attached to the idea of light. The vague breathing of the ocean was audible. This silence palpitated obscurely. Gilliatt, silent also, watched all these blocks of fog grouping themselves overhead, and the deformity of the clouds in construction. On the horizon brooded and spread out a band of ash-colored mist, and in the zenith another of lead-colored livid strips hung from the clouds above upon the fogs below. The whole background, which was composed of the wall of clouds, was wan, milky, earth-colored, gloomy, indescribable. A thin, whitish, transverse cloud, which had come from some unknown source, cut the high, gloomy wall from north to south. One of the extremities of this cloud trailed in the sea. At the point where it touched the confusion of the waves, a dense red vapor was visible. Below the long, pale cloud, small clouds, very low and perfectly black, were flying in opposite directions from each other, as though they knew not what to do. The mighty cloud in the background increased in all parts at once, darkened the eclipse, and continued its lugubrious interposition. Only a porch of clear sky was left in the east, behind Gilliatt, and that was about to close.

Without the impression that there was any wind, a strange diffusion of grayish down passed by, scattered and in morsels, as though some gigantic bird had just been plucked of its plumage behind that wall of shadows.

A platform of compact blackness had formed, which touched the sea at the extreme horizon, and there mingled with the night. Something could be felt advancing towards one. It was vast and ponderous and ferocious.

The obscurity thickened. All at once, a tremendous peal of thunder burst forth.

Gilliatt himself felt the shock. There is somewhat of the dream in thunder. This brutal reality in the region of visions has something terrifying about it. One thinks that one hears the fall of a piece of furniture in the chamber of giants.

No electric flash accompanied the peal. It was like black thunder. Silence settled down again. There was a sort of interval, as when one is taking up position. Then, huge, shapeless flashes of lightning made their appearance slowly, one after the other. These flashes were dumb. No roar. At each flash, everything was lighted up. The wall of clouds was now a cavern. There were vaults and arches. Silhouettes were to be distinguished there. Monstrous heads were roughly outlined; rocks seemed to stretch themselves forward; elephants bearing turrets vanished when one had caught a glimpse of them.

A column of fog, erect, round, and black, surmounted by a white vapor, simulated the smoke stack of a colossal sunken steamer, hissing and smoking below the waves. Sheets of cloud undulated. One fancied that one beheld folds of giant flags. In the centre, beneath crimson denseness, was buried, motionless, a nucleus of fog, dense, inert, impenetrable to the electric sparks, a sort of hideous fœtus in the womb of the tempest.

Gilliatt suddenly felt a gust ruffling his hair. Three or four large splashes of rain flattened themselves around him on the rock. Then came a second thunderclap. The wind rose.

The expectation of the shadow was at its height; the first clap of thunder had stirred the sea, the second rent the wall of cloud from top to bottom, a hole appeared, the whole pent-up flood rushed toward it, the crevice became an open mouth, full of rain, and the vomiting forth of the tempest began.

It was a frightful moment.

Downpour, hurricane, fulgurations, fulminations, waves to the very clouds, foam, detonations, frantic writhings, cries, hoarse rattles, hisses, all at once. An unchaining of monsters.

The wind blew as though it were thunder. The rain did not fall, it dropped down bodily.

For a poor man caught, like Gilliatt, with a loaded boat in a space between rocks in the open sea, no crisis could be more menacing. The danger of the tide over which Gilliatt had triumphed was as nothing beside the danger of the tempest. This was the situation:—

Gilliatt, around whom everything was precipice, displayed at the last minute, and in the face of supreme peril, a wise strategy. He had taken his basis of operations from the enemy; he had associated himself with the reef; the Douvres reef, formerly his adversary, was now his second in this immense duel. Gilliatt had subjected it to himself. Out of this sepulchre, Gilliatt had made his fortress. He had fortified himself in that formidable dwelling of the sea. He had entrenched himself in this tremendous ruined castle of the deep. He was blockaded, but walled in there. He had, so to speak, set his back against the reef, face to face with the storm. He had barricaded the strait, that street of the waves. It was, moreover, the only thing to do. It appears that the Ocean, which is a despot, can also be brought to reason with barricades.

The boat could be regarded as in safety on three sides. Narrowly pressed between the two interior faces of the reef, crossmoored, it was protected on the north by the little Douvre, on the south by the great Douvre. Savage cliffs, more accustomed to causing shipwrecks than to preventing them. On the west it was protected by the screen of beams moored and spiked to the rocks, a tried barrier, which had conquered the rude flood tide of the sea, a veritable citadel gate, having for jambs the very columns of the reef, the two Douvres themselves. Nothing was to be feared on that side. It was on the east that the danger lay.

On the east, there was nothing but the breakwater. A breakwater is a pulverizing apparatus. There must be at least two hurdles. Gilliatt had had time to construct only one. He was building the second in the tempest itself.

Fortunately, the wind came from the northwest. The sea is guilty of awkwardness. This wind, which is the ancient nor'wester, had but little effect on the Douvres rocks. It assailed the reef crosswise, and impelled the waves into neither the one nor the other of the two narrow entrances of the defile, so that, instead of entering a street, it dashed against a wall. The storm had made its attack badly.

But the attacks of the winds are shifting, and some sudden change was to be looked for. If it veered to the east before the second lattice-work of the breakwater was constructed, the peril would be great. The invasion of the lane between the rocks by the tempest would be accomplished, and all would be lost.

The frenzy of the storm continued to increase. The whole tempest is blow upon blow. Therein lies its power; therein also lies its defect. By reason of its fury it leaves a hold to intelligence, and man defends himself; but amid what destruction! Nothing is more monstrous. No respite, no interruption, no time, no pause for taking breath. There is an indescribable cowardice in this prodigality of the inexhaustible. One feels that it is the lungs of the infinite which are blowing.

The whole immensity in tumult hurled itself upon the Douvres reef. Numberless voices were heard. But who cries out thus? The ancient panic terror was present. At moments it seemed to speak, as though some one were issuing a command. Then, clamors, clarions, strange trepidations, and that grand, majestic howl which mariners term "the call of the Ocean."

The indefinite and fleeting spirals of the wind whistled as they convulsed the sea; the waves became disks beneath these eddies, and were flung against the rocks like gigantic quoits hurled by invisible athletes. The enormous foam streamed over all the rocks. Torrents above, foam below. Then the roars redoubled. No uproar of men or beasts can give an idea of the mingled din of these displacements of the sea. The clouds roared like cannon, the hailstones rattled like machine-guns, the surges leaped on high.

At certain points the wind seemed motionless; at others, its velocity was twenty fathoms a second. The sea was white as far as the eye could reach; ten leagues of soapsuds filled the horizon. Doors of fire opened. Some clouds seemed burned by other clouds, and resembled smoke above the pile of red clouds which appeared like burning coals. Floating configurations came in contact and amalgamated, changing each other's shapes. An incommensurable flood of water streamed down. The rattle of musketry firing by squads was heard in the firmament. In the middle of the canopy of gloom there was a sort of huge overturned basket whence fell, pell-mell, the waterspout, hail clouds, purple fire, phosphoric gleams, darkness, light, flashes of lightning,—so formidable are these inclinations of the abyss.

Gilliatt appeared to be paying no attention to it. His head was bent over his work. The second hurdle was beginning to rise. To every clap of thunder he replied by a blow of his hammer. The cadence was audible amid this chaos. He was bareheaded. A gust had carried away his galley cap.

His thirst was burning. He probably had fever. Pools of rain had formed around him in the hollows of the rocks. From time to time he took water in the hollow of his hand and drank. Then, without even looking to see what the storm was about, he set to work again.

Everything might depend on one moment. He knew what awaited him if he did not complete his breakwater in season. What was the use of wasting a minute in watching the approach of the face of death?

The confusion around him was like a boiling cauldron. There was uproar and racket. At times the thunder seemed to be descending a stairway. The electric percussions returned incessantly to the same points of the rock, which was probably veined with diorite. There were hailstones as large as a fist. Gilliatt was forced to shake the folds of his peajacket. His very pockets were full of hail.

The storm was now from the west, and beat against the barrier of the two Douvres; but Gilliatt had confidence in this barrier, and rightly. This barrier, made of the great forward piece of the Durande, received the shock with an elastic rebound; elasticity is a resistance; the calculations of Stevenson establish the fact that against the water, which itself is elastic, a mass of timbers of any desired dimensions, joined and chained together in a certain way, makes a better obstacle than a breakwater of masonry.

The barrier of the Douvres fulfilled these conditions; it was, moreover, so ingeniously moored that the wave, when striking it, was like the hammer which drives in the nail, and pressed and consolidated it against the rock; to demolish it, it would have been necessary to overthrow the Douvres themselves. In fact, the gale only succeeded in sending a few jets of foam across the obstacle to the boat. On this side, thanks to the barrier, the tempest ended in a spitting. Gilliatt turned his back on that effort. He tranquilly heard that useless rage behind him.

The flakes of foam flying from all directions resembled wool. The vast and angry water overflowed the rocks, mounted above them, entered into them, penetrated the network of interior fissures, and emerged again from the granitic masses by narrow orifices, a sort of inexhaustible mouths, which sent forth peaceful little fountains amid this deluge. Here and there, threads of silver fell gracefully into the sea from these mouths.

The hurdle to reinforce the eastern barrier was nearing completion. A few knots more of rope and chain, and the moment approached when that barrier would also be in a state to contend.

All at once a great light appeared, the rain ceased, the clouds dispersed. The wind had just shifted; a sort of lofty, twilight window opened in the zenith, and the lightning was extinguished; one might have thought it was the end. It was the beginning.

The wind had jumped from southwest to northeast.

The tempest was about to begin anew with a fresh troop of hurricanes. The north was about to deliver an assault—a violent assault. Mariners call this transition "the return gale." The south wind has more water, the north wind more thunder and lightning.

The aggression, coming now from the east, was about to attack the feeblest part.

This time, Gilliatt ceased his work and looked around him.

He placed himself erect on a projection of overhanging rock behind the second hurdle, which was almost completed. If the first section of the breakwater were carried away, it would crush the second, which was not yet consolidated, and in this demolition it would crush

Gilliatt. Gilliatt, in the place which he had chosen, would be crushed before seeing his boat, the engine, and all his work ruined in this engulfment. Such was the contingency. Gilliatt accepted it and sternly wished it.

In this shipwreck of all his hopes, to die first was what he desired; to die the first, so to speak; for the machinery produced on him the effect of a person. With his left hand he lifted his hair which had been plastered in his eyes by the rain, clasped his good hammer with the full power of his fist, threw himself back in a menacing attitude and waited.

He had not long to wait.

A clap of thunder gave the signal, the pale opening in the zenith closed, a burst of the deluge hurled itself down, all became dark again, and there was no longer any torch but the lightning. The sombre attack came.

A powerful surge, visible in the fast-following flashes of lightning, rose in the east beyond "the Man" rock. It resembled a great roll of glass. It was glaucous and foamless and striped the whole sea. It advanced towards the breakwater. As it approached, it swelled; it was like some broad cylinder of darkness rolling over the ocean. The thunder kept up a dull rumbling.

This swell reached "the Man" rock, broke in twain against it, and passed on. The two fragments, rejoined, formed but one mountain of water now, and, instead of being parallel to the breakwater, it became perpendicular to it. It was a wave taking the form of a beam.

This battering ram flung itself upon the breakwater. The shock gave vent to a roar. All was covered with foam.

Unless one has seen them, one cannot imagine these snowy avalanches which the sea precipitates, and under which it engulfs rocks more than a hundred feet in height, such, for example, as the Grand-Anderlo in Guernsey, and the Pinnacle in Jersey. At Sainte-Marie de Madagascar it leaps over the point of Tintingue. For some moments the mass of water drowned everything. Nothing was visible save a furious accumulation, a vast foam; the whiteness of the winding-sheet waving in the wind of the sepulchre, a mass of noise and storm beneath which extermination was at work. The foam dispersed. Gilliatt was still standing erect.

The barrier had held firm. Not a chain was broken, not a nail wrested from its place. The barrier had displayed, under trial, the two qualities of breakwaters; it had been as flexible as a hurdle and as solid as a wall. The surf had dissolved into raindrops before it.

A stream of foam, gliding along the zigzags of the strait, died away under the boat.

The man who had made this muzzle for the ocean took no repose.

Fortunately, the storm wandered for a while. The frenzy of the waves returned to the walled parts of the reef. This was a respite. Gilliatt profited by it to complete the rear hurdle.

The day terminated in this labor. The storm continued its violences in the flank of the reef, with mournful solemnity. The urn of water and the urn of fire which exist in the clouds poured out incessantly, without becoming empty. The high and low undulations of the wind resembled the movements of a dragon.

When night arrived, it was already there; it was not perceptible.

However, the darkness was not complete. Tempests, illuminated and darkened by lightning, have intermittences of the visible and the invisible. All is white; then, all is black. One is present at the exit of spectres and at the re-entrance of shadows.

A phosphoric zone, ruddy with the northern aurora, floated like a ray of spectral flame behind the density of the clouds. The result was a vast blanching. The breadths of the rain were luminous.

These brilliancies helped Gilliatt and directed him. Once he turned round and said to the lightning: "Hold the candle for me."

By the aid of this light, he was able to raise the rear hurdle even higher than the forward hurdle. The breakwater was almost complete. As Gilliatt was mooring to the final beam a strengthening cable, the gale struck him straight in the face. This made him raise his head. The wind had abruptly shifted round again to the northeast. The assault of the eastern entrance began again. Gilliatt cast a glance at the open sea. The breakwater was on the point of being assailed once more. There came another burst of sea.

This blow of the surges was harshly dealt; a second followed it; then another, and still another; five or six in a tumult, almost together; at length, a final and terrible one.

The last, which was like an accumulation of forces, bore some indescribable resemblance to a living thing. It would not have been difficult to imagine in that swelling and that transparency, aspects of gills and fins. It flattened itself and crushed itself on the breakwater. Its almost animal form there tore itself in a secondary spurt. On that block of rocks and timbers there was something like the vast crushing of a hydra. As the swell died away, it devastated. The water seemed to cling and bite. A profound trembling moved the reef. A roar, like that of beasts, was mingled with it. The foam resembled the saliva of a leviathan.

When the foam subsided, it allowed its ravages to be seen. This last attempt at scaling had done some work. This time the breakwater had suffered. A long and heavy beam, torn from the forward hurdle, had been hurled over the rear barrier, upon the overhanging rock chosen for a moment by Gilliatt as his post of combat. Fortunately, he had not mounted it again. He would have been struck dead.

There was one peculiarity in the fall of this beam, which, by preventing the timber from rebounding, saved Gilliatt from its leaps and counter blows. It even proved useful to him again, as the reader will presently see, in another manner.

Between the projecting rock and the interior escarpment of the defile there was an interval, a great gap, bearing a considerable resemblance to the notch made by an axe, or to the split of a wedge. One of the ends of the beam hurled into the air by the billows had lodged in this gap as it fell. It had enlarged the gap.

An idea occurred to Gilliatt.

It was to bear down on the other end.

The beam, lodged in the crack of the rock, which it had enlarged, projected straight from it like an outstretched arm. This sort of arm was prolonged parallel to the interior wall of the defile, and the free end of the beam was distant from this point of support about eighteen or twenty inches. A good distance for the effort to be made.

Gilliatt planted himself firmly with feet, knees, and fists against the cliff, and placed his two shoulders to the enormous lever.

The beam was long, which increased the power of the lever. The rock was already started. Nevertheless, Gilliatt was obliged to make four efforts. As much perspiration as rain dripped from his hair. The fourth effort was frantic. A hoarse noise in the rock followed, the gap, prolonged into a fissure, opened like a jaw, and the heavy mass fell into the narrow space of the defile with a terrible noise, an echo to the claps of thunder.

It fell straight, if this expression is possible, that is to say, without breaking.

Let the reader picture to himself a menhir precipitated in one piece.

The lever beam followed the rock, and Gilliatt came near falling with it, since all gave way at once beneath him.

The bottom was much encumbered with boulders at this spot, and there was but little water. The monolith landed, with a splash of foam which reached Gilliatt, between the two great parallel rocks of the strait, and formed a transverse wall, a sort of hyphen between the two cliffs. Its two ends touched; it was a little too long, and its summit, which was of friable rock, was crushed as it fell into position. The result of this fall was a singular pocket, which may be seen at the present day. The water behind this barrier of stone is almost always tranquil.

This was a still more invincible barrier than the section of the forepart of the Durande, adjusted between the two Douvres.

This barrier came in opportunely.

The attacks of the sea continued. The waves always wax obstinate over an obstacle. The first screen was injured and was already beginning to come unjointed. One mesh broken in a breakwater becomes serious injury.

The enlargement of the aperture is inevitable, and there is no means of repairing the breach. The swell would sweep away the worker.

An electric flash which illuminated the reef revealed to Gilliatt the havoc which had been made in the breakwater, the beams thrown out of position, the ends of cords and chains beginning to swing in the wind, and a rent in the centre of the apparatus. The second hurdle was intact.

The block of stone, so powerfully cast by Gilliatt into the space behind the breakwater, was the most solid of barricades, but it had one defect; it was too low. The billows could not break it, but they could cross it.

Raising it higher was not to be thought of. Only masses of rock could be superimposed on this stone barrier to any purpose; but how were they to be detached, how moved, how raised, how piled up, how fastened? Timber-work may be added, but not rocks.

Gilliatt was not Enceladus.

The lack of height in this little isthmus troubled Gilliatt.

This defect was not long in making itself felt. The gusts no longer ceased their assaults upon the breakwater; they did more than rage, one would have said that they devoted themselves to its destruction. A sort of trampling could be heard upon that much-shaken framework.

All at once, a fragment of a binding-strake, detached from the dislocated barrier, leaped from beyond the second hurdle, flew over the transverse rock, and landed in the defile, where the water seized it and carried it into the windings of the lane. Gilliatt lost sight of it. It is probable that the fragment of beam struck the boat. Fortunately, in the interior of the reef, the water, enclosed on all sides, hardly felt the external turmoil. There was but little swell and the shock could not be very severe. Moreover, Gilliatt had no time to attend to this injury, if injury there were; all sorts of dangers rose at once, the tempest was concentrating itself upon the vulnerable point, a catastrophe lay before him.

The darkness was profound for a moment, the lightning ceased, sinister connivance; the cloud and the sea became one; there came a dull crash.

This crash was followed by an uproar.

Gilliatt thrust his head forward. The hurdle which formed the front of the barrier was stove in. The tips of the beams could be seen leaping in the waves. The sea made use of the first breakwater to effect a breach in the second.

Gilliatt felt what a general would feel on seeing his vanguard driven in.

The second barrier of beams resisted the shock. The rear armament was strongly bound and counter-buttressed. But the broken hurdle was heavy, it was at the mercy of the waves, which dashed it forward, then snatched it back; the ligatures which remained prevented its falling apart and maintained for it its entire volume, and the qualities which Gilliatt had imparted to it as a weapon of defence resulted in making of it an excellent engine of destruction. From a shield, it had been converted into a club. Moreover, it was bristling with breaks, the ends of timbers projected from it in every direction, and it was as though covered with teeth and spurs. There could be no blunt weapon more formidable and more fitted to be handled by the tempest.

It was the projectile, and the sea was the catapult.

The blows followed each other with a sort of tragic regularity. Gilliatt, standing thoughtfully behind this door barricaded by himself, listened to these knocks of death as it sought entry.

He reflected bitterly, that, had it not been for the smoke stack of the Durande, so fatally retained by the wreck, he would at that moment be in Guernsey, which he would have reached that morning, and in port, with the boat in security and the machinery saved.

The thing he had feared was realized. The breach took place. It was like a death rattle. All the timber-work of the breakwater at once, the two armaments confounded and crushed together, came in a hollow spout of billows and dashed against the stone barrier like a chaos on a mountain, and there paused. It was no longer anything but a heap, a shapeless thicket of beams, penetrable by the waves, but still pulverizing them.

This conquered rampart went through the death struggle heroically. The sea had shattered it, it broke the sea. Though overthrown, it remained efficacious to some extent. The rock which formed the barrier, an obstacle impossible to withdraw, held it by the foot. The defile was, as we have said, very narrow at this point; the victorious whirlwind had thrust back, mingled and piled up all the breakwater in a block, in that choked entrance; the very violence of the thrust, by heaping up the mass and ramming the broken ends of some into the others, had made of this demolition a solid ruin. It was destroyed but impregnable. A few pieces of wood only had been torn away. The waves scattered them. One passed through the air very close to Gilliatt. He felt the wind from it on his brow.

But several great surges, those great surges which return with imperturbable regularity in storms, leaped over the ruins of the breakwater. They fell into the pass and, in spite of the elbows made by the alley, raised the level there. The water in the strait began to be angrily agitated. The mysterious kiss of the waves and rocks began to be accentuated.

How was this agitation to be kept from propagating itself as far as the boat?

Not much time would be required for these gusts to set the whole water inside in a tempest, and a few dashes of the sea would scuttle the boat and send the engine to the bottom.

Gilliatt meditated and shuddered.

But he was not disconcerted. No defeat was possible for that soul.

The hurricane had now found the point, and plunged frantically between the two walls of the strait.

All at once, some distance behind Gilliatt, a crash more frightful than all that Gilliatt had heard up to that time, resounded and prolonged itself in the pass.

It was in the direction of his boat.

Something fatal was taking place there.

Gilliatt ran towards it.

From the eastern entrance where he stood, he could not see the boat, because of the zigzags in the lane.

At the last turn he halted, and waited for a flash of lightning.

The flash came and showed him the situation.

The dash of the billows from the east had been answered by a gust of wind on the western entrance. A disaster was outlined there.

The paunch had suffered no visible injury; moored as it was, it was but little exposed; but the carcass of the Durande was in distress.

The ruin, in such a tempest, presented a large surface. It was entirely out of the water, in the air, exposed to disaster. The hole which Gilliatt had made in it, in order to extract the machinery, had completed the weakening of the hull. The keelson was cut through. The skeleton's vertebral column was broken.

The hurricane had breathed upon it.

Nothing more was required. The platform of the bridge had folded like a book opening. The dismemberment was complete. It was this crash which had reached Gilliatt's ears through the storm.

What he beheld on his approach appeared almost irremediable.

The square incision which he had made had become a wound. Of this cut the wind had made a fracture. This transverse break cut the wreck in two; the after part, adjoining the boat, had remained firm in its vise of rocks. The forward part, that which faced Gilliatt, was hanging suspended. A fracture is a hinge, so long as it holds good. This mass was oscillating on its breaks as though on joints, and the wind was swaying it to and fro with a doleful noise.

Fortunately, the boat was no longer beneath it.

But this swaying shook the other half of the hull which was still wedged and motionless between the two Douvres. The distance between shaking and wrenching loose is not great. With the persistence of the wind, the dislocated part might suddenly drag down the other, which almost touched the boat, and all, boat and engine, would be engulfed in this overthrow.

Gilliatt had this before his eyes.

It was a catastrophe.

How was it to be averted?

Gilliatt was one of those who snatch the means of safety from the danger itself. He pondered for a moment.

Gilliatt went to his arsenal and took his axe.

The hammer had worked well, now it was the axe's turn.

Then Gilliatt climbed upon the wreck once more. He took footing on the part of the bridge which had not given way and, bending over the precipice between the two Douvres, he set to work to finish off the broken beams and to cut what bonds still remained on the hanging hull.

The operation consisted in completing the separation of the two fragments of the wreck, in freeing the half which remained solid, and in casting into the water what the wind had seized. It was more perilous than difficult. The hanging portion of the wreck, dragged down by the wind and by its own weight, now adhered only at a few points. The wreck, as a whole, resembled a diptych, one half-hanging fold of which was beating against the other. Five or six pieces of the framework only, bent and splintered but not broken still held together. Their fractures creaked and yawned more widely at every backward and forward movement of the blast, and the axe had, so to speak, only to aid the wind. The small number of these attachments, which constituted the facility of the work, also constituted its danger. All might give way at once beneath Gilliatt.

The storm attained its highest point. The tempest had been only terrible, it became horrible. The convulsion of the sea was communicated to the sky. The cloud had hitherto reigned sovereign, it seemed to execute what it willed, it gave the impulse, it drove the waves to frenzy, while itself preserving an indescribable sinister lucidity. Below it was madness, above it, wrath. The sky is the breath, the ocean is only the foam. Hence the authority of the wind. The hurricane is a genius. In the meanwhile, the intoxication of its own horror had confused it. It was no longer anything but a whirlwind. It was blindness giving birth to night. There is a moment of frenzy in storms; it is a sort of delirium of the sky. The abyss no longer knows what it is doing. It darts its lightnings blindly. Nothing more frightful. It is the hideous hour.

The trepidation of the reef was at its height. Every storm has a mysterious orientation which it loses at that moment. This is the dangerous point in a tempest. At that instant, said Thomas Fuller, "the wind is a raging madman." It is at that moment in tempests that the continuous discharge of electricity takes place which Piddington calls "the cascade of lightning." It is at that instant that there appears in the blackest of the cloud, to spy upon the universal terror, that circle of blue light which the ancient Spanish mariners called the Eye of the Tempest, *el ojo de tempestad.* This dismal eye rested on Gilliatt.

Gilliatt, on his side, watched the clouds. Now he raised his head. After each blow of the axe, he straightened himself up haughtily. He was, or he seemed to be, too completely lost for pride not to come to him.

Did he despair? No. Before the supreme access of rage in the ocean, he was as prudent as he was bold. He set his feet only on the solid points of the wreck. He risked his life and preserved it. he, also, was in a paroxysm. His vigor had been increased tenfold. He was frenzied with intrepidity. The blows of his axe sounded like challenges. He appeared to have gained in lucidity what the tempest had lost. Pathetic conflict. On the one hand the inexhaustible, on the other the indefatigable. It was a struggle to see which could compel the other to loose its hold.

The terrible clouds took the shape of gorgon masks in the immensity, every possible form of intimidation was produced. The rain came from the waves, the foam from the clouds, the phantoms of the wind bent down, the faces of meteors grew crimson and were eclipsed, leaving the obscurity more monstrous after they had vanished; there was nothing now but one downpour, coming from all quarters at once; all was ebullition; the mass of gloom overflowed; the cumulus, charged with hail, ragged, ash-colored, appeared to be seized with a whirling frenzy; there was in the air a sound as of dry peas being shaken about in a sieve; the inverse currents of electricity observed by Volta exercised their fulminating play from cloud to cloud; the prolongations of the thunder were terrible, the flashes of lightning came near to Gilliatt. He seemed to astonish the abyss. He came and went on the quivering Durande, making its deck tremble beneath his steps; striking, hewing, cutting, axe in hand, pallid in the lightning, hair streaming, barefooted, in rags, his face covered with the spittle of the sea, he was great in this cesspool of thunder.

Adroitness alone can contend against the delirium of forces. Adroitness was Gilliatt's triumph. He desired the simultaneous fall of all the dislocated fragments. To this end, he weakened the hinge fractures without wholly severing them, leaving some fibres which sustained the rest. All at once he paused, holding his axe aloft. The operation was complete. The entire piece detached itself.

This half of the carcass of the Durande sank between the two rocks, below Gilliatt who stood erect on the other half, leaning forward and watching. It plunged perpendicularly into the water, splashed the rocks, and came to a halt in the narrow passage before touching bottom. Enough remained out of the water to rise above the waves by more than twelve feet; this vertical platform formed a wall between the two Douvres; like the rock cast across a little higher up in the strait, it allowed barely a slipping of foam to filter past its two extremities; and this was the fifth barricade improvised by Gilliatt against the tempest in that street of the sea.

The blind hurricane had aided in this last barricade.

He was glad that the contraction had prevented this barrier from reaching quite to the bottom. This left it more height. Moreover, the water could pass beneath the obstacle which deprived the waves of their force. What passes beneath does not leap over. Therein lies, in part, the secret of floating breakwaters.

Henceforth, whatever the clouds might do, there was nothing to fear for the boat and the engine. The water around them could no longer be disturbed. Between the enclosure of the Douvres, which covered them on the west, and the new barrier which protected them on the east, no attack from either sea or wind could reach them.

Gilliatt had snatched safety from catastrophe. The clouds, in short, had assisted him.

This thing done, he took in the hollow of his hand a little rain water from a pool, drank, and said to the clouds: "Blockhead!"

It is an ironical joy for militant intelligence to prove the vast stupidity of these furious forces ending in good turns rendered, and Gilliatt felt that immemorial desire to insult one's enemy which goes back to Homer's heroes.

Gilliatt descended into the boat, and took advantage of the flashes of lightning to examine it. It was time that succor should be rendered to the poor bark; it had been sadly shaken during the last hour, and was beginning to give way. In that hasty glance, Gilliatt perceived no injury. Nevertheless, it was certain that it had been subjected to violent shocks. The water once calmed, the hull had righted itself; the anchors had held fast; as for the machinery, its four chains had supported it admirably.

As Gilliatt was completing his survey, a whiteness passed close to him and plunged into the gloom. It was a sea-mew.

There is no better apparition in storms. When the birds arrive, it signifies that the storm is subsiding.

Another excellent sign, the thunder redoubled.

The supreme violences of the tempest disorganize it. All mariners know that the last burst is rough but brief. The excess of thunder announces the end.

The rain suddenly ceased. Then there was nothing but a surly growl in the clouds. The storm ended like a plank falling to the earth. It broke, so to speak. The immense machinery of the clouds broke apart. A crevice of clear sky separated the shadows. Gilliatt was astonished. It was broad daylight.

The tempest had lasted nearly twenty hours.

The wind which had brought it carried it away. Fragments of obscurity were diffused over the horizon. The broken and flying fogs massed together pell-mell, in a tumult, from one end to the other of the line of clouds. There was a movement of retreat, a long, diminishing muttering could be heard, a few last drops of rain fell, and all that gloom, full of thunders, departed like a horde of terrible chariots.

Suddenly, the sky became blue.

Gilliatt realized that he was weary. Sleep swoops down upon fatigue like a bird of prey. Gilliatt allowed himself to relax and to fall into the boat without choosing his place, and fell asleep. He remained thus for several hours, inert and stretched at length, scarcely distinguishable from the beams and timbers among which he lay.

BOOK FOURTH
THE PITFALLS OF THE OBSTACLE

I
THE HUNGRY MAN IS NOT THE ONLY HUNGRY ONE

WHEN he awoke he was hungry. The sea was growing calmer. But sufficient agitation lingered in the open ocean to render an immediate departure impossible. Moreover, the day was too far advanced. In order to reach Guernsey before midnight, with such a cargo as that carried by the paunch, it was necessary to start in the morning.

Although pressed by hunger, Gilliatt began by stripping himself, the only means of getting warm.

His garments were drenched by the storm, but the rain water had washed out the salt water, which now made it possible for them to dry out.

Gilliatt retained only his trousers, which he turned up to the knees.

Here and there, on the projections of the rocks around him, he spread out his shirt, his peajacket, his tarpaulin, his leggings, and his sheepskin, fastening them down with stones.

Then he bethought himself of eating.

Gilliatt had recourse to his knife, which he took great pains to sharpen and to keep always in good condition, and he detached from the granite several sea lice, of nearly the same species as the round clams of the Mediterranean. As the reader knows, these are eaten alive.

But, after so many labors, which had been so varied and so rough, it was a meagre pittance. He had no more biscuit. As for water, he no longer lacked that. He was more than refreshed, he was inundated.

He took advantage of the fact that the tide was ebbing to prowl among the rocks in search of crawfish. He had seen enough of them there to hope for a successful hunt.

But he did not reflect that he could no longer cook anything. If he had taken the trouble to go to his storehouse he would have found it broken in by the rain. His wood and coal were drenched, and of his stock of tow, which stood him in stead of tinder, there was not a thread which was not wet. There was no means of lighting a fire.

Moreover, the bellows were disorganized; the blower of the forge hearth was broken away, the storm had sacked the workshop. With the tools which had escaped injury, Gilliatt might, at a pinch, still work as a carpenter, not as a blacksmith. But Gilliatt was not thinking of his workshop for the time being.

Drawn in another direction by his stomach, he had set out in search of his repast without further thought. He wandered, not out in the direction of the gorge of the reef, but outside, among the breakers. It was in that direction that the Durande had struck on the rocks ten weeks before.

For the search in which Gilliatt was engaged, the outside of the reef was better than the inside. Crabs have a habit of crawling out in the air at low water. They are fond of warming themselves in the sun. These deformed creatures love midday. Their exit from the water into the full light is a singular thing. The way they swarm is almost exasperating. When one sees them with their awkward, oblique gait, crawl heavily from fold to fold, up the lower stages of the rocks, like the steps of a staircase, one is forced to confess that the ocean has its vermin.

However, that day the hermit crabs and crawfish had hidden themselves. The tempest had thrust back these solitaries into their hiding-places, and they were not yet reassured. Gilliatt held his knife open in his hand, and, from time to time, tore off a shell fish from under the seaweed. He ate as he walked.

He could not be far from the spot where Sieur Clubin had been lost.

Just as Gilliatt was making up his mind to resign himself to sea-urchins and sea-chestnuts, a splash was made at his feet. A huge crab, frightened by his approach, had just dropped into the water. The crab did not sink so deeply that Gilliatt lost sight of it.

Gilliatt set out on a run after the crab along the base of the reef. The crab sought to escape.

Suddenly, he was no longer in sight.

The crab had just hidden in some crevice under the rock.

Gilliatt clung to the projections of the rock, and thrust forward his head to get a look under the overhanging cliff.

There was, in fact, a cavity there. The crab must have taken refuge in it.

It was something more than a crevice. It was a sort of porch.

The sea entered beneath this porch, but was not deep. The bottom was visible, covered with stones. These stones were smooth and clothed with algæ, which indicated that they were never dry. They resembled the tops of children's heads covered with green hair.

Gilliatt took his knife in his teeth, climbed down with his hands and feet from the top of the cliff, and leaped into the water. It reached almost to his shoulders.

He passed under the porch. He entered a much worn corridor in the form of a rude pointed arch overhead. The walls were smooth and polished. He no longer saw the crab. He kept his foothold, and advanced through the diminishing light. He began to be unable to distinguish objects.

After about fifteen paces, the vault above him came to an end. He was out of the corridor. He had here more space, and consequently more light; and besides, the pupils of his eyes were now dilated; he saw with tolerable clearness. He had a surprise.

He was just re-entering that strange cave which he had visited a month previously.

Only he had returned to it by way of the sea.

That arch which he had then seen submerged was the one through which he had just passed. It was accessible at certain low tides.

His eyes became accustomed to the place. He saw better and better. He was astounded. He had found again that extraordinary palace of shadows, that vault, those pillars, those purple and blood-like stains, that jewel-like vegetation, and, at the end, that crypt, almost a sanctuary, and that stone which was almost an altar.

He had not taken much notice of these details, but he carried the general effect in his mind, and he beheld it again.

Opposite him, at a certain height in the cliff, he saw the crevice through which he had made his entrance on the first occasion, and which, from the point where he now stood, seemed inaccessible.

He beheld again, near the pointed arch, those low and obscure grottoes, a sort of caverns within the cavern, which he had already observed from a distance. Now he was close to them. The one nearest to him was dry and easily accessible.

Still nearer than that opening he noticed a horizontal fissure in the granite above the level of the water. The crab was probably there. He thrust in his hand as far as he could and began to grope in this hole of shadows.

All at once he felt himself seized by the arm.

What he felt at that moment was indescribable horror.

Something thin, rough, flat, slimy, adhesive, and living had just wound itself round his bare arm in the dark. It crept up towards his breast. It was like the pressure of a leather thong and the thrust of a gimlet. In less than a second, an indescribable spiral form had passed around his wrist and his elbow, and reached to his shoulder. The point burrowed under his armpit.

Gilliatt threw himself backwards, but could hardly move. He was as though nailed to the spot; with his left hand, which remained free, he took his knife, which he held between his teeth, and holding the knife with his hand, he braced himself against the rock, in a desperate effort to withdraw his arm. He only succeeded in slightly disturbing the ligature, which resumed its pressure. It was as supple as leather, as solid as steel, as cold as night.

A second thong, narrow and pointed, issued from the crevice of the rock. It was like a tongue from the jaws of a monster. It licked Gilliatt's naked form in a terrible fashion, and suddenly stretching out, immensely long and thin, it applied itself to his skin and surrounded his whole body. At the same time, unheard-of suffering, which was comparable to nothing he had previously known, swelled Gilliatt's contracted muscles. In his skin he felt round and horrible perforations; it seemed to him that innumerable lips were fastened to his flesh and were seeking to drink his blood.

A third thong undulated outside the rock, felt of Gilliatt, and lashed his sides like a cord. It fixed itself there.

Anguish is mute when at its highest point. Gilliatt did not utter a cry. There was light enough for him to see the repulsive forms adhering to him.

A fourth ligature, this one as swift as a dart, leaped towards his belly and rolled itself around there.

Impossible either to tear or to cut away these shiny thongs which adhered closely to Gilliatt's body, and by a number of points. Each one of those points was the seat of frightful and peculiar pain. It was what would be experienced if one were being swallowed simultaneously by a throng of mouths which were too small.

A fifth prolongation leaped from the hole. It superimposed itself upon the others, and folded over Gilliatt's chest. Compression was added to horror; Gilliatt could hardly breathe.

These thongs, pointed at their extremity, spread out gradually like the blades of swords towards the hilt. All five evidently belonged to the same centre. They crept and crawled over Gilliatt. He felt these strange points of pressure, which seemed to him to be mouths, changing their places.

Suddenly a large, round, flat, slimy mass emerged from the lower part of the crevice.

It was the centre; the five thongs were attached to it like spokes to a hub; on the opposite side of this foul disk could be distinguished the beginnings of three other tentacles, which remained under the slope of the rock. In the middle of this sliminess there were two eyes gazing.

The eyes were fixed on Gilliatt.

Gilliatt recognized the octopus.

II
THE MONSTER

TO believe in the octopus, one must have seen it.

Compared with it, the hydras of old are laughable.

At certain moments, one is tempted to think that the intangible forms which float through our vision encounter in the realm of the possible certain magnetic centres to which their lineaments cling, and from these obscure fixations of the living dream, beings spring forth. The unknown has the marvellous at its disposal, and it makes use of it to compose the monster. Orpheus, Homer, and Hesiod were only able to make the Chimæra: God made the octopus.

When God wills it, he excels in the execrable.

The wherefore of this will affrights the religious thinker.

All ideals being admitted, if terror can be an object, the octopus is a masterpiece.

The whale has enormous size, the octopus is small; the hippopotamus has a cuirass, the octopus is naked; the jararaca hisses, the octopus is dumb; the rhinoceros has a horn, the octopus has no horn; the scorpion has a sting, the octopus has no sting; the scorpion has nippers, the octopus has no nippers; the ape has a prehensile tail, the octopus has no tail; the shark has sharp fins, the octopus has no fins; the vespertilio vampire has wings armed with barbs, the octopus has no barbs; the hedgehog has quills, the octopus has no quills; the swordfish has a sword, the octopus has no sword; the torpedo fish has an electric shock, the octopus has none; the toad has a virus, the octopus has no virus; the viper has a venom, the octopus has no venom; the lion has claws, the octopus has no claws; the hawk has a beak, the octopus has no beak; the crocodile has jaws, the octopus has no teeth.

The octopus has no muscular organization, no menacing cry, no breastplate, no horn, no dart, no pincers, no prehensile or bruising tail, no cutting pectoral fins, no barbed wings, no quills, no sword, no electric discharge, no virus, no venom, no claws, no beak, no teeth. Of all creatures, the octopus is the most formidably armed.

What, then, is the octopus? It is the cupping-glass.

In open sea reefs, where the water displays and hides all its splendors, in the hollows of unvisited rocks, in the unknown caves where vegetations, crustaceans, and shell fish abound, beneath the deep portals of the ocean, the swimmer who hazards himself there, led on by the beauty of the place, runs the risk of an encounter. If you have this encounter, be not curious but fly. One enters dazzled, one emerges terrified.

This is the nature of the encounter always possible among rocks in the open sea.

A grayish form undulates in the water, it is as thick as a man's arm and about half an ell long; it is a rag; its form resembles a closed umbrella without a handle. This rag gradually advances towards you, suddenly it opens; eight radii spread out abruptly around a face which has two eyes; these radii are alive; there is something of the flame in their undulation; it is a sort of wheel; unrolled, it is four or five feet in diameter. Frightful expansion. This flings itself upon you.

The hydra harpoons its victim.

This creature applies itself to its prey, covers it, and knots its long bands about it. Underneath, it is yellowish; on top, earth-colored; nothing can represent this inexplicable hue of dust; one would pronounce it a creature made of ashes, living in the water. In form it is spiderlike, and like a chameleon in its coloring. When irritated, it becomes violet in hue. Its most terrible quality is its softness.

Its folds strangle; its contact paralyzes.

It has an aspect of scurvy and gangrene. It is disease embodied in monstrosity.

It is not to be torn away. It adheres closely to its prey. How? By a vacuum. Its eight antennæ, large at the root, gradually taper off and end in needles. Underneath each one of them are arranged two rows of decreasing pustules, the largest near the head, the small ones at the tip. Each row consists of twenty-five; there are fifty pustules to each antenna, and the whole creature has four hundred of them. These pustules are cupping-glasses.

These cupping-glasses are cylindrical, horny, livid cartilages. On the large species they gradually diminish from the diameter of a five-franc piece to the size of a lentil. These fragments of tubes are thrust out from the animal and retire into it. They can be inserted into the prey for more than an inch.

This sucking apparatus has all the delicacy of a keyboard. It rises, then retreats. It obeys the slightest wish of the animal. The most exquisite sensibilities cannot equal the contractibility of these suckers, always proportioned to the internal movements of the creature and to the external circumstances. This dragon is like a sensitive plant.

This is the monster which mariners call the poulp, which science calls cephalopod, and which legend calls the kraken. English sailors call it the "devil fish." They also call it the "bloodsucker." In the Channel Islands it is called the *pieuvre.*

It is very rare in Guernsey, very small in Jersey, very large and quite common in Sark.

A print from Sonnini's edition of Buffon represents an octopus crushing a frigate. Denis Montfort thinks that the octopus of the high latitudes is really strong enough to sink a ship. Bory Saint Vincent denies this, but admits that, in our latitudes, it does attack man. Go to Sark and they will show you, near Bréchou, the hollow in the rock where, a few years ago, an octopus seized and drowned a lobster fisherman. Péron and Lamarck are mistaken when they doubt whether the octopus, since it has no fins, can swim.

He who writes these lines has seen with his own eyes, at Sark, in the cave called the Shops, an octopus swimming and chasing a bather. When killed and measured, it was found to be four English feet in spread, and four hundred suckers could be counted. The dying monster thrust them out convulsively.

According to Denis Montfort, one of those observers whose strong gift of intuition causes them to descend or to ascend even to magianism, the octopus has almost the passions of a man; the octopus hates. In fact, in the absolute, to be hideous is to hate.

The misshapen struggles under a necessity of elimination, and this consequently renders it hostile.

The octopus when swimming remains, so to speak, in its sheath. It swims with all its folds held close. Let the reader picture to himself a sewed-up sleeve with a closed fist inside of it. This fist, which is the head, pushes through the water, and advances with a vague, undulating movement. Its two eyes, though large, are not very distinct, being the color of the water.

The octopus on the chase, or lying in wait, hides; it contracts, it condenses itself; it reduces itself to the simplest possible expression. It confounds itself with the shadow. It looks like a ripple of the waves. It resembles everything except something living.

The octopus is a hypocrite. When one pays no heed to it, suddenly it opens.

A glutinous mass possessed of a will, what more frightful? Glue filled with hatred.

It is in the most beautiful azure of the limpid water that this hideous, voracious star of the sea arises.

It gives no warning of its approach, which renders it more terrible. Almost always, when one sees it, one is already caught.

At night, however, and in breeding season, it is phosphorescent. This terror has its passions. It awaits the nuptial hour. It adorns itself, it lights up, it illuminates itself; and from the summit of a rock one can see it beneath, in the shadowy depths, spread out in a pallid irradiation,—a spectre sun.

It has no bones, it has no blood, it has no flesh. It is flabby. There is nothing in it. It is a skin. One can turn its eight tentacles wrong side out, like the fingers of a glove.

It has a single orifice, in the centre of its radiation. Is this one hole the vent? Is it the mouth? It is both.

The same aperture fulfils both functions. The entrance is the exit.

The whole creature is cold.

The Mediterranean jellyfish is repulsive. It has an odious contact, this animated gelatine which envelops the swimmer; into which the hands sink, where the nails scratch, which one rends without killing, and tears off without pulling away, a sort of flowing and tenacious being which slips between one's fingers; but no horror equals the sudden appearance of the octopus,—Medusa served by eight serpents.

No grasp equals the embrace of the cephalopod.

It is the pneumatic machine attacking you. You have to deal with a vacuum furnished with paws. Neither scratches nor bites; an indescribable scarification. A bite is formidable, but less so than a suction. A claw is nothing beside the cupping-glass. The claw means the beast entering into your flesh; the cupping-glass means yourself entering into the beast.

Your muscles swell, your fibres writhe, your skin cracks under the foul weight, your blood spurts forth and mingles frightfully with the lymph of the mollusk. The creature superimposes itself upon you by a thousand mouths; the hydra incorporates itself with the man; the man amalgamates himself with the hydra. You form but one. This dream is upon you. The tiger can only devour you; the octopus, oh, horror! breathes you in. It draws you to it, and into it, and bound, ensnared, powerless, you feel yourself slowly emptied into that frightful sack, which is a monster.

Beyond the terrible, being devoured alive, is the inexpressible, being drunk alive.

Science first rejects these strange animals, according to her habit of excessive prudence, even in the presence of facts; then she decides to study them; she dissects them, she classifies them, she catalogues them, she labels them; she procures specimens of them; she exhibits them under glass in museums; they enter into her nomenclature; she describes them as mollusks, invertebrates, radiates. She fixes their relationships a little beyond squids, a little this side of cuttlefish; she finds for these salt-water hydras an analogous one in fresh water, the argyronectus; she divides them into great, medium, and small species; she admits the small species more easily than the great ones, which is, moreover, in all branches, the tendency of science, which likes rather to be microscopic than telescopic; she looks to their construction and calls them cephalopods; she counts their antennæ, and calls them octopods. That done, she leaves them. Where science abandons them, philosophy takes them up.

Philosophy, in her turn, studies these beings. She goes less far and farther than science. She does not dissect them; she meditates upon them. Where the scalpel has worked, she plunges in the hypothesis. She seeks the final cause. Profound perplexity of the thinker. These creatures almost inspire uneasiness in regard to the Creator. They are hideous surprises. They are the joy-disturbers of contemplation. In desperation man verifies their existence. They are the deliberate forms of evil. What is one to do in the presence of these blasphemies of creation against itself? Towards whom shall one turn for the solution?

The Possible is a terrible matrix. Mystery becomes concrete in monsters. Fragments of shadow spring from that mass, immanence, are rent, detached, roll, float, are condensed, borrow from the circumambient blackness, undergo unknown polarizations, take on life, compose for themselves some indescribable form out of darkness and some soul out of miasm, and depart, spectres among living things. It is something like shadows converted into monsters. To what purpose? What end does this serve? Once more the eternal question.

These animals are phantoms as well as monsters. They are proved, and yet improbable. They are, because they exist; if they were not, reason would be justified. They are the amphibia of death. Their improbability complicates their existence. They border on the human frontier, and people the region of Chimæras. You deny the vampire, the octopus appears. Their swarming is a certainty which disconcerts our assurance. Optimism, which is the truth, nevertheless almost loses countenance before them. They are the visible extremes of black circles. They mark the transition from one reality to another. They seem to belong to that beginning of terrible beings of which the dreamer catches a confused vision through the loophole of night.

These continuations of monsters, first into the invisible, then into the possible, have been suspected, perceived perhaps, in deep ecstasy and by the intent eye of magi and philosophers. Hence, the conjecture of a hell. The demon is the tiger of the invisible. The wild beast that preys on souls has been described to the human race by two seers; one named John, the other, Dante.

If, in fact, the circles of shadows continue indefinitely, if after one ring there follows another, if this augmentation persists in unlimited progression, if this chain exists, which we for our part are determined to doubt, it is certain that the octopus at one end proves Satan at the other.

It is certain that an evil thing at one end proves evil at the other.

Every evil beast, like every perverse intelligence, is a sphinx.

A terrible sphinx propounding the terrible enigma. The enigma of evil.

It is this perfection of evil which has caused great minds sometimes to incline towards belief in a dual God, towards the formidable double-headed deity of the Manichæans.

A piece of Chinese silk, stolen during the last war from the palace of the Emperor of China, represents the shark devouring the crocodile, which is devouring the serpent, which is devouring the eagle, which is devouring the swallow, which is devouring the caterpillar.

All nature which we have before our eyes is devouring and devoured. The prey prey on each other.

But learned men, who are also philosophers, and consequently optimists, find or think they find an explanation. Among others, Bonnet of Geneva, that mysterious, exact mind who was opposed to Buffon, as Geoffroy

Saint-Hilaire was later on to Cuvier, was struck with this idea of the final purpose. The explanation is this: universal death entails universal interment. Those who devour are those who bury.

All beings enter into each other. To decay is to nourish. Frightful cleaning of the globe. Man, a carnivorous animal, is also a burier. Our life is made up of death. Such is the appalling law. We are sepulchres.

In our twilight world, this fatality of order produces monsters. You say: To what purpose? To this.

Is this the explanation? Is this the reply to the question? But then, why not another order? The question returns.

Let us live; agreed.

But let us endeavor to have death a progress to us. Let us aspire to less gloomy worlds.

Let us follow conscience which leads us thither.

For, let us never forget, the best is only found by the better.

III

Another Form of Combat in the Gulf

SUCH was the creature in whose power Gilliatt had been for several moments.

This monster was the inhabitant of that grotto. It was the frightful genius of the place. A sort of sombre demon of the water.

All these magnificences had horror for their centre.

A month previously, on the day when, for the first time, Gilliatt had made his way into the grotto, the dark outline of which he had caught a glimpse in the ripples of the water was this octopus.

This was its home.

When Gilliatt, entering that cave for the second time in pursuit of the crab, had perceived the crevices in which he thought the crab had taken refuge, the octopus was lying in wait in that hole.

Can the reader picture that lying-in-wait?

Not a bird would dare to brood, not an egg would dare to hatch, not a flower would dare to open, not a breast would dare to give suck, not a heart would dare to love, not a spirit would dare to take flight, if one meditated on the sinister shapes patiently lying in ambush in the abyss.

Gilliatt had thrust his arm into the hole; the octopus had seized it.

It held it.

He was the fly for this spider.

Gilliatt stood in water to his waist, his feet clinging to the slippery roundness of the stones, his right arm grasped and subdued by the flat coils of the octopus's thongs, and his body almost hidden by the folds and crossings of that horrible bandage. Of the eight arms of the octopus, three adhered to the rock while five adhered to Gilliatt. In this manner, clamped on one side to the granite, on the other to the man, it chained Gilliatt to the rock. Gilliatt had two hundred and fifty suckers upon him. A combination of anguish and disgust. To be crushed in a gigantic fist whose elastic fingers, nearly a metre in length, are inwardly full of living pustules which ransack your flesh.

As we have said, one cannot tear one's self away from the octopus. If one attempts it, one is but the more surely bound. It only clings the closer. Its efforts increase in proportion to yours. A greater struggle produces a greater constriction.

Gilliatt had but one recourse, his knife.

He had only his left hand free; but, as the reader knows, he could make powerful use of it. It might have been said of him that he had two right hands.

His open knife was in his hand.

The tentacles of an octopus cannot be cut off; it is leathery and difficult to sever, it slips away from under the blade. Moreover, the superposition is such that a cut into these thongs would attack your own flesh.

The octopus is formidable; nevertheless, there is a way of getting away from it. The fishermen of Sark are acquainted with it; any one who has seen them executing abrupt movements at sea knows it. Porpoises also know it; they have a way of biting the cuttlefish which cuts off its head. Hence, all the headless squids and cuttlefish which are met with on the open sea.

The octopus is, in fact, vulnerable only in the head.

Gilliatt was not ignorant of this fact.

He had never seen an octopus of this size. He found himself seized at the outset by one of the larger species. Any other man would have been terrified.

In the case of the octopus as in that of the bull, there is a certain moment at which to seize it; it is at the instant when the bull lowers his neck, it is the instant when the octopus thrusts forward its head, a sudden movement. He who misses that juncture is lost.

All that we have related lasted but a few minutes. But Gilliatt felt the suction of the two hundred and fifty cupping-glasses increasing.

The octopus is cunning. It tries to stupefy its prey in the first place. It seizes, then waits as long as it can.

Gilliatt held his knife. The suction increased.

He gazed at the octopus, which stared at him.

All at once the creature detached its sixth tentacle from the rock, and, launching it at him, attempted to seize his left arm.

At the same time it thrust its head forward swiftly. A second more and its mouth would have been applied to Gilliatt's breast. Gilliatt, wounded in the flank and with both arms pinioned, would have been a dead man.

But Gilliatt was on his guard. Being watched, he watched.

He avoided the tentacle, and, at the moment when the creature was about to bite his breast, his armed fist descended on the monster.

Two convulsions in opposite directions ensued, that of Gilliatt and that of the octopus.

It was like the conflict of two flashes of lightning.

Gilliatt plunged the point of his knife into the flat,

viscous mass, and with a twisting movement, similar to the flourish of a whip, describing a circle around the two eyes, he tore out the head as one wrenches out a tooth.

It was finished.

The whole creature dropped.

It resembled a sheet detaching itself. The air-pump destroyed, the vacuum no longer existed. The four hundred suckers released their hold, simultaneously, of the rock and the man.

It sank to the bottom.

Gilliatt, panting with the combat, could perceive on the rocks at his feet, two shapeless, gelatinous masses, the head on one side, the rest on the other. We say "the rest," because one could not say the body.

Gilliatt, however, fearing some convulsive return of agony, retreated beyond the reach of the tentacles.

But the monster was really dead.

Gilliatt closed his knife.

IV

Nothing Is Hidden and Nothing Is Lost

It was time that Gilliatt killed the octopus. He was almost strangled, his right arm and his body were violet in hue; more than two hundred swellings were outlined upon them; the blood spurted from some of them here and there. The remedy for these wounds is salt water, Gilliatt plunged into it. At the same time he rubbed himself with the palm of his hand. The swellings subsided under this friction.

As he retreated and plunged more deeply into the water, he had, without perceiving it, approached a sort of vault already noticed by him, near the crevice where he had been seized by the octopus.

This vault extended obliquely and above water, beneath the great walls of the cave. The boulders which had accumulated there had raised the bottom above the level of ordinary tides. This aperture was a tolerably large flattened arch; a man could enter by stooping. The green light of the submarine grotto penetrated thither and illuminated it faintly.

As Gilliatt was rubbing his swollen skin, he chanced to raise his eyes mechanically.

His glance penetrated into this vault.

He shuddered.

It seemed to him that he saw, at the extremity of that hole, in the gloom, a sort of face laughing.

Gilliatt was ignorant of the word hallucination, but acquainted with the fact. The mysterious encounters with the improbable, which we call hallucinations in order to extricate ourselves from the difficulty, exist in nature. Whether as illusions or realities, visions exist. He who has the gift beholds them. Gilliatt was a dreamer, as we have said. He had the grandeur of being at times a seer like a prophet. One cannot, with impunity, be a dreamer in solitary places.

He thought it might be one of those mirages by which, nocturnal man that he was, he had more than once been deceived.

The cavity presented the shape of a lime-kiln with tolerable exactness. It was a low niche, like the handle of a basket, whose abrupt coving gradually contracted to the end of the crypt, where pebbles, fragments of boulders, and the vault of the rock joined, and where the pocket ended.

He entered, and bending his head, directed his steps towards what lay at the bottom.

Something was really grinning. It was a death's-head.

There was not only the skull, there was the skeleton also.

A human skeleton was lying in this cave.

The glance of a bold man, in such encounters, desires to know the real state of the case.

Gilliatt cast his eyes around him.

He was surrounded by a multitude of crabs.

This multitude moved not. It had the aspect which a

dead ant-hill would present. All these crabs were inert. They were empty shells.

These groups, scattered here and there, formed shapeless constellations on the pavement of stone which encumbered the vault.

Gilliatt had walked over them without seeing them, his eyes being fixed elsewhere.

At the extremity of the crypt which Gilliatt had reached, they were still thicker. It was a motionless bristling of antennæ, legs, mandibles. Open claws stood stark upright and closed no more. Their bony shells no longer stirred beneath their crust of spines; some were turned over, and showed their livid cavities. This pile resembled an affray of besiegers, and lay massed together like a thicket.

Beneath this heap lay the skeleton.

Beneath this confusion of tentacles and scales, the cranium was visible with its sutures, the vertebræ, the thigh bones, the shin bones, the long, jointed fingers with their nails. The cavity of the ribs was full of crabs. Some heart had once beaten there. Marine moulds draped the eye-sockets. Limpets had left their slime in the nostrils. Moreover, there was in this nook of the rocks neither seaweeds nor grasses nor a breath of air. No movement. The teeth grinned.

The disturbing point about laughter is the mocking imitation of it which the skull makes.

This marvellous palace of the abyss, inlaid and incrusted with all the gems of the sea, had ended by revealing itself and telling its secret. It was a lair, the octopus dwelt there; and it was a tomb, a man lay there.

The spectral immobility of the skeleton and the creatures around it oscillated vaguely by reason of the reflection of the subterranean waters which trembled over this petrifaction. The crabs, a frightful, confused mass, appeared as if in the act of finishing their repast. The shells seemed to be eating the carcass. Nothing could be more strange than the dead vermin on the dead prey. Sombre continuations of death.

Gilliatt had before his eyes the larder of the octopus.

Melancholy vision, wherein the profound horror of things allowed itself to be caught in the very act. The crabs had devoured the man, the octopus had devoured the crabs.

There was not a vestige of clothing near the corpse. He must have been seized naked.

Gilliatt, attentive and scrutinizing, began to remove the crabs from the man. Who was this man? The body had been admirably dissected. One would have pronounced it an anatomical preparation; all the flesh had been removed, not a muscle remained, not a bone was lacking. Had Gilliatt belonged to the profession, he might have authenticated the fact. The denuded periostea were white, polished, and rubbed up, as it were. They would have been like ivory had it not been for some greenish patches of seaweed. The cartilaginous partitions were delicately smoothed down and spared. The tomb sometimes produces such sinister jeweller's work as this.

The corpse was virtually interred beneath the dead crabs; Gilliatt disinterred it.

All at once he bent over hastily.

He had just caught sight of a sort of band around the vertebral column.

It was a leather belt which had evidently been buckled round the man's abdomen when he had been alive.

The leather was mildewed. The buckle was rusted.

Gilliatt drew the belt towards him. The vertebræ resisted, and he was obliged to break them in order to obtain it. The belt was intact. A crust of limpets had begun to form upon it.

He fingered it and felt a hard object, square in form, in the interior. Such a thing as undoing the buckle was not to be thought of. He split the leather with his knife.

The belt contained a small iron box, and a few gold pieces. Gilliatt counted twenty guineas.

The iron box was a sailor's old tobacco box, which opened with a spring. It was much rusted and very securely closed. The spring, completely oxidized, no longer worked.

His knife once more extricated Gilliatt from his dilemma. A thrust from the point of the blade caused the cover of the box to fly off.

The box opened.

There was nothing in it but paper.

A little package of very thin sheets folded in four covered the bottom of the box. They were damp but not spoiled. The box, hermetically sealed, had preserved them. Gilliatt unfolded them.

They were three bank notes for a thousand pounds sterling each, making altogether seventy-five thousand francs.

Gilliatt folded them up again, replaced them in the box, took advantage of the small space which remained to add the twenty guineas, and closed the box again, as well as he could.

Then he began an examination of the belt.

The leather, originally glazed on the outside, was rough on the interior. On that unfinished background some letters were traced in thick ink. Gilliatt deciphered these letters: "SIEUR CLUBIN."

V

IN THE INTERVAL WHICH SEPARATES SIX INCHES FROM TWO FEET, THERE IS ROOM TO LODGE DEATH

GILLIATT replaced the box in the belt and put the belt in the pocket of his trousers.

He left the skeleton to the crabs, with the dead octopus beside it.

While Gilliatt had been engaged with the octopus and the skeleton, the rising tide had flooded the entrance to the passage. Gilliatt could get out only by diving under the arch. He managed it without difficulty; he knew the exit and he was a master of these gymnastics of the sea.

The reader has had a view of the drama which had taken place six weeks before. One monster had seized another. The octopus had caught Clubin.

This had been, in the inexorable gloom, what might almost be called the encounter of hypocrisies. At the bottom of the abyss, these two existences, made up of waiting and of shadows, had come into violent collision, and one, which was the beast, had executed the other, which was the soul. Sinister justice.

The crab feeds on carrion, the octopus feeds on crabs. The octopus arrests in its passage any swimming animal, a dog or a man, if it can, drinks his blood and leaves the dead body at the bottom of the water. Crabs are the necrophagous beetles of the sea. Decaying flesh attracts them; they come; they eat the corpse; the octopus eats them. Dead things disappear in the crab, the crab disappears in the octopus. We have already pointed out this law.

Clubin had served the octopus as bait.

The octopus had held him down and drowned him; the crabs had devoured him. Some wave had thrust him into the cave, at the bottom of whose niche Gilliatt had found him.

Gilliatt retraced his steps, fumbling among the rocks in search of sea urchins and whelks, as he no longer desired any crabs. It would have seemed to him as though he were devouring human flesh.

Moreover, his only thought was to sup as well as possible before setting out. Henceforth, nothing detained him. Great tempests are always followed by a calm, which sometimes lasts many days. No danger now existed on the side of the sea. Gilliatt was resolved to set out on the morrow. It was important to keep the barricade between the Douvres in place during the night, because of the tide; but Gilliatt intended to remove this barrier at daybreak, to push the boat clear of the Douvres, and to set sail for Saint-Sampson. The light breeze which was blowing from the southwest was precisely the wind which he needed.

The first quarter of the May moon was beginning; the days were long.

When Gilliatt, having finished his prowling among the

rocks and almost satisfied his appetite, returned to the gap between the Douvres where his boat lay, the sun had set, the twilight was livid with that half moonlight which may be called the light of the crescent; the tide had attained its height, and was beginning to ebb again: the smoke stack of the engine, rising upright above the paunch, had been covered by the foam of the tempest with a layer of salt, which shone white in the moonlight.

This reminded Gilliatt that the squall had thrown a great deal of rain water and sea water into his boat, and that, if he wished to set out on the morrow, he must bail out the paunch.

He had noticed, when he quitted the boat to go in pursuit of crabs, that there were about six inches of water in the hold. His bailing scoop would be sufficient to throw out this water.

On reaching the boat, Gilliatt gave a start of terror. There were nearly two feet of water in the boat.

A formidable fact, the boat was leaking.

It had gradually filled during Gilliatt's absence. Loaded as it was, twenty inches of water was a dangerous addition. A little more and it would sink. If Gilliatt had returned one hour later, he would probably have found only the mast and smoke stack out of water.

Not a moment could be spared for deliberation. He must find the leak, stop it up, then empty the boat, or at least relieve it. The pumps of the Durande had been lost in the shipwreck; Gilliatt was reduced to the bailing scoop of the paunch.

He must find the leak, first of all. That was the most urgent point.

Gilliatt set to work instantly, without even giving himself time to dress again, all shivering as he was. He was no longer conscious of either hunger or cold.

The boat continued to fill. Fortunately, there was no wind. The slightest swell would have sunk it.

The moon set.

Gilliatt searched for a long time, groping, bent, half submerged in the water. At last he discovered the injury.

During the storm, at the critical moment when the paunch had twisted round, the strong bark had come somewhat violently in contact with the rocks. One of the projections of the little Douvre had made a fracture in the hull on the starboard side.

This leak was vexatiously, one might say treacherously, situated near the joints of two riders, and this, together with the confusion of the storm, had prevented Gilliatt's perceiving the injury, in his obscure and rapid survey at the height of the tempest.

The fracture had this alarming feature, that it was large; and this reassuring feature, that although submerged for the moment by the inward increase of water, it was above the water line.

At the instant when the crack had opened, the waves had been rudely shaken in the strait, the water had dashed through the breach into the boat, the boat beneath this extra load had settled several inches, and even after the waves had subsided, the weight of the water which had filtered in, by raising the water line, had kept the leak under water. Hence the imminence of the danger. The water had increased from six inches to twenty. But if the leak could be stopped, the boat could be bailed out; the bark once emptied, it would rise once more to its normal water line, the fracture would be out of water and thus dry, repair would be easy or, at least, possible. Gilliatt, as we have already said, still had his carpenter's tools in fairly good condition.

But what uncertainty before reaching that point! what perils! what evil chances! Gilliatt heard the water inexorably gushing in. A shock and all would sink. What wretchedness! Perhaps it was already too late.

Gilliatt blamed himself bitterly. He should have perceived the injury at once. The six inches of water in the hold should have warned him. He had been stupid to attribute those six inches to the rain and foam. He reproached himself for having slept, for having eaten; he almost reproached himself with the tempest and the night. All was his fault.

These harsh self-reproaches were uttered as he went to and fro about his work, and did not prevent his giving it careful attention.

The leak was found, that was the first step; to stop it was the second. Nothing more could be done for the moment. Carpentering cannot be done under water.

One favorable circumstance was that the break in the hull had taken place in the space comprised between the two chains which stayed the smoke stack on the starboard. The stuffing could be fastened to these chains.

Meanwhile, the water was gaining. The depth was now over two feet.

The water rose above Gilliatt's knees.

VI
De Profundis ad Altum

GILLIATT had at his disposal, in the reserve of the rigging of the boat, a tolerably large tarpaulin, provided with long lashings at its four corners.

He took this tarpaulin, fastened two corners of it by means of the lashings to the two rings of the chains of the smoke stack, on the side of the leak, and flung the tarpaulin overboard. The tarpaulin fell like a table cloth between the little Douvre and the bark and sank in the waves. The pressure of water endeavoring to enter the hull forced it against the hull and upon the hole. The more the water pressed, the closer the tarpaulin clung. It was glued by the water itself upon the fracture. The wound was dressed.

This tarred canvas interposed between the interior of the hold and the billows without. Not another drop of water entered.

The leak was covered, but not calked.

It was a respite.

Gilliatt took the scoop and set to bailing the paunch. It was high time to lighten it. This work warmed him up a little, but his fatigue was extreme. He was forced to admit to himself that he should not be able to finish, and that he should not succeed in bailing out the hold. Gilliatt had hardly eaten, and he had the humiliation of feeling himself exhausted.

He gauged the progress of his work by the fall of the level of the water to his knees. This fall was slow.

Moreover, the leak was only interrupted. The evil was palliated, not repaired. The tarpaulin, thrust into the fracture by the water, was beginning to form a tumor in the hull. It resembled a fist beneath that canvas, seeking to burst it. The canvas, being solid and well tarred, resisted; but the swelling and the tension were augmenting, and it was not certain that the canvas would not give way, and the tumor might burst at any moment. The irruption of the water would recommence.

In such a case, as ships' crews in distress are aware, there is no other resource than stuffing. Rags are taken, of every sort that comes to hand, everything that is known in the technical language as "service," and as many as possible of them are thrust into the crevice of the tarpaulin tumor.

Of this "service," Gilliatt had none. All the strips and oakum which he had stored up had either been employed in his work or dispersed by the gale.

At the most, he might have found a few remains by ransacking the rocks. The boat was sufficiently relieved to admit of his leaving it for a quarter of an hour; but how was such a search to be made without light? The darkness was complete. There was no longer any moon; nothing but the sombre, starry heavens. Gilliatt had no dry rope wherewith to make a wick, no tallow to make a candle, no fire to light it, no lantern to screen it. All was confused and indistinct in the bark and on the reef. The water could be heard swashing against the wounded hull; but not even the hole was visible; it was with his hands that Gilliatt discovered the increasing tension of the tarpaulin. Impossible to prosecute, in such darkness, a faithful search for the bits of canvas and cordage scattered among the rocks. How was he to glean these fragments when he could not see clearly? Gilliatt gazed sadly at the night. All those stars, and no candle.

The liquid mass within the bark having diminished, the pressure from without was increased. The swelling of the tarpaulin grew larger. It grew more and more distended. It was like an abscess ready to burst. The situation, improved for a moment, had again become threatening.

A plug was absolutely necessary.

Gilliatt had nothing but his clothes.

He had placed them to dry, as it will be remembered, on the salient rocks of the little Douvre.

He went and gathered them up and placed them on the rail of the paunch.

He took his tarpaulin coat, and kneeling in the water, he thrust it into the crevice, pressing back the swelling of the tarpaulin outwards, and, consequently, emptying it. To the tarpaulin he added the sheepskin; to the sheepskin, his woolen shirt; to his shirt, his peajacket. Everything went the same way.

He had on but one garment, he took this off, and with his trousers he enlarged and strengthened the plugging. The stopper was made and seemed to answer the purpose.

This plug extended beyond the edge of the breach with the tarpaulin for its envelope. The water, desirous of entering, pressed against the obstacle, spread it out usefully on the fracture, and consolidated it. It was a sort of exterior compress.

In the interior, the centre alone of the swelling having been thrust back, there remained all around the breach of the crevice and of the plug a circular pad of the tarpaulin, all the more adherent because the very inequalities of the fracture retained it. The leak was stopped.

But nothing could be more precarious. Those sharp projections of the fracture which fastened the tarpaulin might pierce it, and through those holes the water would enter again. Gilliatt would not even perceive it in the darkness. It was hardly probable that that plug would last until daylight. Gilliatt's anxiety assumed a different form, but he felt it increasing at the same time that he felt his strength decreasing.

He set to bailing the hold again, but his exhausted arms could hardly lift the scoop full of water. He was naked and shivering.

Gilliatt felt the sinister approach of the end.

One possible chance crossed his mind. Perhaps there was a sail in the offing. A fisherman who should happen to be passing through the Douvres waters, might come to his assistance. The moment had arrived when an assistant was absolutely necessary. With a man and a lantern all might be saved. Two of them could easily bail out the hold; as soon as the bark was water tight and no longer overflooded, she would rise, she would regain her water line, the crevice would be above the water, repairs could be made, the plug could immediately be replaced by a section of planking, and the provisional apparatus placed on the fracture by definite repairs. If not, he must wait until daybreak, wait all night! Fatal delay which might prove ruinous. Gilliatt was in a fever of haste.

If, by chance, some ship's lantern was in sight, Gilliatt could make signals from the summit of the Douvres. The weather was calm, there was no wind, a man moving against the starry background of the sky stood a chance of being noticed. The captain of a ship, or even the skipper of a fishing boat, does not sail the waters of the Douvres by night without pointing his glass at the reef by way of precaution.

Gilliatt hoped that he might be seen.

He scaled the wreck, grasped the knotted rope, and ascended the great Douvre.

Not a sail on the horizon, not a light. The water was deserted, as far as he could see.

No assistance possible, and no resistance possible.

Gilliatt felt himself disarmed, a thing which had not happened with him up to that moment.

Dark fatality was now his master. He, with his boat, with the engine of the Durande, with all his labor, with all his success, with all his courage, he belonged to the gulf. He had no longer any means of continuing the struggle; he became passive. How was he to prevent the tide coming, the water rising, the night continuing? That plug was his only reliance. Gilliatt had worn himself out and stripped himself to make it, and complete it; he could neither fortify it nor render it firmer; such as the plug was it must remain, and fatally, all his effort having come to an end. The sea had at its discretion that hasty apparatus applied to the leak. How would that inert thing behave? It was now the plug which was combating, it was no longer Gilliatt. It was that rag, it was no longer that mind. The swelling of the waves was sufficient to reopen the fracture. More or less pressure; the whole question lay there.

All was going to be solved by a blind struggle between two mechanical quantities. Gilliatt could henceforth neither aid the auxiliary nor stop the enemy. He was no longer anything but spectator of his life or his death.

Gilliatt, who had been a providence, was, at the supreme moment, reduced to an inanimate resistance.

None of the trials and terrors which Gilliatt had undergone approached this one.

On arriving at the Douvres reef, he had beheld himself surrounded and seized, as it were, by solitude. This solitude did more than environ, it enveloped him. A thousand menaces had shaken their fists at him simultaneously. The wind was there, ready to blow; the sea was there, ready to roar; impossible to stop that mouth, the wind; impossible to deprive of its teeth that monster, the sea.

Yet he had struggled; a man, he had contended hand to hand with the ocean; he had wrestled with the tempest.

He had held his own against still other anxieties and necessities.

He had become familiar with all manner of distress; without tools, he had been obliged to perform great works; without aid, to move burdens; without science, to solve problems; without provisions, to eat and drink; without bed or roof, to sleep.

On that reef, a tragic rack, he had been put to the question in turn by the diverse torturing fatalities of Nature: a mother when it seems good to her, an executioner when she chooses.

He had conquered isolation, conquered hunger, conquered thirst, conquered cold, conquered fever, conquered work, conquered sleep. He had encountered objects in coalition to bar his passage. After privation, the elements; after the sea, the tempest; after the tempest, the octopus; after the monster, the spectre.

Melancholy final irony. In that reef whence Gilliatt

had reckoned on emerging in triumph, Clubin, dead, came to gaze upon him with a mocking laugh.

The sneer of the spectre was justified. Gilliatt beheld himself lost. Gilliatt beheld himself as dead as Clubin.

Winter, famine, fatigue, the wreck to dismember, the engine to remove, the blows of the equinox, the wind, the thunder, the octopus,—all these were nothing as compared to the leak.

Against the cold one can use, and Gilliatt had used, fire; against hunger, the shell fish from the rocks; against thirst, rain; against the difficulties of salvage, industry and energy; against he sea and the storm, the breakwater; against the octopus, his knife;—against a leak, nothing.

The hurricane left him this sinister farewell. A last reprisal, a traitorous thrust, the underhand attack of the conquered on the conqueror. The tempest in its flight shot this arrow to the rear. Defeats turned about and dealt a blow.

It was the underhand stab of the abyss.

One can combat with the tempest, but how combat a leakage?

If the plug yielded, if the leak opened again, nothing could prevent the boat from sinking. It was the ligature on the artery unloosened. And the paunch once at the bottom of the water with that heavy load, the engine, there would be no means of raising it. This heroic effort of two titanic months was ending in annihilation.

To begin anew was impossible. Gilliatt had no longer either forge or materials. Perhaps at daybreak he would behold his whole work sink slowly and irremediably into the gulf.

It is a frightful thing to feel a dark force beneath one.

The gulf drew him to itself.

His boat submerged, nothing would be left to him but to die of cold and hunger as that other had done, the shipwrecked sailor of "the Man" rock.

For two long months, the intelligences and providences which are in the invisible had been witness of this: On the one hand, the expanse, the waves, the winds, the lightnings, the atmospheric phenomena; on the other, a man. On the one side, the sea; on the other, a soul. On the one side, the infinite; on the other, an atom.

And there had been a battle.

And behold, perhaps this marvel had come to naught.

Thus ended in impotence this unprecedented deed of heroism; thus ended in despair this formidable combat, the struggle of nothing against everything, this Iliad of one.

Gilliatt gazed into space in despair. He had no longer even a garment. He was naked in the presence of immensity.

Then, in the despondency of all that unknown vastness, no longer knowing what was wanted of him; confronting the gloom; in the presence of that impenetrable obscurity; in the uproar of the waters, the billows, the waves, the surges, the foams, the squalls; beneath the clouds, beneath the gusts, beneath the vast scattered force; beneath that mysterious firmament of wings, of stars, of tombs; beneath the intent possibly hidden in these excesses having around him and beneath him the ocean, and above him the constellations;—beneath the unfathomable, he gave way, he renounced all, he flung himself flat upon his back on the rock, with his face to the stars, vanquished, and, clasping his hands before the terrible profundity, he cried to the infinite: "Mercy!"

Hurled to earth by immensity, he prayed to it.

He was there alone, in that darkness, on that rock, in the midst of that sea, overcome by exhaustion, resembling a man who has been struck by lightning, naked as a gladiator in the circus; only, instead of the arena, having the abyss; instead of wild beasts, shadows; instead of the eyes of the populace, the gaze of the unknown; instead of vestals, stars; instead of Cæsar, God.

It seemed to him, that he felt himself dissolving in cold, fatigue, weakness, in prayer, in the gloom, and his eyes closed.

VII

There Is an Ear in the Unknown

SEVERAL hours elapsed.

The sun rose, dazzling.

Its first ray lighted up a motionless form upon the plateau of the great Douvre. It was Gilliatt.

He still lay outstretched on the rock.

That frozen and stiffened nudity no longer even shivered. His closed eyelids were pallid. It would have been difficult to say whether he was not a corpse.

The sun seemed to gaze upon him.

If this naked man were not dead, he was so near it that the slightest cold wind was sufficient to put an end to him.

The wind began to blow warm, and vivifying; the springlike breath of May.

Meanwhile, the sun mounted higher in the deep blue sky; its less horizontal rays grew crimson. Its light became heat. It enveloped Gilliatt.

Gilliatt did not stir. If he breathed, it was with that feeble, dying respiration which would hardly cloud a mirror.

The sun continued its ascent, its rays falling less and less oblique upon Gilliatt. The wind, which had at first been merely warm, was now hot.

That rigid and naked body still remained devoid of movement; but the skin seemed less livid.

The sun, as it approached the zenith, fell perpendicularly on the plateau of the Douvre. A prodigality of light was poured from the heights of heaven; the vast reflection of the glassy sea was added to it; the rock began to grow warm, and revived the sleeper.

A sigh heaved Gilliatt's breast.

He lived.

The sun continued its caresses, which were almost ardent. The wind, which was already the wind of the south and of summer, approached Gilliatt like a mouth breathing gently.

Gilliatt stirred.

The calmness of the sea was inexpressible. It murmured like a nurse beside her child. The waves seemed to be cradling the reef.

The sea birds, who knew Gilliatt, flew above him uneasily. This was no longer their former wild uneasiness. There was something indescribably tender and fraternal about it. They uttered little cries. They seemed to be calling him. A sea-mew that liked him, no doubt, was so familiar as to come quite close to him. It began to speak to him. He seemed not to hear. It jumped upon his shoulder, and pecked gently at his lips.

Gilliatt opened his eyes.

The birds, content and shy, flew away.

Gilliatt sprang to his feet, stretched like a lion awakened, ran to the edge of the platform, and looked down into the passage between the Douvres beneath him.

The boat was there, intact. The plug had held firm; the sea had probably not disturbed it much.

All was saved.

Gilliatt was no longer weary. His strength was renewed. His swoon had been a sleep.

He bailed out the boat, made the hold dry, and raised the leak above the water line, dressed himself once more, drank, ate, was joyous.

The leak, examined by daylight, required more labor than Gilliatt would have believed. It was a rather serious injury. The whole day was not too much for Gilliatt to repair it.

On the following day at dawn, after having removed the barriers and opened the exit from the pass once more, clothed in his rags which had got the better of the leak, wearing Clubin's belt with the seventy-five thousand francs, standing erect upon the mended boat beside the machinery which he had saved, Gilliatt left the Douvres reef with a good wind and a propitious sea.

He steered his course for Guernsey.

At the moment when he was quitting the reef, any one who had been there might have heard him singing in a low tone the air of "Bonny Dundee."

PART III

DÉRUCHETTE

BOOK FIRST
NIGHT AND MOON

I
THE BELL OF THE PORT

THE SAINT-SAMPSON of to-day is almost a city; the Saint-Sampson of forty years ago was almost a village.

When the spring had come and the long winter evenings were over, people cut evenings short and went to bed at nightfall. Saint-Sampson was an ancient curfew parish, having preserved the habit of blowing out its candle early.

People there went to bed and rose with the day. These ancient Norman villages imitate the habits of their fowls.

Let us mention in addition that Saint-Sampson, with the exception of a few rich bourgeois families, has a population of quarry-men and carpenters. The port is a port for repairing. All day long they quarry stone or hew beams; here the pick, there the hammer. A perpetual handling of oak and of granite. By evening they drop with fatigue and sleep like lead. Heavy work brings heavy slumbers.

One evening in the beginning of May, Mess Lethierry, after having, for several moments, gazed at the moon through the trees and listened to Déruchette's step as she walked alone in the cool of the evening in the garden of les Bravées, retired to his chamber, opening towards the port, and went to bed. Douce and Grâce were already in bed. Every one was asleep in the house except Déruchette. Every one in Saint-Sampson was also asleep. Doors and shutters were everywhere closed. There was no passing to and fro in the streets. A few lights, like the blinking of eyes about to close, gleamed redly here and there from the small windows in the roofs, a sign of the retiring of the servants. It was already some time since nine o'clock had rung out in the old ivy-draped Roman clock-tower which shares with the church of Saint-Brelade in Jersey the singularity of bearing as its date four ones, IIII; which signifies "eleven hundred and eleven."

Mess Lethierry's popularity in Saint-Sampson had been the result of his success. Success gone, a void had resulted. We are forced to believe that bad luck is contagious, and that people who are not fortunate have the plague, so speedily are they placed in quarantine. The handsome sons of good families avoided Déruchette. The isolation around les Bravées was now such that they had not even learned in the house the little scrap of local news which had set Saint-Sampson in commotion that day. The rector of the parish, the Reverend Joë Ebenezer Caudray, was rich. His uncle, the magnificent Dean of St. Asaph, had just died in London. The news had been brought by the mail-sloop *Cashmere,* which had arrived from England that very morning, and the mast of which could be seen in the roadstead of Saint-Pierre-Port. The *Cashmere* was to set out for Southampton the next day at noon, and, it was said, was to carry with it the reverend rector, recalled to England in haste to be present at the official opening of the will, not to mention the other pressing demands in connection with taking possession of a great inheritance. All day long, Saint-Sampson had been carrying on a confused dialogue. The *Cashmere,* the Reverend Ebenezer, his dead uncle, his wealth, his departure, his possible promotions in the future, had formed the burden of the buzzing. A single house, not being informed, had remained silent,—les Bravées.

Mess Lethierry had thrown himself into his hammock all dressed. Flinging himself into this hammock had been his resource ever since the wreck of the Durande. Stretching out on his pallet is something to which every prisoner has recourse, and Mess Lethierry was the prisoner of his grief. He went to bed; it was a truce, a space for taking breath, a suspension of ideas. Did he sleep? No. Did he keep watch? No. Properly speaking, for the last two months and a half,—two months and a half had elapsed since the disaster,—Mess Lethierry had been like a somnambulist. He had not yet recovered possession of himself. He was in that mixed and confused state with which those who have undergone great affliction are acquainted. His reflections were not thought, his sleep was not repose. During the day he was not fully awake. At night he was not asleep. He was up and had gone to bed; that was all. When he was in his hammock a measure of oblivion came to him; he called this sleeping; chimæras floated over him and within him; the nocturnal cloud, filled with confused faces, traversed his brain; the Emperor Napoleon dictated his memoirs to him; there were several Déruchettes; queer birds were in the trees; the streets of Lons-le-Saulnier became serpents. Nightmare was the respite from despair. He passed his nights in dreaming and his days in reverie.

He sometimes remained a whole afternoon motionless at his window,—which, as the reader will remember, opened on the port,—with his head bent, his elbows on the stone, his ears resting on his fists, his back turned to the whole world, his eyes fixed on the old iron ring fastened in the wall of his house, to which the Durande had formerly been moored. He was watching the rust collect on that ring.

Mess Lethierry was reduced to the mechanical function of living.

The most valiant of men, on being deprived of their realizable idea, come to that pass. It is the result of an existence which has been rendered void. Life is the voyage, the idea is the itinerary. Where there is no longer an itinerary, one stops short. The goal is lost, force is dead. Fate holds an obscure discretionary power. It can touch even our moral being with its wand. Despair is almost the destitution of the soul. Very great spirits alone resist. And yet . . .

Mess Lethierry meditated continually, if absorption can be called meditation, at the base of a sort of precipice of troubles. Heartbroken words escaped him, like the following: "All that remains for me is to ask from above my ticket of departure."

Let us note a contradiction in this nature, as complex as the sea, of which Lethierry was, so to speak, the product: Mess Lethierry did not pray.

To be powerless is in itself a kind of force. In the presence of our two great blindnesses, destiny and nature, it is in his powerlessness that man has found his chief support, prayer.

Man makes his terror lend him succor; he demands aid of his fears; anxiety counsels him to kneel.

Prayer is an enormous force, peculiar to the soul, and of the same species as mystery. Prayer addresses itself to the magnanimity of the shadows; prayer looks at the mystery with the very eyes of the shadow, and before the powerful intentness of that suppliant gaze, one feels that it is possible to disarm the Unknown.

This possibility once realized is a consolation in itself. But Mess Lethierry did not pray.

While he was happy, God existed for him in flesh and blood, one might say; Lethierry spoke to Him, pledged his word to Him, almost shook hands with Him from time to time. But in Lethierry's unhappiness, God was eclipsed, a not infrequent phenomenon. This happens when one has made for one's self a good God, who is a good fellow.

In the state of mind in which Lethierry then was, there existed for him but one clear vision, Déruchette's smile. Beyond that smile, all was dark.

For some time past, no doubt on account of the loss of the Durande, the counter-shock of which she felt, this charming smile of Déruchette's had become more rare. She appeared thoughtful. Her birdlike and childlike pretty ways had disappeared. She was no longer seen to make a curtsy in the morning at the sound of the day-break gun, and say to the rising sun "Boom! . . . day. Pray take the trouble to enter." She wore a very serious air at times, a sad thing in this sweet being. Nevertheless, she made an effort to smile at Mess Lethierry and to divert him, but her gayety grew more tarnished from day to day, and became covered with dust, like the wing of a butterfly with a pin through its body.

Let us add that either out of grief for her uncle's grief, for there are such things as reflected sorrows, or for other reasons, she seemed now to incline greatly towards religion. In the days of the former rector, M. Jaquemin Hérode, she had only gone to church, as the reader knows, four times a year. She was very assiduous there now. She never missed a service, either on Sunday or on Thursday. The pious souls of the parish beheld this amendment with satisfaction. For it is great good fortune when a young girl, who runs so many risks from men, turns towards God.

This at least causes the poor parents to feel more at ease on the score of love affairs.

In the evening, whenever the weather permitted, she strolled for an hour or two in the garden of les Bravées. She was almost as pensive there as Mess Lethierry, and always alone.

Déruchette was the last to go to bed. This did not prevent Douce and Grâce from always keeping an eye upon her, through that instinct for watching which is common to domestics; spying relieves the tedium of serving.

As for Mess Lethierry, in that abstracted state of his mind, these little alterations in Déruchette's habits escaped him. Moreover, he had not been born a duenna. He did not even notice Déruchette's punctual attendance at the parish services. Always tenacious in his prejudices against things and people pertaining to the clergy, he would have viewed this frequentation of church with no pleasure.

It was not because his own moral condition was not in process of modification. Grief is a cloud and changes its form.

Robust souls, as we have just said, are sometimes, by certain blows of ill fortune, almost if not wholly thrown off their bearings. Virile characters, like Lethierry, react in a given time. Despair has ascending degrees. From prostration one mounts to despondency, from despondency to affliction, from affliction to melancholy. Melancholy is a twilight. Suffering melts into it in sombre joy.

Melancholy is the happiness of being sad.

These mournful alterations were not made for Lethierry; neither the nature of his temperament nor the character of his unhappiness was adapted to these delicate shades. But at the moment when we find him again, the reverie of his first despair had been, for about a week, tending to dissipate; without being less sad, Lethierry was less inert; he was still sombre, but he was no longer gloomy; a certain perception of facts and events had come back to him; and he had begun to experience something of that phenomenon which may be called the re-entrance into reality.

Thus, during the day, in the lower room, he did not listen to the people's words but he heard them. Grâce came in triumph one morning to tell Déruchette that Mess Lethierry had broken the wrapper of a newspaper.

This half acceptance of reality is, in itself, a good symptom.

It is convalescence. Great misfortunes stun. It is in this way that one emerges from the shock. But this amelioration first produces an aggravation of the evil. The previous state of dreaminess blunted the suffering; one saw indistinctly; one felt but little; now the vision is clear, one escapes nothing, one bleeds at everything. Pain is accentuated by all the details which one perceives. One beholds all again in memory. To remember all is to regret all. There are all sorts of bitter aftertastes in this return to the real. One is better and, at the same time, worse. This was Lethierry's experience. His sufferings were more distinct.

It was a shock which had restored Mess Lethierry to the sense of reality.

Let us describe what this shock was.

One afternoon about the fifteenth or twentieth of April, the two knocks which announced the postman had been heard at the door of the big room of les Bravées. Douce had opened the door. It was, in fact, a letter.

This letter came from the sea. It was addressed to Mess Lethierry. It was postmarked Lisbon.

Douce had carried the letter to Mess Lethierry, who was shut up in his chamber. He had taken the letter, placed it mechanically on the table, and had not glanced at it.

This letter remained a full week on the table, with its seal unbroken.

But one morning it chanced that Douce said to Mess Lethierry,—

"Monsieur, shall I brush the dust off from your letter?"

Lethierry appeared to wake up.

"All right," said he.

And he opened the letter.

He read as follows,—

AT SEA, MARCH 10.

MESS LETHIERRY, of Saint-Sampson:

You will be glad to receive tidings of me. I am aboard the *Tamaulipas,* bound for Nevercome-back. Among the crew there is a sailor, Ahier-Tostevin, of Guernsey, who *will* come back, and who will have some things to tell you. I take advantage of our speaking the ship *Hernan Cortez,* bound for Lisbon, to send you this letter.

Be astonished, I am an honest man.

As honest as Sieur Clubin.

I am bound to believe that you know what has occurred; nevertheless, it may not be superfluous for me to inform you.

Here it is.

I have restored your money to you.

I borrowed from you, somewhat irregularly, fifty thousand francs. Before leaving Saint-Malo, I handed to your confidential man, Sieur Clubin, three bank notes of a thousand pounds each, making seventy-five thousand francs.

You will, no doubt, find this reimbursement sufficient. Sieur Clubin protected your interests and took your money with energy. He struck me as very zealous, which is my reason for notifying you.

Your other confidential man,

RANTAINE

P.S. Sieur Clubin had a revolver, which explains why I have no receipt.

Touch a torpedo, touch a charged Leyden jar, and you will experience what Lethierry felt on reading this letter.

Beneath that envelope, in that sheet of paper folded in four, to which he had paid so little attention at first, there was a commotion.

He recognized the writing, he recognized the signature. As for the fact, at the first moment he understood nothing about it.

Such a commotion it was, that it set his mind on its feet again, so to speak.

This phenomenon of the seventy-five thousand francs confided by Rantaine to Clubin, being an enigma, was the useful feature of the shock, in that it forced Lethierry's brain to work. Conjecture is a healthy occupation for the mind. Reason is awakened, logic is called forth.

For some time past, public opinion in Guernsey had been occupied in rejudging Clubin, that honest man for so many years, so unanimously regarded with esteem. People began to question and to have their doubts; there were wagers laid for and against. Singular lights had been thrown on the subject. Clubin began to be illuminated, that is to say, he became black.

A judicial investigation had taken place in Saint-Malo to learn what had become of coastguardsman number 619. Legal perspicacity had gone astray, which is frequently the case. It had started with the supposition that the coastguardsman must have been enticed away by Zuela, and embarked on board the *Tamaulipas* for Chile. This ingenious hypothesis had gone astray in many respects. The shortsightedness of justice had not even perceived Rantaine. But during the investigation, the examining magistrates had come upon other trails.

This obscure affair was complicated. Clubin had entered into the enigma. A coincidence, perhaps a connection, had been established between the departure of the *Tamaulipas* and the loss of the Durande. Clubin had been recognized in the wineshop of the Dinan gate, where he thought he was not known; the keeper of the shop had talked. Clubin had bought a bottle of brandy.

For whom?

The gunsmith of the Rue Saint-Vincent had talked. Clubin had bought a revolver.

Against whom?

The landlord of the Jean Tavern had talked. Clubin had been inexplicably absent.

Captain Gertrais-Gaboureau had talked. Clubin had been determined to set out, although warned, and aware that he was going to meet the fog.

The crew of the Durande had talked. In fact, a full cargo was not taken, and the stowage was badly done, a piece of negligence easy to understand if a captain desires to wreck his vessel.

The Guernsey passenger had talked. Clubin had fancied that he was wrecked on the Hanways.

The people of Torteval had talked. Clubin had gone thither a few days before the loss of the Durande, and had strolled towards Plainmount, close to the Hanways. He carried a valise.

"He went away with it, and he returned without it."

The bird-nesters had talked. Their story might seem to have some connection with Clubin's disappearance, provided only that smugglers were substitutes for the ghosts.

Lastly, the haunted house of Plainmont itself had spoken. People determined to investigate the matter had climbed up into it, and had found there,—what? That same valise of Clubin's.

The Douzaine of Torteval had seized the bag and had it opened. It contained provisions, a spyglass, a chronometer, a man's clothing, and linen marked with Clubin's initials.

All this was construed in the gossip of Saint-Malo and of Guernsey, and ended in a decision of something like barratry.

The confused features of the case were brought together; they proved a singular disregard of advice, an acceptance of the chances of the fog, a suspicious negligence in the stowage, a bottle of brandy, a drunken helmsman, a substitution of the captain himself for the helmsman, a turn of the helm which was very awkward, to say the least. The heroism of remaining on the wreck became knavery.

However, Clubin had mistaken the reef. The intention of barratry admitted, the choice of the Hanways was understood, the coast easily reached by swimming, a sojourn in the haunted house while awaiting an opportunity to escape. The valise, that provision for emergencies, completed the proof. By what bond this adventure was connected with that of the coastguardsman could not be perceived. Some connection was suspected, nothing more. In connection with that man, the guard number 619, a glimpse of a whole tragic drama was to be seen. Perhaps Clubin had played no part in it, but he could be perceived in the side scenes.

All was not explained by barratry. There was an unemployed revolver. This revolver probably belonged to the other affair.

The scent of the people is fine and just. Public instinct excels in these restorations of the truth made of bits and morsels. Only, in these facts, whence probable barratry stood forth, there existed serious uncertainties.

All held good, all agreed; but the basis was lacking.

No one wrecks a vessel for the pleasure of wrecking it. No one runs all those risks of the fog, the reef, swimming, concealment, and flight, without some interest in the matter. What could have been Clubin's interest?

His act was seen, but not his motive.

Hence, a doubt in many minds.

Where there is no motive, it seems as though there were no act.

The gap was an important one.

This gap had just been filled by Rantaine's letter.

This letter gave Clubin's motive. Seventy-five thousand francs to steal.

Rantaine was the *Deus ex machina*. He had descended from the clouds with a candle in his hand.

His letter furnished the final gleam of light.

It explained all, and announced in addition a witness,—Ahier-Tostevin.

A decisive point, it explained the employment for the revolver. Rantaine was, undoubtedly, thoroughly posted in the matter. His letter permitted one to lay one's finger on the whole.

No extenuation was possible to Clubin's villainy. He had premeditated the shipwreck, and the proof was the valise carried to the haunted house. And even supposing him to be innocent, admitting the wreck to be accidental, ought he not at the last moment, having made up his mind to sacrifice himself on the wreck, to have handed the seventy-five thousand francs for Mess Lethierry, to the men who were escaping in the long-boat? The evidence was startling. What had become of Clubin now? He had probably been the victim of his mistake. He had doubtless perished on the Douvres reef.

This structure of conjectures, very nearly answering, as it will be seen, to the reality, occupied Mess Lethierry's mind for many days. Raintaine's letter rendered him the service of forcing him to think. There was a first shock of surprise, then he made the effort at reflection. He made a still more difficult effort,—to obtain information. He was obliged to listen to, and even to seek conversation. At the end of the week, he had become practical to a certain extent; his mind had regained coherence, and was almost restored. He had emerged from his troubled state.

Admitting that Mess Lethierry had ever been able to entertain any hope of reimbursement from Rantaine, this letter had caused his last chance to vanish.

It added to the catastrophe of the Durande this new shipwreck of seventy-five thousand francs. It put him in possession of that money just enough to make him feel its loss. This letter revealed to him the very bottom of his ruin.

Hence a new suffering, and a very acute one, which we have just pointed out. He began—a thing which he had not done for two months—to take an interest in his household, in what was to become of it, in what must be reformed about it. Petty annoyances at a thousand points, almost worse than despair. To undergo your misfortune in detail, to dispute, foot by foot, with an accomplished foe, the ground which it has just wrested from you, is odious. Misfortune can be accepted in the mass, not piecemeal. The great total may overwhelm, but the detail tortures. Just now catastrophe struck you like a thunderbolt, now it trifles with you.

It is humiliation aggravating ruin. It is a second and hideous desolation added to the first, one step nearer annihilation. After the shroud, the rag.

There is no sadder thought than that one is diminishing.

To be ruined seems simple. A violent blow, the brutality of fate, that is catastrophe once for all. So be it. One accepts it. All is over. One is ruined. Very well, one is dead. Not at all. One is alive. One perceived it on the very next day. To what? To pin-pricks. Such and such a passer-by does not salute you, the merchants shower down their bills upon you, yonder is one of your enemies, laughing. Perhaps he is laughing at Arnal's last pun, but all the same, that pun only seems so charming to him because you are ruined.

You read your fall even in glances of indifference. The people who used to dine with you consider three courses too much on your table; your defects are apparent to every one; cases of ingratitude no longer wait, but proclaim themselves; every fool has foreseen what has happened to you, the malicious rend you, the worst pity you.

And then, a hundred petty details. Nausea follows tears. You have drunk wine, you must now drink cider. Two servant maids. That is one too many. This one must be discharged, and that one work harder. There are too many flowers in the garden; potatoes must be planted. You have been in the habit of giving fruit to your friends; you will now have it sold in the market. As for the poor, they are no longer to be thought of; are you not poor yourself?

Dress, a painful question. Deprive a woman of a ribbon, what torture! Refuse adornment to her who gives you her beauty. To act like a miser! Perhaps she will say to you: "What, you have taken the flowers from my garden, and now you are taking them from my bonnet!" Alas! to condemn her to faded gowns! The family table is silent. You fancy that those around you are angry with you. Beloved faces are careworn. This is what coming down in the world means. You must die again each day. To fall is nothing, it is the furnace. To come down is a slow fire.

Collapse is Waterloo; diminution is Saint Helena. Fate, incarnate in the shape of Wellington, still retains some dignity; but when it becomes Hudson Lowe, what meanness! Destiny becomes a contemptible dastard. One beholds the man of Campo Formio quarrelling about a pair of silk stockings. Humiliating Napoleon, who humiliated England.

Every ruined man traverses these two phases, Waterloo and Saint Helena, reduced to humbler proportions.

On the evening to which we have referred, and which was one of the first evenings in May, Lethierry, leaving Déruchette strolling in the garden by moonlight, went to bed sadder than ever.

All those petty and unpleasant details, complications of lost fortunes, all these preoccupations of the third order, which begin by being insipid and end by being gloomy, were rolling about in his mind. Disagreeable accumulation of miseries.

Mess Lethierry felt his fall to be irremediable. What was to be done? What was to become of him? What sacrifices must he impose on Déruchette? Which should he dismiss, Douce or Grâce? Should he sell les Bravées? Should they not be reduced to quitting the island? To be nothing, where one has been everything, is in every truth an intolerable descent.

And the idea that all was over! To recall those trips which bound France to the Archipelago, those Tuesdays of sailing, those Fridays of return, that throng upon the quay, those great cargoes, that industry, that prosperity, that direct and proud navigation, that machinery into which man puts his will, that all-powerful boiler, that smoke, that reality! The steamer is the compass completed; the compass indicates the straight road, the steamer follows it. The one proposes, the other executes.

Where was she, his Durande, his magnificent and sovereign Durande, that mistress of the sea, that queen which made him king! To have been in his country the man of ideas, the man of success, the man of revolution! to renounce it! to abdicate! To exist no longer! to become a laughing stock! To be an empty sack which once was filled! To belong to the past when one has been the future, to end in the haughty pity of idiots, to see the triumph of routine, obstinacy, the beaten track, egotism, ignorance! To behold the going and coming of the old-fashioned coasters, the sport of the waves, stupidly begin again; to see the antiquated grow young again; to have wasted his life; to have been a light, and to suffer eclipse!

Ah! how beautiful upon the waves had been that proud smoke stack, that prodigious cylinder, that pillar with a capital of smoke, that column grander than the Vendôme column, for upon the one there is only a conquered man, while upon the other there is Progress! The ocean had been subdued. It was certainty on the open sea. This had been seen in that little isle, in that little port, in little Saint-Sampson? Yes, it had been seen. Indeed, it had been seen and it would never be seen again!

All this throng of regrets tortured Lethierry. There are mental sobbings. Never, perhaps, had he felt his loss more bitterly. A certain stupor follows these acute attacks. Beneath this weight of sadness he fell into a doze.

He remained for about two hours with closed eyes, sleeping a little, thinking much, feverish. These stupors hide an obscure and very fatiguing labor of the brain. Towards the middle of the night, about midnight, a little earlier or a little later, he shook off this doze. He woke, he opened his eyes, his window faced his hammock, he beheld an extraordinary thing.

A form was in front of his window. An unprecedented form. The smoke stack of a steamer.

Mess Lethierry sat upright with a sudden movement. The hammock oscillated as in the agitation of a tempest. Lethierry gazed. There was a vision in front of the window. The port, flooded with moonlight, was framed in its panes, and against that brightness, quite close to the house, there was outlined, upright, round, and black, a superb silhouette.

The funnel of an engine was there.

Lethierry sprang out of his hammock, ran to the window, raised the sash, leaned out and recognized it.

The smoke stack of the Durande was before him. It was in its old place. Its four chains held it moored to the rail of a boat in which, beneath it, a mass of complicated form could be distinguished. Lethierry retreated, turned his back to the window, and fell back upon the hammock in a sitting posture.

He turned round again, and again he beheld the vision.

A moment later, in the time required for a flash of lightning, he was on the quay, lantern in hand.

To the Durande's former mooring-ring was moored a bark bearing, a little towards the stern, a massive block from which the smoke stack rose straight before the window of les Bravées. The bow of the bark ran out beyond the corner of the wall of the house, flush with the quay.

There was no one on the boat.

This bark had a form peculiar to itself, which all Guernsey could have described. It was the paunch.

Lethierry leaped into it. He ran to the mass which he perceived beyond the mast. It was the engine.

There it was, complete, entire, intact, squarely planted on its cast-iron flooring; the boiler had all its rivets; the paddle-shaft was set up on end and lashed near the boiler; the brine-pump was in its place, nothing was missing.

Lethierry inspected the engine.

The lantern and the moon aided each other in lighting him. He passed the whole mechanism in review. He saw the two boxes which stood beside it. He looked at the paddle-shaft.

He went to the cabin. It was empty.

He returned to the engine and touched it. He thrust his head into the boiler. He knelt down in order to look inside.

He set his lantern in the furnace, and its light illuminated the whole mechanism, and almost produced the optical illusion of a lighted engine.

Then he burst into a laugh, and, drawing himself up, with his eyes riveted upon the engine, his arms outstretched towards the funnel, he cried, "Help!"

The port bell was situated on the quay, a few paces distant, he ran to it, seized the chain, and began to jerk the bell furiously.

II
Again the Port Bell

GILLIATT had, in fact, arrived at Saint-Sampson after nightfall, nearer ten o'clock than nine, after a trip devoid of incident, but a little slow, owing to the weight of his cargo.

Gilliatt had calculated the hour. The half-flood had made. There was moonlight and water, so that he could enter the port.

The little harbor was asleep. A few vessels were anchored there, their sails brailed upon the yards, topsails furled, and without lights. At the further end several fishing boats under repair were visible on the careenage. Great dismasted and stripped hulls, lifting above their planking, pierced with openings here and there, the curving points of their denuded framework, bearing a strange resemblance to dead beetles lying on their backs with their legs in the air.

As soon as he had passed the mouth of the harbor, Gilliatt examined the port and the quay. There was no light anywhere, either at les Bravées or elsewhere. There were no passers-by, with the exception, perhaps, of a man who had just entered or left the parsonage. And even then, one could not be sure that it was a person, since the night blurs all that it draws, and the moonlight never makes anything otherwise than indistinct. Distance added to the obscurity. The parsonage of that day was situated on the other side of the port, on the place where a covered shipyard has been constructed at the present day.

Gilliatt had quietly come alongside of les Bravées, and

had moored the paunch to the ring of the Durande, under Mess Lethierry's window.

Then he had leaped over the rail and landed.

Gilliatt, leaving the paunch at the quay behind him, turned the corner of the house, passed through one little street, then another, did not even glance at the branch of the path which led to the Bû de la Rue, and in a few moments he halted in that nook of the wall where there were wild mallows with rose-colored flowers, in June, holly, ivy, and nettles.

It is there that, hidden under the brambles, seated on a stone, many a time on summer days, and for long hours together, and for whole months, he had gazed over the wall, which was so low as to tempt him to step across, at the garden of les Bravées, and through the branches of the trees at two windows belonging to a certain chamber of the house. He found his stone, his nettle, the wall as low, the nook as dark as ever, and there he crouched down, crawling in like an animal reëntering its hole, rather than walking. Once seated, he made no further movement. He gazed.

Again he beheld the garden, the paths, the clumps of bushes, the beds of flowers, the house, the two windows of the chamber. The moon showed him this dream. It is terrible that one should be forced to breathe. He did what he could to keep from doing so.

It seemed to him that he beheld a phantom Paradise. He was afraid it would all fly away. It was almost impossible that these things should really be before his eyes, and if they were there, it could only be with the imminent danger of vanishing, always pertaining to things divine. A breath, and all would be dissipated; Gilliatt trembled at this thought.

Quite close to him, in the garden, at the edge of a walk, was a wooden bench painted green. The reader will remember this bench.

Gilliatt gazed at the two windows. He thought of the possible slumbering of some one in that chamber. Behind that wall, some one was sleeping. He would have liked to be elsewhere. He would have preferred to die rather than to go away. He thought of a breast that rose in breathing. She, that mirage, that whiteness in a cloud, that floating obsession of his mind, she was there! He thought of the inaccessible who was asleep and so near, and within reach, as it were, of his ecstasy; he thought of the impossible woman sleeping, and visited also by visions; of the creature longed for, distant, indiscernible, with her eyes closed and her brow in her hand; of the mystery of the slumber of the ideal being; of the dreams possible to a dream.

He dared not think beyond that, and yet he did; he ventured into almost disrespectful familiarity in his reverie, the quantity of feminine form which an angel can have disturbed him, the hours of night emboldened timid eyes to furtive glances, he was vexed with himself for going so far, he feared to profane by reflection upon it; in spite of himself, forced, constrained, quivering, he gazed into the invisible. He endured the thrill and almost the pain, of picturing to himself a petticoat on a chair, a mantle flung on the carpet, a girdle loosened, a fichu. He imagined a corset with its lace trailing on the ground, stockings, garters. His soul was in the stars. The stars are made for the human heart of a poor man like Gilliatt no less than for the human heart of a millionaire. Up to a certain degree of passion, every man is subject to profoundly dazzling impressions. If his be a wild and primitive nature, this is all the more true. An uncultivated mind is most susceptible of reverie.

Ecstasy is a fulness which overflows like any other. The sight of those windows was almost too much for Gilliatt.

All at once he beheld her herself.

From amid the branches of a thicket which had already been made dense by the spring, there came forth, with an ineffable, spectral, and celestial slowness, a figure, a robe, a divine face, almost a radiance under the moon.

Gilliatt felt himself grow weak; it was Déruchette.

Déruchette approached. She paused. She retreated several steps as though to return, paused again, then came back and seated herself on the wooden bench. The moon shone through the trees, a few clouds wandered among the pale stars, the sea murmured to the gloom in a low tone, the town was asleep, a mist was rising from the horizon, the melancholy was profound.

Déruchette inclined her head, with that pensive glance which gazes attentively at nothing; she was seated in profile; she was almost bareheaded, having a cap, but untied, which allowed a view of the commencement of hair on the nape of her dainty neck; she was mechanically twisting one string of this cap round her finger, the half gloom outlined her statue-like hands; her gown was of one of those shades which by night appear white; the trees rustled as though sensible of the enchantment which emanated from her; the tip of one of her feet was visible; in her downcast lids there was that vague contraction which indicates a repressed tear, or a thought suppressed; her arms had the ravishing indecision of not knowing where to rest themselves, something floating was mingled with her whole attitude, it was a gleam rather than a light; the grace of a goddess; the folds of the bottom of her skirt were exquisite, her adorable face was rapt in virgin meditation. She was so near that it was terrible. Gilliatt could hear her breathe.

In the darkness a nightingale was singing. The stirring of the wind among the branches set in motion the ineffable silence of the night. Déruchette, pretty and divine, appeared in this twilight like the resultant of these rays and these perfumes; this immense and scattered charm ended mysteriously in her, and was there concentrated, and in her was it flowering. She seemed the flower-soul of all that shadow.

All that shadow hovering about Déruchette weighed upon Gilliatt. He was bewildered. What he felt transcends words; emotion is always new, and words have been always in use; hence the impossibility of expressing emotion. There is such a thing as the overwhelming of rapture. To see Déruchette, to see her herself, to see her dress, her cap, to see the ribbon which she was rolling round her finger,—can such a thing be imagined? Was it possible he was near her? He heard her breathe—so she did breathe? Then the stars breathe.

Gilliatt was thrilled. He was the most miserable and the most intoxicated of men. He knew not what to do. The delirium of beholding her was annihilating him.

What! was she really there, was he really here? His ideas, dazzled and fixed, rested upon this creature as upon a precious stone. He gazed at that neck and hair. He did not even tell himself that all was now his, that in a short time, to-morrow, perhaps, he should have the right to take off that cap, he should have the right to untie that ribbon. He had never for a moment conceived such an excess of audacity as to dream of that. To touch with the thought is almost the same as to touch with the hand. Love was to Gilliatt what honey is to the bear, a delicate and exquisite dream. He thought confusedly. He did not know what possessed him. The nightingale sang. He felt as if he were about to expire.

To rise, to leap over the wall, to approach, to say, "it is I," to speak to Déruchette,—such an idea never occurred to him. If it had occurred to him, he would have fled. If anything approaching a thought did succeed in making its way through his mind, it was this, that Déruchette was there, that he needed nothing more, and that this was the beginning of eternity.

A noise aroused her from her reverie, and him from his ecstasy.

Some one was walking in the garden. Who it was could not be seen, because of the trees. It was the footstep of a man.

Déruchette raised her eyes.

The steps drew near, then ceased. The person who had been walking had stopped. He must be very close at hand. The path on which the bench stood wound between two clumps of bushes. The person was there, in that passage, a few paces from the bench.

Chance had so arranged the denseness of the branches that Déruchette could see while Gilliatt could not.

The moon cast a shadow on the ground from the thicket to the bench.

Gilliatt saw this shadow.

He looked at Déruchette.

She was very pale. Her half open mouth gave vent to a cry of surprise. She had half risen from the bench and fallen back upon it. There was a mixture of fright and fascination in her attitude. Her astonishment was an enchantment full of fear. She wore upon her lips almost the radiance of a smile, and in her eyes a gleam of tears. She was as though transfigured by a presence. It did not seem as though the being whom she beheld could be of this earth. The reflection of an angel was in her gaze.

The being, who was only a shadow to Gilliatt, spoke. A voice proceeded from the thicket, sweeter than the voice of woman, but a man's voice, nevertheless. Gilliatt heard these words,—

"Mademoiselle, I see you every Sunday and Thursday; I am told that formerly you did not come so often. It is a remark which has been made, and I beg your pardon. I have never spoken to you, it was my duty; to-day I speak to you, it is my duty. I must first address myself to you. The *Cashmere* sails to-morrow. This is why I am come. You walk in your garden every evening. It would be an ill thing in me to know your habits, if I did not cherish my present intention. Mademoiselle, you are poor; after to-morrow I shall be rich. Will you have me for your husband?"

Déruchette clasped her hands like a suppliant, and gazed at the man who was speaking to her, mute, with fixed eyes, trembling from head to foot.

The voice continued,—

"I love you. God has not made the heart of man to keep silence. Since God promises eternity, it is because he wishes man not to be alone. There is for me one woman on earth: it is you. I think of you as of a prayer. My faith is in God, and my hope is in you. The wings which I have, you wear. You are my life, and my heaven already."

"Monsieur," said Déruchette, "there is no one in the house to answer you."

The voice rose again,—

"I have cherished this sweet dream. God does not forbid dreams. You produce upon me the effect of glory. I love you passionately, mademoiselle. You are holy innocence. I know that this is the hour when all your household are asleep, but I had no choice of any other moment. Do you remember the passage in the Bible which was read to us? Genesis, chapter twenty-five! I have thought of it ever since. I have often read it over. The Reverend Hérode said to me: 'You need a rich wife.' I answered him, 'No, I need a poor wife.' Mademoiselle, I speak to you without approaching you. I will even retreat farther back if you desire that my shadow should not touch your feet. You are the sovereign, you shall come to me if you will. I love and I wait. You are the living form of benediction."

"Monsieur," stammered Déruchette, "I did not know that I had been noticed on Sundays and Thursdays."

The voice continued,—

"One cannot contend against angelic things. Love is all the law. Marriage is Canaan. You are the promised land of beauty. O full of grace, I salute you."

Déruchette replied,—

"I did not think that I was doing any more harm than other people who were constant in attendance."

The voice pursued,—

"God has set his intentions in the flowers, in the dawn, in the spring,—it is his will that we should love. You are beautiful in this sacred gloom of night. This garden has been cultivated by you, and in its perfumes there is something of your breath. Mademoiselle, the meetings of souls do not depend upon themselves. It is no fault of ours. You were present, nothing more; I was there, nothing more. I have done nothing but feel that I loved you. Sometimes my eyes were raised to you. I was in the wrong, but what was I to do? It was while looking at you that it all came about. One cannot help one's self. There are mysterious wills above us. The first of temples is the heart. The terrestrial paradise to which I aspire is to have your soul in my house; do you consent to it? As long as I was poor, I said nothing. I know your age, you are twenty-one. I am twenty-six. I go to-morrow; if you refuse me, I shall not return. Be my betrothed, will you? My eyes have already put this question to you more than once, in spite of me. I love you, answer me. I will speak to your uncle as soon as he can receive me, but I turn to you, first of all. It is to Rebecca that one pleads for Rebecca. Unless you do not love me."

Déruchette bent her head and murmured,—

"Oh! I adore him!"

This was spoken so low that only Gilliatt heard it.

She remained with bowed head, as if by hiding her face in the shadow she could conceal her thoughts.

A pause ensued. The leaves on the trees did not stir. It was a solemn and peaceful moment when the slumber of things is added to the slumber of beings, and when the night seems to be listening to the heart throbs of nature. In this musing-time there rose, like a harmony completing silence, the immense murmur of the sea.

The voice began again,—

"Mademoiselle."

Déruchette started.

The voice continued,—

"Alas! I am waiting."

"For what are you waiting?"

"Your reply."

"God has heard it," said Déruchette.

Then the voice became almost sonorous, and, at the same time, sweeter than ever. These words proceeded from the thicket, as from a burning bush,—

"Thou are my affianced bride. Rise and come. May the blue canopy wherein lie the stars be present at this acceptance of my soul by thy soul, and may our first kiss be mingled with the firmament!"

Déruchette rose, and remained motionless for a moment, her gaze riveted before her, no doubt upon another's eyes. Then, with slow steps, her head erect, her arms drooping, and her fingers outspread, as when one treads upon unfamiliar ground, she went toward the thicket and disappeared.

A moment later, instead of one shadow on the sandy walk there were two. They were mingled together, and Gilliatt saw at his feet the embrace of these two shadows.

Time flows from us as from an hourglass, and we have no consciousness of its flight, especially at certain supreme moments. On the one hand, this couple, who were ignorant of the presence of this witness, and who did not see him; on the other hand, this witness who did not see this couple, but who knew that they were there,—how many minutes did they remain thus in that mysterious suspense? It would be impossible to say.

All at once, a distant noise broke forth, a voice shouted,

"Help!" and the port bell sounded. It is probable that this intoxicated and celestial happiness did not hear the tumult.

The bell continued to ring. Any one who sought Gilliatt in the corner of the wall would not have found him there.

BOOK SECOND
GRATITUDE PLAYS THE DESPOT

I
JOY SURROUNDED BY ANGUISH

MESS LETHIERRY rang the bell furiously. All at once he stopped. A man had just turned the corner of the quay. It was Gilliatt.

Mess Lethierry ran to him, or to speak more accurately, flung himself upon him, seized his hand between his own, and gazed into his eyes for a moment in silence. The silence of an explosion that knows not where to break forth.

Then, violently shaking and pulling him, and straining him in his arms, he made Gilliatt enter the lower room of les Bravées, with his heel pushed back the door, which remained half open, seated himself or rather fell upon a chair beside a large table lighted by the moon, whose reflection vaguely whitened Gilliatt's face, and, in a voice which was composed of mingled bursts of laughter and sobs, he cried,—

"Ah! my son! the man of the bagpipe! Gilliatt! I knew well that it was you! The paunch, parbleu! Tell me about it. So you went! You would have been burned a hundred years ago. It is magic! Not a screw is missing. I have already looked at everything, recognized everything, handled everything. I guess that the two paddle wheels are in those two boxes. Here you are at last! I have just been looking for you in the cabin. I rang the bell. I was in search of you. I said to myself: 'Where is he, that I may devour him?' One must admit that extraordinary things take place. This creature has returned from the Douvres reef. He brings me back my life. Thunder! You are an angel. Yes, yes, yes, 'tis my engine. No one will believe it. They will see it and will say: 'It is not true.' All is there, indeed! Everything is there! Not a screw thread is missing. Not a bolt is lacking. The tube for the feed pipe has not budged. It is incredible that it should have suffered no injury. It only needs a little oiling. But how did you manage it? And to think that the Durande will go again! The wheel-shaft is dismounted as though by a jeweller. Give me your word of honor that I am not mad."

He stood erect, took breath, and went on,—

"Swear that to me. What a revolution! I pinch myself. I feel plainly that I am not dreaming. You are my child, you are my boy, you are my good Providence. Ah! my son! To go and get my rascally engine! On the open ocean! In that snare of a reef! I have seen very queer things in my life. I have never seen anything like this. I have seen Parisians who were devils. I scorn the idea that they could do that! 'Tis worse than the Bastille. I have seen the gauchos tilling the pampas, they have for a plough the branch of a tree with an elbow to it, and for harrow, a fagot of thorns drawn by a leather rope, and with these they harvest grains of wheat as large as hazel nuts. 'Tis a mere trifle by the side of you. You have performed a miracle, in very truth. Ah! the scamp! Come, throw yourself on my neck! We shall owe you the whole prosperity of the country. How they will growl in Saint-Sampson! I am going to busy myself instantly with making the boat over again. 'Tis astounding there is nothing broken about the connecting rod. Gentlemen, he has been to the Douvres. I say the Douvres. He went all alone. The Douvres! the worst stumbling-block in existence. Do you know? have they told you? it has been proved, it was done intentionally; Clubin sank the Durande for the sake of swindling me out of some money which he was to bring me. He got Tangrouille drunk! 'Tis a long tale, I will tell you about his piracy some other time. I, stupid brute that I am, had confidence in Clubin. He was caught, the rascal, for he shouldn't have gotten away. There is a God, scoundrels! You see, Gilliatt, instantly, presto! we'll have our irons in the fire and rebuild the Durande. We will add twenty feet to her. They build boats longer now. I will buy timber at Danzig and Bremen. Now that I have got the machinery, I can get credit. Confidence will return."

Mess Lethierry paused, raised his eyes, with that look which sees heaven through the ceiling, and muttered between his teeth: "There is one."

Then he placed the middle finger of his right hand between his eyebrows, with the nails resting on the bridge of his nose, which indicates a project passing through the brain, and went on,—

"Never mind; in order to begin again on a grand scale, a little ready money would have been the thing for me. Ah! if I only had my three bank notes, the seventy-five thousand francs which that brigand of a Rantaine returned to me, and which that brigand of a Clubin stole from me!"

Gilliatt silently fumbled for something in his pocket, and placed it before him. It was the leather belt which he had brought back. He opened it, and on the table spread out the belt, on the inside of which, by the light of the moon, they could decipher the word "Clubin"; he drew from the pocket of the belt a box, and from the box three bits of folded paper, which he unfolded and handed to Mess Lethierry.

Mess Lethierry examined the three pieces of paper. It was light enough to render the figures "1000" and the word "thousand" perfectly visible. Mess Lethierry took the three notes, placed them on the table, side by side, looked at them, looked at Gilliatt, remained speechless for a moment, and then came something like an eruption after an explosion.

"That too! You are a prodigy! My bank notes! All three! a thousand each! My seventy-five thousand francs! Did you go to hell itself? It is Clubin's belt. Pardieu! I read his filthy name on it. Gilliatt brings back the machinery plus the money! That's something worth putting in the newspapers. I shall purchase timber of the best quality.—I guess you must have found his carcass. Clubin rotted in some corner.—We will get the fir at Danzig and the oak at Bremen; we will have it well planked, we'll put the oak inside and the fir outside. In former times they did not build ships so well, and they lasted longer; it is because the wood was better seasoned, because they did not build so many. Perhaps we will make the hull of elm. Elm is good for the parts under water. It rots a thing to be sometimes dry and sometimes wet; elm wants to be always wet, it feeds on water. What a beautiful Durande we are going to fit out! They can't dictate terms to me. I shall have no further need for credit. I have the sous! Has the like of this Gilliatt ever been seen before? I was flat on the earth, dead. He sets me on my pins again! And I was not thinking of him in the least! He had escaped my mind. It all comes back to me now. Poor fellow!

"Oh! by the way, you know, you are to marry Déruchette."

Gilliatt placed his back against the wall, like a man who is tottering, and said very low but very distinctly,—

"No."

Mess Lethierry gave a start.

"How's this, no?"

Gilliatt replied,—

"I do not love her."

Mess Lethierry went to the window, opened it, closed it again, returned to the table, took the three bank notes, folded them, placed the iron box on top of them, scratched his head, seized Clubin's belt, flung it violently against the wall, and said,—

"There's something the matter."

He thrust his two fists into his pockets, and repeated,—

"You don't love Déruchette! So it was for me that you played the bagpipes?"

Gilliatt, with his back still to the wall, turned pale like a man near his end. As he grew pale, Lethierry grew red.

"Here's an imbecile! He does not love Déruchette! Well, make up your mind to love her, for she shall marry no one but you. What devil of a story are you telling me? Perhaps you think I believe it? Are you ill? Very well, send for the doctor, but don't talk nonsense. It is not possible that you should have had time to quarrel already, and to get angry with her. It is true that lovers are so stupid! Come, have you any reasons? If you have any reasons, tell them. One does not make a goose of one's self without having a reason for it. But, however, I have cotton in my ears, perhaps I heard wrong; repeat what you said."

Gilliatt replied,—

"I said no."

"You said no. He sticks to it, the brute! There's something the matter with you, that's certain! You said no! Here's stupidity that surpasses the limits of the known world. Men get ducked for less than that. Ah! so you don't love Déruchette? Then it was for love of the old man that you have done all you have done! It was for papa's fine eyes that you went to the Douvres, that you have endured cold, that you have been hot, that you have been dying of hunger and thirst, that you have eaten the vermin of the rocks, that you have had fog, wind, and rain for a bedchamber, and that you have accomplished the task of bringing me back my engine as one brings back to a pretty woman her canary bird which has escaped. And the tempest of three days ago! Do you suppose that I don't appreciate the matter! You have had a hard time! It was while pursing up your mouth in heart shape towards my old noddle that you hewed, cut, turned, veered, dragged, filed, sawed, built, invented, planned, and performed more miracles all alone by yourself than all the saints in paradise! Ah! idiot! Yet you have bored me enough with your bagpipe. It is called a 'biniou' in Brittany. Always the same tune, you brute! Ah! you don't love Déruchette? I don't know what's the matter with you. I recall it all quite well now; I was there, in the corner; Déruchette said: 'I will marry him!' And she shall marry you! Ah! you don't love her! On reflection, I don't understand it at all. Either you are mad or I am. And here he never says a word. It can't be permitted to a man to do all that you have done, and then to say at the end of all: 'I don't love Déruchette.' One does not do people a service for the sake of putting them into a rage. Well, if you won't marry her, she shall remain a spinster. In the first place, I need you myself. You shall be the pilot of the Durande. Do you imagine that I am going to let you off like this? No, no, no, dear heart, I shall not let you go. I have got you. I won't even listen to you. Where is there a sailor like you? You are my man. Come, say something!"

In the meantime, the bell had roused the household and the neighborhood. Douce and Grâce had risen and had just entered the room, with an air of stupefaction, and without uttering a word. Grâce had a candle in her hand. A group of neighbors, bourgeois, mariners, and peasants, who had run out in haste, stood outside on the quay, staring in amazement and petrifaction at the smoke stack of the Durande in the paunch. Some, on hearing Mess Lethierry's voice in the big room, began to slip in silently, through the half-open door. Between the faces of two gossips was thrust the head of Sieur Landoys, who always had the good luck to be where he would have regretted being absent.

Great joys ask nothing better than to have witnesses. The rather scattered support which a crowd offers pleases them, they start afresh from it. Mess Lethierry suddenly perceived that he had people around him. He welcomed the audience at once.

"Ah! here you are, you fellows. 'Tis very lucky. You know the news. This man has been there, and has brought it back. Good-day, Sieur Landoys. Just now, when I woke up, I espied the smoke stack. It was under my window. Not a nail is missing in the thing. They make pictures of Napoleon; for my part, I prefer this to the battle of Austerlitz. You get out of bed, good people. The Durande comes to you while you are asleep. While you are putting on your nightcaps and blowing out your candles, there are people who are heroes. Some are a pack of cowards and idlers, they coddle their rheumatism; fortunately, that does not prevent there being madmen. These madmen go where it is necessary, and do what must be done. The man of the Bû de la Rue has just arrived from the Douvres rocks. He has fished up the Durande from the bottom of the sea, he has fished up the money from Clubin's pocket, a hole that was still deeper. But how did you do it? But you had the very devil against you, wind and sea, sea and wind. 'Tis true that you are a sorcerer. Those who say that are not so stupid, after all. The Durande has come back! tempests may rage, now; this cuts them out. My friends, I announce to you that the shipwreck is no more. I have examined the machinery. It is like new, perfectly whole! The steam valves work as though on wheels. One would declare it a thing made only yesterday morning. You know that the waste water from the engine is taken outside the boat by a tube placed in another tube, through which the cold water passes as it enters the boiler, in order to utilize the heat; well, those two tubes are there. The whole engine! And the paddle wheels too! Ah! you shall marry her!"

"Marry whom? the engine?" asked Sieur Landoys.

"No, the girl. Yes, the engine. Both. He shall be doubly my son-in-law. He shall be the captain. Good day, Captain Gilliatt. He's going to have a ship, a Durande! We're going to do business with it. There will be trade, and circulation, and commerce, and cargoes of cattle and sheep! I wouldn't give Saint-Sampson in exchange for London. And here's the author. I tell you that 'tis a great adventure. It will be read on Saturday in Father Mauger's gazette. Gilliatt the Cunning is a crafty fellow. What louis-d'ors are these?"

Mess Lethierry had just observed through the crack in the cover, that there was gold in the box which lay on the bank notes. He took it, opened it, emptied it into the palm of his hand, and placed the handful of guineas on the table.

"For the poor, Sieur Landoys, give these sovereigns in my name to the constable of Saint-Sampson. You know about Rantaine's letter? I showed it to you; well, I have the bank notes. Here's the wherewithal to purchase oak and fir, and to do carpentry. Look! Do you remember the weather of three days ago? What a massacre of wind and rain! The sky fired cannon. Gilliatt received that in the Douvres. But it did not prevent his unhooking the wreck as I unhook my watch. Thanks to him, I have become some one again. Father Lethierry's galliot is going to resume its service, ladies and gentlemen. A nutshell with two wheels and a pipe. I have always been crazy over that invention. I have always said to myself: 'I'll make one of them.' It dates from a long time back! 'Tis an idea which occurred to me in Paris, in the café at the corner of the Rue Christine and the Rue Dauphine, while reading a journal that spoke of it. Do you know that it would not embarrass Gilliatt to put Marly's machine in his fob and walk off with it? That man is of wrought iron, of tempered steel, of diamond, a mariner in good earnest, a smith, an extraordinary fellow, more astonishing than the Prince of Hohenlohe. I call him a man of mind. None of us amount to much. Sea dogs—that's you, that's myself, that's all of us; but the lion of the sea is here. Hurrah, Gilliatt! I know not what he has done, but he certainly has been a devil of a fellow, and how can you suppose that I would not give him Déruchette!"

Déruchette had been in the room for the last few moments. She had not uttered a word, she had not made a sound. She had entered like a shadow. She had seated herself, almost unnoticed, on a chair behind Mess Lethierry, as he stood there loquacious, stormy, joyous, talking loudly and with many gestures. Shortly after her, another mute apparition had entered. A man dressed in black, with a white tie, with his hat in his hand, had halted in the opening of the door. There were now many candles in the group, which had swelled slowly. These lights illuminated from one side the man clad in black; his profile, of a young and charming complexion, was outlined against the dark background with the purity of a medallion; he leaned his elbow on the corner of a panel of the door, and rested his brow on his left hand, an unconsciously graceful attitude, which set off the height of the brow by the smallness of the hand. There was a fold of anguish at the corner of his contracted lips. He scrutinized and listened with profound attention. Those present having recognized the Reverend Ebenezer Caudray, rector of the parish, had drawn aside to let him pass, but he had remained on the threshold. There was hesitation in his attitude, and decision in his glance. This glance occasionally met that of Déruchette. As for Gilliatt, either by accident or intentionally, he stood in the shadow, and only a very confused glimpse could be had of him.

At first, Mess Lethierry did not see M. Ebenezer, but he did see Déruchette. He went to her and kissed her with all the ardor which a kiss on the brow can contain. At the same time, he extended his arm towards the dark corner where Gilliatt stood.

"Déruchette," said he, "you are rich, and there is your husband."

Déruchette raised her head in bewilderment, and looked into the darkness.

Mess Lethierry continued,—

"The wedding will take place immediately; to-morrow, if possible. We will have a dispensation, and, besides, the formalities are not difficult here; the dean does what he pleases, and one is married before one has time to cry, 'Look out!' It is not as it is in France, where there are banns and publications and delays, and all the folderols. And you can boast of being the wife of a brave man, and there's nothing to be said. He's as a sailor should be, and I thought of him from the very day that I saw him come back from Herm with the little cannon. Now he has come back from the Douvres with his fortune and mine, and the fortune of the country; he is a man who will be talked about some day, more than you think possible. You said, 'I will marry him'; you shall marry him, and you will have children, and I shall be a grandfather, and you will have the good fortune to be the lady of a fine fellow who works, who is useful, who is astonishing, who is worth a hundred others, who saves the inventions of others, and who is a providence. And you, at least, will not, like nearly all the rich, proud hussies of this countryside, have married a soldier or a priest; that is to say, a man who kills or a man who lies. But what are you doing in your corner, Gilliatt? We can't see you. Douce! Grâce! everybody, some light. Illuminate my son-in-law like the day. I betroth you, my children, and here is your husband, and here is my son-in-law; he is Gilliatt of the Bû de la Rue, the good fellow, the great sailor, and you shall have no other husband, and I will have no other son-in-law. I pledge my word again on it, to God Almighty. Ah! there you are, monsieur le curé, you shall marry these young people for me."

Mess Lethierry's eye had just fallen on the Reverend Ebenezer.

Douce and Grâce had obeyed. Two candles placed on the table lighted Gilliatt from head to foot.

"How handsome he is!" cried Lethierry.

Gilliatt was hideous.

He was as he had been when he had emerged, that same morning, from the Douvres reef, in rags, with tattered elbows, a long beard, bristling hair, eyes red and bloodshot, skin peeling off his face, bleeding hands, and with bare feet. Some of the pustules made by the octopus were still visible on his hairy arms.

Lethierry contemplated him.

"He is my true son-in-law. How he has fought with the sea! he is all in rags! What shoulders! what paws! How handsome you are!"

Grâce ran to Déruchette and supported her head. Déruchette had just fainted.

II
The Leather Trunk

Saint-Sampson was on foot at daybreak, and Saint-Pierre-Port began to arrive. The resurrection of the Durande created in the island a commotion comparable with that made in the south of France by la Salette. A crowd had assembled on the quay to stare at the smoke stack projecting from the paunch. They would have liked to see and touch the machinery a little, but Lethierry, after having made a fresh and triumphant inspection of the engine by daylight, had stationed two sailors in the boat, with others to prevent all approach. Moreover, the smoke stack was enough to look at. The crowd marvelled. People talked about nothing but Gilliatt. His surname of Cunning was commented upon and emphasized; admiration was given to ending in this phrase,—

"It is not always agreeable to have in the island people capable of doing things like that."

From the outside, Mess Lethierry could be seen seated at his table in front of his window, writing, one eye on his paper, the other on the engine. He was so absorbed that he only interrupted himself once to call Douce and inquire after Déruchette. Douce replied,—

"Mademoiselle has risen and gone out."

Mess Lethierry had said,—

"She does well to take the air. She was rather ill last night because of the heat. There were a great many people in the room. And then, the surprise, the joy,—and the windows were shut, besides. She is going to have a fine husband."

And he began to write again. He had already signed and sealed two letters addressed to the most notable timber merchants of Bremen. He was just completing the sealing of the third.

The sound of a wheel on the quay made him raise his head. He leaned out and saw a boy pushing a wheelbarrow out of the path which led to the Bû de la Rue. This boy was going in the direction of Saint-Pierre-Port. In the wheelbarrow there was a yellow leather trunk studded with pewter and copper nails in patterns.

Mess Lethierry hailed the boy.

"Where are you going, boy?"

The lad halted, and replied,—

"To the *Cashmere.*"

"What for?"

"To carry this trunk."

"Well, you shall carry these three letters also."

Mess Lethierry opened the drawer of his table, took out a bit of cord, tied crosswise into one packet the three letters he had just written, and tossed the package to the boy, who caught it in both hands.

"You will say to the captain of the *Cashmere,* that it was I who wrote them, and that he is to take good care of them. There are for Germany. Bremen via London."

"I shall not speak with the captain, Mess Lethierry."

"Why?"

"The *Cashmere* is not lying at the quay."

"Ah!"

"She is in the roads."

"Quite right. Because of the sea."

"I can only speak to the skipper of the small boat."

"You will put my letters in his care."

"Yes, Mess Lethierry."

"At what hour does the *Cashmere* sail?"

"At twelve o'clock."

"At noon to-day, the tide rises. She has the tide against her."

"But she has the wind with her."

"Boy," said Mess Lethierry, pointing his forefinger at the smoke stack of his engine, "do you see that? that laughs at wind and tide."

The boy put the letters in his pocket, seized the handles of the wheelbarrow once more, and resumed his way towards the town. Mess Lethierry shouted: "Douce! Grâce!"

Grâce opened the door a little way.

"What's wanted, Mess?"

"Come in and wait."

Mess Lethierry took a sheet of paper and began to write. If Grâce, as she stood behind him, had been curious and had leaned over his shoulder while he was writing, this is what she might have read:—

"I have written to Bremen for timber. I have appointments all day with carpenters, for the estimates. The rebuilding will proceed rapidly. Do you, on your side, go to the dean and get the license. I wish the marriage to take place as soon as possible; it would be better to have it immediately.

"I am busy with the Durande, do you busy yourself with Déruchette."

He dated and signed it. "Lethierry."

He did not take the trouble to seal the note, but simply folded it in four and handed it to Grâce.

"Carry this to Gilliatt."

"To the Bû de la Rue?"

"To the Bû de la Rue."

BOOK THIRD
DEPARTURE OF THE CASHMERE

I
THE HAVELET QUITE CLOSE TO THE CHURCH

SAINT-SAMPSON cannot have a crowd without Saint-Pierre being deserted. A curious thing at any given point is a suction pump. News travels rapidly in small communities; the great matter in Guernsey, beginning with sunrise, was to go and take a look at the Durande's smoke stack in front of Mess Lethierry's windows. Every other event was eclipsed in the presence of this one.

Eclipse of the death of the Dean of St. Asaph; there was no longer any question of the Reverend Ebenezer Caudray, nor of his sudden wealth, nor of his departure by the *Cashmere*. The engine of the Durande brought back from the Douvres, such was the order of the day. People did not believe it. The shipwreck had appeared extraordinary, but salvage seemed impossible. They vied with each other in making sure of the fact with their own eyes. Every other occupation was suspended. Long files of bourgeois in families, from the *vésin* (neighbor) to the Mess, men, women, gentlemen, mothers with children, children with their dolls, betook themselves along all the roads towards "the thing to see," at les Bravées, and turned their backs on Saint-Pierre-Port.

Many shops in Saint-Pierre-Port were closed; in the Commercial Arcade there was absolute stagnation of sales and negotiations; all attention was absorbed by the Durande; not a merchant had made his first sale, with the exception of a jeweller, who was much amazed to have sold a wedding ring, "to a sort of man who seemed in great haste, and who had inquired of him where the house of monsieur the dean was situated."

The shops which remained open were places for gossip, where the miraculous salvage was noisily discussed. Not a promenader on the Hyvreuse, which is now called, no one knows why, Cambridge Park; no one in High Street, which was then called Grand' Rue; nor in Smith Street, which was then called the Rue des Forges; no one in Hauteville; the Esplanade itself was deserted. One would have taken it for Sunday. A royal highness on a visit, reviewing the militia at Ancresse, would not have emptied the town more thoroughly. All this disorder in consequence of a mere "nothing at all" like that Gilliatt, made grave men and correct persons shrug their shoulders.

The church of Saint-Pierre-Port, a triple gable in juxtaposition with transept and spire, is situated at the water's edge near the extremity of the port, almost at the very landing. It welcomes those who arrive and bids the departing God-speed. This church is the capital letter of the long line which the façade presents to the town.

It is, at the same time, the parish church of Saint-Pierre-Port, and deanery of the whole island. It has for its officiating priest the surrogate of the bishop, a clergyman endowed with plenary powers.

The haven of Saint-Pierre-Port, a very fine and very large harbor at the present day, was at that epoch, and even only ten years ago, less considerable than the port of Saint-Sampson. There were two huge, cyclopean, curving walls, starting from the shore on starboard and port and almost uniting at their extremities, where there was a small, white lighthouse. Below this lighthouse a narrow entrance, still having the double ring of the chain which closed it in the Middle Ages, gave passage to ships.

Let the reader picture to himself the half-open claw of a lobster—this was the haven of Saint-Pierre-Port. This claw took from the abyss a little sea, which it forced to remain quiet. But when there was an east wind the waves poured through the narrow channel, the harbor was covered with a choppy sea, and it was wiser not to enter. This is what the *Cashmere* had done that day. She had anchored in the roads.

When the wind was from the east, vessels preferred to take this course, especially as it relieved them from port dues. In that case, the boatmen licensed by the town, a brave tribe of mariners whom the new port has driven to beggary, came with their boats to the landing, or to stations on the beach, to pick up the voyagers, and transported them and their baggage, often through very rough seas, and always without accident, to the ships about to sail. The east wind is a slanting wind, very good for the trip to England; the vessel rolls, but does not pitch.

When the ship to sail was in the port, every one embarked in the port; when it lay in the roads, a person had his choice of embarking from one of the points on the shore near the moorings. There were "unlicensed" boatmen in all the inlets.

The Havelet was one of these inlets. This tiny harbor was quite close to the town, but so deserted that it seemed very far off. It owed its solitude to being encased in the lofty cliffs of Fort George, which commands this retired cove. The Havelet could be reached by many paths. The most direct skirted the edge of the water; it possessed the advantage of leading to town and to the church in five minutes, and the inconvenience of being covered by the waves twice a day. The other paths, more or less abrupt, plunged into the crevices of the cliffs.

The Havelet lay in shadow, even in broad daylight. Blocks out of the perpendicular overhung it on all sides. It bristled with a dense mass of nettles and undergrowth which formed a sort of gentle night over this disorder of rocks and waves; nothing could be more peaceful than this inlet in calm weather, nothing more tumultuous when the water was rough. There were tips of branches there perpetually damp with foam. In spring, it was full of flowers, nests, perfumes, birds, butterflies, and bees. Thanks to recent improvements, these things no longer exist; they have been replaced by fine, straight lines;

there are bits of masonry, quays, and little gardens; embankments have become popular; taste has executed justice on the singularities of the cliffs and the irregular-shaped rocks.

II
All in Despair

IT was a little before ten o'clock in the morning, "a quarter before," as they say in Guernsey.

The flood of people seemed to be increasing at Saint-Sampson. The population, fevered with curiosity, streamed to the north of the island, and the Havelet, which lies on the south, was more deserted than ever.

Nevertheless, a boat and boatman were to be seen there. In the boat there lay a travelling bag. The boatman seemed to be waiting.

The *Cashmere* could be seen lying at anchor in the roads, but as it was not to start until noon, no preparations for getting under sail were visible as yet.

If any one passing along the staircase paths of the cliff had listened, he would have heard a murmur of words in the Havelet, and, if he had leaned over the overhanging rocks, he would have seen, some distance from the boat, in a nook formed of rocks and branches, where the eye of the boatman could not penetrate, two persons, a man and a woman,—Ebenezer and Déruchette.

Those obscure niches on the sea coast which tempt maidens to the bath are not always as solitary as they are supposed to be. People are sometimes seen and listened to. Those who take refuge and shelter there can easily be followed through the dense vegetation, and, thanks to the multiplicity of paths, the granite and trees which conceal the private meeting may also conceal a witness.

Déruchette and Ebenezer were standing face to face, with their eyes riveted on each other; they clasped each other's hands. Déruchette was speaking. Ebenezer was silent. A tear which had gathered and paused between his lashes, hung there, but did not fall.

Grief and passion were stamped on Ebenezer's religious brow. A poignant resignation was added thereto,—a resignation hostile to faith, though proceeding from it. On that countenance, simply angelic up to that time, there was the beginning of a fatal expression.

He who had hitherto meditated only on dogma, was beginning to meditate on Fate, an unhealthy meditation for a priest. Faith is decomposed in it. Nothing is more disturbing than to bend under the unknown. Man is the sufferer of events.

Life is a perpetual succession! we undergo it. We never know from what quarter fate's abrupt descent will be made. Catastrophes and happiness enter, then depart, like unexpected personages. They have their law, their orbit, their gravitation, outside of man.

Virtue does not bring happiness, crime does not bring unhappiness; conscience has one logic, fate has another; no coincidence. Nothing can be foreseen. We live pell-mell, and in confusion. Conscience is a straight line, life is a whirlwind. This whirlwind unexpectedly casts black chaos and blue skies upon the head of man.

Fate does not understand the art of transitions. Sometimes the wheel turns so rapidly that man hardly distinguishes the interval between one revolution and another, and the bond between yesterday and to-day.

Ebenezer was a believer whose faith was mingled with reasoning, and a priest who was subject to passion.

Religions which impose celibacy know what they are about. Nothing undoes a priest like loving a woman.

All sorts of clouds threw a gloom over Ebenezer.

He gazed at Déruchette too long.

These two beings idolized each other.

In Ebenezer's eyes lay the mute adoration of despair.

Déruchette was saying,—

"You shall not go. I have not the strength for that.

You see I thought that I had strength enough to bid you farewell, but I have not. One cannot be forced to accomplish an impossibility. Why did you come yesterday? You should not have come if you wished to go away. I have never spoken to you. I loved you, but I did not know it. Only, that first day, when Monsieur Hérode read the story of Rebecca, and your eyes met mine, I felt my cheeks aflame, and I thought, 'Oh! how crimson Rebecca must have become!' If any one has said to me yesterday, 'You love the rector,' I should have laughed. That is the terrible thing about our love. It has been like a treason, I paid no heed to it. I went to church, I saw you, I thought that every one was like myself. I do not reproach you; you have done nothing to make me love you; you took no trouble, you looked at me; it is not your fault if you look at people; and that made me adore you. I did not suspect it. When you took the book, it was a light; when others took it, it was only a book. You sometimes cast your eyes on me. You spoke of archangels, and you were the archangel. What you said, I immediately thought. Before you came, I do not know whether I believed in God. Since you came, I have become a praying woman. I said to Douce: 'Dress me very quickly, that I may not miss the service.' And I ran to church. So that is being in love with a man. I did not know it. I said to myself: 'How devout I am becoming!' It is you who have taught me that I did not go to church for the sake of God. I went there for your sake,—that is true. You are handsome, you talk well; when you raised your arms to heaven, it seemed to me that you held my heart in your two white hands. I was mad, I did not know it. If you wish me to tell you your fault, it is this,—having entered the garden yesterday, having spoken to me. If you had said nothing to me, I should have known nothing. You would have taken your departure, I should have been sad, perhaps, but now I shall die. Now that I know that I love you, it is no longer possible that you should go away. Of what are you thinking? You do not appear to be listening to me."

Ebenezer replied,—

"You heard what was said yesterday?"

"Alas!"

"What can I do against that?"

They were silent for a moment. Ebenezer began again,—

"There is but one thing for me to do. To go away."

"And for me to die. Oh! I wish there were no sea, and that there were nothing but heaven. It seems to me that that would arrange everything, our departure would be the same. You ought not to have spoken to me. Why did you speak to me? Then do not go away! What is to become of me? I tell you that I shall die. You will be well advanced, and I shall be in the cemetery. Oh! my heart is broken. I am very unhappy. Yet my uncle is not unkind!"

This was the first time in her life that Déruchette had said "my uncle," in speaking of Mess Lethierry. Up to that day she had always said "my father."

Ebenezer retreated a step and made a sign to the boatman.

The sound of the boat hook could be heard among the boulders, and the step of the man on the edge of his bark.

"No, no!" cried Déruchette.

Ebenezer drew near to her again.

"It must be, Déruchette."

"No, never! For the sake of an engine! Is it possible! Did you see that horrible man yesterday? You cannot abandon me. You are clever, you will find a way. It cannot be that you told me to come and meet you here this morning, with the idea that you would go away. I have done nothing to you. You have no reason to complain of me. Is it by this vessel that you meant to go? I will not have it. You shall not leave me. Heaven is not opened to be thus closed again. I tell you that you shall stay. Besides, it is not yet time. Oh! I love you!"

And pressing herself against him, she crossed the ten fingers of both hands behind his neck, as though to make with her encircling arms a bond for Ebenezer, and with her clasped hands a prayer to God.

He loosed this gentle clasp, which resisted as far as it was able.

Déruchette sank back in a sitting posture on a projecting rock covered with ivy, with a mechanical gesture turning up the sleeve of her gown to the elbow, showing her charming bare arm, with a suffused and pallid light in her eyes.

The boat was approaching.

Ebenezer took her head in his two hands; this virgin had the look of a widow, and this young man had the look of an old man. He touched her hair with a sort of religious care; he fixed his gaze upon her for some moments, then he placed on her brow one of those kisses beneath which it seems as though a star must blossom forth, and, in an accent in which trembled supreme anguish, and in which the rending of a soul could be heard, he uttered this word, the word from the depths,—

"Farewell!"

Déruchette burst into sobs.

At that moment they heard a slow, grave voice saying,—

"Why should you not marry?"

Ebenezer turned his head. Déruchette raised her eyes.

Gilliatt stood before them.

He had just entered by a side path.

Gilliatt was no longer the same man that he had been on the previous evening. He had combed his hair, he had shaved his beard, he had put on shoes, he wore a sailor's white shirt with a broad rolling collar, he was dressed in his newest sailor's clothes. A gold ring could be seen on his little finger. He seemed profoundly calm.

There was a paleness beneath his sunburn.

Suffering bronze—such was this visage.

They stared at him in amazement. Although unrecognizable, Déruchette recognized him. As for the words which he had just uttered, they were so remote from what they were thinking of at the moment, that they made but little impression on their minds.

Gilliatt repeated,—

"Why should you bid each other farewell? Marry. You can go together."

Déruchette started. She trembled from head to foot.

Gilliatt continued,—

"Miss Déruchette is of age. She is dependent upon herself alone. Her uncle is only her uncle. You love each other."

Déruchette interrupted him gently,—

"How comes it that you are here?"

"Marry each other," repeated Gilliatt.

Déruchette began to perceive what this man was saying to her. She stammered,—

"My poor uncle."

"He would refuse if the marriage had not taken place; he will consent when the marriage is already performed. Besides, you are going away. When you return, he will forgive."

Gilliatt added, with a shade of bitterness,—

"And then, he is thinking only of rebuilding his boat. That will occupy him during your absence. He has the Durande to console him."

"I should not like," stammered Déruchette, in a stupor in which joy was discernible, "to leave any unhappiness behind me."

"It will not last long," said Gilliatt.

Ebenezer and Déruchette had been dazzled, as it were. They were recovering themselves now. As their confusion decreased, the sense of Gilliatt's words became apparent to them. A cloud was mingled with them, but it was not to their interest to resist.

One allows those who are saving us to have their way. Objections against a return to Paradise are weak.

In Déruchette's attitude, as she leaned imperceptibly on Ebenezer, there was something which made common cause with what Gilliatt said. As for the enigma of the presence of this man, and of his words which, in Déruchette's mind in particular, evoked many varieties of astonishment, they were side issues. This man was saying to them: "Marry." This was clear; if there were any responsibility, he assumed it. Déruchette felt in a confused way that for many reasons he had the right so to do. What he had said of Mess Lethierry was true.

Ebenezer murmured thoughtfully: "An uncle is not a father."

He was under the influence of a sudden and happy change.

The probable scruples of the clergyman melted and dissolved in this poor, loving heart.

Gilliatt's voice became curt and harsh, and something like the pulsations of fever could be heard in it.

"Instantly. The *Cashmere* sails in two hours. You have time, but you have barely time. Come."

Ebenezer gazed at him attentively.

All at once he exclaimed,—

"I recognize you. It was you who saved my life."

Gilliatt replied,—

"I think not."

"Yonder, at the point of the Banks."

"I don't know the place."

"It was on the very day of my arrival."

"Let us not waste time," said Gilliatt.

"And, I am not mistaken, you are the man we saw last evening."

"Perhaps."

"What is your name?"

Gilliatt raised his voice.—

"Boatman, wait for us. We are coming back. Miss Lethierry, you asked me how it comes that I am here; it is very simple. I walked behind you. You are twenty-one years of age. In this country, when people have attained their majority, and are dependent only on themselves, they can marry in a quarter of an hour. Let us take the path along the water side. It is practicable; the sea will not cover it until noon. But come at once with me."

Déruchette and Ebenezer seemed to consult each other with a glance. They stood beside each other, and did not stir; they were as though intoxicated.

There are such hesitations on the brink of that abyss, happiness.

They understood, as it were, without comprehending.

"His name is Gilliatt," said Déruchette to Ebenezer.

Gilliatt began again with a sort of authority,—

"Why do you tarry? I tell you to follow me."

"Whither?" asked Ebenezer.

"There!"

And Gilliatt pointed towards the tower of the church.

They followed him.

Gilliatt went on before. His step was firm. They walked unsteadily.

As they advanced towards the church, something which was soon to become a smile could be seen dawning on the pure and beautiful faces of Ebenezer and Déruchette. The approach to the church illuminated them.

In Gilliatt's hollow eyes reigned night.

One would have said that he was a spectre conducting two souls to Paradise.

Ebenezer and Déruchette did not fully comprehend what was about to take place. The intervention of the man was the branch at which the drowning wretch clutches. They followed Gilliatt with the docility of despair leaning on the first comer.

He who feels that he is dying is not overscrupulous in making the most of chance.

Déruchette, being more ignorant, was more confident.

Ebenezer pondered.

Déruchette had attained her majority.

The formalities of English marriage are very simple, especially in primitive countries, where the rectors of the parish have almost discretionary power; but, nevertheless, would the dean consent to celebrate the marriage without even inquiring whether the uncle consented? That was the question. One might make the attempt, however. In any case, it was a reprieve.

But who was this man? and if it really was he whom Mess Lethierry had declared to be his son-in-law, on the preceding evening, how was his present course of action to be explained? He, the obstacle, had been converted into providence. Ebenezer yielded himself to it, but he gave to what was taking place the tacit and rapid consent of the man who feels that he is saved.

The path was uneven, sometimes wet and difficult. Ebenezer, in his absorption, paid no heed to the pools of water and the blocks of stone. From time to time, Gilliatt turned and said to Ebenezer,—

"Look out for these stones; give her your hand."

III
The Foresight of Abnegation

HALF past ten sounded as they entered the church. The church was empty on account of the hour, and also on account of the solitude of the town on that day.

At the further end, however, near the table which takes the place of the altar in reformed churches, there were three persons. They were the dean, his assistant, and the registrar. The dean, who was the Reverend Jaquemin Hérode, was seated; the clerk and the registrar were standing.

The Book lay open on the table.

On one side, upon a credence table, lay another book, the parish register, also open, and in it an attentive eye would have observed a freshly written page on which the ink was not yet dry. A pen and an inkstand lay beside the register.

On seeing the Reverend Ebenezer Caudray enter, the Reverend Jaquemin Hérode rose.

"I have been expecting you," said he. "All is ready."

The dean, in fact, wore his ecclesiastical robes.

Ebenezer glanced at Gilliatt.

The reverend dean added,—

"I am at your service, colleague."

And he bowed.

This bow turned neither to right nor left. It was evident from the direction of the dean's visual ray that Ebenezer alone existed for him. The dean did not include in this salutation either Déruchette, who was beside him, nor Gilliatt, who was behind. In his glance there was a parenthesis, into which Ebenezer alone was admitted. The observance of these shades form a part of good order, and consolidate society.

The dean resumed with graciously haughty urbanity,—

"I present you with my double compliments, colleague. Your uncle is dead, and you are taking to yourself a wife; you are rich through the one, and happy through the other. Moreover, now, thanks to the steamer which is to be started again, Mess Lethierry is also rich, which I approve. Miss Lethierry was born in this parish. I have verified the date of her birth in the register. Miss Lethierry has attained her majority and belongs to herself. Moreover, her uncle, who is all the family she has, gives his consent. You wish to be married at once, on account of your departure; that I understand, but, as you are the rector of a parish, I should have desired a little more formality for this marriage. I will abridge it, as a favor to you. The essential may be contained in the summary. The certificate is already prepared upon the register here, only the names remain to be filled in. According to the terms of the law and of custom the marriage can take place immediately after signing. The declaration required by the license has been duly made. I take upon myself a slight irregularity, since the request for the license should have been registered a week in advance; but I yield to necessity and the urgency of your departure. So be it. I will marry you. My assistant shall be the witness for the bridegroom; as for the witness on the part of the bride—"

The dean turned to Gilliatt.

Gilliatt nodded.

"That is sufficient," said the dean.

Ebenezer remained motionless. Déruchette was in an ecstasy, petrified.

The dean continued,—

"Now, there is still an obstacle."

Déruchette made a movement.

The dean went on,—

"The representative, here present, of Mess Lethierry has asked for your license and has signed the declaration on the register," and with the thumb of his left hand the dean designated Gilliatt, which exempted him from articulating that sort of a name,—"the envoy of Mess Lethierry told me this morning that Mess Lethierry, who was too much occupied to come in person, desired that the marriage should take place immediately. This desire, verbally expressed, is not enough. I am unable, on account of having to grant the license, and of the irregularity of which I am assuming the responsibility, to advance so rapidly without making inquiries of Mess Lethierry, or at least unless I am shown his signature. However great may be my good will, I cannot content myself with a message which is repeated to me. I must have some writing."

"Let that not delay us," said Gilliatt.

And he presented a paper to the reverend dean.

The dean seized the paper, ran his eye over it, seemed to skip several lines, doubtless not to the purpose, and read aloud,—

"Go to the dean and get the license. I wish the marriage to take place as soon as possible. It would be better to have it immediately."

He laid the paper on the table and went on—

"Signed Lethierry. The thing would be more respectful if addressed to me. But since a colleague is in question, I will demand nothing more."

Ebenezer looked at Gilliatt again. There are such things as understandings between souls. Ebenezer felt that there was deception here, and he had not the strength to denounce it, nor even an idea of so doing. Either through obedience to a latent heroism of which he caught a glimpse, or because his conscience was stunned by the thunderclap of happiness, he remained speechless.

The dean took the pen and, aided by the registrar, he filled in the blanks of the page written in the register, then straightened himself up, and, with a gesture, invited Ebenezer and Déruchette to approach the table.

The ceremony began.

It was a strange moment.

Ebenezer and Déruchette stood side by side before the minister. Any one who has had a dream in which he was being married, has experienced what they experienced.

Gilliatt stood at some distance, in the shadow of the pillars.

Déruchette on rising in the morning, in her despair, and with a thought of the coffin and the shroud, had dressed herself in white. This attire, associated with the idea of mourning, was suitable for the wedding. A white robe immediately makes a bride. The tomb is also a betrothal.

A radiance emanated from Déruchette. Never had she been what she was at that moment. Déruchette's fault lay in being, perhaps, too pretty, and not sufficiently beautiful. Her beauty sinned—if that is a sin—through excess of grace. Déruchette in repose, that is to say, outside of passion or pain, was, as we have already pointed out in detail, above all pretty. The transfiguration of the charming girl, that is the ideal virgin. Déruchette, rendered greater by love and suffering, had undergone that promotion, if we may be allowed the expression. She had the same candor with more dignity, the same freshness with more perfume. It was somewhat as though a daisy should be changed into a lily.

The moisture of tears scarcely dried was on her cheeks. One, perhaps, still lingered in the corner of her smile. Tears dried, vaguely visible, are a sweet and sombre embellishment for happiness.

The dean, standing beside the table, laid his finger on the open Bible and asked in a loud voice,—

"Is there any objection?"

No one replied.

"Amen," said the dean.

Ebenezer and Déruchette advanced a step towards the Reverend Jaquemin Hérode.

The dean said,—

"Joseph Ebenezer Caudray, will you have this woman to be your wife?"

Ebenezer replied,—

"I will."

The dean continued,—

"Durande Déruchette Lethierry, will you have this man to be your husband?"

Déruchette, in agony of soul from too much joy, like a lamp with too much oil, murmured rather than uttered,—

"I will."

Then, following the beautiful Anglican rite of marriage, the dean glanced about him and put this solemn question to the gloom in the church,—

"Who giveth this woman to be married to this man?"

"I do," said Gilliatt.

A pause ensued. Ebenezer and Déruchette felt a vague oppression through their rapture.

The dean placed Déruchette's right hand in Ebenezer's right hand, and Ebenezer said to Déruchette,—

"Déruchette, I take thee to be my wedded wife, for better for worse, for richer for poorer, in sickness or in health, to love and to cherish until death do us part, and thereto I plight thee my troth."

The dean put Ebenezer's right hand in Déruchette's right hand, and Déruchette said to Ebenezer,—

"Ebenezer, I take thee to be my wedded husband, for better for worse, for richer for poorer, in sickness or in health, to love and to cherish until death do us part, and thereto I plight thee my troth."

The dean resumed,—

"Where is the ring?"

This took them by surprise. Ebenezer, taken unexpectedly, had no ring.

Gilliatt removed the gold ring from his little finger. It was probably the "wedding-ring," purchased in the morning from the jeweller in the Commercial Arcade.

The dean laid the ring upon the book, then handed it back to Ebenezer.

Ebenezer took Déruchette's small, trembling left hand, slipped the ring on the fourth finger, and said,—

"With this ring I thee wed"—

"In the name of the Father, and of the Son, and of the Holy Ghost," said the dean.

"Amen," said the clerk.

The dean raised his voice,—

"You are man and wife."

"Amen," said the clerk.

The dean resumed,—

"Let us pray."

Ebenezer and Déruchette turned towards the table and knelt down.

Gilliatt, who remained standing, bowed his head.

They knelt before God; he bowed beneath fate.

IV

"For Your Wife, When You Marry

On leaving the church, they saw the *Cashmere* beginning to make ready to sail.

"You are in time," said Gilliatt.

They again took the path to the Havelet.

They walked in front; Gilliatt now followed behind.

They were two somnambulists. They had, so to speak, only changed their bewilderment. They knew neither where they were nor what they were doing. They made haste mechanically, they no longer remembered the existence of anything; they felt each other, they could not put two ideas together. In ecstasy, one no more thinks than one swims in a torrent. From the midst of the darkness they had fallen into a Niagara of joy. One might say that they were undergoing the process of introduction to paradise. They did not speak to each other, they were saying too many things with their souls. Déruchette pressed Ebenezer's arm closely to her.

Gilliatt's steps behind them occasionally reminded them that he was there. They were profoundly moved, but they said not a word; excess of emotion resolves itself into stupor. Theirs was delicious but overwhelming. They were married. They were postponing all other thoughts, they would see each other again, what Gilliatt had done was well, that was all. The depths of these two hearts thanked him ardently and vaguely. Déruchette said to herself that there was something for her to unravel in this matter later on. In the meanwhile, they accepted. They felt themselves at the discretion of this decided and abrupt man, who had made their happiness with authority. It was impossible to question him, to talk with him. Too many impressions rushed upon them at once. Their absorption is pardonable.

Facts are sometimes like a hailstorm. The stones riddle you. They stun. The abruptness of incidents falling into existences habitually calm, very speedily renders incidents unintelligible to those who suffer or profit by them. One is not acquainted with one's own adventure. One is crushed without guessing it; one is crowned without understanding it.

Déruchette, in particular, for several hours had been subjected to all commissions; first she had been dazzled by Ebenezer in the garden; then came nightmare, that monster declared to be her husband; then desolation, the angel spreading his wings and on the point of departing; now it was joy, an unheard-of-joy, with an indecipherable background, the monster giving the angel to her, Déruchette; marriage springing from agony; Gilliatt, the catastrophe of yesterday, the salvation of to-day.

She could understand nothing. It was evident that since early morning, Gilliatt's only occupation had been to get them married; he had done everything; he had answered for Mess Lethierry, seen the dean, obtained the license, signed the necessary declaration; this was how it had been possible for the marriage to take place. But Déruchette did not understand it. Moreover, had she understood the how, she would not have understood the why.

All there was to be done was to close her eyes, return thanks mentally, forget earth and life, allow herself to be carried to heaven by this good demon. An explanation was too long, thanks were too little. She held her peace in the sweet intoxication of happiness.

A little, though, remained in them,—sufficient. There are parts of the sponge which remain white under water. They possessed exactly the quantity of lucidity which was requisite for distinguishing the sea from the land, and the *Cashmere* from any other vessel.

In a few minutes they had reached the Havelet.

Ebenezer was the first to enter the boat. At the moment when Déruchette was about to follow him, she experienced the sensation of having her sleeve plucked gently. It was Gilliatt, who had placed his finger on a fold of her dress.

"Madam," he said, "you were not expecting to depart. I thought that you would, perhaps, need dresses and linen. On board the *Cashmere* you will find a trunk which contains articles of clothing for a lady. This trunk came to me from my mother. It was intended for the woman whom I should marry. Permit me to offer it to you."

Déruchette half awoke from her dream. She turned towards Gilliatt. Gilliatt, in a low voice which was scarcely audible, continued,—

"Now, I do not wish to detain you, but you see, madam, I think that I must explain to you. On the day when that misfortune occurred, you were sitting in the parlor, you said some words. You do not remember it; it is quite natural. One is not obliged to remember all the words which one utters. Mess Lethierry was greatly grieved. 'Tis certain that it was a good boat, which had rendered good service. The misfortune of the sea had happened, there was a great commotion in the countryside. These are things which one forgets, naturally. That was not the only vessel which has been lost on the rocks. One cannot think forever of an accident. Only, what I wanted to say to you was this, that when they said: 'No one will go,' I went. They said it was impossible; it was not that which was impossible. I thank you for listening to me for a brief moment. You understand, madam, that, if I went there, it was not in order to offend you. Besides, the matter dates from a long time ago. I know that you are in haste. If one had the time, one would remember, but it would serve no purpose. The story goes back to one day when there was snow. And then, once when I was passing, I thought that you smiled. That is the way it is to be explained. As to last night, I had not had time to go home, I had just come from my work, I was all ragged, I frightened you, you felt ill, I was wrong; that is not the way to make one's appearance before people. I pray you not to be angry with me for it. This is nearly all that I wished to say. You are about to take your departure. You will have fine weather. The wind is from the east. Farewell, madam. You think it natural, do you not, that I should say a little? this is the last minute."

"I am thinking of that trunk," said Déruchette. "But why not keep it for your wife when you marry?"

"Madam," said Gilliatt, "I shall probably never marry."

"That will be a pity; for you are good. Thank you."

And Déruchette smiled. Gilliatt returned her smile.

Then he helped Déruchette to enter the boat.

Less than a quarter of an hour afterwards, the boat containing Ebenezer and Déruchette came alongside the *Cashmere* in the roads.

V

The Great Tomb

GILLIATT followed the water's edge, passed rapidly into Saint-Pierre-Port, then set out again for Saint-Sampson along the seashore, shunning encounters, avoiding the roads, which on account of his achievement were full of peasants.

As the reader knows, he had long had a way of his own of traversing the country in every direction without being seen by any one. He knew the paths; he had made for himself isolated and winding routes; he had the wild habits of the being who feels himself disliked; he held aloof.

He had taken this turn when a small child, on perceiving the scant welcome in the faces of men, and it had afterwards become his instinct to remain apart.

He passed the Esplanade, then the Salerie. From time

to time he turned round and looked behind him at the roadstead and at the *Cashmere,* which had just set sail. There was but little wind. Gilliatt went faster than the *Cashmere.* Gilliatt walked along the rocks of the extreme edge of the water, with bowed head. The flood tide was beginning to rise.

At a certain moment he halted and, turning his back to the sea, he gazed for several minutes at a clump of oak trees beyond the rocks which concealed the road of le Valle. They were the oaks of the spot called the Basses-Maisons. There, in days gone by, Déruchette's finger had written his name, "Gilliatt," on the snow. That snow had melted long ago.

He pursued his path.

The day was more charming than any that there had hitherto been that year. There was something nuptial about the morning. It was one of those spring days when May lavishes herself wholly; creation seems to have no other object than to give itself a festival and to make its own happiness. Beneath all the sounds of the forests as well as of the village, of the wave as well as of the atmosphere, there was a sound of cooing. The first butterflies were alighting on the first roses. All was new in nature,—the grasses, the mosses, the leaves, the perfumes, the rays.

It seemed as though the sun had never shone thus before. The pebbles were freshly washed. The profound song of the trees was sung by birds born yesterday. It is probable that their eggshells, broken by their tiny beaks, still lay in the nest. Newly fledged birds rustled among the trembling branches. They were singing their first song, they were winging their first flight. There was a sweet chatter of all at once,—hoo-pooes, tomtits, woodpeckers, goldfinches, bullfinches, sparrows, and thrushes.

The lilacs, lilies of the valley, daphnes, wisteria, formed an exquisite mixture in the ditches. A very pretty water-lentil, which grows at Guernsey, covered the pools with a carpet of emerald. The wagtails and apple-tree strippers, who make such pretty little nests, were bathing in them. Through the gaps in the vegetation, the blue sky was visible. Some wanton clouds were pursuing each other in the azure, with nymphlike undulations. One fancied that one felt the passage of kisses wafted by invisible mouths. Not an old wall but had its bouquet of wallflowers, like a bridegroom. The plum trees were in blossom, the laburnums were in blossom, white piles which shone and yellow piles which sparkled were visible through the interlacing branches. The spring cast all its silver and all its gold into the immense basket of the foliage. The new shoots were all of a fresh green. Cries of welcome were heard in the air. It was the moment of the swallows' arrival. The clusters of furze bordered the slopes of the hollow roads, while waiting for the clusters of the hawthorn.

The beautiful and the pretty were good neighbors; the superb was completed by the graceful; the great did not embarrass the little; not a note of the concert was lost; microscopic magnificences were in their own plane; in the vast, universal beauty, all was distinguishable as in limpid water. Everywhere, a divine fulness and a mysterious swelling allowed one to guess at the violent and unseen effort of the sap at work.

The things that shone, shone more; the things that loved became more loving. There was something of the hymn in the flower, and of radiance in the noise. The great diffuse harmony was expanding. Things beginning to dawn invited things beginning to gush forth. An impulse which came from below and which came also from on high, moved hearts vaguely, susceptible as they are to the scattered and subterranean influence of the seed-germs. The flower gave obscure promise of fruit, every virgin meditated; the reproductions of beings, designed by the immense soul of the gloom, was roughly outlined in the irradiation of things. Betrothal was going on everywhere. There were marriages without end. Life, which is the female, united with the infinite, which is the male.

The weather was beautiful, light, warm; through the hedges, in the enclosures, laughing and playing children could be seen. Some of them were playing hop-scotch. The apple trees, peach trees, cherry trees, and pear trees covered the orchards with their heaps of pale or crimson tufts. In the grass, cowslips, periwinkles, yarrow, daisies, hyacinths, amaryllis, violets, and veronicas. Blue borage and yellow iris swarmed with those pretty little pink stars which always flourish in a troop, and which for that reason are called "companions." Creatures all gilded ran between the stones. House leeks in flower empurpled the thatched roofs. The toilers of the hives were out. The bee was at work. Space was full of the murmur of seas and the humming of flies. Nature, permeable to the springtime, was moist with voluptuousness.

When Gilliatt reached Saint-Sampson, there was no water as yet at the head of the port, and he could traverse it dryshod, unperceived behind the hulls of the vessels under repair. A cordon of flat stones placed at regular intervals facilitated his passage.

Gilliatt was not noticed. The crowd was at the other end of the port, near the entrance of les Bravées. There his name was in every mouth. They were talking so much about him that they paid no attention to him. Gilliatt passed by, concealed to some degree by the noise which he had created.

From afar he beheld the paunch at the place where he had moored it, the smoke stack of the engine between its four chains, a movement of carpenters at work, confused forms going and coming, and he heard the joyous and thundering voice of Mess Lethierry giving his orders.

He plunged into the small lanes.

There was no one behind les Bravées, all curiosity being in front. Gilliatt took the path which skirted the low wall of the garden. He halted in the corner where grew the wild mallow, again he beheld the stone where he had sat; again he saw the wooden bench where Déruchette had sat. He gazed at the centre of the walk where he had seen the two shadows, who had disappeared, embrace.

He set out again. He ascended the hill of the Château du Valle, then redescended it, and directed his course towards the Bû de la Rue.

Houmet-Paradis was deserted.

His house was just as he had left it that morning, after dressing to go to Saint-Pierre-Port.

A window was open. Through this window the bagpipe could be seen hanging on a nail in the wall.

On the table could be seen the small Bible given,

by way of thanks, to Gilliatt by a stranger, who was Ebenezer.

The key was in the door. Gilliatt stepped up, laid his hand on that key, double locked the door, put the key in his pocket, and walked off.

He went, not in the direction of the land but of the sea.

He traversed his garden diagonally, by the shortest path, with no precautions for the beds, but taking care, however, not to crush the sea-kale which he had planted there because it was a favorite with Déruchette.

He crossed over the parapet and descended among the rocks.

He began to follow, still walking straight ahead, the long and narrow line of reefs which connected the Bû de la Rue with that great obelisk of granite in the middle of the sea, which is called the Beast's Horn. It was there that the chair of Gild-Holm-'Ur was situated.

He strode from one ridge of rocks to another, like a giant on the crests of mountains. Taking such strides on a crest of reefs resembles walking on the ridge of a roof.

A fisherwoman who was prowling barefoot among the pools of water some distance off, and who was just coming on shore, called to him: "Take care, the tide is rising."

He continued to advance.

On reaching that great rock at the point, the Horn, which formed a pinnacle in the sea, he halted. The land ended there. It was the extremity of the little promontory.

He looked.

In the offing a few boats were anchored and fishing. From time to time one could see silver dripping in streams in the sunlight, which indicated the drawing of the nets from the water. The *Cashmere* had not yet arrived opposite Saint-Sampson; she had spread her main topsail. She was between Herm and Jethou.

Gilliatt turned the corner of the rock. He arrived under the chair of Gild-Holm-'Ur, at the foot of that sort of abrupt staircase which, less than three months previously, he had aided Ebenezer to descend.

He ascended it.

The greater part of the steps were already under water. Two or three only were still dry.

He climbed them.

These steps led to the chair of Gild-Holm-'Ur. He reached the chair, looked at it for a moment, covered his eyes with his hand and allowed it to glide slowly from one eyebrow to the other, a gesture by which one seems to wipe out the past, then he seated himself in that hollow of the rock, with the cliff behind his back and the ocean under his feet.

The *Cashmere* was at that moment coming abreast of the great, round, submerged tower, guarded by a sergeant and a cannon, which marks in the channel the halfway point between Herm and Saint-Pierre-Port.

Above Gilliatt's head, in the crevices, some rock flowers waved. The water was blue as far as the eye could reach. The wind being east, there was but little surf around Sark, of which only the western side is visible from Guernsey. France could be seen in the distance, like a mist, and the long, yellow ribbon of the sands of Carteret.

Now and then a white butterfly flitted past. Butterflies have a mania for flying over the sea.

The breeze was very light. All that blue, below as well as above, was motionless. No quiver agitated those serpentine shapes, of a paler or darker azure, which mark the concealed lines of the shoals, on the surface of the sea.

The *Cashmere,* which was but little aided by the wind, had hoisted her studding-sails in order to catch the breeze. She was covered with canvas. But the wind being abeam, the studding-sails compelled her to hug the coast of Guernsey very closely.

She had passed the Saint-Sampson beacon. She reached the hill of the Château du Valle. The moment was at hand when she would double the point of the Bû de la Rue.

Gilliatt watched her approach.

The air and the water seemed lulled to sleep. The tide was rising, not by waves but by swelling. The level of the water rose without palpitation. The stifled sound of the open sea resembled the breathing of an infant.

In the direction of the harbor of Saint-Sampson, small, dull blows, blows of hammers, were heard. It was probably the carpenters preparing the tackle and gear for removing the engine from the boat.

These sounds hardly reached Gilliatt, because of the mass of granite against which his back was placed.

The *Cashmere* approached with the slowness of a phantom.

Gilliatt waited.

All at once a rippling sound and a sensation of cold made him look down.

The water touched his feet.

He lowered his eyes, then raised them again.

The *Cashmere* was quite close at hand.

The cliff in which the rain had hollowed out the chair of Gild-Holm-'Ur was so vertical, and the depth of water was so great there, that ships could without danger, in calm weather, sail within a few cables' lengths of the rock.

The *Cashmere* arrived. She rose up and seemed to grow upon the water. It was like the enlargement of a shadow. The rigging stood out black against the sky in the magnificent rocking of the sea. The long veils which had been thrown across the sun for a moment, became almost rosy, and assumed an ineffable transparency. The waves murmured indistinctly. Not a sound troubled the majestic gliding of that silhouette. One could see all on deck as though one were there one's self.

The *Cashmere* almost grazed the rock.

The helmsman was at the rudder, a cabin boy was climbing the shrouds, several passengers, leaning on the bulwarks, were contemplating the serenity of the weather, the captain was smoking. But Gilliatt saw nothing of all this.

On the deck there was one corner full of sunlight. It was on this point his eyes were fixed. In that sunlight were Ebenezer and Déruchette. They were seated close to each other. They were crouching down gracefully side by side, like two birds warming themselves in a ray of midday sun, on one of those benches, covered with a small tarred awning, which well-ordered vessels offer to passengers, and upon which one reads, when the vessel is English: *For ladies only.*

Déruchette's head was on Ebenezer's shoulder; Ebenezer's arm was passed around Déruchette's waist; they were holding each other's hands, fingers interlaced in fingers. The shades between one angel and another were discernible on those two exquisite faces formed of innocence. One was the more virginal, the other more starlike. Their chaste embrace was expressive. All of marriage was there, and also all purity. That seat was already an alcove, and almost a nest. At the same time it was a halo; the sweet halo of love fleeing in a cloud.

The silence was celestial.

Ebenezer's eyes returned thanks and contemplated; Déruchette's lips moved; and in that charming silence, as the wind was blowing on shore, at the rapid moment when the sloop was gliding past, a few fathoms from the chair of Gild-Holm-'Ur, Gilliatt heard Déruchette's tender and delicate voice saying,—

"Look! It seems as though there were a man on the rock."

This apparition passed.

The *Cashmere* left the point of the Bû de la Rue behind her and plunged into the deep ripples of the waves. In less than a quarter of an hour, her masts and sails described upon the water only a sort of white obelisk growing ever smaller on the horizon. The water reached Gilliatt's knees.

He watched the sloop sail away.

The breeze freshened on the open sea. He could see the *Cashmere* run out her lower studding-sails and staysails, in order to profit by this increase of wind. The *Cashmere* was already beyond the waters of Guernsey. Gilliatt never took his eyes from it. The water came to his waist.

The tide was rising. Time was passing.

The sea-gulls and cormorants flew uneasily around him. One would have said that they were seeking to warn him. Perhaps, in those flocks of birds, there was some sea-gull which had come from the Douvres, and had recognized him.

An hour elapsed.

The wind from the open sea did not make itself felt in the roadstead, but the *Cashmere* dwindled rapidly. From all appearances, the sloop was going at full speed. She was already nearly abreast of the Casquets.

There was no foam around the rock of Gild-Holm-'Ur, no wave beat the granite. The water swelled peacefully. It had almost reached Gilliatt's shoulders.

Another hour elapsed.

The *Cashmere* was now beyond the waters of Alderney. The Ortach rock concealed her for a moment. She passed behind the rock, then came out again, as from an eclipse. The sloop fled away to the north. She gained the open sea. She was nothing but a point now, with the scintillation of a light, owing to the sun. The birds uttered little cries to Gilliatt.

Only his head was now visible.

Gilliatt, motionless, watched the *Cashmere* as she vanished.

The tide was nearly full. Evening was drawing on. Behind Gilliatt in the roadstead some fishing-boats were returning.

Gilliatt's eyes, fastened to the sloop in the distance, remained fixed. That fixed eye resembled nothing that can be seen upon earth. In that calm and tragic pupil, there lay the inexpressible. That gaze contained the entire quantity of appeasement which an unrealized dream leaves; it was the melancholy acceptance of a different fulfillment.

The flight of a star must be followed by a similar gaze.

From moment to moment, celestial darkness increased beneath those lids whose visual ray remained fixed upon a point in space. The immense tranquillity of the shadow rose in Gilliatt's deep eyes, at the same time as the infinite water around the rock of Gild-Holm-'Ur.

The *Cashmere,* which had become invisible, was now a speck mingled with the mist. One needed to know where it was in order to be able to distinguish it.

Little by little this speck, which was no longer a form, grew pale.

Then it dwindled.

Then it disappeared.

At the moment when the vessel vanished on the horizon, the head disappeared under water. There was nothing left but the sea.

Selected Bibliography

Other Works by Victor Hugo

Cromwell, 1827 play
The Last Day of a Condemned Man, 1829
Hernani, 1830 play
The Hunchback of Notre-Dame, 1831 (Signet Classic 0-451-52222-2)
Les Contemplations, 1856 poetry
Les Misérables, 1862 (Signet Classic 0-451-52526-4)
William Shakespeare, 1864
Ninety-Three, 1874
The End of Satan, 1886
God, 1891

Biography and Criticism

Brombert, Victor. *Victor Hugo and the Visionary Novel.* Cambridge, MA.: Harvard University Press, 1984.

Grant, Elliott M. *The Career of V. Hugo.* Cambridge, MA.: Harvard University Press, 1945.

Grant, Richard B. *The Perilous Quest: Image, Myth, and Prophecy in the Narratives of Victor Hugo.* Durham, NC.: Duke University Press, 1968.

Houston, John Porter. *Victor Hugo*. Boston: Twayne, 1988.

Maurois, André. *Olympio: The Life of Victor Hugo.* Trans. Gerard Hopkins. New York: Harper, 1956.

Peyre, Henri. *Victor Hugo: Philosophy and Poetry.* Trans. Roda P. Roberts. University, AL.: University of Alabama Press, 1980.

Richardson, Joanna. *Victor Hugo.* London: Weidenfeld & Nicolson, 1976.

Robb, Graham. *Victor Hugo.* New York: Norton, 1998.